ALSO BY JOHN THORNDIKE

Anna Delaney's Child

THE
POTATO
BARON

THE
POTATO
BARON

JOHN
THORNDIKE

Villard Books
New York
1989

FIC
Thorndike

Library of Congress Cataloging-in-Publication Data

Thorndike, John.
The potato baron.

I. Title.
PS3570.H6497P68 1989 813'.54 88-40468
ISBN 0-394-57712-4

Manufactured in the United States of America

9 8 7 6 5 4 3 2

First Edition
Book Design by Timothy O'Keeffe

For JJT, who always let us choose

ACKNOWLEDGMENTS

Thanks to Alison Acker, Lady Borton, Pat Frederick, Beth Isacke, Peter Livingston, Jane Maier, Joseph Thorndike, Bill Whitehead and all the members of the Canyon Club. This book would not be the same without them.

My thanks as well to the Virginia Center for the Creative Arts, the Ragdale Foundation and the Leighton Artist Colony in Banff, Canada: three havens where writing came easier.

THE
POTATO
BARON

ONE

Pooler color was yellow. Everyone knew that. The farmhouse, the barns, the storage houses, the trucks—even the farm's mailbox was painted yellow. For almost a hundred years everything at Pooler Farm had been the same color. Yet on the sunny spring morning his wife left him, Austin Pooler flipped through the color chart at Vignon's Paint Store and told Earl he wanted ten gallons of heliotrope paint.

"Heliotrope?" Earl said. His eyes traveled up Austin's forearm as far as the elbow, then fell back.

Austin didn't speak. He tapped his finger, blunt as a new potato, on a square of bright purple.

"But you use custard yellow," Earl said. "Right here, number 2340. I sold this paint to your grandfather."

"Just mix it up, Earl. Ten gallons. I'll sign for it."

Though Austin usually enjoyed going into Earl Vignon's store, with its painty smell and worn wooden floors, everything about the place now offended him: the frayed linoleum counter, the mixing machines spattered with paint, the disarray of brushes and rollers.

Earl, who had long had a hand in the upkeep of the Poolers' landmark yellow buildings, pouted like a five-year-old. "What can you paint with this?" he asked, staring down at the color chart.

Austin was not in the mood. "My mother-in-law," he said. "And when I finish with her I'll do the trees around my house."

Just above his collar Earl's neck began to quiver. "You know what you're getting here?"

Austin remembered that a year ago Earl's only son had died in a construction accident. Maybe that was why Earl looked so different. He had gone bald overnight. The skin lay over the top of his head as smooth and pink as a new scar.

"I'll find something to paint," Austin said. The desire to offend the old man, which had overwhelmed him upon entering the store, now vanished.

Earl grumbled behind the counter as he mixed two five-gallon cans of heliotrope paint and stirred them with an electric drill. Austin signed a receipt, hoisted the cans onto the back of his pickup and drove out of town.

He drove too fast, accelerating through the gravel curves of Pooler Road until the rear wheels of his pickup began to drift. There were no fences or livestock here, only woodlots, a pair of round ponds and dark potato fields, all recently plowed. Between the fields and the road grew rye grass, cinquefoil and yellow galinsoga—all weeds to a potato man. Austin Pooler had driven this road a thousand times, maybe ten thousand times. It bore his name.

"*Goddamn*," he said, and smacked the dash with the heel of his palm. "Goddamn it to son of a bitch." He reached into his shirt pocket and touched the letter he had found on the kitchen table earlier this morning, after flying back from Portland. He had read the letter twice, then folded the single sheet of blue stationery into sixteenths and stuck it into his pocket.

No counselor, no minister, no psychiatrist could have comforted Austin as surely as the V-8 growl of his old Dodge Power Wagon. He had bought the truck twenty years ago, a month after getting married, and for some time it was a household joke as to which would last longer, the marriage or the Dodge. Fay said the marriage, but Austin insisted the truck was stronger than both of them. When he kicked the bucket, he told her, she could use the Dodge to carry him up to the Pooler ridgetop cemetery. "Whatever you do, keep me away from those funeral parlors. I don't even care if there's a coffin. Just slip me into the ground."

"And if I go first," Fay made him promise, "I want you to throw my ashes into the ocean. I'm serious. Don't bury me up here in Aroostook County."

All that had been settled years ago.

Past the ancient hemlocks at the farm gate, the nineteenth-century Pooler farmhouse looked out over the valley. The house was sturdy, but no longer entirely plumb. To the north and south of the yellow buildings wide potato fields rose from the valley floor to the top of the ridge. The luminous April morning had not yet reached ten o'clock.

Austin parked outside his equipment barn, lifted down the two cans of paint and set them next to Jules Derosier, the hired man. Jules looked up from a compressor and spray pump attached to the power takeoff on a small John Deere. He sucked in his cheeks, making his thin face thinner.

"That stuff better be latex," he said. "It took me an hour to clean the gum out of this pump."

"The last batch was latex," Austin said.

"Hmmp."

Though Jules had a small wiry frame, he hated to work in cramped quarters or make fine adjustments to machinery. He happily split the largest tractors in half to do transmission or hydraulic repairs, but if he had to replace the points on an old distributor, or fix a leak in the crawl space beneath his house, his hands would shake and he'd grind his molars. If his watch broke he threw it away. He preferred not to think of something that small being fixed.

He gave Austin's yellow Dodge a critical look. "You got some rust there. You want me to touch up that truck while I'm at it?"

"Just the potato house," Austin said.

Jules rummaged in the tractor toolbox for a pair of pliers to loosen the paint caps. Austin, who knew what was coming, stepped into the bermed windowless storage house. The cool air smelled sweet; there was no hint of rot from the Kennebecs piled in back. Prices had gone up ten cents a hundred the week before, so Austin had sold. Now the house was barely a third full.

Most of Austin's potatoes were stored behind his packing shed in the town of White Pine, in new metal houses with precise control over temperature and humidity. The crop didn't keep quite as well in these older houses, and warm weather was approaching. All the same, Austin sold his last farm stock reluctantly. He liked to keep some potatoes close by, something he could touch. Occasionally—more times than Fay knew—he came out to the house at night and crawled gently onto the great pile of tubers. He lay back in the dark, alone, reaching about with his hands and smelling the Aroostook earth.

Sometimes he let his son, Blake, scramble over the pile as well. The Maine Anti-Bruise Campaign, of which Austin was an advisory member, would not have been pleased. But Austin didn't believe a sneakered eight-year-old boy could do any more harm to the potatoes than the rubberized belts of harvesters, graders and bin pilers. Besides, an Aroostook son should have plenty of contact with potatoes.

Standing alone in the dark house, Austin jerked back his foot. It was only a cat, twining its black tail around his ankle. A second strawberry cat joined the first, and the two of them padded over the concrete floor toward the back of the house.

The cats hung around because of Fay. She was the one who set out food and water for them, and cared for them when they were sick or hurt. She particularly liked the wildest of them: the half-feral cats that disappeared into the woods all summer, returning only to mate with the domestic barn cats in a screeching series of late-night courtships.

"Hey, Austin."

He stepped back outside to find Jules pointing with digust at the two open cans of paint. In the direct sunlight, the color looked fierce.

Jules stood with his palms on his hips. Earl knuckled this one up good. Look at this fool paint."

"That's heliotrope."

"*Helio*-what? It looks like a whore's bathroom."

"Nice and bright," Austin said. "Something new."

Jules laughed. "You got a mistake here, right? You got somebody else's paint?"

Austin looked at him without speaking.

Jules's smile faded. "You gotta be kidding. Everybody knows what color we use. You can see this house ten miles off. The whole valley can see it."

"My grandmother had some wallpaper with this color in it," Austin said with a shaky voice. He was already sorry he'd bought this crazy paint. All he wanted to do was go inside and read Fay's letter again. "What do you know about whores' bathrooms anyway?"

Jules, who was six inches shorter than Austin, stood up to his full height and clattered his pliers onto the metal bed of the pickup. "Twenty-eight years I've worked here," he said. "I'll admit, Austin, you always bring in a good crop, but sometimes you don't know basswood from asswood about how to run a farm. I know, it's not my position. But who in dead-dog hell would paint his storage house purple?"

"Heliotrope." Austin said. "Latex heliotrope. Just run some water through the sprayer when you finish."

"Jesus and Mary. You should stop going to those Potato Board meetings. Every time you come back you've got a new plan."

"Like the geese."

"Yeah, like the geese. And the jazz. That was something."

Austin had dreamed up some fairly eccentric schemes in the past, such as turning weeder geese loose in the fields to eat the redroot pigweed, dock and lamb's quarters. Another year he had set up an experimental plot and broadcast an endless loop of Charlie Parker and Clifford Brown tapes over a patch of young potato vines, hoping to stimulate their growth. The results were indecisive.

"You going to start painting?" he asked Jules. "Or you want me to do the job?"

Jules looked at the cans as if they held raw sewage. "I don't know as I've got the stomach for it."

Austin turned away and walked to his kitchen, tapping his

chest pocket to make sure the letter from Fay was still there. Crocuses and violets had come up along the edge of the lawn, and the first maple leaves, barely an inch across, trembled in the sunshine overhead. Robins hopped across the grass, and a mourning dove sauntered ahead of Austin around the side of the house.

Sometimes a cat killed a dove and ate it. Only a week before, Fay had led Austin out to the lawn and shown him a telltale pile of feathers and down. Though Fay liked birds, her eyes were bright. "I saw it happen," she said. "It was one of those woods cats. It killed the dove, then started at the neck and ate both ways."

Back at the potato house the John Deere came to life, followed by the wheezing sound of the compressor. Jules moved about his job stiff-backed and slow, as if he knew he was being watched. Austin sat down at the kitchen table. Shit, he thought, I don't want a purple barn.

He took Fay's letter out of his breast pocket, smoothed its creases and laid it on the table where he had found it earlier this morning after coming back from Portland.

> *Dear Austin,*
>
> *I'm sorry to leave this way, sneaking off while you're down at the Potato Board meeting, but I didn't want to make a scene about going, especially in front of Blake. I've found a place in town—house-sitting at the Ledyards'—and Blake and I will be staying there for a while.*
>
> *We moved last night, and today I'm taking him off for a long weekend. We probably won't get back until late Monday night. I want to put a little distance between me and the farm, and let you get used to the idea that I don't live there anymore.*
>
> *Next week you start planting. I guess I always knew you'd plant this year—and maybe you'll never stop. Maybe you'll always live on your farm, the way*

*you want to, and always grow potatoes. Not me. I
don't know where I'll be six months from now, but
it won't be here. I've spent my last winter in the
County.*

*But don't make out like I'm leaving you,
because I'm not. I'm leaving the farm behind, and
White Pine and a lot of friends, but not you. I never
wanted to break up our family.*

*I know you pretty well, Austin, so I know you
could read this letter and still think it will all blow
over. It won't. I'm going to leave Maine and I hope
you'll come with me. I've talked about this for a
couple of years and given you plenty of warning,
but I don't think you ever believed me. Maybe this
will be enough to wake you up.*

Love,

Fay

Austin pushed away the blue sheet and stared from a
distance at his wife's small handwriting. It was true. She had
told him many times she wanted to go—and maybe he hadn't
listened. But what was there to listen to? To the mad notion that
he should abandon the farm his great-great-grandfather had
bought in 1891? That he should tag along through the trash and
chaos of the modern world until Fay discovered where she
wanted to go, and what she wanted to do there?

Usually his wife agreed with him about the rest of the
country. She said Cleveland, where she was born, was the city
where rivers burned. She said Wilmington, where she grew up,
had been rubbed raw between Philadelphia and Baltimore.

Austin stood up and kicked his chair against the wall. She
had never said anything about taking their son.

After first reading the letter he had checked the closets and
dressers upstairs. Almost all her clothes had been taken, and
half of Blake's.

He tried to imagine where she could have gone for four days. South, probably. Everyone always went south. People acted as if Portland stood at the gates of heaven.

In fact, Portland was trash, and south of Portland worse. With every mile the land became more crowded, all the way to the degraded depths of Boston. And from there, in an uninterrupted chain as far as Newport News, Virginia, the cities mounted each other like pigs in a crowded pen. Austin hated even to fly over that part of the world.

What if it was a man? The thought entered Austin's chest like a blade. Maybe some man was behind all this talk about leaving, and Fay didn't have the courage to tell him. Maybe it was that gallic Casanova they had met at the teachers' conference last fall in Orono. He had put the rush on Fay the whole weekend, showing them photos of his wife and daughter in Bordeaux even as he slid his arm around Fay's waist.

"Quite a body on that frog," Fay had said on the way home. She was not above teasing her husband from time to time. Austin tried to remember the guy's name: Jean-Claude something, or Jean-Paul.

He took off the city clothes he had left Portland in this morning, tossed them on his dresser and pulled out a pair of work pants. At 6′3″ and 195 pounds, Austin hadn't lost or put on any weight since his last year in high school. He had unruly dark brown hair, blue eyes, a small cleft in his jaw and a celebrated oversized pair of ears. A patch of dark hair the size of an open hand grew on his otherwise smooth white chest. His only jewelry was a gold wedding ring that hadn't been off his finger since the day he married. No glasses, no birthmarks, no scars of consequence, never a broken bone. He had had chicken pox once, at the age of nine, but had never stayed in a hospital and hadn't caught a cold in ten years. Loudly, recurrently and to all who would listen, he attributed his good health to a diet rich in potatoes.

Could Fay possibly have been writing to that licorice-eyed, high-waisted Frenchman? Who else could there be?

Outside he found Jules climbing down from the bucket of a second tractor, from where he had sprayed the storage house's wooden end wall. The hired man's hog-nosed respirator and defiant stance made him look like a riot cop. The sun bore down on the two old balsam firs next to the potato house, and on the scandalous paint job. Jules turned off the tractor and compressor.

"It is kind of bright," Austin admitted.

"Looks like shit." Jules folded his arms and stared out over the valley.

Austin stuck his hands under his armpits and worked the driveway gravel with his toe. "Don't bishops wear robes this color?" he asked. He went on scoring a little furrow into the drive. Out on Pooler Road a truck went by, kicking up dust. "Fay always liked purple. She has a purple dress."

"Look, Austin, I just work here. I'll paint the house any fly-high color you want, but don't go telling me you picked out this here helio-trope because the bishop wears purple or because Fay owns some kind of dress."

"Earl Vignon was kind of annoyed himself. "

"He sunk awful low selling you a color like this."

"He didn't have any choice. I made him do it."

Jules leaned the spray gun against the tractor, pulled the respirator over his head and inspected its filter. "You know, Austin, you're a Pooler, so I guess you can do anything you want. In this whole town there's not much bigger or better than a Pooler. But when people see this barn they won't need Earl Vignon to tell them you've gone off the deep end."

Austin worked up his nerve. "These last couple of days," he said, "you didn't happen to talk to Fay, did you?"

"Nope." Jules folded his sleeves back over his dark arms. "I had the rock picker over on the McCaslin fields. I didn't see her."

"She went off with Blake somewhere. I don't know where."

For the first time since discovering the two cans were full of purple paint, Jules looked directly at his boss. "They coming back soon?" he asked.

"Monday, she says." Austin jammed his booted toe into the drive, two, three, four times in succession. "Sometimes I think she gets angry at me for going down to Portland. She thinks I spend too much time with the Potato Board."

"You do. We start planting in another week. We are going to plant, aren't we?"

"Does the governor of Maine eat potatoes? Of course we're going to plant."

The spring air rustled Austin's hair, grown long over his collar, and mixed the fragrance of crocus blooms with the odor of paint. The songs of sparrows and nuthatches carried across the lawn. The two men stood side by side under the bright purple of the storage house. Owner and hired man, they had worked together since Austin was fifteen. For years they had talked about farm plans and White Pine gossip, and occasionally about a small family crisis of their own. But neither of them had ever reported that his wife wanted to leave the County. Hands deep in their pockets, the two men eased a couple of inches farther apart.

With the start of planting only a week away there was plenty for Austin to do. He could have examined the seed stock or tested the cutting machines and planters. Instead, he stalked about the house until Jules went home for lunch, then got into his truck and drove into town a second time, headed for his mother's.

The air was clean, the fields vacant, the horizon lined with poplars. In the windless sky above, clouds hung as white as shirts. But all Austin could think of was his absent wife and son. He knew the town would talk. After all, he was a Pooler. His grandfather had been mayor of White Pine, and their farm was the second largest in all of Aroostook County—that topmost section of Maine that most people in the state referred to simply as "the County."

Though Austin drove an old pickup with a docked exhaust system and wobbling headlights, he did so by choice. Everyone knew he was rich. Though he dressed like any other farmer, and though his pickup looked like wrack and ruin compared to his hired man's new gas-shocked, high-riding Chevy, everyone knew Austin was rich where it counted, in land and farm machinery. In addition to eighteen hundred acres of land he owned the big Pooler enclave on the east side of the valley, a packing shed and two new potato houses in town, and a prodigious collection of implements: three new Lockwood potato harvesters, two new planters and the best cushioned pilers, sorters, washers and baggers. His giant yellow equipment barn was crammed with cultivators, bulk tanks, sprayers, rock pickers, liquid-manure tanks, disks and subsoilers, as well as six John Deere tractors, all in perfect condition.

He was a member of the National Potato Council and the Maine Potato Board. Like his father and grandfather before him he had graduated from Harvard. His electives were history, anthropology and Latin, with a major in botany. He liked to say he had majored in potatoes—and in fact, he spent most of his junior and senior years in the botany labs on Divinity Avenue, doing research on *Rhizoctonia solani,* black scurf. To this day he was a known fanatic on the subject of tubers. Thirty years after Maine had yielded its ascendancy to the irrigated fields of Idaho, Austin steadfastly upheld his family's ancestral zeal for Aroostook potatoes.

Bypassing the center of town, he drove to his mother's house, a small two-story on a quiet street of maples, lilacs and manicured lawns. He parked on the asphalt drive, aware, as usual, that his truck looked out of place in such an orderly neighborhood. That had always pleased him. Indeed, it was one reason he still drove his old Dodge. It was a farm truck and didn't belong anywhere near the suburbs.

Austin didn't stop to embrace his mother at the front door, as he sometimes did, but pushed on into the kitchen.

"Give me a minute," Rose called in to him from the vestibule. When alone at home she wore a pair of waffle-soled running shoes, but when someone came to visit she changed into leather walkers.

Austin browsed through the kitchen. He opened and shut the icebox, looked at the entries on Rose's calendar and rummaged through the cabinets.

"Do you want some lunch?" she asked. "It's almost twelve." At sixty-six, Rose was still an agile woman. She weighed less than 110 pounds and had only one natural breast. After the operation her hair had turned pure white.

"You know all about it, don't you?"

"I've got some chicken salad," Rose said. "It's already made. All about what?"

"About Fay leaving."

"Quit speaking in code, Austin. Leaving for where?"

"This letter was on the kitchen table when I got home this morning. She says she's moving out. And she took Blake."

Rose, whose eyes were still as good as Austin's, sat down at the table and read Fay's small script. Her Adam's apple scuttled up and down like a crab.

"So she finally did it. You think it's for good?"

"Of course it's not for good. But if you knew this was coming, you could have told me."

Rose gave him back the letter. "I've talked to Fay about this for years, but she never told me about moving to the Ledyards' or going away this weekend."

Austin picked up a copy of *House and Garden*, rolled it into a cylinder and thumped it on the table like a club. Rolling and unrolling the magazine, he sat down at the table opposite his mother. "I never thought she'd actually do it," he said. "She didn't give me any warning. I just came home from Portland and found that letter. I don't even know where she is."

Rose sighed. She stood up and pulled a bowl out of the refrigerator. "If I didn't know men were born blind, I'd think you weren't even trying. You better pay attention, Austin, because Fay has been telling you about this for months. Sure, she comes over and talks to me. But I've heard her tell you all this myself. She wants to live somewhere else. Sometimes I think a potato's got better eyes than you do."

"What are you talking about?" He turned in his chair and stared out the kitchen window through a border of green leaves, searching the backyard as if his wife and child might have camped there for the weekend. "All right," he said, "she told me. But I never thought she'd actually go. She doesn't even know what she wants to do."

"She'll find something. It's not that hard."

"What do you mean? You mean some other man?"

"No, I don't mean some other man. Here, eat this." Rose slid an oversized chicken-salad sandwich across the table to her son.

"But she talked about it."

"She talked about leaving. She told me the same things she told you. But she never said she was going to move into White Pine. After all, I'm your mother. She'd come over and complain sometimes about the six-month winters and her exile from the rest of the world. Because I understood her. Sometimes I think I've put up with all that long enough myself."

"Now you sound just like her. But you're a Pooler. You've lived almost your whole life up here."

"I'm not a Pooler, I'm a Barnes. Go ahead, eat that sandwich. As a matter of fact, I've been thinking about taking back my own name."

"You mean Hilary Rose?"

"No, I mean Barnes. I've put up with Pooler my whole life. *Pooler*. I never did get used to it. Lord, my feet hurt in these shoes."

By the time she came back wearing her Nikes, Austin had finished his sandwich. He carried his plate to the sink and washed it like a teenager, ignoring the other dishes. "You two have been in cahoots the whole year," he said.

"She has been talking about calling herself Fay Hallwick again, it's true."

"Christ on a crutch. What is it with women these days?"

"Don't start in on that, Austin. We just want to live closer to the civilized world."

"Civilized? What are you talking about? South of Bangor they're all barbarians and terrorists. They've got rivers down there you could walk across. And bureaucrats, Jesus Christ. The last time I went to a government office in Augusta there were a hundred guys sitting around in three-piece suits and a hundred women painting their nails. Nobody does anything until five o'clock, and then they go shopping. They're *consumers*."

"Some of them buy your potatoes."

"Maybe. I'm not sure they know enough to eat potatoes. But you know it's a trash heap down there. *This* is civilization."

"It is to you. But Fay wants to live somewhere else—and I think I might too."

"What's she going to do? And what about Blake and Maggie?"

"Do you want to hear what I've got to say?" Rose asked. "Or do I have to stand here and repeat it until you listen?"

"Listen to what?"

"I'm leaving too. I'm going to spend the summer on Long Island."

"Rump on a dog. You're not."

"I am."

"With Dossett?"

Rose nodded. "He's been calling me every week. Even before his wife died he used to write and ask how I was doing."

Rose knew Jack Dossett from the old days, when Dossett and Austin's father were both members of the National Potato Council. Dossett had grown up farming on the sandy South Fork of Long Island. He was a local kid on a tractor, he plowed his family's land right up to the honeysuckled fences of the wealthy summer residents.

Dossett's father had managed a construction company through the thirties and forties and put all his profits into land. During the war the family made good money off spuds. Right into the fifties, when land prices were rising fast, Dossett Senior continued to buy. Eventually the influx of New Yorkers drove prices beyond his reach, but by the time he died in 1970, Jack Junior was sitting on a fortune. It was an uncommon fate for a potato grower.

"Let's put it this way," Dossett said, the last time Austin talked to him about the potato business on Long Island. "I still call myself a farmer, but the real crop out there is land. Every once in a while I pinch off five acres for about a million and drop the money into my grandchildren's trust funds. I only let go of a little at a time, the way De Beers lets go of diamonds. I never sell off so much in one place that the fields lose that quaint look."

Dossett still planted about fifty acres of potatoes near Sagaponack and did much of the work himself. He liked to get up on one of his old Massey Fergusons and disk and plant the same fields he had plowed as a teenager.

"The winters are mild on Long Island," Rose said.

"He probably has some Javanese girl warm up his sheets for him before he goes to bed, so his feet don't get cold."

"Austin, you mind your tongue about Jack Dossett."

"You going to wear those running shoes to the Maidstone Club?"

"I might. You got anything else nasty to say?"

Austin sagged back in his chair, his legs bent below him. "I thought you'd know where Fay went. I guess I better shut up."

Rose stood behind him. She rested her hands on his shoulders and her chin on the top of his head. "I'm sorry Fay wants to leave. I guess she might have hung on in White Pine until she outlived you, the way I did your father. But times change."

Austin drove north out of town, headed nowhere. Instead of helping, the visit to his mother's had made things worse. The constriction of his heart had spread through his body so even his fingers and toes ached.

He should have taken Fay on more vacations in the winter. He should have offered to live half the year in Maine—the potato months from May to October—and the other half somewhere else. But that would never work, because Blake was in school and Fay was teaching. Fay could always quit, of course. But what of brown-haired, gap-toothed, eight-year-old Blake? He could hardly go to school in two different towns.

Their daughter, Maggie, was in her first year at Rhode Island School of Design. Instead of coming home in June, she was flying straight to Wyoming to work in a hotel for the summer. Austin had been unhappy about that, but now he was just as glad. He didn't want her to see what Fay was up to.

Along the Aroostook River's dark pools, a lone gaitered fisherman flicked his line for trout. Ice-out had come only two weeks before. On the bank above the river the dense afternoon sunlight lit up stands of larch and black ash. Austin wasn't much good at fishing. Occasionally he took Blake, who loved it.

Austin didn't want either of his children to lose touch with home. In part that was because he attributed most of the world's problems to people who lived without land. He watched their disasters on the evening news: an abusive husband in handcuffs, a wife charged with leaving her newborn in a dumpster, a teenager too drunk to talk. Austin based his politics on geography. He thought the major tensions of the world would be diffused if the Israelis and the Palestinians and the peasants in El Salvador all had land.

But now even his mother wanted to leave White Pine. It enraged him how she trotted out that old argument about the mild winters down south. If she was so eager to throw herself into hell, why didn't she go all the way down to Florida? Why stop halfway on Long Island?

The beat of his heart jumbled up his thoughts. Without planning to, he found himself driving along the river road toward Lauren Sorrell's. He knew he shouldn't talk to anyone in the state he was in, yet he slowed down and turned into Lauren and Charley's driveway.

"I always know it's you," Lauren said as he walked up to the house. She stood in the doorway smiling. "No one could mistake the sound of that truck." They shook hands on the front porch—a peculiar gesture, Austin thought, after thirty-five years of friendship—and Lauren stepped back to let him into the house. "I hope it's not your return. I hardly see you anymore, except for taxes."

Lauren ran an accounting business out of her home and did Austin's taxes every year. In return Austin seeded her husband's potatoes. Charley wasn't much of a farmer, but he liked to keep his hand in. He liked to lean back in his desk chair at the processing plant and talk about how his crop was coming along.

"I thought you might be out in the garden," Austin said. "The day's so pretty. As pretty as you are."

She looked away, her color rising. This was not how they usually spoke. Indeed, he hadn't planned on saying anything like that.

"Too many late filers," she said. "I've been tied up with a dozen returns. You haven't had a call from the IRS, have you?"

"God forbid. Those guys would sue the Pope for tax evasion. They probably have."

She lifted a coil of hair away from her neck and twirled it through her fingers. It was a gesture unchanged since high school. "So what are you doing out this way?" she said.

"A little business. Just driving around."

They sat at the dining-room table, looking across the road at Charley's twenty-acre potato field. Lauren kept her hands in the pockets of her sweater, a baggy woolen cardigan.

They had been lovers in their last year of high school. And before that they had been friends since the first and second grades. All three of them had been friends: Austin and Charley played on the same basketball and baseball teams, year after year, with Lauren one grade behind them. Starting when she was thirteen, she went steady with Austin for a year, then Charley for a year, then back to Austin—until Charley managed to lock onto her for two straight years in high school.

Even then they were all friends. In the spring term of his senior year Austin asked her out to a party. He was president of the senior class and had already been accepted at Harvard. The party was nothing special, and Austin wasn't trying to steal her away from Charley—yet parked afterward on a dark street in town, she had turned to him and pressed the soft weight of her breasts into his hands. He unbuttoned her blouse and raised her dress above her knees. After making out for an hour, she lifted the gold chain from her neck, unfastened Charley's class ring and replaced it with Austin's.

Over the next month they spent a lot of time in the back seat of Lauren's Fairlane. It was planting season, and every day after school Austin drove a tractor. Lauren would meet him in the fields at dusk with a pizza or submarine sandwich, and they'd drive her car to some sequestered spot. They'd eat dinner on the hood, then climb into the back seat to kiss and talk and touch each other.

They first made love in a motel in Edmundston, Canada, across the border from Fort Kent. Lauren made him promise not to tell anyone, ever—yet almost immediately the fact that they had slept together was common knowledge. Charley knew, their classmates knew, the whole town seemed to know. And to Austin there was no mystery as to how the news got out, because Lauren had begun to radiate sex with every step she took. Her smooth calves showed it, her wide smile and the way she flung her skirts about as she walked into her classrooms and sat down.

What people in the town had not figured out since then was that five times in the last twenty years he and Lauren had repeated the act. Certainly Fay didn't know, or Charley. Several times Austin had come close to telling Fay, but he never had—because after each time Lauren had sworn him to secrecy with a binding oath.

Sitting at the table with her now, he wondered if he might lean forward and kiss her and take her straight into the bedroom. He wasn't at all sure, for they hadn't made love in over six years. Perhaps sex for them was a thing of the past. He had never understood what it meant anyway. The word *adultery* had never seemed to apply to what he did with Lauren. And never, in all these years, had he figured out what sex had to do with their friendship, or their friendship with sex.

But if he went to bed with her now, later she would hear that Fay had moved into town and she'd understand why he had come visiting this afternoon. In fact, it wasn't sex he wanted, but to tell Lauren what Fay had done. He didn't have the nerve.

"I'm going to have trouble getting over to do Charley's planting this year," he said. "It's not the time involved, but ring rot. I was just down in Portland with the Potato Board. They don't think certified seed producers should lend out equipment or work anyone else's fields."

That was a lie. The board members had simply talked, as they always did, about general sanitation and the terrors of ring rot.

"You don't loan us your planter," Lauren said. "You do all the work yourself. I thought you or Jules would be coming over next week. Didn't you already talk to Charley about it?"

"I sure did. But it seems the problem took a bad turn last year down in Mars Hill. And using my equipment on someone else's fields is the fastest way to pick up the disease and spread it around."

"We've never had ring rot on this field, Austin, and you know it."

"All it takes is one volunteer plant from an infected tuber. It's too big a risk. You know what the inspector would do if he found a single diseased plant on one of my fields?"

"Yes, I know."

"I don't think I can risk it."

"And I can't believe you didn't tell us until now. It's going to put Charley in a hell of a bind."

"I'm sorry about that," Austin said. "I just got back this morning. I don't think I knew how serious it was."

Lauren made the old cliché true, she was beautiful when angry. Her eyebrows arched and her face darkened. She didn't say anything.

Later she would figure it all out as surely as if he had slept with her. He felt dizzy. He should never have come here, because his friendship with Lauren was not something he wanted to lose. As abruptly as he had turned into her drive, he coughed up a good-bye and left the house.

Halfway back toward town the view opened up toward the eastern side of the valley. There, a few miles off, was Pooler Farm: the yellow house among the maples and hemlocks, the big yellow equipment barn and the one heliotrope potato house, bright as a billboard.

TWO

On Monday night Austin lay on his couch at home, unable to read or watch television. All evening the phone had rung unanswered when he dialed the Ledyards' number. At eleven o'clock he took off his clothes and went to bed but couldn't sleep.

At midnight he got up, his heart racing, put his clothes back on and drove to town. As quietly as possible he cruised past the Ledyards' house. The lights were off, but Fay's van was parked in the driveway. At least she had come back on the promised date.

Late the next afternoon, after school was out, he drove back into town. It embarrassed him to call upon his wife like a suitor. He parked a block away and hoped no one would see him standing at the door of the Ledyards' house.

Blake ran out first and jumped into his arms. "Hi, Dad! Mom and I went to Quebec!"

Austin held his son's compact little body to his chest. It seemed as if the boy had been away for months. "Did you? Did you have fun?"

"We went on the ferryboat twice over to Lévis. And we ate in a fancy restaurant where I had to wear a coat and tie. I ate a whole steak."

"A porterhouse with béarnaise sauce," Fay said. She stood behind her son out of Austin's reach, wearing a printed circle skirt and a white blouse. She still had her hair pinned up from work. "It cost a small fortune. How are you doing?"

"I'm okay, I guess."

"Come on in. Have you ever been here?"

"We ate dinner here once. Duck or something. It was years ago. I put the car into a snowbank on the way home."

"That's right, I forgot. I heard at school they wanted someone to look after the place while they're gone."

"Which is how long?" Austin asked.

"July sometime."

Fay held the reins now. Or the cleaver. With a single stroke she had divided their marriage in two.

"Blake, why don't you watch television for a while?" she suggested. "And then maybe your dad will take you out to the farm and cook French fries for you."

After the boy left, she said, "I don't think we should talk these things over in front of him, do you?" Austin stepped forward to embrace her, but she met him with an upraised palm. "Not now. I want to keep a little distance. It took me a long time to do this, and I don't want to throw it away the first time you come over and look sad."

"Do I look sad?" He felt much worse than sad. "I guess I do."

They sat at opposite ends of the long sofa while Fay told him about her weekend in Quebec. "I did some shopping," she said.

"I noticed the new skirt," he said. "Walk around in it and let me see."

"I don't think so."

He felt dizzy. He felt as if his heart were being stepped on. "Was there a man in Quebec?"

"There was no man." Fay crossed her arms over her chest. "Nothing new has happened, you know."

Austin nodded. His body had dropped away below him.

"I've lived in your world for twenty years," she began. "So I think it's only fair for you to give me the next five or ten. That's kind of a joke, but only kind of. You know what I want, don't you?"

He knew he should have, so he kept nodding. He knew the minute she said the words he would remember everything—but until she actually said them, his mind stayed furiously blank.

"I want to choose something on my own," she said. "It doesn't matter that much what it is, as long as *I* choose it. Because all these years I've been living your life, in your town with your family. And I don't want to stay here until I'm sixty-six years old the way your mother has."

"She's leaving."

"I know," Fay said. "I talked to her about it."

"Is that what you want, to go off and live with some other guy?"

"Austin, you're not listening. There are plenty of men out there—and I've had a few invitations. But that's not what I want. I want you to come with me. I really do."

She looked as attractive as she had in years. Her hair fell to her shoulders, and her skirt to the top of her calves. Her blouse was open at the throat. She had dressed up for his visit, he thought. Yet her look was hard, almost pained, and when he made a move toward her along the couch, she raised her hand and held it up between them like a traffic cop.

"Don't, Austin."

"Don't what?"

"I know what you think. You think if I'd just relax, we'd both feel better. But I don't want to relax. I've got too much to do."

Though she held herself stiffly upright, wedged into the far corner of the couch, she didn't sound very sure of herself. For a moment Austin thought he could turn her around. "You didn't miss me in Quebec?"

"I missed you a lot," she said, the words spilling out in a tumble. "I kept remembering the last time we were there with Maggie. It was kind of sad this time, just me and Blake."

He breathed in. This was what he wanted to hear. Of course Fay had her doubts. She clutched one hand in the other and stared at the floor, her eyebrows jumping.

"I didn't know where you were," he said.

But when she looked up a minute later, her face was composed. "Just because I got a little lonely doesn't mean I'm going back to the farm. Even if I get horribly lonely, I'm not going back. Sure, half of me could pack up my things and drive out with you tonight—but I'm not going to."

"I wasn't asking you to do that," he said.

"No, but you think I should. And you think this is all some terrible plot of mine. That's the look you get when we talk about it. But this hurts me too. I don't want my life split apart any more than you do."

"But who's splitting us apart?"

She stood up and walked across the living room. With her back to him she looked as slim and distant as a fish in midstream. She turned abruptly. "This is not something *I'm* doing. It's something *we're* doing. It pisses me off that you don't see that."

"I don't. I don't see it."

"Then tell me this. Are you going to plant this year?"

"Fay, please. What else can I do?"

Her expression hardened as if set in a mold. "You could listen to what I've been saying for the last two years. You could start with that. You could acknowledge for once that you've even thought about it." Her voice had risen and now shook.

He started to speak but she cut him off. "I'm glad you want to talk, Austin. I want to talk more myself—but not now. Come another day, whenever you want. You don't have to call first and there won't be any men here. I hope we can work things out about Blake."

And with that the conversation was over. Because he was going to plant potatoes—the same as every other year of his adult life—she had nothing more to say to him. The interview was closed, and they had never so much as touched hands. Five minutes later he drove home with Blake to make dinner in his empty farmhouse.

Against one wall of the kitchen Austin had built a pair of giant wooden dispensers, one for baking potatoes and the other for fryers, both of them large enough to hold a full bushel of spuds. From either dispenser the tubers rolled out like giant gumdrops onto a tray below. While Blake washed some Green Mountains, Austin heated olive oil in a deep pan.

"You should have come with us, Dad. It was great."

"I should have. What else did you do?"

"Walked around the harbor and the old town and up to the Château."

"The Frontenac."

"Yeah, that one. And we stayed in a hotel where Mom said you and Maggie and her went to last year."

"The Brisquard. That's your mom's favorite hotel. So how do you like it over at the Ledyards' house?"

"It's okay."

"Just okay?"

"Yeah, it's all right. Here, these are all washed. Call me when dinner's ready. I'm going to see if that robin's nest is still there with the eggs in it." A moment later he was out the door.

Austin let him go. He didn't want to start complaining to his son, or saying that the whole thing was Fay's idea or that the reason he hadn't gone to Quebec was because he hadn't been invited.

After dinner Blake took a bath, then let himself be rubbed down with a towel. He went loose in his father's hands, making engine sounds with a wavering pitch: *wahwoo wahwoo wahwoo*. He put on his pajamas, brushed his teeth, peed, drank a glass of water, adopted a sprinter's crouch at the end of the hall and ran down the varnished plank floors to jump onto his bed.

"And now *Lieutenant Hornblower?*" Austin said.

"Yes. And you have to keep reading until I'm asleep. You have to."

Blake curled up against his chest. When Austin started too far back on the crimped page, Blake immediately corrected him. "You already read that."

He must have been tired, for after only a few minutes he closed his eyes. Austin read another page, then stopped to watch his son drift off. His breath was sweet, his skin transparent. Should something wake him now he would be up for another hour—but if he were left undisturbed for ten more minutes, a hand clap beside his ear would fail to rouse him. An hour more and he would lie in the uttermost depths of sleep.

Austin sat beside the bed for twenty minutes. Then he went

downstairs and opened a James Ready. He sat in the darkened living room with the beer in his hand, thinking about Fay's history.

For a full decade she had thrown herself into the job of planting and harvesting potatoes. She tilled fields, talked to brokers and drove the heaviest bulk body trucks. She thought of herself as a liberated woman—one who could work like a man. And then suddenly, after ten years at Austin's side, she had had enough.

From the start she had always taken a six-week break from the long potato season and gone to stay with her family in the Hallwicks' summer house on Nantucket. Austin managed to break away at the start of August, and he flew down to join his wife and daughter on the island. After two weeks they all drove home together. Year after year they followed the same schedule.

But one summer in mid-August when it came time to pack up the van and head back to White Pine, Fay didn't want to go. She said Maggie could miss the August start of school. The kids never learned anything then anyway, because after four weeks the schools closed down again so everyone could pick potatoes.

"And from now on," Maggie announced at the dinner table in support of her mother, "I'm going to be independent." She was nine years old, with long, skinny legs and a haircut almost as short as a boy's.

Mother and daughter, Austin thought. God knows what things they shared behind a man's back. But he left them and flew back to White Pine by himself. After Labor Day, with the start of harvest only ten days off, he flew down again to bring his family home. But Fay still wasn't ready. Maggie could go back, she said, but she was staying.

"What are you talking about?" Austin said. "The summer's over. They're going to close down everything on the island. They already have."

"The stores stay open. Plenty of people live here year-round. And I want to see what it's like in the fall. Do you know I've come here every year of my life and never once stayed past Labor Day?"

Austin held out his hands. "So?"

"So not this year. This year I'm going to see what the ocean looks like when the summer is over and everyone has gone."

The island was peaceful in September, and the nights cool. The truth was that if it hadn't been for harvest, Austin would rather have come at this time of the year himself. He understood how Fay might want to sit alone up on the Siasconset headlands and watch the ocean in a new season. But he worried about her wild look. Her clothes were rumpled and her hair uncombed. When he tried to argue with her, she looked right through him. Her family had all gone home.

He had asked her then too if there was some other man. Of course not, she said. She just wasn't ready to leave yet.

So Austin flew back to White Pine with Maggie and entered the monthlong ordeal of harvest. For a while he called Fay every night, until she told him, "For godsake, Austin, I'm not carrying on some affair. It's just me and the ocean. Do your harvest and let me take a break from it. I'm happy here alone. I'm having a wonderful time."

When he flew down again in mid-October, she let him drive her home. She had done enough camping in the unheated house and had watched enough waves. But she had also decided something about her life on the farm.

"I've planted and harvested with you for ten years," she said. "I always liked it, but now I've had enough. I want to do some work of my own. First I'm going to go back to school to get my teaching certificate. And then—I've been thinking. How would you like to have another child?"

"I thought you'd never ask," he said, laughing. He had wanted a second child for years, almost from the time Maggie was born. "We might have a boy."

"We might," she said, holding him by the chest. "But you never know."

So this was not the first time Fay had chafed under life in northern Maine and the Pooler obsession with potatoes. Austin set his beer on the floor beside the couch. Ten years ago, he thought, everything had worked out for the best. But now it didn't look good. Fay was older. She wasn't going to get sidetracked by either a job or another child. Austin threw himself at the problem over and over, but didn't see how this could ever turn out well.

Austin knelt on the chill floor of the barn, connecting one of his big Lockwood planters to a tractor. In the first hour of dawn the trees above the farmhouse showed only as silhouettes against the pale sky. Jules drove up with his truck lights on. He was slight, he seemed no larger than a child as he slid out from behind the wheel of his oversized pickup. He set his quart Thermos of coffee on the concrete floor and thumped one of the large, cleated tractor tires with his fist.

"Jesus and Mary," he said. "I love the first day."

Austin secured the three-point hitch with a set of linchpins. "Maybe this year Jesus and Mary will take care of the beetle."

"Maybe they will." Jules stood by the open door and raised his chin, testing the weather against his throat. There was ground fog in the valley, but it wouldn't last. "Your father was the same way," he said. "He hated religion. He'd as soon have eaten rocks as go to church."

"We used to go at Easter," Austin said. "When's the last time you went to mass?"

"Cathy goes for me. She even confesses my sins. But then I say the Hail Marys and Our Fathers. I can polish those off by the dozen out on the tractor. I always save some up for planting." He gave a rare ingenuous smile.

"Come on, Jules, you don't believe in that rigmarole."

"I don't know. What's the harm in saying a few prayers?"

"If you married a Buddhist," Austin said, "would you spin those little prayer wheels?"

"What wheels? I just keep the peace. I say those Hail Marys the same way I jump up after dinner and wash the dishes. I'd just as soon sit back awhile and give 'em a rest, but Cathy wants them done on the instant. She gets all heated up if they lie around in the sink for ten minutes. And since it's no big deal to me, I go along with the program. You know, it's married life."

Austin understood that Jules, who rarely came out with such a long speech, was making an indirect offer to talk about Fay.

But Austin wasn't ready yet. He didn't know what he could say about it except that Fay wanted to leave—and that just by planting potatoes, the same as he did every spring, he might be sealing his own fate. He clicked home the hydraulics and gave the tractor a cursory inspection.

Fifteen minutes later the first two members of the planting crew drove up in an old Malibu and a Plymouth Fury. Seven more followed soon after. Three workers ran the seed-cutting machines in the barn, two rode over the bins on either planter and two more ferried the seed and fertilizer out to the tractors. In all, seven men and two women stood in a semicircle on the drive. In the granite light, wisps of vapor rose into the air from their white faces. It was not yet 6:00 A.M.

Austin read them their rights and duties. "We start at six o'clock, take a full hour off for lunch and quit at seven. Everything over eight hours a day is time and a half, and on weekends—as long as you don't miss any days—it's double time. We still serve lunch here, same as my father did. Same as my grandfather."

Few growers paid as well as Austin. For their part he asked his crew to put in eighty-four hours a week for three straight weeks, or until the job was done. With enough overtime everyone showed up every day.

Though ten years had passed since Fay last helped with the planting, she had never failed, at this exact hour of the first morning, to emerge from the house with a steaming pot of coffee and a trayful of doughnuts. As Austin spoke, a few members of the crew turned to have a look at the yellow Pooler house.

He started them off without any more talk. Almost all of them had worked for him before. First they loaded Katahdin seed into the four hoppers on each planter, then topped off the fertilizer bins with pelletized 10-20-16. The sun had not yet cleared the top of the ridge when Austin planted his first thirty feet of seed. He jumped down to check the spacing and found, in the ridged soil behind the closing disks, a sliced potato every ten inches and a band of fertilizer on either side of the seed. In the cool moist soil the tubers gave off a mineral odor.

He drove precisely, listening to the click and drag of the planter, making a tight curve at either end of the field and aligning himself for each new pass with the hydraulic row marker. For the first time in days his anxious heartbeat slowed. He forgot about the troubled phone calls and visits he'd been having with Fay.

The fields were never so broad and empty as when plowed but not yet planted. Fenced only by poplar and birch and fir, they were topped by leviathan skies. At the bottom of the valley the rivers still ran raw with mud after last week's rain. Austin loved the barbaric look of the land in early May, and the fact that he was taming it.

The crew settled in and the job assumed its endless rhythm: drive and turn, drive and turn, pause and load. Six hundred acres, twenty-two fields and a dozen varieties of seed. In the first few hours, always a delicate time, there were no breakdowns.

Cathy Derosier arrived at noon with a full hot lunch: fried chicken, peas and baked potatoes. After eating, while the others slept out their hour, Austin walked along the edge of a woodlot. The weather was benign. A partridge drummed his mating call on a log, then scuffled off among the chokecherries. With the tractors quiet Austin could hear the calls of redwing blackbirds and grosbeaks.

All afternoon freshly cut seed potatoes the size of jumbo eggs arrived at the field in barrels. The long rows combed Austin's thoughts clean. Once he said the Lord's Prayer, stumbling only at the end.

Beneath the coulters and disks of the planter, the earth was moist and friable. The soil smelled of life: of bacteria and fungi and paramecia. For Austin, on such a spring day there was only one thing in the world to do, and that was plant. He drove and drove, he didn't care if seven o'clock never came. Behind the tractor's hypnotic drone he gave up worrying about Fay. Here in the fields there were few choices to be made, for in the spring a man planted. Later in the season, if no one paid attention, the plants might wither in a drought, or the Colorado potato beetle might eat them to the stems, or they might wilt under late blight. Perhaps even later, one's wife and child might decamp. But in the Aroostook spring, if a man had land and a tractor and potato seed, he planted.

At forty-three, though he had done this all his life, Austin's urge to plant was as strong as ever. Maybe stronger now that it was under attack. He wanted to raise more and more potatoes. And until recently, when Fay had convinced him to get a vasectomy, he had also wanted to raise more children. A third child, at least. Year after year they had talked it over. She was adamant and finally he gave in. And only a couple of years later she started talking about leaving.

He had always loved Fay pregnant. Smooth-skinned, dreamy and self-absorbed, she had almost no concern for the rest of the world. The second time, with Blake, she had spent the entire summer on Nantucket, and Austin had gone for four weeks instead of two. That was the summer of cherries and black-berries. Fay sat in a sagging captain's chair, Thoreau's *Cape Cod* propped on her swollen belly, picking cherries out of a bowl and spitting the stones into her hand. The sunlight lay across the pine floor of her parents' house, and the dusty window screens were marked, after squirt-gun wars between eleven-year-old Maggie and a friend, by dark paisley swirls. In front of the house, beyond a miniature lawn ringed by beach plums, lay the cliff, the surf and the Atlantic Ocean.

Fay read. She slept through the afternoons and stayed up half the night with Thoreau and D. H. Lawrence. The world revolved elsewhere, without her. She was immune, for once, to her mother's schedule of parties, tennis and walks to the ocean. She did exactly as she pleased. Pregnant, flat-footed, her lustrous dark hair pulled back from her temples, she padded about the house like a native queen. She asked for blackberries and cottage cheese. Austin took them to her chair in the living room, then stood in the kitchen and watched her read. She had forgotten he was there.

He didn't care. He loved to watch her that way. In the evenings he lay with his head next to her belly, hoping to feel the prod of a tiny foot against his temple. Nothing disturbed him in those halcyon days. Fay had yet to say, even as a joke, that one day she wanted to live somewhere other than Aroostook County.

To Jules, Austin often spoke as if his summer vacation were a duty, a family obligation that tore him away from the fields. In fact he always liked Nantucket when he got there. He loved the desolate beaches when the fog rolled in, the cobalt hydrangeas, the Norfolk pines and grey shingled houses. He swam and played tennis. He played a little golf with some guys he knew—and finally came to admit, after a dozen years, that he liked the game. With the least tailwind he could drive the ball 250 yards.

In recent years, since her husband's death, Lina Hallwick had turned relentlessly social. She liked Fay to join her at the Nantucket Yacht Club for a morning game of doubles, after which they ate a fashionable lunch in town. Austin thought it was an affront to the world's poor to spend forty dollars apiece on a lunch. Fay demurred. She said it was part of being a daughter.

Austin could not always distinguish between what Fay did to please her mother and what she did of her own desire. Fay liked to go to cocktail and dinner parties, with or without him. She liked to play tennis in a little flared skirt that showed off her underwear. Sometimes she played a game in the morning and wore the skirt all day long.

After twenty years of marriage Austin still thought his wife was beautiful. Of course, he wasn't blind. He knew her looks were fading. Every summer, without a trace of malice, an exuberant new crop of high-school and college girls slipped into miniscule bikinis, made up their already flawless skins and nudged Fay further into a category with no sure name. She was a grown-up, a mother, no longer in her thirties—but certainly not yet middle-aged. There were still times when every man at a party wanted to talk to her—but also cold winter mornings in Maine when she stumbled out of bed with a cough and a papery skin.

She had started jogging and skiing after Blake's birth, and was thinner at forty-two than she had been at thirty-two. Her waist was like a young girl's, though her wrists and ankles were heavy. She looked like a folk painting, large at the extremities.

For Austin, she moved with a grace that could not be captured in photographs. At night she could still excite him just by lowering a nightgown over her shoulders, then reaching up below it and pulling off her underwear. Sometimes all it took was for her to kneel at the foot of their bed, half-dressed and legs askew, and stare at him.

Year after year they had had some of their greatest sex in the Nantucket summer house. Not inside the house itself—whose uninsulated plank walls allowed even simple conversations to carry from room to room—but where they regularly slept, on the screened-in summer porch. There, especially on windy nights, the battering ocean masked the noises they made in bed.

Only last summer they had come home late from a party and found the house dark and everyone asleep. Fay had watched him undress, then stripped off her own clothes and laid them on a chair. She made him get off the bed and stand behind her as she crouched on the edge of the mattress, her elbows pushed down, her loose hair hiding her face. Austin leaned against her, planting and withdrawing in strokes as slow as oil. Fay dropped her head and was silent—until a cry escaped her. The first was no louder than the surf beyond the cliff, but it was followed by other, louder cries.

Austin gathered up a couple of blankets and led her outside across the lawn past a gap in the beach plums. She lay in a crouch, in a sandy depression not twenty feet from the top of the cliff. He started over, warming her up like a machine gone cold. First he opened her with his fingers, then with his palm, then with his mouth. He ate her in time with the whistling surf, coursing the length of her vagina with his tongue. Finally he entered her again. He spoke to the back of her neck.

"Do you want your mother to hear?"

"Of course not."

"Do you?"

"Well." She laughed as if drunk. The wind carried off her words into the night. "It wouldn't hurt her. Sometimes I think it would do some good. I don't know what gets into me here. I never scream at home."

"Sometimes a little," he said.

"Only when you tease me. *Oh,* don't move. Don't move at all."

Austin pressed his mouth against the cool flesh of her shoulders. "What if I have to get up and stretch my legs? I might want to have a look at the sea."

"You could carry me with you. I love you, Austin. I love it when you come down from Maine, and I hate it when the summer ends. I'm never ready to go back."

He pressed the front of his thighs against the back of hers, lifting her forward with each stroke. The wind had grown cold on his back. When Fay grew still and silent he let his own orgasm come through. He caught up to her just at the end. Afterward they lay tangled on the sand, the blankets pulled over them, the night suddenly cold.

"I mean it," she said. They lay facing the Atlantic. "I hate it when the summer ends. I don't want to go back."

"You want to stay on into the fall, the way you did ten years ago."

"No, it's bigger than that."

A week later they drove home and Fay went back to teaching the second grade, and they did not have a good year in White Pine. Some years are better than others, Austin told himself. But the winter came early and stayed late, and almost for the first time in their marriage they argued.

When he got home from the fields that night Fay's van was in the drive and Fay in the kitchen cooking dinner: spaghetti and frozen broccoli, her own from last summer. She turned toward him but didn't stop work. "Hi, Austin. Was it a good first day?"

"Not too bad."

He didn't know if he was glad to see his wife or not. He was, but it didn't seem fair that here she could come and go at will, while at the Ledyards' house he felt like an intruder.

"I had a few things to pick up out here," she said. "And I thought Blake might want to spend the night with you. Then we got hungry and I decided to cook for all of us."

"Can I, Dad? I want to sleep out here."

"You can always spend the night, any time you want. If your mom's busy, I'll come in at the end of the day and get you."

"And I want you to read to me."

"Good. We've been falling behind with *Lieutenant Hornblower*."

"You're not reading ahead, are you?"

"Not a page. Though sometimes I want to."

After dinner Austin put his son to bed and read to him. By the time he came downstairs it was long since dark. Fay had cleaned up after dinner and was outside loading some kitchenware and books into her van.

"I worry about Blake," she said. "He pretends everything's fine, but I don't think he really understands what's going on."

"What *is* going on?"

"You know what's going on, because I told you. I'm leaving."

"And this is the civil way to do it? A couple of boxes at a time? First you move into White Pine, and then it's on to Portland."

Fay pushed her hair back and held it away from her face with a clip. "I guarantee you I won't move to Portland. It's too close."

"So when are you going to make this big move to wherever?"

"Not before I finish teaching. When school is over in June, I'll give them notice."

"I can't believe it."

"I know you can't. That's why I'm so patient with you and why I tell you everything over and over. Because you're a slow learner."

"You're angry," he said. "It's because I started planting."

She took his arm in hers and held it to her side. "I never get angry at you. I wish I did sometimes, but I just get sad."

"Because I don't listen."

"No, because I'm asking you to stop doing what you love most. I don't hate it when you plant, I like it. I almost called Cathy to find out what field you were in so Blake and I could drive out and see you after school."

"I missed you this morning with coffee and doughnuts," he said.

She dropped his arm and looked up at him without blinking. "I'm sorry about this, Austin. It's the saddest thing I've ever done."

He wanted to believe her. "Maybe we could live in two different places. Six months here for the potatoes and then the other half somewhere you want to be."

Fay stood next to her van, watching the moonlight on the empty fields. The clear skies threatened frost, and the night was already cool. She gathered her sweater to her throat. "I don't know. Maybe you could come visit me for six months."

"I could. I could do that."

"No, I don't think so. I don't see how that could work. I don't want to be just a failed part of Aroostook County—you know, one of those wimpy out-of-staters who can't take the winters and has to go where it's warm. Because it's more than that. I want to start my own life from the ground up. And I want you and Maggie and Blake to be part of it. I must be dreaming."

"Sometimes I think you've just . . . had enough of me," Austin said.

She opened her arms to him and held him against her chest. Her hair smelled different. Maybe it was from living in another house and sleeping in another bed. He wanted to go on holding her.

But she didn't let him. Only a minute later she took a step back and raised her hand.

"Fay . . ."

"Palm out," she said. "It's still palm out."

They had worked out their first hand signs years ago at parties, where a palm turned out meant don't-worry-about-me-I'm-doing-fine, and a palm turned in meant come-rescue-me-from-this-bore. By now there were a dozen variations to the signs, including palm out with a crossed thumb: let's-get-out-of-here; and palm in held close to the heart: I'm-feeling-amorous. Fay's current gesture, however, was just the traffic-cop palm, not the least bit subtle.

Austin wrapped his arms around his own chest. "How long is this going to go on?"

"I don't know, but that's how I feel. Palm out. If it changes I'll let you know."

"We hardly touch anymore," he said.

Fay closed the side door of the van. From one moment to the next she was all business. "You think sex could solve all this."

"Fay, that's unfair. I've never been like that. I didn't say anything about sex—I just said we don't touch anymore. I miss it. I miss talking to you."

"Things change." She got into the van and started the engine. Once behind the wheel she softened a little.

"The trouble is, I'm afraid to be affectionate with you. I think if I'm affectionate we'll have sex, and if we have sex I'll lose everything. I could give in again, you know. It would be a lot easier than all this. But I've been giving in to you for two years, so sex is going to have to wait until I'm stronger. Maybe it'll be easier for me after I've moved to . . . Seattle, or Tucson or Santa Barbara."

"That's where you're going?"

"I don't know, Austin. Those are just places I've thought about. I don't know what I'm doing."

"You could hardly go any farther away."

"Probably anywhere I think of is going to be far away."

"What if I promised you no sex?"

Fay laughed from behind the wheel. "Austin, you can still get to me."

"We could just hug a little," he said.

"I do love you. For everything we've ever done, I love you."

"Then the next time, a hug or two."

"I don't know. Good night, Austin."

They talked on the phone every couple of days and traded Blake back and forth—but there were no hugs. They never so much as brushed arms. They were like characters in a soap opera, Austin thought: they had secrets, they couldn't talk, they were nervous all the time.

One night he ran into Fay and Blake at the supermarket. Blake, who had seen his truck in the parking lot, ran down the aisles looking for him. Austin picked him up and Blake clung to him with his arms and legs. Maybe that's how Fay got by without needing any hugs, he thought: She had Blake, every day.

Fay came along behind with an empty cart. Austin's was almost full. "You're really stocking up," she said. "Is all that yours?"

"Once-a-month shopping. And I've got some things for Blake in here too. Like pistachio ice cream, because he's the weird one in the family."

"Mmm, pistachio. The best," Blake said. He hung from his father's neck and looked into his cart. "And Peanut Butter Bonkers!"

Austin was about to ask him if he'd like to come out to the farm for the night when he caught sight of the town's most relentless gossip, Sue Randall, approaching past the frozen pizzas. "I'll meet you outside," he told Fay. Before she could answer, he wheeled his cart around and headed for the checkout counters with Blake still hanging from his neck.

Maybe the whole town already knew what was going on between him and Fay. Maybe—but Austin didn't want Sue Randall to see them buying separate groceries. A dozen people had already asked him about his purple storage house, and that was bad enough.

He and Blake sat at the edge of the parking lot on a concrete stop, eating pistachio ice cream with their fingers.

"Don't tell your mom," Austin said. "We're supposed to have better table manners than this."

Fay caught them but didn't care. She was already mad. Or maybe cold, which was worse. She threw her groceries in the van and told Blake to get in.

"But I'm going to Dad's. We already decided."

"Then go get in his truck. Go ahead, he'll be over in a minute. Take the ice cream." She was hard as hickory.

"What's got into you?" Austin said when Blake had gone.

"You're completely out of it. Is that what you're going to feel when I'm gone—embarrassed because somebody finds out? Why not think about *us* instead? Why not think about whether or not we can keep this marriage together?"

"I don't want people talking about us. I don't see why they should."

"Austin, this is Fay, your wife. I'm talking to you. I'm telling you that you don't have that much time to wake up."

"Fay, take it easy. We're in the middle of town."

"You're never going to learn. You're not paying attention. Go ahead then, take Blake with you—but *you* take him to school in the morning. And think about what's going on before the next time we meet."

After that night a week passed and he didn't see her, or Blake either. Planting took too much time. He worked all day, cooked dinner and kept his records. He tumbled into bed at ten and rose well before dawn the next morning. In the past he had always had Fay's help during planting. He had paid her back during the winters, when he did almost all the cooking and cleaning.

He missed Blake. He talked to him a couple of times on the phone and made plans for a little camping trip as soon as the planting was done. Then something came up that Austin needed to ask Fay's advice about. It was only an excuse to see her, he knew.

Dick Lachance had come over to the farm one night and offered to sell Austin a hundred acres of land at four hundred dollars an acre. Four hundred dollars was way, way under the market for developed potato land. Even if Austin never touched a plow to it, the piece would be a great investment.

So he invited himself over to Fay's for dinner one night, and after Blake was asleep Austin told her about Lachance's offer. "No one could lose money at that price," he said. "Even with troubles in the potato industry, land values have been going back up. And Maine farmland is doing better than most places in the country."

Fay nodded. Her expression was flat, unreadable.

"You know that field. It sits up above the McCaslin piece."

"I know where it is."

"And there's a woodlot at one end that's got some good timber in it. Lachance needs the cash or he'd never let it go so cheap."

Fay never moved or spoke. She sat on the Ledyards' couch with her feet raised to the coffee table. She looked like an atheist trapped in church. But Austin went on. He thought he had a trump.

"That was the field we drove up to after Blake was born. Do you remember that? You had him all wrapped up in a white blanket, and we walked out along the furrows and laid him down. It was warm for so late in the fall."

"I remember."

"And we left him there for a few minutes. He was asleep. We walked off a hundred yards and came back and pretended we found him there. Do you remember that? We pretended he was someone else's little baby and we'd just stumbled across him. Well, that's the same field Lachance wants to sell."

Fay put one foot on the floor, then the other, and stood up. "Get out," she said.

"Why? What's the matter?"

"Just go on out the door."

"Fay, what's wrong?"

"You're completely mad. I'm talking about moving away and still trying to have a life with you, and you come around telling me you want to buy more land. You've got too much land already. What do you need any more for? I've had it, Austin."

"But, Fay . . . "

"Don't press me. *Palm out*," she said and held up her hand. "Go home and think this one over. See if you can wake up on your own, because I've said everything I have to say. Just go."

He drove home knowing he'd made another mistake. And only a week later she left town.

T H R E E

This time, perhaps because she wanted the delay, Fay sent her letter through the mail. Austin drove back from the fields, picked up the mail at his box on Pooler Road and went straight in to start dinner. He had already sliced up the potatoes and heated the pan before he paused to leaf through the pile of bills and junk mail. And there, in Fay's handwriting on a blue envelope, was his name and address. It was the same stationery as last time.

Dear Austin,

I never thought I'd leave out of anger, but I was furious the day you came over. More land. *How much land do you need? And what did you think, that another hundred acres would hold me back?*

I'm going. For a long time I hoped to make this move with you, but you're planting potatoes again—as I should have known you would—and I can't wait any longer. I'm sorry, Austin.

And I know you're going to be angry, because I'm taking Blake with me. There's no excuse, I just have to have him. I've wrestled with it but I can't leave without him.

Imagine how Blake would see it if I left him behind. He'd think I didn't want him anymore. No matter what I said or wrote to him, he'd think I'd abandoned him. But he won't have to feel that way about you, because you'll be at home the same as always.

Can you see how unfair it all is about Blake? The cards are stacked against me if I want to go somewhere else and be with my son. You have all his friends here, his toys, the house, baseball on the lawn—everything. It may be unfair for me to take him, but it's just as unfair to think I have to leave him.

I've written Maggie, so she knows I'm going. I haven't changed my mind about the long run, you know. I still hope all of us will be together—though not here.

After the dust settles, I'll send you word on how we're doing. Maybe where we're headed isn't the best place for me in the long run—it probably isn't—but all the same, I won't be coming back to live in White Pine.

Love,

Fay

Austin turned off the stove and threw his potatoes into the compost bucket. "The Bronx and Queens," he swore. "*Goddamn you, Fay.*"

He ran upstairs to look at her closet and at Blake's. He thought a few more clothes were gone, but he couldn't be sure. She'd been taking things bit by bit.

He phoned the Ledyard house but there was no answer. He dialed his mother's number but hung up before it started to ring. He didn't even want Rose to know.

Both their passports were missing from the file cabinet. Austin searched twice, but his was the only one there. His heart drove through his chest. He sat down at his desk and tried to think.

He dialed the Hallwicks' house on Nantucket but the number was temporarily disconnected. Of course, for the house would not have been opened yet for the summer. Fay wouldn't go to Nantucket anyway, that was too easy. She wouldn't go to her mother's either.

Not to Portland, not back to Quebec and surely not to Boston or New York. Not even Fay would stoop that low.

He flipped through the unpaid bills that had piled up on his desk since the start of planting season, and ripped open the one from the telephone company. There were calls listed from before the time Fay moved out of the house, and several of them were to her sister in Amherst. In fact, altogether there had been eight calls made to Carolyn's number—one of them at three in the morning. Austin could not remember that Fay had ever gotten out of bed at 3:00 A.M. to make a phone call.

Carolyn would be the one to know. He should have figured that out on his own. The number was in his hand, so he called her.

"Hi, this is Carolyn. Thanks for calling and please leave a message after the tone. You can speak as long as you like."

He went outside and sat on a lawn chair, ignoring the mosquitoes and flies. Periodically he got up to call his sister-in-law's number.

"Hi, this is Carolyn. Thanks for calling and please—"

"*Goddamn it, Carolyn,* I know you're screening these calls. Fay, are you there? Just pick up the phone for a minute, will you? I want to know how Blake is. Carolyn? Fay?"

No one ever answered.

Early the next morning, before the first light showed above the ridge, Austin dressed, packed and ran down the stairs. The kitchen windowpanes were shiny black. He had skipped dinner the night before, so he cooked himself a full breakfast of home fries, eggs and toast. Before driving off he left a note for Jules on the barn blackboard. They'd have to manage the last couple of planting days without him.

The fields along Route 1 were fenceless, the same as on Pooler Road. As far as Houlton this was all potato country. And even before sunrise, as an early pearl light turned lemon over the Canadian border, a few tractors stalked across the land. Bob Palenk's blue Ford stood out like a jay in the middle of a tan field. Austin waved at him, but Palenk had his eye on his planter. He was a hard-working, careful farmer, lost in the true fancy of spring.

Along the interstate south of Houlton the woods closed in on the County's last open fields. A few villages, a final few acres of cleared land and then nothing but trees. Whenever the road lifted off the forest floor, Austin made out the top of Mount Katahdin thirty miles to the west.

Austin wanted to cry but couldn't. He pushed his truck to seventy-five, trying to shake himself into tears, but they wouldn't come. He needed Fay's help.

The week his father died she had taught him how to cry. Anthony Pooler lay in the hospital after his heart attack, not recovering. Austin went every day to watch him breathe. There was no other sign of life.

Pacing around his house, Austin felt as if his ribs were being pried apart. He could hardly touch his children, or even look at his mother. He was a wreck.

"Austin, come here."

Fay sat down with him on their bed, kneeling face to face. He thought for a moment she wanted to make love—for sometimes they sat like that before sex, just watching each other. But that wasn't it. Fay stared at him but paid no attention to his body. Her eyes drew back into her skull. Her brows thrust forward and her mouth grew long. As Austin watched, the first tears came into her eyes. She took his hands in hers. A minute later her body began to shake, her breaths came hard and then she was sobbing, almost soundlessly, directly into his face.

Without a thought he began to cry himself. Outside of movies it was something he had rarely done in his entire adult life. Fay didn't say a word. He cried and cried, calling up before him the vision of his father's inert form in the hospital bed. And every day until Anthony Pooler died, and often in the weeks that followed, Fay would take Austin's hand and lead him upstairs to their bedroom. There, the same as the first time, she showed him the way. It got so his tears would spring out within seconds of getting onto the bed—but he always needed to be with her. He never learned to do it alone. So now, when he wanted to cry about Fay, he couldn't do it.

Six hours after leaving home he dropped down out of Maine into the little wing of New Hampshire that touched the ocean. He skirted Boston on 495 but could not altogether avoid the suburbs, the traffic and the hazy blue air. Tired of driving, he stayed in the left lane of Route 2 and risked a ticket halfway across Massachusetts.

Approaching Amherst the back way, along the quiet stretches of road near Quabbin Reservoir, he had to admit to himself that a few attractive places still existed in southern New England. Here, for example, a few thousand acres had somehow been overlooked by the developers. They must have been waiting for the population to rise another percent.

Fay's van was parked in Carolyn's driveway just as he had expected. But no one was home and the van was locked. Austin hadn't thought to bring a key. Indeed, besides the one they always left in the ignition, he didn't know if there was another key. One of Blake's sweaters lay on the front seat along with a book of travel games and a paper bag from McDonald's. Suddenly he had an image of his son's bleak future: fast food wherever they went.

Sheltered from the street by a profusion of climbing roses, Austin sat down in a cushioned chair on his sister-in-law's front porch. Sunlight flickered onto the green wooden floor while unseen insects droned and ticked through the still air. He sat back and closed his eyes.

He dreamed he was paddling down the Saint John with Thoreau—but in a modern, flame-red canoe. The seats were made of old railroad ties and the thwarts of baseball bats. "Wake up," Henry David said and laid his hand on Austin's shoulder. "Wake up."

It was Carolyn, gently shaking him. "Austin, wake up. Do you want something to drink? You sure didn't waste any time getting down here."

"Unnh." He hated waking up out of afternoon naps. They always left him groggy and confused.

"Fay thought you'd be too busy with planting to leave."

"What do you mean, too busy? Where are they?" He struggled up out of the chair, uncrimping his damp neck. His voice sounded to him as if he spoke through a bat of insulation.

"You don't look so good, Austin. You want something to drink? How about a glass of juice?"

"Where is she?"

"I'll get you something."

He stood up and glared at her. "You think I drove five hundred miles to sit on your porch and drink carrot juice? Just tell me where Fay went with my son."

"I can't do that."

Without waiting for him to speak, she went inside and came back with a pitcher of apple-and-cranberry juice. Austin was thirsty. He downed two cold glasses.

"It's simple," Carolyn said. "It's not like maybe I'll tell you and maybe I won't. I'm her sister and I'm not going to tell you."

They sat down face to face in two chairs. Carolyn looked nothing like her older sister. She had short blond hair, a thin neck and small hands, and a mouth that had never filled out. Her thin lips promised a tight hold on secrets.

Already he understood that he had come to Amherst in vain. He wasn't going to win this one. On the drive down that was not something he had allowed himself to imagine. "What about Blake?" he said. "You think he's happy about this?"

"Blake will get by."

"It's probably against the law," Austin said.

"So you're going to call the cops?"

47

"Carolyn, for Chrissake. At least tell me how he looked."

"He looked all right."

"Was he worried?"

"I don't think so. We played chess. He's gotten much better."

"You know I'm going to find them. Why don't you just make it easier and tell me?"

She gave a minimal shake of her head and poured him another glass of juice. Next door a man started a rototiller and began to chew up a miniature garden. The noise filled the air for a moment, then settled down to a drone. "Why don't you let her be for a couple of months?" Carolyn said. "She just wants to try some other life, and you get so steamed up about things it's probably hard on her. Listen, you want a beer? I'm going to fix dinner."

He didn't want a beer or dinner or any of this damn talk. But not knowing what else to do, he stayed in his chair.

They barely spoke over the meal. Carolyn served rice, broccoli, tempeh—a bunch of birdseed as far as Austin was concerned. There wasn't a potato in the house. Afterward, as she wrote lesson plans for the next day, he washed the dishes. Her concentration enraged him. He imagined sneaking up behind her and howling in her ear. Maybe she'd blurt out "France!" or "San Francisco!" or wherever it was Fay had gone.

He let a plate slip out of his wet fingers onto the floor. It bounced once into the air and smashed into twenty pieces. Carolyn looked up. She said, "There's a broom in the closet."

Long after she went to bed Austin lay on the couch, his legs bent to make a fit. Though the night was still, the house creaked and moved. The hot-water heater clicked in its alcove. The refrigerator hummed for a few minutes, then shuddered to a stop. Cats seemed to pad around in the dark on the polished floor, but there were no cats. Some bug scuttled across the window next to Austin's head, scratching its carapace on the metal screen. Finally he got up and lowered the sash. He sought a fresh line on the couch but couldn't sleep.

An hour passed, then another, and still he couldn't sleep. In his bare feet he tiptoed out to the porch and walked to his truck. Maple trees in full leaf darkened the street, and the lights were all off in the houses nearby. All the same, he felt exposed in only his underwear. He found his six-cell flashlight and gave it a test, clicking it on and off, twice. Everything made more noise at night: the flashlight, the truck door, the creak of the porch steps. Even his heart, banging away inside his chest, seemed loud enough to wake up Carolyn. Austin's hands began to sweat. Stripping off his undershirt, he shielded the end of the flashlight and turned its muted bulb onto Carolyn's desk.

In the top left drawer were envelopes, stamps, a compass, a pair of scissors and a bottle of ink. In the middle drawer some keys, a cluster of felt pens, a gross of yellow pencils and several letters, none from Fay. He looked for a Rolodex or an address book. As silently as possible he closed the middle drawer and began to open the one below it.

Bright as a flashbulb, the overhead light went on. Carolyn stood at the foot of the stairs, her hand on the switch. "There's nothing written down anywhere in this house," she said. "And you have no right to look through my desk." She wore a tee-shirt and white cotton pajama bottoms, heavy enough for winter.

Austin wheeled and threw his flashlight at the window. His own reflection danced for an instant in the glass, then burst. The flashlight, held by the screen, bounced back into the room and dropped onto the floor.

"You could go through a lot of dishes and glass before this is over," she said.

"But you're so damn calm, aren't you?"

She brought him the broom and dustpan. While he put his undershirt back on and cleaned up the broken glass, she added water to the kettle and set it on the stove.

They sat at the kitchen table, their cups of tea steaming incongruously in the warm night.

"What time is it?" he asked.

"Almost two."

"I'll pay for the window."

She nodded.

"Fay has always had a good life in White Pine," he said. "She stays as busy as I do. She's got a family and a big house and she says she likes teaching. What more does she want?"

"Austin, don't play dumb with me. We both know what Fay wants. And you might as well help her by getting out of the way. Then, if she wants you back, you can join her somewhere."

"What do you mean, *if* she wants me back? She's been trying to get me to go with her for a year."

"But you didn't." Carolyn lifted herself up on the chair and curled her feet under her legs.

"So why can't I go with her now?" Austin said.

"Because you waited too long. And because now you don't know where she is."

"It's some man, isn't it?"

Carolyn raised her chin an eighth of an inch and gave him a blank look.

He wanted to throw his teacup across the room. Something about Carolyn's small contained movements had always made him squirm. Sitting across from her in the still kitchen, he felt like a boy under a barber's sheet forced to endure a summer haircut.

He had always feared her a little because of how different she was from Fay. She seemed to carry about, as if balanced on a small plate, a tidy contentment about her life. She owned her own house and kept it in strict order. She made her decisions in an instant and never questioned them later. In the early seventies she had chosen some eccentric paths: macrobiotic diets, drug use and a three-year affair with an older woman. She never made a joke of those times or dismissed them. Now, like Fay, she was a teacher—but in high school, with advanced-placement students. She thought White Pine, Maine lay pretty close to the end of the world.

All the same, she had spent a great deal of time with the two Pooler children. She adored Blake and treated Maggie like a sister. Over the years she had been more than generous in looking after them.

And no matter how well Austin thought he knew her she could still surprise him. "How about this for odd timing," she said. "I've been thinking about getting married."

"You and Stefan?"

"We've been together for five years now."

"You wouldn't give up your house."

"Maybe."

"I can't believe it. I thought you two didn't agree about kids."

"We're still talking that one over. If I could give birth to a five-year-old I think Stefan would go for it."

"No shortcuts," Austin said. "Not if you want the five-year-old of your choice. You have to start at day one and go through the mill."

Carolyn leaned forward on her elbows. "Do you know how much I love your son?" She spoke so quietly at first that Austin had trouble hearing her. "Have I ever really told you? Of all the people in the world, I think the one I love most is Blake."

Though she had never come out and said it before, he already knew.

"Whenever he comes to visit we play a game together. We've been doing it since he was three. We walk out to the fields past the old dairy and start creeping toward each other through the grass. Sometimes we circle around a little, but you can't stand up. You're only allowed to creep. I love how Blake does it. His little butt stays right on the ground like a salamander. In the spring, when the grass is tall enough, we sometimes lose sight of each other—but then I hear him scurrying along, and all of a sudden we're face to face. We're tense, like a couple of lions. It isn't Amherst, Mass. any longer, but Africa, and we're both lions. We get closer and closer. I move my head to the right, and he moves the same way. We stalk each other, one hand at a time, then a leg. We wait, and I can hear him breathe. The whole game might take an hour. We crouch, ready to spring—and at the same instant we leap into the air and put our nails at each other's throats. He doesn't hurt me but he growls and puts his mouth to my neck and pretends to chew on me. I love him, Austin. He's God's perfection of child. We played that game the day before yesterday."

Tears had not come to Austin on the drive down but they came now. He cried because of his son's secret life. Right now, somewhere, he was doing something Austin knew nothing about.

Carolyn finished her tea as he stopped crying. "If Blake means so much to you," he said, "how can you let Fay just carry him off? What if something happens to them?"

She ignored his question. "If you fight her, you're going to lose," she said. "Her mind's made up."

"But I can't leave my whole life behind."

"Fay did when she moved to White Pine."

"But she was barely twenty-two. And she wanted to live there. What else did she have?"

"She had her family," Carolyn said. "Same as you."

"But it's different when you've got kids. You love Blake so much but you lead Fay on. I can't understand it."

"Believe me, I didn't put Fay up to this one. This particular escapade was her own idea."

"*Escapade*," Austin said. "What escapade is that?"

Carolyn folded her hands and looked down at the linoleum. "She's probably dicking that Frenchman from Bordeaux."

His sister-in-law glanced at him with a faint questioning look on her eyebrows. She couldn't have faked something that subtle, Austin thought. So maybe it wasn't that sleazy frog after all. Maybe it was someone else.

"Obviously it's a man," he said. "Anyone can see that."

Her expression never changed—but one foot, where it was tucked under her other thigh, arched slowly back. Austin stared at it until Carolyn noticed. She reached down and pretended to massage her toes.

So he was right. Fay had fallen in love with someone and never told him. His heart beat all over his rib cage. It beat like an animal trying to get out.

Carolyn had had enough. "I have to go back to bed," she announced. "If I'm sleepy in class tomorrow, the kids will eat me alive. I'll leave the house unlocked and you can look through the whole place if you want—though I guarantee you there's nothing here. The key to the van is by the back door."

"You keep it. Won't Fay need it?"

"I don't think you'll see her in New England anytime soon."

Back at his farm Austin thought about the impossible. First he spread out Fay's two letters on the smooth surface of his desk and read them another time. The blue paper was already growing soft. Then he went outside and lay down on the grass under a sky of drifting clouds. Across the valley, vapor lights dotted the western slope like supernovas.

He tried to imagine where Fay might want to live. Certainly she'd choose a town with more money and flair than White Pine. Aside from Seattle and Tucson and Santa Barbara, the only places he could remember her talking about were Santa Fe and Key West. And the only one of those towns he had ever been to was Santa Barbara, on a conference trip a couple of years ago. It was pretty, all right. Fay said it looked like paradise on earth. Every curb, every driveway, every bush was manicured. A nice house rented for three thousand a month.

She could be in Hawaii, or out of the country somewhere. She had her passport. She could be testing the waters in Brazil, or on the Italian Riviera.

Tired of fighting the bugs, Austin got up off the grass and went inside to call his daughter.

"Hi, honey, it's your dad again."

"Hi, Dad. You doing okay?"

"Pretty good, I guess. All things considered. I suppose you're as busy as ever."

"That's all right. I can talk."

Things had gone well for Maggie during her first year at the Rhode Island School of Design. She was a tall athletic girl, a diligent student and sure of her own attractiveness. But now, at the end of the year, her mother had gone on the lam. In the last few days Austin had phoned her a half-dozen times.

"You've got enough money? Got your flight booked for Wyoming?"

"Dad, I'm as organized as you are. I use those same little spiral notebooks."

"You haven't heard anything, have you?"

"She said she might not write for a while. Maybe she will after I'm out West."

"When you're far from Maine," he said.

"It's no further than Rhode Island by phone."

"What if she wrote and told you where she was?"

"Mom wouldn't put me on the spot like that. That's why she didn't let me know where she went in the first place."

"But what if she did. Would you tell me?"

"Of course."

"Sworn on the eyes of Mr. Potato Head?"

"You're such a cornball, Dad. But yes, sworn on the eyes of Mr. Potato Head. And on the sun and the moon and the stars, honor bright and no crossed fingers. I promise if I get even a postcard, I'll tell you where it's from."

"What about your brother. Don't you worry about him?"

"Blake's in good hands, Dad."

"Maybe. But I'm not so sure about your mother."

"Oh, Dad."

"Well, I'm not."

For a while the line was silent. Austin walked through his living room dragging the telephone cord behind him. "Do you think it was fair for her to just lift him like that?" He knew he shouldn't be asking Maggie this.

There was an even longer pause on the line. "Mom never made me take sides," Maggie said. "And I don't want to now."

"Okay, sorry. But how about you? Have you had enough of White Pine?"

"Of course not. Though I doubt if I'd find too many jobs up there. Hey, I'm coming back for Labor Day, aren't I? No matter where Mom is. And then I've got three more years of college."

"And then?"

"Then I want to see the world."

"Same as your mother," he said.

"I guess. Of course, Mom farmed half her life up there, and I don't think I was ever cut out to be a farmer. There aren't too many women farmers."

"Some. And a lot who help out."

"Yeah."

"Well, I never thought you would. You never showed much interest in it and you were always good at drawing. Now with Blake I can't tell."

"Don't lean on him, Dad."

"All right, I must be losing it. But don't worry, because I know times are changing. It's almost un-American for a kid to take over the family business anymore. What have you got going this weekend?"

"A big rock-and-roll party out on the Cape. My roommate's going and she's the designated driver, so don't worry about that."

"There's a band?"

"The Slimeheads and the Weasel Wonders."

"Is that one band or two? I'm out to lunch on this stuff."

"You're hanging in there like a trooper, Dad. Those are two new groups out of Boston—and if you were here I'd take you."

"You wouldn't. You'd die of embarrassment."

"No way," she said. "I'd take you right out on the dance floor."

"Then *I'd* die of embarrassment."

"Now you're slipping. When I come for Labor Day we better do some square-dancing at least."

"We should. Or there's always Nick Spud and the Spudniks. They play a little rock-and-roll. Okay, grown-up girl. I know you're probably going out to the Cape with Tom. Just be careful. It's not just driving anymore. Think of all those diseases."

"Believe me, they never let us forget. They practically give us a whole course in AIDS protection here. I'm going with Tom *and* my roommate, and I'm always careful about everything. I'm not your average teenager, remember?"

"That's what I always said."

"If I hear anything from Mom, I'll let you know right away. I'm not giving up on her."

Austin hung up and stood with the telephone in his hand in the middle of the room. Every time he called Maggie she sounded more convinced that her mother had done something completely sensible.

He didn't know what to do. He could hardly think about his family breaking up. It was like death, it happened to other people, it was inconceivable.

Saturday was not a good day for Austin. First he got his pickup stuck and had to have Jules winch him out. Then he got a letter from Fay's mother, Lina.

"I know how upset you are," she wrote, "but that's no reason for you to doubt my word. I do not know where Fay is. She wrote me a letter, but that was from Amherst the day before she left. Only Carolyn knows. I'm sure Fay picked her because she's the only one brave enough to face you eye to eye and not tell.

"I have to say, Austin, that while I have no wish to see my grandchildren come from a broken home, I must think first of my daughter. For two decades now Fay has endured the harsh weather and extreme isolation of northern Maine—which is longer than most women could have borne it. I feel that her patience has been a tribute to your qualities as a husband and father, and to the respect she holds for your family. But finally the pendulum has swung, and I assume she will choose a life closer to the world she grew up in. I only hope you will adapt to her needs, as she has long adapted to yours, and that you'll join her when she calls."

Mother of dogs. Austin balled up the letter and threw it across the room. "The pendulum has swung." That stupid twit, she'd been waiting for this to happen for twenty years. "You will adapt to her needs." Damned if he would. He'd adapted the whole time, what did she think marriage was all about? He picked the letter up off the floor, read it a second time and then burned the thing in the kitchen sink.

In a rage Austin ran out to the barn and brought back a spading fork and a hoe. Below the kitchen window, all along the east side of the house, Fay had her flower garden. The peonies were already up, as well as begonias and amaryllis.

The soil, rich with old manure and mulch, took the spading fork to the shank. Austin went after the peonies first, wrenching the plants out and throwing them aside like weeds. Then dahlia bulbs, sedums, and phlox. It looked as if a tornado had swept down the bed.

Fay would howl. She'd stick a pitchfork through his chest.

The disturbed earth gave off a decaying, faintly acidic odor. Old-timers in the County had limed according to taste, by placing a bit of soil on their tongue. Austin, when the ground was moist, could go them one better and calculate the pH by smell alone. For Fay's garden, 5.9 he thought. Maybe 6.0.

When the soil was completely clear of plants he picked out a bowlful of Green Mountains from the kitchen dispenser and hoed a six-inch furrow down the center of the bed. He got down on his knees to nestle each potato into the furrow, one by one. In all of agriculture there was no lovelier job. The soil, long ago cleared of every rock and twig, was smooth as chocolate cake.

Austin had barely finished mounding up the earth over his potato seed when Charley Stoddard's new pickup turned in through the farm gates. It stopped sharply in front of the house, its tires biting on the limestone pebbles of the drive.

"Say hey, Pooler, how's life treatin' you?" Charley strode across the lawn, a smile fixed on the forward edge of his face. He paid no attention to the heliotrope potato house. With each manly step his bootheels sank into the unmown grass.

Ten years ago, after a single season in Idaho, Charley had returned to White Pine with a closetful of cowboy boots: ostrich and snakeskin boots, insulated winter boots with ribbed treads, Mexican boots with canted heels, all kinds of pointy-toed western boots. The ones he had on now were made of elephant skin. "Indestructible," Charley had told him. "Cost about the same as an old pickup."

Lauren once confided to Austin that her husband's little toes had been cramped inside his boots for so long that they no longer spread out flat, even in the shower.

"Don't you think it's an insult to Maine," Austin said, "to walk around in Idaho boots?"

Charley gave a loud flat laugh. He raised his eyebrows at the freshly mounded soil. "Potatoes," he said. "Fay always had such a nice display here."

"Didn't she."

"I hear she and that young boy of yours are out of state."

"They're visiting friends."

"No trouble, I hope."

"Nope, no trouble." Austin tried to say the words as simply as possible, but they came out with a wheeze.

Charley drew his gut in far enough to slide both thumbs inside the elastic waistband of his pants. By now the one-ounce smile on his face had drifted off.

"I got my twenty acres in," he said. "But you sure waited long enough before telling us you couldn't do the job. And that line of crap you gave Lauren about ring rot. You think she didn't see through that? You know damn well we've never had any ring rot in that field."

Austin attacked where he could. "You know the rumor going around town? Word has it that you've been buying more of those Prince Edward Island potatoes."

"Hell, Austin, you know I'm just the plant manager. Starr Foods out in Idaho makes decisions like that."

"The year we graduated from high school there were twenty-five hundred potato farmers in this county. Now it's down to nine hundred. Where do you think it's going to end if you keep making French fries out of Canuck potatoes?"

"But look at their price," Charley said. "They're beating yours by half. Anyway, it's no big deal if every once in a while I buy a few thousand hundredweight from a broker on PEI. I got forty-five workers out at the plant now. I've got to think about them, too."

"You better, because they could all be out of a job before long. You keep buying those PEI and New Brunswick spuds and the whole industry will go under up here. They'll move that plant of yours down to New Jersey."

"They'd pay me down there the same as here."

Austin stared at him. "You're crazy. But you're not so crazy you could live in New Jersey. They'd crush you like a bug down there."

"The hell they would."

"You'd take your family to a place like that?"

"Wake up, Austin. This isn't the only part of the world, you know. In fact, a lot of people think the weather up here sucks, and the good movies never come and we're too far out in the boondocks. It's like Alaska without the money."

"You'd make Lauren live in a place like that?"

Charley took a step forward in his cowboy boots. "Shut up about Lauren. She's done the last taxes she'll ever do for you. And I'll decide what's best for my wife and kids."

After a moment's hesitation Austin plunged in. "You'll never forgive me for getting to Lauren first, will you? You'll worry about that for the rest of your life. You think she cheated you out of something so now you've got a right to punish her."

Charley stared. His neck swelled up like a frog's. They hadn't talked about this in two decades.

"You're flapping your mouth, Pooler. I'll bet you don't even know where Fay is. You got a wife on the loose, a potato house the color of joe-pye weed and you want to talk about *my* family. You better think about your own first, pal."

"You don't know anything about it," Austin said. He put his hands in his pocket, then folded them across his chest.

"Look at this place," Charley said. "It's going to pieces. You ought to get somebody out here to mow the grass. *This* is the showplace farm of northern Maine? You got some troubles, Pooler, so don't start talking about my wife." He backed up three steps, as if Austin were a dangerous animal, then turned and headed for his truck.

Austin watched him drive off. "New Jersey, shit," he said.

FOUR

This time Austin planned ahead. He lifted an aluminum cap onto his truck and anchored it to the bed with four C-clamps. He threw in a foam pad and his sleeping bag, a Coleman stove, some pots and pans, a water jug and an entire bushel of potatoes.

"I'll be back in ten days," he told his hired man.

"You're headed south," Jules said.

"I'll phone back every couple of nights in case you run into trouble."

"I won't. Don't worry about it."

"Well, I might be longer than ten days. If anyone asks for me, just tell them I'm out of state. It's no business of theirs anyway."

"No, it's not."

The next day, after a trip to the bank, he slipped a wad of cash and traveler's checks into his briefcase, along with his passport, his high-school copy of the *Hammond World Atlas,* an old Michener, his son's *Lieutenant Hornblower* and, in case the wait got bad, Redcliffe N. Salaman's *The History and Social Influence of the Potato.*

Shortly after noon he packed some clothes into an old Bean canvas bag and climbed into his pickup's tattered front seat. Like his clothes and haircuts, Austin's truck was serviceable but not quite up to Holiday Inn standards. The wheel wells and headlight sockets had started to rust out, and the transmission only stayed in reverse as long as he kept his hand on the bouncing shift lever. The odometer read 210,000 miles, but the engine had yet to be worked on below the valve gasket. Even the rings were original equipment. Austin loved his truck for the miles it had traveled—but like his marriage, he thought, it needed some work.

He did seventy-five on the interstate, the same as always: no cops, no traffic, a full tank of gas. Farther south the traffic would build, for everything that left Maine funneled down this road: potatoes and lumber and lobster and blueberries. Dead deer splayed over car roofs, antiques headed for Boston, old lobster pots and spinning wheels. Old couples headed for Florida and wives on the run.

He didn't want to lose Fay. He had never believed, before this, that he might. He had never even considered it. Because for the entire twenty years of their marriage they had always stood by each other. Fay had almost never failed him. True, she had lost interest herself in farming—but she had never fought his devotion to potatoes.

He remembered the time at a Nantucket party, a couple of years before Blake was born, when he fell into talk with a banker from Colony Trust. The guy made $150,000 a year and let Austin know it. After that was established he wanted to talk about the comical subject of potatoes.

"Really, let me get this clear," he said. "Six hundred acres of potatoes? On one farm? It sounds a bit obsessive. What do you do with them all?"

The guy was Boston North Shore. Hopeless, really. But Austin never sidestepped the subject of potatoes. "Don't you eat them?" he asked. "You should eat potatoes every day. They're three percent protein and they've got every essential amino acid except cysteine and methionine—and you can get those two from milk. You can live on milk and potatoes alone. I did it once for forty days."

"Forty days? They must have written that up in the paper. Hey, Frank, come over and listen to this."

"As a matter of fact," Austin said, "it was in the *White Pine Argus*."

The banker's friend joined them and quickly picked up the spirit of the game. "A farmer!" he said. "I've never met an actual American farmer. Don't you feed something like fifty-three other people in the world? It sounds so noble."

"Nobility's got nothing to do with it."

"Then you *like* to do this," Frank said.

Austin paused. He was starting to feel like a bear in a zoo. "Of course I like to do it. But not everyone would. You know, *'De gustibus non disputandum est'*."

Frank opened his eyes. "A potato farmer who speaks Latin. This is too, too wonderful. Where did you go to school, man?"

"Harvard. Class of '67." Austin rarely let that drop, but he had the mistaken idea it might get these two off his back.

"My God," the banker said, "we're practically classmates! And ever since Harvard you've been growing potatoes?"

"As my father did before me. And his father, and his."

At that moment Fay came up and took his arm. She must have been listening. Austin introduced them.

"And you live up there too?" Frank asked her, incredulous.

"Way, way, way, way up in Aroostook County," Fay said.

She was dressed for dinner in a knit yellow sheath and gold earrings. She leaned on Austin's arm and slowly curled a stockinged, high-heeled foot around one of his calves.

"Are you two interested in potatoes?" she asked. She sounded as breathless as a girl who'd popped out of a cake.

"Yes . . . sure, potatoes," Frank said. "We've been hearing all about them."

"So you know all about the essential amino acids?"

"We should," Frank said. He could hardly listen to her. He just stared.

"Austin knows everything about potatoes," she said. "Everything."

Austin didn't know what to think. Her knee was sliding up behind his own, and Frank's eyes looked like yo-yos, running up and down her body.

"I like a man who's passionate about his work," Fay said. "Don't you think that's important?"

Oh yes, they agreed, very important. She could have been Mata Hari preparing to remove her veils. She stared briefly at the men's blue party pants, one covered with little ducks and the other with tiny whales. By now some other people were listening in to the conversation.

"My husband, I should tell you, is an extremely passionate man. I mean that he's passionate by nature. He could only work at something he believed in, like growing potatoes. Something of real value to the world. Compare that to working in a bank or an investment house. Certainly there's no passion in that. Perhaps, from time to time, a little enthusiasm. But underneath it's only greed."

Her leg came back from around his knee. She dropped his arm and stood like a schoolgirl in front of the two men, her hands held lightly behind her back. "As a matter of fact, it's pretty obvious. It's all over your auras. There's nothing there but greed. How do your wives stand it?"

Later that evening Austin asked her about those auras.

"You know I can't see auras any more than you can," she said. "But didn't they look like greedy guys to you? I bet they're the same in bed too. Just a couple of old-fashioned, sarcastic, power-hungry guys. Not my type at all."

After six straight hours on the highway Austin stopped in Leominster, Mass. for a bowl of chili, some French fries and a cup of coffee. The coffee was a mistake. Parked later that evening near Quabbin Reservoir, he had trouble dropping off to sleep. A couple of mosquitoes got into the cap with him and droned. He couldn't find them with his flashlight and they wouldn't land. And he was nervous. What he had in mind was probably dishonorable, and certainly against the law.

By nine-thirty the next morning he was already waiting on Carolyn's street in Amherst, his engine pinging softly under the hood. Broad bars of sunlight lay across the street between the houses. Austin didn't think the mailman would have come and gone by this hour.

The carrier, who didn't show up until almost noon, turned out to be a woman. She wore a blue postal shirt, blue Bermuda shorts, black shoes and high black socks. Austin squeezed down a little behind the wheel of his truck, but she never looked over at him. She worked one side of the street and then the other, walking from sidewalk to porch to sidewalk, over and over, without ever cutting across a lawn.

A couple of people retrieved their mail immediately. The street was a quiet one. An occasional car rolled past on the smooth asphalt, and an old man walked his dog. Austin forced himself to wait. Finally he got out of his truck, walked idly along the street and nipped up onto Carolyn's porch. There the arbor vitae helped screen him from the neighbors.

He found a magazine and five envelopes: a bill from the gas company, something from a bank and the rest junk mail. No letters. He slipped everything back into the box, put his hands in his pockets and stepped casually down from the porch. He walked around the block and returned to his truck the long way.

Shit. Though it was unlikely, he had hoped to find a letter the first day. He drove around to the back side of UMass and staked out a place he thought he might park his truck for the night. He didn't want to be spotted by his sister-in-law.

Before dark that evening, with the first excitement of the trip still with him, he cooked home fries on his camp stove and ate them off the truck's tailgate. The next morning he woke early, but waited until Carolyn would have left for school. He walked into town for breakfast, read on an Amherst bench until twelve-thirty and then walked to Carolyn's. Again junk mail and bills. There was a letter from New York City, but the handwriting wasn't Fay's.

The second night he made potato soup for dinner with onions, milk and cheese. Then a long walk through the dark protected streets of town. He had already done enough reading.

The next night, after a third fruitless day at the mailbox, he went to a movie at UMass—and the next afternoon to a matinee in town. If Carolyn saw him the game was over, so when the shows let out he headed straight back to his truck.

On Saturday he stayed away from her mailbox. He walked and read and waited, wondering how long he could stand such an inactive life.

Late that afternoon he heard some yells from the softball fields beyond the trees. He wandered over but paused at a distance to inspect the players, for it was a coed game. He doubted that Carolyn played softball, but he checked anyway. She was nowhere in sight. For a while he stood along the left-field line, until someone called out to him, "Hey, you want to play?"

It was one of the women, veering toward him on her way to the outfield. "We're down one," she said, "and there's a lot of ground to cover."

Austin raised his hands. "No glove."

"You can borrow one. Here." She ran back to the other team's bench and threw him a worn Rawlings.

"I haven't played in a couple of years," he warned her.

"Take right field. You can't go wrong out there."

He did, though, the next inning, when a left-handed hitter banged a line drive straight at him. The ball took a bad hop, smacked him in the shoulder and spun off to one side. The batter went to second.

"Don't worry," she said at the end of the inning. "We'll get 'em. Loosen up."

They sat on an aluminum bench behind a fence along the first-base line. The woman wore a Boston Red Sox shirt and a pair of tight nylon shorts. She was blond and high-breasted, much younger than Austin.

His first two times at bat he popped up into the infield. "Keep your eye on the ball," she told him as he came on deck a third time. "Swing easy."

He did, and almost without effort drove the ball into deep left, clear over the outfielder's head. He lit out for first in his jogging shoes and khaki pants as the ball rolled to the fence. He steamed around second, almost ran out of the base path onto the grass and was waved home by the third-base coach.

"Stand up, stand up!" his teammates yelled as he bore down on the plate. "Inside the park!"

He leaned on the bench, breathing hard. The blond woman grabbed his arm. "You really tagged that one. I knew you could do it."

"I did," he said. "I hit that ball! That guy was cheating in, he thought I'd pop it up again. What a sprint!" A couple of minutes went by before he fully caught his breath.

She must be someone's girl, he thought, and looked over the men on the team. He couldn't tell. For the final inning she switched positions and played right-center, next to Austin. They trotted out together, making softball talk. "Let's play some D now," she said. "Just three more outs and we've got 'em."

They squeaked out a win at 9–8. After the game, around a cooler, she introduced Austin to the rest of the team and invited him to join them for ribs and beer. "Come on," she said. "You don't have anywhere else to go."

Austin climbed into her car, his caution blown away like seeds off a dandelion, and they caravaned it down to a restaurant on the Hadley road.

Her name was Marilyn Tzobik. "So big, but not too big," she said with a laugh. She must have said that a thousand times, he thought, but it came out so naturally he felt as if he were the first person to ever hear it. They drank some beer and ate crinkle-cut French fries and barbecued ribs, and after dinner the two of them wound up at a separate table on the patio.

"Are you married?" she asked.

He had forgotten about his ring. "I'm separated," he said. "And I've got two kids. How about you?"

"No husband and no kids. But I'd like to do that before it's over."

"Before what's over?"

She laughed. "I don't know, all this fun."

She was twenty-five maybe, not much older. She didn't ask Austin's age, so he never found out if he would have lied about that too. Of course, looking strictly at the facts, he *was* separated. He didn't even know where Fay was. *Abandoned* would have been the exact word.

He told her he was only in town for a few days, on business.
"I stay in my truck," he said. "It's parked out past the diamonds."

"In *that?*" she asked later, after driving him back to his
Dodge.

"That's my home away from home."

"Goddamn, what's home look like? This thing's beat to piss."

Austin laughed. "Do you have *any* inhibitions?"

"Not too many. Does it run?"

"Sure it runs. Runs like a deer. Want to go for a drive? If it
weren't so far I'd show you home. It might surprise you."

"That's hard to do," she said. "Where is home?"

She walked to the front of the truck and back, giving it a full
inspection. Austin, meanwhile, inspected her. Her legs were
phenomenal, the absolute embodiment of youth. Her face too.
She looked like she'd never heard of jealousy or guilt.

"Home is a farm in northern Maine," he said. "Eighteen
hundred acres of the best Caribou gravelly loam."

"Is that right? My grandparents farmed in New York State.
They're still out there. I like farms." For a moment she jingled
the keys in her hand. Then she leaned over and kissed him on the
cheek. "Want to go to a pretty place tomorrow? It's over on the
river."

"I do." He didn't hesitate at all.

"Good. Be here at noon and I'll pick you up."

Austin had occasionally imagined that at some National
Potato Council meeting or a seed producers' conference he might
meet a beautiful young woman in the hotel bar and follow her
upstairs to an anonymous room. But it was only a fantasy, and in
twenty years of marriage nothing like that had ever happened to
him.

He was stretched out under the cap reading when Marilyn
drove up the next day at noon. She wore a pair of knee-length
shorts, white sandals and a half-unbuttoned blouse the color of
marigolds. She leaned into the back of his truck, pinched his big
toe and said, "Come out, come out, Austin, we're going
swimming."

He closed his book, jumped out onto the pavement and folded
up the tailgate.

"You live in a truck," she said. "And you're still here!"

"Do I need a suit?"

"Don't be silly."

She drove him to the Connecticut River near Sunderland. There they parked her car by the road and walked down to the water along a tractor path through waist-high corn. It was nice ground, Austin thought: a fast-warming sandy loam protected from frost by the river. Probably some of the best corn land in New England. He and Marilyn walked side by side, their arms occasionally brushing. He felt as youthful and fresh as the translucent blades of corn. At the bottom of a shaded path they emerged beside the Connecticut.

The broad sunlit river moved south in gentle swirls. Marilyn leaned against the mottled trunk of a sycamore, took off her sandals and all her clothes and waded in.

My God, Austin thought. Fay still had a great body—but Marilyn was in another league altogether. She was edible at a distance. He wondered if she even knew. Of course she knew.

"Doesn't look like any inhibitions at all," Austin said as he unbuttoned his shirt.

"Hey, I've got a few. I grew up Catholic. But I try never to let 'em show. Come on, the water's great."

They swam upstream against the current, then drifted down feet-first to their landing. Standing naked on the gravel shingle, they kept a little apart. Marilyn's remarkable young breasts stood out in the sunlight, tipped by two pale nipples. Austin grew dizzy trying to keep his eyes on her face.

She laughed as if she knew he was struggling. "If we had a couple of tubes," she said, "or a little raft, we could drift all the way down to Hadley."

He wanted to do that: get into a raft with this ingenuous young woman and drift and drift.

They lay down side by side on the gravel on two towels, not touching but talking and laughing. When a pair of canoes came down the middle of the river she raised her eyebrows but didn't move. They stayed where they were, naked, and waved to the canoeists.

"This is the way to live," Austin said.

"You bet. Flaunting it."

For an hour almost everything she said made him smile or laugh outright. She lay beside him naked, tanned all over, her light brown pubic hair curling between her legs. He snuck a few looks but there was nothing to see, really: her legs, some hair, the bluish veins that ran through the stretched flesh over her hipbones. Nakedness was an idea, and he didn't know what it meant anymore. After a while they jumped back into the river and swam across to the other side.

He took her out to dinner in Northampton, and then she drove him back to his truck. "Would you like to come in for a few minutes?" he joked. "Have a cup of coffee, see my place?" He got out and unlocked the cap and dropped the tailgate for them to sit on.

She leaned against him in the near-dark. No kisses, no more talk, no nudity. She had used up her initiative. He heard her sandals drop onto the pavement: clack, clack. The night was 10 degrees warmer than it would have been in White Pine.

"I kind of lied to you," he said, sitting up a little straighter. "I'm not really here on business."

"Well, I won't let it bother me."

"The truth is, I came to steal somebody's mail."

She nestled her chin against his shoulder as if she were going to sleep.

"I'm trying to find my wife," he said. "We're not really separated."

She lay a hand on his leg. From toe to armpit the hairs on his flesh stood up.

"Or we are separated," he said, "but it wasn't my idea."

"Austin, what are you telling me this for?"

"I don't know," he said. "I guess I'm nervous."

"So you want me to be nervous too. Okay, I'll sit up and get nervous." She straightened up beside him and drummed her fingers against the corrugated aluminum wall of the cap.

He didn't want it to end like this. He wanted it to be daylight again and to drift down the Connecticut in a rubber raft, naked and hidden from the shore. He wanted to lie back and stare at Marilyn, at every part of her body, while she told him stories about her childhood summers at her grandparents' dairy farm and the trip she took last fall to the Wind River Range.

But nothing was simple. Certainly not love or sex. Everything led to something else—and right now, Marilyn led somewhere he didn't want to go.

"You don't even know me," he said. "Don't you worry about AIDS? You think it's safe to take up with just any guy who comes along?"

"I don't have AIDS and I don't go out with just anyone. You're married, aren't you? I doubt if you have AIDS. A married guy from northern Maine—that sounds pretty safe to me. Anyway, I'm careful. I'm into safe sex."

"There is no safe sex," Austin said. "Safer maybe, but not safe."

"Well, relax. I was happy just sitting here." She settled down a little closer to him and linked her arm through his. Her hair still smelled of the river. In the dark it still looked blond, but too bright to be natural. "You are a peculiar man," she said. "You're surprising me after all."

Austin stood up. He was crazy, this woman was offering him everything. "I'm trying to find my wife," he said. "She took my son with her."

"Okay, okay." Marilyn stood up too. She reached around with her toes and stepped back into her sandals. "Look, Austin, I'm sorry about your wife. I didn't know how bad it was. It sounds terrible."

"What if right now she's doing this?" he said. "What if she's sitting outside in the dark with some guy? I bet she is."

That was the vision that had come to him at the moment Marilyn sat down beside him on the tailgate: of Fay walking through the streets with some man, sitting on a bench with some man, kissing some man.

Marilyn reached into her pocket and grabbed her keys. "When am I going to learn? Married men. It's always the same." She took a step toward her car.

"Sure, you better go. You're just a girl anyway. What are

you, twenty-five? No kids to think about, no family. Don't get mixed up with some guy like me who wants to stare at your legs and then tell you all about his wife."

"Shut up, Austin."

"No, really, you should get a raft and float down the river with somebody else. Have a ball. Take all your clothes off and do any damn thing you feel like. To hell with AIDS, don't worry about that. Find some single guy from way up north—Baffin Bay or Greenland or somewhere—some horny guy who's just got to be safe. Take him out on the river and jump on him. Oh God, Marilyn, you're a gorgeous woman. I must be out of my mind."

"You *are* out of your mind." She got into her car and started the engine. "Maybe marriage does it." Without another word she drove away.

When her taillights disappeared, Austin pulled his bushel of potatoes out from the truck. He threw one into the woods, and then another and another. *"Fuck this,"* he screamed. *"Fuck this shit."* He could hear the potatoes rain down through the branches and leaves onto the ground below. He threw until the basket was empty.

More junk mail and bills the next day in Carolyn's mailbox. Austin's body ached at having nothing to do. He read until his eyes dropped and tried to forget what had happened with Marilyn the night before. He wanted to work. He wanted to put in ten hours on a tractor, hilling and cultivating potatoes.

Jules told him over the phone that he'd hired another man, temporary. "Relax, Austin. Stay as long as you have to. I'll keep things running smooth. You think I'm the kind of guy who'd paint a building purple?"

Tuesday marked a full week in Amherst. Austin drove into town, one eye out for cops, and parked down the street from Carolyn's house. At eleven-thirty the letter carrier appeared with the same bulging leather bag. She climbed Carolyn's porch. After fifteen minutes Austin walked up the street, skipped onto the porch and opened the box. Junk mail, junk mail, a wedding invitation, junk mail, an insurance bill—and a letter from Fay.

It was a pale blue aerogram bordered by red and white

stripes, addressed to Carolyn in Fay's orderly hand. On the back it said, "Hallwick, c/de Raigosa Menéndez, Apartado 536, Mérida, Estado de Yucatán, México."

He had her! He stuffed the letter into his front pocket and almost ran back down the street to his truck. Mexico, goddamn. What the hell was she doing in Mexico? It was a good thing he had money and his passport: He could fly out of Boston and be there tomorrow, maybe tonight. He laid the letter on the seat next to him and stared at it as he drove out of town.

But who did Fay know in Mexico? She didn't speak any more Spanish than he did. The letter said, "c/de Raigosa Menéndez." That must be in charge of. He'd never heard her talk about anyone named Menéndez.

At the lookout over the reservoir he carefully tore open the folded, single sheet of blue paper. "Dear Carolyn," it began. Then:

> I was so glad to get your letter. After all, you're my only contact, and home seems a million miles away. Not that I worry about that, because I like it. I want it to be a million miles away.
>
> This is completely different from going as a tourist. At the Potato Institute in Lima, for example, almost everyone spoke English, but here almost no one does except for Ricardo. Even his daughters can only say a few words out of a book. I thought half the people would know English because they're so close to the U.S. They've studied it but they can't speak it.
>
> I've been listening to my tapes, so now I can say things like, "Where is Don Ricardo?" and "Let's go to the beach," and "I can't speak Spanish." No puedo hablar español.
>
> Sometimes I go to the market with Teresa, the maid, and do the shopping with her. She goes

*every day after breakfast and only buys what she
wants for that day: strips of meat, tomatoes, little
tomatillos, soft cheese, squash, chayote and fruit.
Even the rice and beans she buys each day.
Ricardo is funny about tortillas, he almost never
eats them. For breakfast he likes the little rolls
they call* pan francés. *They're made fresh every
day but turn perfectly stale by dinnertime, when
you can slice them in two like nuggets of
Styrofoam. Blake eats them with butter and strawberry jam. Morning or night, it makes no difference to him.*

*Hundreds of women sell at the market, but
Teresa buys from the same stalls every day. Every
once in a while she balks at a price and moves on,
but not very often. Everyone knows her and calls her
Doña Teresa. She calls me Doña Fe. A few days ago
she introduced me to two of the women she buys
from in the market. One sells fruit and the other
vegetables, and they sit up behind their mounds
of produce like ancient queens. Like Mayan
priestesses—if there were priestesses. I love the dignity of these two women, and how they run their
own businesses. When I show up now, they ask me
how I am.* "¿Como está la señora?" *I get as far as*
"Muy bien, gracias," *and they take off in reams of
Spanish while I stand there nodding my head.*

*The funny thing is, I love everything about
this place. I love being where almost no one knows
me, and those who do make a fuss over the
smallest things.* "Tan rosadita la señora," *one of
the women said yesterday, and touched my hair. It*

*was because my hair has turned a little red with
the sun—rosada.*

*Ricardo and I are doing well. Really, I'm just
getting to know him.*

*A few things seem odd in this house, or
certainly not what you'd find in the U.S. Ricardo
is absolutely imperious with the help. There's
Teresa and Rigoberto, the gardener, and Cecilia,
the girl who looks after the children. All three of
them work fourteen-hour days with only one day
off a week, and Ricardo orders them around in a
tone of voice I wouldn't use on a dog.*

*But with me he's always attentive and charm-
ing, so I haven't said anything about it. I try to
remember it's a different culture.*

*Blake is getting along fine—though I have to
admit he misses Austin. I don't know what to say
to him sometimes when he asks about Ricardo.
After we'd been here a week he asked me, "Who is
Ricardo?" almost as if they hadn't met. I think he
meant, What's Ricardo's role in all this, and what
are we doing in his house?*

*You know Blake. He's so clever, and his little
mind works overtime. Maybe it was a mistake to
bring him—Austin must be furious. But I'd built
up so much steam over the last couple of years that
finally I had to run, and damned if I was going to
leave Blake behind. Anyway, now it's done.*

*No more room on this letter, so I'll close and
mail it. Please write with news, and best burn this.*

Love,

Fay

Fuck this bitch, Austin thought. He could hardly believe it. She had written an entire letter, paragraph after paragraph in miniature print, and hardly said a word about him. Day and night he had thought of almost nothing but Fay—and all she could talk about was how glad she was to get away from Maine. And then Blake. God knows what he was going through down there.

Austin lay down across the front of his truck, close to tears. He imagined his son sitting at an empty table in a Mexican house full of servants, eating bread like Styrofoam with strawberry jam on it.

He reread the letter word for word, trying to figure out who the hell this guy Ricardo was and where Fay had met him. But except for the last few lines the letter was impervious. It could almost have been written by some college girl spending her junior year abroad.

At least he had found her—even if she was living in Mexico with some rich asshole spic named Menéndez. A guy who treated his servants like dogs. Austin lay on his seat for ten minutes, then stood outside in the mild New England breeze. The nerve endings in his hands and feet had closed down. Finally he stuck the letter back in his pocket and took off for Boston.

He drove as fast as he dared. The old Power Wagon's fenders billowed out, the knobby tires howled on the smooth road, and halfway through the trip the pickup's throaty exhaust system began its biennial disintegration. By the time he drove into the heat and grime of the Callahan Tunnel, the roar of the Dodge was sensational. He stepped on the gas, then announced his disdain for Somerville, Charlestown, Boston and every other rathole city in the area by abruptly letting up on the pedal: BLAM BLAM BLAM BLAM. Inside the confines of the tunnel it sounded like war. He kept it up all the way to the airport, defying but never seeing any cops.

The rusted remains of the muffler hung from a single strand of metal. Lying on his back, he wrenched the thing free and chucked it out from under the pickup. He lowered it into a trash barrel meant for paper cups and candy wrappers.

In the full compass of human institutions few were as despicable to Austin as airlines and airports. Logan, Kennedy,

O'Hare: they were all blights on the land. At some other time he might have admitted to a certain fondness for the little commuter line that flew from Portland to White Pine. But this was Boston, the pit of New England. He expected the worst.

There were long lines, of course. And when he got to the counter, the people nearby listened in to his plans. The agent was a pale woman in her thirties with bad skin, a tight white collar and a ribbon tie.

"Where would you like to go in Mexico?"

"Mérida. I think it's in the Yucatán."

"That's correct. It's quite lovely there. I went there myself last year on vacation."

"People go there on vacation?"

She paused, perhaps sizing him up for a terrorist. His hands were still smeared with grime and rust from the defunct muffler. He might have come on a bomb assignment.

"I can give you a five-thirty P.M. to Miami, and you can fly Mexicana to Mérida tomorrow morning."

"I want to get there tonight, as soon as possible."

"Do you have cash or a credit card?" She sounded doubtful.

"Does McDonald's sell fries?"

"I do have people waiting, sir."

Austin leaned forward and asked, softly but clearly, "How do you work in this light all day? Everyone looks blue in here."

"The only other possibility would be to go through New Orleans."

Of course she had heard him. She called up another screen but there was no way he could get to Mérida tonight. So instead of sleeping in Miami, a city he barely knew and had no wish to see, he booked an early morning flight out of Logan with only a two-hour layover in Florida. He put the charge on his Master-Card, folded the ticket into his wallet and walked off into the airport lobby.

What could be simpler? He was going to Mexico to find his wife, who was living with some guy named Menéndez.

That evening Austin went back to Cambridge for the first time in twenty-one years. He had passed through Boston often enough, and a couple of times he'd driven down Storrow Drive and looked across at the college. But since the day he graduated, he hadn't set foot in Harvard Square. Now he parked his truck on Mass. Ave. and walked out of the city into the calm of the Yard. Grays Hall, where he'd lived as a freshman, looked exactly the same. Sever Hall looked the same, and Memorial Church, and the statue of John Harvard and the steps of Widener Library. All the same.

He had lost track of almost every friend from Harvard. His closest friend, Jim Laub, had been dead for almost twenty years now.

He sat down on the broad steps of Widener. Students came and went, some carrying the same green book bags Austin had used as an undergraduate. Squirrels chattered in the trees and skittered across the lawns, many of which had been roped off with stakes and yellow tape. Graduation was coming up.

Austin rarely felt nostalgic about his years in Cambridge, but now a bitterness surprised him. It rose clear into his throat. It wasn't Harvard though, it was Jim Laub. It was Jim Laub being dead.

He stood up and walked back out of the Yard into Harvard Square. A couple of blocks down Brattle Street he found a small French restaurant—not one he remembered—and took a table by the window. He ordered a steak and thought about his roommate.

At the end of their sophomore year Austin had offered him a summer job on the farm. Jim had grown up in the Bronx in a tight-knit Jewish family that thought of Cambridge as the outer rim of the enlightened world. Austin persuaded him that Aroostook County would be an experience, something he should do as part of his education. So early one June the two of them drove up to White Pine in Austin's pickup. Even at Harvard Austin drove a truck.

Jim's first couple of weeks on the farm were lonely and difficult—but he had forgotten that by the time he returned to Harvard for his junior year.

"What a place!" he told everyone. "They're in a time warp up there that covers decades, maybe centuries. It looks like northern

Russia. The whole town lives and breathes potatoes, and guess who's at the top of the pile? The Poolers!"

Jim told jokes about the County. He laughed at the North-country Fair, at the potato barrel-rolling contests, at a play put on by the Chamber of Commerce and even at the "tatahs for dinnah" accent that was common in southern Maine but rare in Aroostook.

Yet he liked it enough to go back a second summer. He confided to Austin that his main goal in life was to get laid, and he figured he had a better chance up in Maine than anywhere else. Too shy around the feisty girls from Radcliffe, he had never had any luck in Cambridge. And the previous summer, at least, he had come close.

Lauren Sorrell was by then already engaged to Charley Stoddard—so that was a closed door. But Austin knew every girl in town. More than once Jim had heard the unmistakable, unbelievable sounds of lovemaking come out of the backseat of the new Pooler Buick when they had double-dated at the drive-in. Austin had set him up with a number of different girls, and Jim probably figured it was only a matter of time.

Things got off to a flying start the first weekend of the second summer when they took Connie Burk and Joanne Weems to a party in someone's basement and Jim made out a little with both girls. On the way home, at two-thirty in the morning, his hand had already dropped from Connie's breasts to the top of her thighs when Sheriff Bill Perleau caught Austin doing eighty-five down the Caribou road. The sheriff didn't even bother to check Austin's license, but shined his flashlight in the face of both girls, who were barely out of high school. He ordered the girls into his cruiser, and before taking them home escorted the two Harvard boys back to the farm and delivered them to William Wayman Pooler, Austin's sleepy grandfather.

Jim was impressed at how easily Austin got off the handle—until the next morning when old WWP gave the boys a special Sunday job. They had to spread out and cover a fifty-barrel load of rotten potatoes, all by hand. Normally it was a chore carried out with an end loader, manure spreader and chisel plow, but Granddad Pooler sent the boys off with only a pickup truck and a pair of garden forks.

Hung over to begin with, both Austin and Jim threw up in the first twenty minutes. The smell of decay enveloped them as they tromped through the mushy spuds, forking the potatoes out onto the field and covering them with soil.

"Ten more minutes and I would have had my hand in her pants," Jim said. "I know she wants it. And now I'm barfing over a load of rotten potatoes."

Austin didn't say anything. He knew if his grandfather was in a bad mood that night, he might tell them the strip was in the wrong place, and they would spend the next day moving the potatoes twenty yards east or west. Driving back to the farm at the end of the day he told Jim, "Make sure you look exhausted. Don't say a word."

William Pooler made them stand for inspection on the front lawn. He looked over their smeared rubber boots, turned up his nose at the rotten smell of their clothes and walked around them like a drill sergeant. There was, Austin thought, a faintly amused look on his face.

"You have a nice time today with those rots?" He looked Jim in the eye.

"I puked," Jim said.

"Just once?"

"Yessir."

"And your buddy here, Austin. Did he clear his system out?"

"Yessir."

"It's kind of far away from the Bronx here," William said, his hands on his hips. "You think you can make it through another summer?"

Jim hesitated.

"Do you?"

"I look at it as part of my education," Jim claimed.

"Is that right? I'm glad to hear that. It makes me think I've applied the proper discipline. So you didn't resent spending your day off burying those fetid spuds?"

"Not at all," Jim said. "I was eager to do it. It's always been my dream to serve an apprenticeship under Attila the Hun."

Austin, standing to one side, jerked back his head in surprise. But an instant later the old man started laughing. He slapped

Jim Laub across the shoulders hard and told him he had some guts after all—for a city boy.

"Tell you what," he said. "You two can have next Saturday off to take those young potato-blossom queens to the fair." He turned to his grandson and stabbed a broad forefinger against his chest. "But Austin Pooler, don't you *ever* let me hear you've been driving that fast again. You got that? Now you two go wash up. You smell like death."

Jim Laub finally got laid that summer—six or seven times. He went back to Harvard talking up Aroostook County big, and Connie Burk became legend. He made it sound as if he'd bedded down a princess of the realm, rather than a skinny, hot-breathed farm girl who'd never been farther south than Augusta. But he also talked about potatoes, and farming in general, with unmistakable respect.

Austin finished his steak and sat back in his chair, looking out at the Brattle Street traffic. Fucking Vietnam, he thought. Laub was the only person he knew who'd been killed in the war—but one friend was all it took.

After a cup of decaf he wandered among the houses. He didn't return to the Yard but strayed as far as the Charles before getting back in his truck and heading for the airport. His exhaust system thundered as he cruised down Memorial Drive past Dunster House.

It was at a Dunster House mixer that Jim Laub had introduced him to Fay Hallwick, when they were seniors and she was a junior at Wellesley. By the time Austin got to the mixer, Jim had already worked Fay into a corner of the room. But newly confident after his summer adventures with Connie Burk, he waved Austin over and introduced him. Fay nodded and shook Austin's hand. Jim continued with his embroidered descriptions of northern Maine and Pooler Farm, but Austin hardly listened. For her posture, for her skin and for the perfect camber of her lips, he instantly desired this young woman.

"She's got eyes for you," Jim told him later that night.

"But you're interested."

"I was, but I owe you. Besides, she forgot all about me as soon as you came up. She couldn't get enough of you. She loved hearing you talk."

"You think so?"

"Ask her out. My God, that mouth and those eyes. Ask her out, you'll see."

The following Sunday Austin picked her up in his truck at Wellesley College and took her for a drive up near the New Hampshire border. They had missed the peak of the foliage, but a few of the maples were still bright red. Fay wore an old pair of jeans and an oversized shirt. On the way, sitting at the far end of the seat, she wove her hair into a single long braid and played the end of it through her fingers.

"Potatoes," Austin said, pointing toward a tan field covered with long, hilled rows.

"Where?"

They stopped beside the field and got out. Fay didn't bother with a coat, though there was a cool afternoon breeze. It ruffled her hair, lifting the few strands that had already escaped from her braid. After watching how Austin climbed over the woven fence she did the same, swinging out her leg at the top and jumping down to the dry ground. Her boots knocked up a little puff of dirt. The vines had been chemically desiccated and lay folded over each other, grey and limp.

"These are potatoes?" she said.

A few yards out Austin dropped to his knees and pushed his right hand into the mounded soil. Scooping and grabbling, he brought out a single, clean-skinned potato. Fay crouched beside him, her legs drawn up against her chest. She took the round white tuber in her hand.

"You mean the ground is full of these?" She looked as amazed as if he had plunged a hand inside his chest and pulled out one of his lungs.

"Kennebecs," he said. He dug another few inches and pulled out two more potatoes. She held the three of them in her hands, rolling them over, smelling them, feeling their weight.

"I can't believe it."

He laughed. Jim was right about her mouth, it was beautiful. He wanted her to talk so he could watch her lips move. He dug his big hands into the row, pulling out a dozen potatoes, then a dozen more.

"You're digging up the crop," she said. "Don't."

He crouched on the dry sunny ground. This serious young woman, whom he had yet to touch, had given him an erection in the middle of the potato field. "The owners won't mind," he said. "They've got ten tons to the acre here. Anyway, we'll bury them again."

Two years later, when he and Fay were already married and living on Pooler Farm, Jim Laub was shot down over the Gulf of Tonkin.

That night Austin slept in his truck, the same as every night of the trip so far, in one of the outlying parking lots at the airport. His pulse settled slowly under the continuous wail of jet engines, as one plane after another either braked to a stop or clawed its way up into the lit sky. A hot breeze puffed through the lot, and the truck's aluminum cap hummed and vibrated. He had trouble going to sleep. Twice he got up to take a leak on the pavement, pissing between two parked cars. In the end the night was longer than his worries, and he slept.

He slept, in fact, right through dawn, and woke to the alarm on his watch. The parking lot had cooled overnight, but just above the smoggy eastern skyline the sun was already lodged in the sky like a hot coin. Austin's clothes were rumpled and his hair in disarray. He was headed the wrong direction, he thought. He should be going back to White Pine. But he put on his jogging shoes, locked the truck cap and carried his canvas bag to the shuttle bus stop.

Before the flight there was time for breakfast in the airport—though he immediately regretted the two eggs and fries. The eggs were small and runny, and the "home fries" a miniature oval patty. On the back of the bill, where invited to leave a comment, he wrote, "The home fries were crap. Can't you use fresh potatoes?" He signed it Austin Wayman Pooler, White Pine, Maine.

On the plane they served him a second breakfast, including an identical orange patty of deep-fried potatoes. Austin sat by the window next to a businessman in a tie and white shirt.

"Not much of a breakfast, is it?"

"Pretty poor," the man said. He had been reading a memo before the meal was served, but had stuffed the papers back into his briefcase.

Austin twisted around in his seat until he almost faced the businessman. He tapped on the fries with his fork. "I wouldn't call these things potatoes at all. They're just grease and salt. They could just as well be corn fries." Austin speared the patty and held it up in the air.

Busy with a croissant, the businessman glanced over and raised his eyebrows. On his forearms, where he had rolled back his sleeves, the dark mat of hair was so thick it made the skin beneath look green.

"They flash-fry these things," Austin explained, holding the patty to his nose. "And instead of changing the oil, they filter it. Some of these restaurants use the same oil for thirty days. Hell, you'd change the oil in your car more often than that if you drove it all day long. Wouldn't you?"

The man moved his elbow off the armrest between them. "I'm having a little weight problem with all this traveling," he said. "I try to stay away from potatoes."

Austin jerked in his seat. "You've got to be kidding. Don't you know anything about nutrition? Complex carbohydrates should be the basis of every diet—and potatoes are the best there are. Just stay away from the oil. And stay away from those croissants and butter."

"You . . . ah . . . sell potatoes?"

"I *grow* potatoes. And I eat them every day. Look at this." Austin thumped his belly beneath the fold-out table. "I haven't gained a pound in twenty years. Does your wife cook for you?"

"I'm recently divorced. Look out!"

Austin's coffee cup landed sideways on his tray and splashed all the way over onto his neighbor's croissant. The man reached up and pulled the button for the stewardess.

"Sorry about that," Austin said. "Here, here's a napkin. If you spend all your time in meetings and on airplanes eating shit like this, no wonder you put on weight. Where do you live? Do you have a garden?"

"I used to. Right now I'm in an apartment."

"Oh Jesus, an apartment. How do you stand it? But even there . . ."

"Can I help you?" A stewardess in slacks and a long apron leaned in from the aisle.

"Coffee spill," the man said. He pointed at Austin's tray. "And . . . is this a full flight?" He looked back over his shoulder.

"I'm afraid it is," she said. "But I'll see what I can do. I'll just get something to clean this up."

A moment later she returned with a small towel and the *Globe*, which she practically stuffed into Austin's hands. "We'll be in Miami before you know it," she said to them both.

As soon as his tray was cleared the businessman made a show of going back to work. Austin read the paper: the obituaries, the editorials and the commodity prices. Potatoes were down three cents a hundred. Halfway through the flight, as the plane bored along at thirty-two thousand feet, he fell asleep.

The Miami airport did not look as if it belonged in the same country as Logan International. More than half the crowd was Latin. The men wore pressed trousers, leather shoes, polo shirts and guayaberas. The women were decked out in high heels, tight dresses and expensive, formfitting jeans. Immediately outside the terminal a resplendent sun lit up patches of spiky grass. Austin walked around among the palm trees and coleus. It was hot.

After checking in with Mexicana, he filled out his tourist card, bought a Spanish phrase book and some Halazone pills and pulled two hundred dollars off his MasterCard. He didn't call Jules. He should have done so the night before, because at this hour Jules would be in the fields. Anyway, Austin didn't want to explain right now that he was on his way to Mexico. Not until he got there and found Fay.

After boarding there was an hour's delay. The plane was hot inside, and the Miami air thick and humid. Austin kept to himself this time and didn't speak at all to the older, perfumed woman in the seat beside him. He didn't know if he could, for she was clearly from Mexico. He read the *Miami Herald*: the obituaries, the editorials, the commodity prices.

Again he slept, waking only when the plane dropped its nose and the engines changed pitch. They began a long slow descent. The captain, with only a trace of a Spanish accent, reported the weather in Mérida: clear skies and 88 degrees. The plane dropped, leveled and dropped again. A stewardess minced down the aisle, spraying behind her with an aerosol can of Black Flag.

"We are happy to protect you and the Republic of Mexico," the captain explained, "from any pests or insects accidentally brought on board the aircraft."

Austin, who was hardly squeamish on the subject of insecticides, covered his face with his hands as the Black Flag mist drifted down over passengers, seats, pillows and drinks. If he had caught that much exposure in the field, he would have stopped work to wash up.

Close to shore, the water of the Gulf turned a brilliant light blue. Mérida, to his surprise, lay inland. They flew over miles of flat forested land, almost unpopulated, before dropping down for a smooth landing.

In the past, whenever Austin had traveled to South America with the Potato Council, someone had always met him at the airport to speed him through customs and take care of his visa. And once he was there, an interpreter was always available if he wanted to talk to someone who spoke no English. Consequently his Spanish had barely advanced past *buenos días* and *muchas gracias*.

A warm breeze blew through the Mérida terminal. Signs on the wall, repeated often, read NO FUMAR and NO ESCUPIR. No Smoking and no something. A big banner, stretched over one wall, proclaimed, LA CORTESÍA AYUDA AL PROGRESO. Something about progress. For the first time it occurred to Austin that finding Fay might not be so easy.

He waited in line, looking away from the few Americans who had gotten off the plane.

"How many days will you stay in Mexico?" An immigration official studied his passport and tourist card.

"I'm not sure. Not too long."

"You have money?"

"Plenty of money," Austin said. He opened his wallet. "And I've got traveler's checks and a charge card."

The official gave him a little wave: no need to pull them out. "You will visit the ruins?"

"Yes, I'm . . . I'm on vacation."

"Very good. I will give you ninety days." He wrote 90 on the card and stamped it with a round blue seal. "Please follow to customs," he said, with a slight list of his head.

The customs inspector pointed at Austin's old waterproofed canoe bag. "¿Sólo ésta?"

"This is all I've got."

Without opening the bag, the man marked it with blue chalk and waved Austin on. At the door to the main part of the terminal four or five young men, all chattering in broken English, made as if to take the bag from him.

"Taxi? You want taxi? You go to Mérida, you go to Chichén Itzá?"

He held tightly to his luggage, suddenly exhausted. Turning away from the taxis, buses and crowds of people, he found a little café off the main lobby. He ordered an orange soda by pointing at a sign, and sat down where he could look out over the runway. It was late in the afternoon and the sun, as bright as the Day-Glo color of his drink, was fast approaching the horizon. He felt, as Fay had written to Carolyn, a million miles away from New England. He had planned to go straight to Apartado Street to confront Fay and this asshole Ricardo, and to hold Blake in his arms. But he was too tired, too surprised, too unsure of himself. He decided to wait until morning.

He remembered, as he stood up to pay for his drink, that he had no pesos. He gave the waitress, an Indian-looking girl not much older than Blake, a dollar bill. She took it without a glance, gave it to a woman at the cash register and brought him back two bills and three coins. He left the coins on the table and picked up his bag.

Immediately someone was on him. *"¿El centro?* You go to Mérida? There is a bus to the Plaza Principal. Come."

Austin yielded his bag to a man who could not have stood over five feet tall. He guided Austin to an old VW van. There was only one other passenger so far. With great care the man placed the bag in the luggage compartment, and Austin gave him the wrinkled paper money left over from the soda. Four or five other people got into the van but paid him no attention. He began to nod. He felt as drugged as if he'd taken a sleeping pill. He wanted to orient himself as they drove into the city, but an unstoppable lethargy took hold of him. Finally his head slumped against the window and he fell into his third nap of the day.

He didn't know how long the trip was, but the skies were dark by the time they pulled into Mérida's main square. Austin paid the driver with a five-dollar bill and was given another collection of coins and bills in return. His head felt as if it were sheathed in tissue. He walked into the plaza and sat down on a bench.

Even in the middle of the plaza Mérida seemed crowded and noisy. Children, both scruffy and well dressed, ran up and down the lighted paths and played under the almond trees. Two Indian-looking men carrying bundles of nylon hammocks stopped in front of Austin and held up a sample.

"¿Quiere el señor una hamaca? Son muy finas."

"No, no thanks. I just got here."

He didn't understand a word from anyone. A lottery seller parked in front of him briefly, holding out a clipboard with sheaves of tickets.

"Tengo el nueve. Tengo el tres y el siete."

Austin looked down at the ground until the man drifted off. Almost immediately the lottery salesman was replaced by a kid selling gum. *"Chicles, ¿no quiere chicles?"* Then another boy came by with a rack of sunglasses, and another with a box of blue and yellow Bic pens. Austin shook his head. They all looked six or seven, younger than Blake.

A pair of middle-aged tourists walked by talking as freely in English as if they were home in Texas. Austin looked away to make sure they wouldn't catch his eye. He didn't want to stand out like them—though he knew he probably did. His height, to begin with. At 6'3" he was a good foot taller than many of the Mexicans passing by. And his running shoes looked funny, and his old canvas luggage. He had shoved the bag underneath his bench but kept one foot in constant touch with it.

Even in the hot overused air of the Mexican night his head gradually cleared. Somewhere in this city, he thought, his wife sat in a chair drinking coffee, or changed her clothes for dinner, or puzzled her way through a local newspaper. Blake was here too.

Austin headed away from the plaza down an uneven narrow street. Buses rocked by, awash in diesel fumes. Their rearview mirrors passed only inches from pedestrians on the crowded sidewalks. The stores were still open. Austin looked for a quiet restaurant and eventually found a half-dozen in a row, all with menus posted in both Spanish and English. He entered one and was seated at a table near a patio lush with palms and bougainvilleas.

Half the diners looked like tourists, but Austin relaxed. Inside the restaurant he didn't feel so exposed. The sound of the street could barely be heard, and the waiter spoke some English.

There were hamburger and steak on the menu, but Austin tried the *mixiotes,* "chicken cooked in local cactus." He had fully woken up. Avoiding the water, he drank another soda and had a cup of coffee. After the meal he asked the waiter, almost in a whisper, "Is there a hotel nearby?"

"Oh yes, the Gran Hotel Colombia is very nice. Is close to here and very nice. I think you like it. El Gran Hotel Colombia."

"Is it expensive?"

"Oh yes, very expensive."

The waiter stood on the balls of his feet, his hands behind his back. The people at the next table were glancing over. "How about something . . . smaller?"

"Yes, we have other hotels, many small hotels. I think you like the Hotel Pandora. Is only two streets from here, very close to the center, very nice."

A sign at the desk of the Hotel Pandora claimed that English was spoken there—but the night clerk, an old man with an exaggerated forward curve to his spine, could say little more

than, "You like a room?" and "Upstairs." He pointed the way up
an aging marble staircase—clearly a relic from an age of greater
glory in the hotel trade. Austin found his own way to room 11,
whose door gave onto the large interior patio. Inside the room
there were two beds, a bureau, a chair and a single slatted
window. The tile floor looked clean and the walls freshly painted.

Austin closed the door and tested the nearest bed. He should
not have been tired after so many naps, but he was. He got up
long enough to brush his teeth and turn on the ceiling fan, then
took off his clothes and crawled under the sheets. Five minutes
later he was asleep.

He woke with a start. What the hell? It took him a minute to
remember where he was. His watch said 12:40. He stood up and
fumbled for the light switch—and saw, in the glare of the
overhead bulb, a dozen cockroaches scurrying for cover. Two
went out the window, some disappeared under the bed and the
rest headed for the bathroom. They were all big, two-inch
cockroaches. Austin grabbed his shoe, jerked the bed to one side
and quickly smashed the two within reach. The rest seemed to
have vanished. Even the bathroom was empty, its tile floors and
walls innocent of insect life. He moved the dresser away from the
wall and opened every drawer, but found no more of the little
bastards.

He put his clothes back on, picked up one of the dead
cockroaches in a wadded piece of toilet paper and carried it
downstairs. The stooped old man had fallen asleep on a cot
behind the desk. When Austin said, "Hey!", he stood up as if he'd
just been resting and came forward looking wide awake. Austin
held up the squashed dead bug in its white shroud. A yellowish
liquid had stained the paper.

"Pues sí, señor. ¿En qué le puedo ayudar?"

"You've got cockroaches everywhere. I think they were on
my face."

The old man glanced upstairs and nodded with a friendly
understanding look. "Sí, hombre, hay miles de estos animales.
We have many many. No se acaban nunca. ¡Es una plaga!" He
smiled, took the wad of toilet paper from Austin and threw the
dead cockroach into a wastepaper basket. From under the

counter he brought out an aerosol can—a copy of the same Black Flag can the stewardess had used on the airplane, but with the name in Spanish: MataMiles. He set it down in front of Austin. "You like?"

Austin wiped his forehead with the back of his hand and gave a disgusted look. The old man smiled benignly. *"¿Qué se puede hacer? ¡Es una plaga!"*

For over an hour Austin lay on his bed with the light on, waiting for some shiny cockroach to venture across the floor. Finally he shut the window, sprayed the drains, closed the bathroom door and fell asleep with the sheet over his face.

Early the next morning, after walking back to the Plaza Principal, he found the city more attractive than it had seemed the night before. A breeze had cleared the air of truck and bus fumes, and the streets had all been watered and swept. The wet broom marks, chased by the early sunlight, were still shrinking back to the storm drains.

Austin bought a city map from one of the newsstands and sat down at a juice bar on the south side of the plaza. Last night he hadn't known south from north. He felt more at ease now, having regained his sense of direction.

The bar had *naranja, toronja, piña, zanahoria, mamey, guava, horchata* and *tamarindo*. Austin chose *piña* from the wall-menu picture of a pineapple.

There was no Apartado Street on the map. In fact, there were almost no named streets in all of Mérida. They were numbered instead. Beyond the downtown area the outlying sections of towns had names like Jardines de Mérida, Prado Norte, Cinco Colonias, Nueva Sambula, Emiliano Zapata. But there were no street names, just numbers. There was no Apartado anywhere.

A driver at the taxi stand stood up from his bench wearing a white guayabera and a dapper straw hat. *"¿Taxi, señor? ¿Para dónde va?"*

Austin pulled Fay's letter out of his pocket, unfolded it and showed the man the address. The driver frowned slightly. *"Pues, caballero, esta dirección es del correo, no más."*

In spite of the man's expression Austin offered to get into his car. But the cabbie waved him off. He raised three fingers and pointed down the street.

"*Se puede caminar al correo. Sólo son tres cuadras. No hay por que tomar taxi, ni para un gringo.*"

A second driver laughed and came forward and the two cabbies stood on either side of Austin, holding up three fingers and pointing repeatedly down the narrow street.

Austin set off walking but found, just as the map indicated, only numbered streets. He walked three blocks, then three more and three more. Finally he doubled around and made his way back to the Hotel Pandora.

A new clerk sat behind the desk, a younger man. Austin borrowed the city telephone directory and sat down with it in a chair next to the pay phone. There were almost a hundred Menéndezes, and three named Ricardo—but none lived on Apartado Street. Austin waited until the lobby was empty save for the clerk, then dialed the first Ricardo Menéndez.

"*Bueno,*" a woman answered. And after a pause: "*Aló, ¿quién habla?*" She could have been a wife, a maid, a daughter. There was no way to tell. "*¿Qué pasa? ¿Quién habla? No sea bruto.*"

She hung up. He called the other two numbers and got two more women, neither one pleased to find herself talking to an empty line.

Back in the plaza he sat on a bench beside the whitewashed trunks of manicured trees. The city stretched out in all directions, as complex as Boston. The airport wasn't even on the map, it was too far away. For the first time the possibility occurred to Austin that he could leave home, fly all the way to Mexico, stay in an old hotel full of cockroaches and still not find his wife.

He set off walking north and east until he came to a more tranquil part of the city. A few broad streets were lined with trees, and some horse-drawn carriages stood beside a narrow park. All the same, he found only the steady progression of numbered streets and avenues shown on the map.

He returned once again to the plaza, thinking that if he was going to spot Fay somewhere in this town, it would be there. He imagined her strolling along beneath the boxed laurels. Just before noon he picked out a couple of rolls at a self-service bakery and ate them off a square of waxed paper on what had become his bench. As he ate, the city came to a stop. Metal screens were unrolled in front of store windows, the number of pedestrians swelled briefly, then the traffic let up and the plaza emptied. Austin walked back to his hotel through the powerful midday heat. He sprayed the bathroom drain with MataMiles and took a three-hour siesta.

The shops didn't open again until four. He cleared his head with a shower, put on a clean white shirt and his best pair of pants and headed for a tourist shop he had seen that morning that had a sign in the window saying ENGLISH SPOKEN. The heat was still oppressive, and after walking only a couple of blocks he began to sweat freely.

He didn't enter the shop immediately, but stood outside inspecting the window display of leather goods, shawls and turquoise jewelry. The woman behind the counter seemed to be alone and the shop empty, so he stepped inside.

The woman had straight black hair and a broad Indian face. She was short, even in high heels, and though she wore a blue skirt and blouse that would not have looked out of place in any U.S. city, Austin could not imagine that she was the one who spoke English, because she looked so thoroughly foreign. Not just Mexican, but Mayan.

"Are you the one who speaks English?"

"Yes, I am. Can I help you?" Her English was good. Better than he had hoped—because he didn't want to have to explain, to someone who might understand all about it, exactly what he was looking for.

"I don't know who to ask," he told her. "I'm looking for a street that's not on the city map. Even the taxi drivers don't know where it is."

He held out Fay's blue aerogram with the address on the back. After only a glance at the letter the young woman said, "This isn't a street, it's a post-office number. How do you say . . . a post-office box. *Apartado cinco treinta y seis.* That's box number five thirty-six."

Her smooth cheekbones shone in the afternoon heat. With the curved point of her fingernail she traced a line on the back of the envelope beneath the name Raigosa Menéndez, leaving a slight indentation on the paper. "You are looking for this person? Have you tried the telephone book?"

"I tried but . . . I couldn't find him. His first name is Ricardo."

She turned on one spiked heel, stepped to a desk in the corner of the room and returned with the phone book. "Do you like our city?"

"I've only been here a day."

"I lived in Philadelphia for one year and a half. I liked it very much. I worked very hard there in a factory, sewing pants. Here, you see? Raigosa Menéndez. Ricardo Raigosa Menéndez." She spun the book around on the counter, holding her finger next to the name Raigosa.

"I thought his name was Menéndez."

"It is, but Menéndez is his mother's name and Raigosa his father's."

Austin did not understand.

"That's how it is in Spanish. Take my name, for example. I am Alicia Morelos Castimóy. That means my father's name is Morelos and my mother's name is Castimóy. The father's name comes first and then the mother's. If I married with someone, I would keep Morelos and give up Castimóy. Then I would be Alicia Morelos de Tal. Do you see?"

"More or less."

She laughed, showing a line of straight white teeth and, almost hidden, one gold incisor. "Are you married?" she asked, tapping his wedding ring with her red fingernail. Her hand moved like a snake, fast and precise.

"I'm supposed to be married. I came here to find my wife." He had no idea what led him to say the one thing he had meant to keep hidden.

"*Ay, por Dios.* And she is with this man, this Ricardo?"

"Yes."

"You don't have a gun, do you?"

"A gun?"

"Sometimes a man gets angry and takes a gun to see another man. It is often in the newspaper. But you are not like that, are you? You seem to be a gentleman."

"What does a gentleman do when he finds his wife with another man?"

The woman rested both hands on top of the telephone book. "It is better to talk than to take a gun."

"I don't have a gun."

"Good. If you have a gun, leave it where you are staying. You are staying in some hotel? After you find your wife and talk to her, if you are sad, you must come back and tell me what happened. I can explain to you about Mexico, and we can have a cup of coffee. I have a Mister Coffee in back. But don't take a gun. Sometimes it feels so bad, but later things will change. Your wife will come back to you. Here, I will write out the address. It's in the Fraccionamiento Campestre, a very beautiful part of town. I think Mr. Raigosa is a rich man."

Austin shook the woman's hand, thanked her and went straight to the taxi stand near the plaza. A different driver was there, lounging against the polished fender of his car. When Austin showed him the Campestre address on the slip of paper, he nodded matter-of-factly and opened the back door for Austin to get in. The wide backseat was newly upholstered and smelled of cleaning fluid. The car was a six-cylinder, three-speed Chevy Caprice, about ten years old, immaculate. A clear vinyl jacket covered the backrest of the front seat like a plastic antimacassar. The cabbie drove as if he expected to leave the car to his grandchildren.

Once the cab was under way, the driver leaned back and asked Austin a couple of questions in Spanish. He could only shrug his shoulders. The city went by in a blur. He no longer cared about the heat or the crowds or the diesel fumes, or understanding the driver. He didn't care if they were headed north or south. His heart was going too fast for any of that. He tried to think of what he would say when he got there.

They entered a residential part of town with wide streets lined with trees and shrubs, and no sidewalks. It looked like wealthy California. There were no pedestrians—not even any maids or gardeners. The taxi stopped in front of a wide low house set among giant rubber trees and a profusion of carefully tended growth.

Austin paid the driver in dollars and waited until he drove off. Then he walked up the curving stone path to the door. His palms were wet. He was no longer thinking, as he had when he first read Fay's letter, about putting his fist through Ricardo's teeth. He was wondering if Ricardo had a gun. He wondered too if he would feel as awkward and humble in Ricardo's house as he had everywhere else in Mexico. Maybe he shouldn't say anything. Maybe he should just take his son in his arms and then decide what to do.

He knocked on the front door and waited. He knocked again, louder. Finally the door was opened by a short older woman so Indian of feature she seemed to be Oriental. She wore an embroidered white dress, earrings in the shape of a figure eight and no shoes.

"¿Sí?"

"Is this the Raigosa Menéndez house?"

The woman ignored his glances over her shoulder. "Don Ricardo no está."

"I'm looking for my wife. No hablo español. I'm looking for my wife and my son. Do you know Fay?"

The woman's submerged black eyes opened a degree. She considered a moment before answering, "La señora Fe tampoco está."

"That's right—Fay. Is she here?"

"No está. Ni ella ni el señor. Salieron en el coche."

Whatever she was saying, it meant no. Austin looked behind her into the house. Over her head he yelled, "Fay!"

"Ya le dije, señor, no está. La señora salió con Don Ricardo y los hijos. No están."

What the hell was she talking about? He considered pushing past her into the house, but she stood squarely in the door frame, her wide bare feet splayed on the mustard-colored tiles. After a silence of almost a minute she stepped past him, abandoning her post, and gestured for him to follow. She walked to the garage and pointed at the empty space. "Se fueron. Vuelven más tarde."

He tapped the crystal on his watch. *"¿Cuando . . .* oh shit. When are they going to come back?"

The woman gave him a shrug as inscrutable as the Mayan empire.

There was nothing to do but wait it out. He walked up the street and back. This was not the impoverished Mexico they wrote about in the papers. There was probably more money in this one neighborhood than in most of White Pine. Austin sat down on the soft earth under an avocado tree across the street from Ricardo's house. He endured the stares of everyone who drove by. He was a big gringo wearing sneakers and a sweat-marked shirt. He stuck out like a wetback in Beverly Hills.

An hour later a large blue Mercedes with tinted glass windows pulled into Ricardo's drive. The front doors opened simultaneously and a man got out of one side and Fay the other. Austin was already halfway across the street when she saw him. Well tanned, in a new dress and heeled sandals, she looked like a wealthy Mexican woman who had spent her whole life around expensive cars and houses.

Austin crossed the street grinning. He tried to stop but couldn't. His mouth was no longer part of his body. Ricardo, perfectly calm, watched him come. He was Fay's height, with a round smooth face and a small moustache. He wore a dark blue suit and tan shoes. He looked like the kind of man who had a gun somewhere: in his glove compartment or a dresser drawer, or even in a holster. Austin, by the time he met them at the front door, had fought his grin back to a smile.

The three of them stood in a triangle. Fay was nowhere near smiling. "How did you find me?" she asked. She sounded angry, even frantic. "I can't believe Carolyn told you."

"Carolyn was loyal to the end. I figured it out on my own."

He had planned to be secretive himself and never to explain how he had found her. He would pretend it was by the sheer force of his desire. But the secret tumbled out. He pulled her letter to Carolyn out of his back pocket and waved it in the air.

Fay grabbed at the letter and missed, then held her arms rigidly at her sides, both hands drawn into fists. "How did you get that letter?"

"You were careful but you weren't careful enough." Austin almost laughed—though even as he spoke he realized that this moment might be his only reward of the trip. "I waited a week for this to come," he said. "A whole week. I went to Amherst and lived in my truck and waited. You didn't think I'd be that clever."

"No, I didn't. I didn't even think you'd go back to Carolyn's after you went down there the first time."

"So she wrote you," Austin said.

"And the last thing I expected was that you'd take any time off from your potatoes."

"What did you think, after stealing Blake? At least you could have warned me about that." His laughter and smiles had passed away. "It was probably illegal."

"Did you finish the planting?"

"Jules finished it with the crew. But what do you care about the farm? You've obviously turned your back on it."

"I can't believe you came down here. I know you've got hay to cut this month."

What surprised her was not that he had found her, but that he had left home in the first place to track her down. What the hell did she expect? Standing upright in her heeled sandals, she now looked puzzled rather than angry. With nothing to carry— no purse or briefcase or sweater—she didn't seem to know what to do with her hands. They kept jerking up to her waist and falling back.

Perhaps noticing her state, Ricardo spoke up for the first time. "You are devoted to have come so far, Mr. Pooler. I'm sure you understand that you've taken us somewhat by surprise."

His English was perfect, with a slight British accent. Austin had seen him before somewhere but couldn't remember where. "Where's my son?" he asked. It was a challenge, not a polite question.

"He's doing fine. We left him with my two daughters at a . . . how do you call it . . . a sleeping party."

"A slumber party," Fay said. She explained it to Austin: "Both boys and girls are invited, and there are chaperones."

"My *son* is at a *slumber* party," he said. He stared at

Fay. "This must go on in Mexico all the time, right? You sleep here, you sleep there, anywhere you damn well feel like. You got a chaperon, Fay?"

She stepped directly in front of him. "Don't start, Austin. You had plenty of time in Maine to listen to me, and you never did."

"You never said you'd do something like this."

"If you'd said you'd go with me, I wouldn't have done this." She stopped to glance at Ricardo. He nodded politely, like someone at a lawn party. Fay looked more like a waitress after a long night. "But you wouldn't leave with me. You wouldn't talk about it, you wouldn't think about it, you didn't even consider it. You ignored me. You ignored everything I said about it for two years. And this spring you had to plant the same as always. You wanted to buy *more* land. So now we're on a different footing."

"A different *footing*," he said. But his sarcasm didn't touch her.

Ricardo, as composed as a mortician, turned and opened the front door. "Mr. Pooler—or may I call you Austin?—please come in for a cup of coffee or a drink. Make yourself at home here. I think inside we could talk this over more easily." He turned to the maid, who had appeared at the other end of the corridor. *"Teresa, tres tazas de café por favor."*

A guy like this didn't need a gun. He could knife you in the heart with his speech. His shoes struck the tile floor as he led them inside. His suit coat was still buttoned.

They sat around a glass-topped table in a patio enclosed by the house but open to the sky. The tropical dusk had come over them with unexpected suddenness.

Fay leaned slightly away from Austin and toward Ricardo. Austin realized with a pang that she was afraid of him. She trusted this smooth-talking cutthroat bastard and was afraid of her husband of twenty years.

Ricardo lit a Winston cigarette. He used a thin silver lighter. "You don't mind, do you? Fay doesn't smoke, but she forgives my weakness."

"And if I minded?"

"I would put it out. A cigarette is a small thing."

"Unlike a wife."

Ricardo exhaled a stream of smoke to one side. Like all his movements, the gesture was precise and moderate. "Let me assure you that Fay is free to leave my house at any time. The door has a lock, but it opens easily from the inside."

Austin stared at her.

"I was going to write you," she said, her voice softer. She turned in her chair to face him. "Blake wrote you a couple of letters and I was going to send them through Carolyn. But please don't think I'm going back to Maine. I'm just surprised you went to all this trouble to find me."

"You thought I'd just say fuck it to twenty years?"

She sat back and dropped her eyes.

"Ah," Ricardo said, "the coffee is served." Nothing disconcerted him: no angry talk, no interruptions by the maid, no bitter looks from Austin. Even his accent was perfect.

Teresa set out three cups and saucers, a kettle of water and a glass-stoppered bottle filled with a dark brown, almost black liquid.

"Esencia de café," Ricardo explained, holding up the bottle. "I own land in Chiapas and every year they send me some of their best beans." He poured a couple of tablespoons of *esencia* in each cup, then added the hot water. "Would you like something to eat?" he asked. *"Teresa, ¿hay pan dulce?"*

"Ya se lo traigo, Don."

Austin asked Fay if she understood this talk.

"Pan dulce is sweet rolls," she said. "I've picked up a few words, but usually we speak English. Blake does much better than I do."

Austin fought against his desire to ask Ricardo questions. He didn't want to show any curiosity—but he wanted to know who he was. Finally he asked, "How did you get an English accent?"

"I went to school in London. And in recent years I have gone there often on business."

"Which is?"

"Records. British rock-and-roll and American top forty, and also a few Mexican groups that sell in New York and London.

Import and export, but mainly import. We have our own label here."

"Apparently you make a lot of money off this business."

Fay interrupted them. "This is not a competition," she said.

Austin stared at her shoulders, crossed by the thin straps of her dress. He stared at her breasts and, through the glass-topped table, the line her underpants made across her hips. She saw him do it, but he kept on looking.

"So you arrived today?" Ricardo said.

"Yesterday afternoon."

"Ah, then you have already found a place to stay."

"At the Hotel Pandora, near the plaza."

"Oh dear. Fay, would you like a roll? Austin? Did they give you a decent room?"

"I woke up in the middle of the night surrounded by cockroaches."

Fay laughed outright. "They're everywhere," she said, "even here. Blake throws little firecrackers at them to scare them off."

"They're like emotions to an Englishman," Ricardo said. "An age-old enemy. We control them but can never totally eliminate them."

"I suppose in Mexico passion rules all," Austin said.

"D. H. Lawrence thought so. But the Pandora is a bit dismal, isn't it? If you would allow me, I could recommend a more comfortable place. It's a small pension run by a friend's aunt. The food is good, and I'm sure it would be much cheaper than your hotel."

"It was on Nantucket, wasn't it?" Austin stood up, banging and almost dislodging the glass tabletop from its frame. "That's where I saw him. At that cocktail party at the Strickmans'."

"That's right," Fay said. "We met there last summer."

"And started screwing there."

Ricardo reached inside his suit coat and for an instant Austin thought he was going to pull out a gun. Instead he withdrew a pen and a monogrammed notepad, on which he wrote the name and address of the Pensión Dorada.

"It's in front of the Parque de las Américas. It's quiet there and I'm sure Doña Luz has the cockroaches under control."

He turned the card onto the table like a poker player laying down an ace. Under the table he crossed one leg over the other, exposing his narrow ankles and expensive tan shoes.

Austin could hardly remember him from the Strickmans' party—just that someone Latin had been there, a man with a black moustache and brown cheeks so smooth they looked as if they had never been shaved.

"I want to talk to Fay alone."

"But of course," Ricardo said. "That sounds quite reasonable. You could take a walk through the neighborhood if you like. It's perfectly safe at night. Or I would loan you my car."

"We'll walk. Fay, will you come?"

"Perhaps a short walk."

There was no question about it. She was afraid of him.

FIVE

They walked along the empty impeccable streets. Overhead, in the hazy night air, moths as big as hands beat against the streetlights.

"This guy Ricardo speaks better English than I do," Austin said.

"His sister lives in England. And he works on it. He'll never say 'sleeping party' again."

A man in a uniform rolled slowly past them on a bicycle. "*Buenas noches*," he said. "*Buenas noches*," Fay answered. He disappeared around the next corner, and a minute later they heard a thin high whistle from his direction, a sound like a tiny clarinet.

"He's a private policeman," she explained. "A *sereno*. He pedals around the neighborhood all night blowing that whistle. It's the sign that all's well—and also that he's on the job. A *sereno* keeps everything serene."

"How cozy."

She stopped in the middle of the street, her arms crossed and her chin raised. "Do you want to talk or do you want to go back?"

He looked down, afraid to challenge her. He had to have this talk. After a moment's silence they continued down the empty street. There were neither cars nor pedestrians. The edge of Austin's vision flickered, and twice he turned his head to see if something was trailing them. There was nothing, or only the moths. After another block Fay drew closer and surprised him by slipping her arm through his. He could feel her breathing beside him: long purposeful breaths with a little burst at the beginning.

They walked past houses half hidden by vegetation. The air smelled of wet soil and new growth. "That's a sapote," Fay said, pointing at a dark tree. "And there's a mango and a saramuyo. I've been learning all the fruits."

Good for you, he almost said. He didn't want to hear about trees or fruits or any other damn thing in Mérida. From somewhere off in the darkness came the remote high whistle of the *sereno*.

"I never thought you'd find me here and . . . see me."

"You mean see you with Ricardo."

She nodded.

"But I did," he said. "So what is this with you and him?"

"He invited me down. It's just a visit. I needed somewhere I couldn't turn around from too easily and go home."

"And of course he's all hot for you."

"Ricardo's been good to me. He's a good listener. And I've had some things to talk about."

"You mean complain about," Austin said.

"Not really. Ricardo never pries. I don't think he wants to hear that much about you or Maine."

Fay's dress clung to her waist in the humid air. They paused under a streetlight, under the flapping moths. "I hope you won't exaggerate what's going on down here," she said.

"What is going on?"

"Probably not as much as you think."

"What are you talking about? You're living with the guy."

"Come," Fay said. She led him to the curb and sat down beside him. "It's not that easy leaving home. I'm not sure what will happen with Ricardo, but I'm certainly not going to settle down in *his* house and *his* life. I want to find my own."

"You've told him that?"

"Of course. I wouldn't have come without telling him that first."

"But you're in love with him."

"You're relentless. I like him but I'm not in love with him. Austin, you and I and Blake could have been traveling around together right now. I asked you a hundred times. Quit worrying so much about me and Ricardo."

"What if you get pregnant or pick up some disease?"

She stretched out her legs and rested their weight on the pointed heels of her sandals. "I'm extremely careful."

He couldn't talk for a minute because his heart went so fast. It made him dizzy, how beautiful she looked. "And after this," he managed to say, "will you want to see me again?"

"I'll always want to see you again. We have two children and we've lived together for twenty years. We're still married. And up until a few weeks ago I was doing everything I could to get you to leave the farm with me. So quit making it Ricardo versus you."

The *sereno*, blowing his whistle, approached from the other direction. Directly in front of them he did a figure eight on his bicycle, said *"Buenas noches"* once again and rode off down the street.

"What about Blake?" Austin said. "Don't you care what he sees?"

She took her wedding ring and spun it slowly on her finger. At least she still wore it. "I do care," she said. "And I've tried to be careful."

"But he's not blind. He knows what's going on."

Fay brought her knees up and enclosed them in her arms, wrapping her dress tightly against her legs. "I guess he does. But he's been a great traveler. I don't really think it's been that hard on him. He's hardly talked about the farm at all."

"He's eight years old. Don't hand me this shit."

She hugged her knees. "Okay, he misses you. Maybe more than I thought he would. But I couldn't leave him. You think this is all a lark for me, but it was scary coming down here. I wanted to be with my son."

She cried silently, then wiped her tears away with her forearm.

Austin waited. He didn't want to be swayed. "What about Maggie?" he asked.

"I couldn't tell her where I was going."

"The last time I called she was headed for some party on the Cape with a rock group called the Weasel Wonders. Does that sound like a nice bunch of guys to you?"

"I'll write her in Wyoming. I doubt if she'll get into any trouble out there."

"Just because Maggie's eighteen," he said, "I don't think we should turn her loose."

"Austin, I'm not turning her loose—or you, for that matter. Or I wouldn't if you'd listen to me."

A car passed by, blinding them momentarily with its headlights. There was no wind, no temperature, no weather at all.

"It's been pretty hard to listen to you in the last few weeks."

"I'm sorry, Austin. I really am, I'm sorry. I still love you." She reached across to him and slipped her arm around his neck. "Maybe I should tell you that every day, because you forget so easily."

He sat still for a moment, then pressed her against his chest. He kissed her hair, the side of her face, her neck. He said, "We could borrow Ricardo's car."

She pushed him away and stood up. "Don't be an idiot." Turning abruptly, she marched off down the street, the vengeful heels of her sandals striking the asphalt pavement.

Austin caught up to her and apologized, but she wouldn't listen. The *sereno* passed by once again and circled them on his bicycle, his eye on Austin. After that they didn't speak until they got back to Ricardo's. At the door Fay unwound enough to say coldly, "I hope you spend some time with Blake. He'll be back tomorrow."

Ricardo answered their knock himself and asked, as if blind, "Did you have a good talk?" The bastard knew Austin hadn't gained any ground. "Do stay for dinner," he said. "We're having a local dish, *pok chuk*. We usually eat about ten."

"No. But tomorrow I want to see my son."

"By all means. You must borrow my car and take him to the beach at El Progreso. The two of you will have a wonderful day."

"You are one nervy son of a gun," Austin said.

Ricardo raised his eyebrows politely. "Son of a gun. I believe that's an American expression."

"I believe it is. Like piss ant and cocksucker."

The smallest ripple of emotion passed over Ricardo's face. "Fortunately," he said, "English swearwords carry little emotional weight for me. But with your proclivity for vulgar language, if you ever learn any Spanish you may run into trouble in the streets."

Fay, standing to one side, looked unhappy. Austin felt defeated. Two minutes later he left for the Hotel Pandora.

The first rumblings of the city woke him after a night filled with cockroaches, or dreams of cockroaches. By six-thirty sunlight had flooded his room through the small jalousie window, dispelling all insects, real or imaginary.

After breakfast he changed some money, then climbed into a taxi and gave the driver Ricardo's card with the address of the Pensión Dorada. He didn't like the idea of taking help from Ricardo, but he didn't want to spend another night worrying about cockroaches.

"El día es bonito," Austin said in the taxi. He had been reading his Spanish phrase book over breakfast: It's a pretty day.

"Muy bonito a esta hora. Después hace calor."

It was hopeless. The driver chatted with him, but he couldn't pick up a single word.

Doña Luz, who ran the Pensión Dorada, spoke English, after a fashion. "This is your house," she said, two or three times. She showed Austin a quiet room on the north side of the building and told him it was "very fresh, very nice for sleep." The house was cool and clean and filled with plants. And just as Ricardo had promised, the price of a room, including breakfast, lunch and dinner, was less than what he had paid for a night at the Hotel Pandora.

After unpacking his few clothes into a dresser, he walked back out into the heat of the day and found another cab. He had to show the driver Ricardo's address, for he still wasn't sure of his numbers. *"Uno, dos, tres, cuatro,"* he murmured, on the short trip to El Campestre.

He was halfway up the path to the house when Blake ran outside. Barefoot, wearing only red shorts and a tee-shirt, he tore down the path like a track star, his head raised in the air.

"Here he comes!" Austin said.

Sure of being caught, Blake took off from the ground and flew against his father's chest. "I knew you'd come to see me! I knew you would! I wrote you letters."

Austin pressed his son's face to his cheek. Blake wrapped his legs around his waist and held on to his ears.

"Aunt Carolyn took us to the plane and we flew over the ocean," he said. "I have a *big* room here. Have you been at home, Daddy? In our house?"

"Right at home, the whole time. And then I went to Amherst, the same as you, and then I flew down here. Maybe even in the same plane."

"Did you see all the little boats on the water? That's what I wrote in my letter. I wrote it all by myself."

"I missed you," Austin said. "Do you have fun here? You look bigger."

"I am. Mom says I'm growing up fast."

"Is your mom here?"

"No, she went out with Ricardo. But Teresa has the key to the car, so we can go to the beach. You know there are two girls here? But we're not going to the beach with them, just you and me. They already know that. They don't speak English anyway."

The two girls, both older than Blake, sat at the glass-topped table in the patio. Blake held tightly on to Austin's hand as he announced, "*Es mi papá.* That means you're my dad."

Both girls rose to shake Austin's hand. One said, "*Tanto gusto,*" and the other, "*Encantada.*" They were thin and dark-haired. They must have been curious about him, Austin thought, but they didn't show it.

"Can you talk to them?" he asked Blake.

"No."

"But you told them I was your dad."

"I know some words. *Plátanos fritos* means fried bananas."

"What about their mother?"

"She died. There's a picture of her in their room. Come here, Dad, I want to show you something."

Blake led him through the back door, past a second patio and out into a small garden. In the very first row were six potato plants just out of the ground, all properly hilled.

"I bought them in the market and washed them in case they had any of that inhibitor stuff on them. Ricardo said it was too hot for potatoes here, but they came up."

Austin knelt, put his arms around Blake and held him to his chest. "Have I told you recently that you're the greatest boy ever? That you're the king of eight-year-olds?"

"I showed Teresa how to cook French fries too. She didn't put enough oil in. But she's getting better at it."

Teresa, with no expression whatsoever, gave Austin the key to the Mercedes. He had brought his map, and they had no trouble finding the road to El Progreso. After Austin's old pickup, the Mercedes accelerated and cornered like a leopard.

Blake turned on the radio and the air-conditioning, lowered the windows, opened the sunroof and moved the antenna up and down. "This car's got everything, Dad." Then he was silent for a moment. "But it's not as much fun as a tractor."

"Are you kidding? This is the hottest car I've ever been in. You could do a hundred in this thing and never know it."

"Yeah! Let's go!"

"We better not. We might crash and destroy it."

"Let's crash it up, Dad! Ricardo can get another one easy. He's *rich*. Let's do a hundred!"

For a brief stretch Austin put the car up to 160 kilometers per hour. They sped over the newly surfaced road like a cue ball on a pool table, zipping past walls of jungle. Then, as bicycles and dogs and pedestrians began to show up along the side of the road, Austin slowed down. Before long they had entered the outskirts of El Progreso.

As far as progress went, the town had made an uneven start. Crumbling pastel houses baked in the sunshine, a man with a horse and cart delivered a new sofa wrapped in plastic, and empty hardware and shoe stores stood open to the bleached sidewalks. There was none of the commotion of downtown

Mérida. Two men wrapped in sheets, sitting in a barbershop, stared at the Mercedes as it passed by.

The car kept Mexico at a distance. The Poolers could see out through the tinted glass, but no one could see in. After two days of being on display—a 6'3" gringo with fair skin and light brown hair—Austin found it restful.

West of town near the little village of Chelem they stepped out of the air-conditioned car onto the bright sand. The heat struck Austin like a fist, though Blake hardly seemed to notice. He knew the ropes. He showed his father how to rent a thatched palapa where they could change their clothes and sit in a hammock in the shade. Blake put on his bathing suit and Austin an old pair of tennis shorts. Then they sprinted over the burning sand and plunged into the blue Caribbean.

"See, Dad, it's great. Now that you're here, we can come every day."

Austin hadn't had time to think about what came next. He tried to imagine, as he splashed about in the warm salt water, what he would tell Jules when he phoned home. First, that Fay was in Mexico and was going to stay here for a while. And second, that he had moved into a little pension—three meals a day included—and was getting to know the Yucatán.

Jules's comment to that would be silence. Austin might just as well report back that he'd decided on a career move to Hoboken, New Jersey, where he planned to do taxidermy on rats and stray dogs.

Women came by the hut with soft drinks, beer, fruit, pork rinds and little meat sandwiches on deep-fried tortillas. Blake knew what was safe to eat and what wasn't.

"Doesn't Ricardo eat everything?"

"No, he says some of it's dirty."

"How about those girls? Do you get along with them?"

"They're okay. Sonia's nice to me sometimes. Isabel talks on the telephone and I can never understand her. She's too old."

"How old?"

"Thirteen."

Blake had brought a tennis ball and they played catch in the shallows. Afterward they lay side by side in the palapa's wide hammock, rocking and talking. With his arm around his father's neck Blake said, "I didn't know Mom was going to Mexico. I would have told you if I knew."

"Don't worry about that. I found you, didn't I? You think I'd stay away very long from the king of eight-year-olds?"

"Is that what Grandpa used to tell you, Dad? When you were a kid? *No, gracias,*" Blake sang out.

Another woman had come by with a tray of soft drinks. As she disappeared down the beach, they could see her through the slat walls of the palapa. The hut was like Ricardo's car: you could see out but no one could see in.

"He might have said something like that. Of course, he didn't have you for a kid."

"He had *you,* and you're the best dad."

"Maybe. But in those days I was just a scruffy little woodchuck. I didn't even know how to tie my own shoes."

"I can tie them when I have to," Blake said. "But I like it when you do it for me."

"Maybe when you grow up you'll be a logger or a farmer, and every morning before work you'll have to come over to my house to get your shoes tied."

"No, Dad. Just for now while I'm a kid. It's so easy for you."

They rocked in the shade of the palapa, swam and rocked and swam again. They stayed all day.

On the way home, in the cool relief of the Mercedes, Blake stretched out across the front seat and put his head on his father's lap. "I'm not really tired, Dad. I could have stayed there some more. I'm just going to close my eyes for a minute."

The next time he looked down, Blake was asleep. His tanned knees and feet were covered with little scars, the battle wounds of an active boy. Austin rested a hand on his chest, all the way back to Mérida. And there, not wanting to wake him, he parked in the street a couple of blocks up from Ricardo's house and sat for almost an hour, letting his boy sleep.

Now began an unusual set of days for Austin Pooler. He lived in the Pensión Dorada, did no work of any kind, saw his son almost every day and his wife almost never. He borrowed Ricardo's car and drove Blake to the ruins at Uxmal and Chichén Itzá, and again to the beach at Chelem. Within the city they went by taxi or bus to soccer games, museums and movies. They had fun, but it was public fun—not like laughing and screaming at home as they beat on each other with rolled-up newspapers. They couldn't very well do that at Ricardo's house, or in Austin's small room at the Pensión Dorada.

One afternoon they went to the Kukulkán Stadium and watched a pair of Mexican teams play spirited noisy baseball.

"This is where they discovered Fernando Valenzuela," Austin said.

"Yeah? I know that guy. He pitches for L.A."

"He used to pitch right here until someone came in with a radar gun and clocked his fastball at ninety-five miles an hour."

"How about my team in White Pine?" Blake asked. "How are they doing this year?"

"I don't know. I'm sorry, I should have asked before I left."

They sat on the bleachers as the stadium emptied after the game, eating the last of a picnic lunch packed by Ricardo's maid. Teresa was fond of Blake and had been trained by Ricardo never to let the children eat foods from street vendors. So every day she prepared a lunch for both Blake and his father. Today there were green mangoes with salt, American cheese sandwiches on white Pan Bimbo, small ripe nances, an avocado and two bottles of Orange Crush.

A couple of street dogs worked the aisles, searching for scraps of food. Austin threw them the remains of his sandwich and then shooed them off. They perched a few yards away, ever alert, their skinny backsides barely resting on the concrete.

"Teresa treats you pretty well, doesn't she?"

"She's nice. I can't understand her, but she cooks me *plátanos fritos* anytime I want."

Teresa had also become the buffer between Austin and Fay. Either Fay was out when he came to get Blake, or she let Teresa preside at the front door while she kept out of sight in back. It was like doing business with a lawyer who was too busy to answer any questions personally, and who fobbed you off onto one of the firm's underlings, someone who had no clear grasp of the problem at hand.

"How about Ricardo?" Austin asked his son.

Here he was on dangerous ground. It did seem fair, though,to make sure his child was being well taken care of.

"He's mean sometimes," Blake said.

"What does he do?"

"He yells at his kids. In Spanish. Sometimes he makes them cry for nothing."

"He doesn't make you cry, does he?"

"No."

"And your mom. Is he good to her?" Now he was on quicksand.

"He's okay."

Austin got up and ran the dogs off. So much for trying to squeeze information out of Blake. "When I go back to Maine," he told his son, "you could either stay here or come with me. I'm going to talk to your mom about it."

"I want to go with you."

"I thought you might."

Blake swung his legs back and forth and stared at the infield. "Are you and Mom going to get divorced?" From the sound of his voice he was holding back tears.

"I hope not. But we might be separated for a while." Austin put his arm around his son's small shoulders. They didn't give. He just sat there rocking his feet and staring, his hands pinned beneath his legs.

"I want her to come home," the boy said.

"Me too. But I don't think she will. She wants to live somewhere else and maybe find a new job."

"Here?"

"I don't think so. This is more like a visit."

Blake relaxed his tight little shoulders and crawled into Austin's lap. He hadn't cried. On the infield the shadows reached as far as the pitcher's mound. The heat of the day was passing.

"I don't want you and Mom to fight. Or you and Ricardo to fight."

"We won't," Austin assured him.

Other than in a simple fistfight, he couldn't imagine beating Ricardo at anything here on his home ground.

Mérida was wild about baseball. There were several local teams, and every afternoon there was a U.S. game on the television with commentary in Spanish. Sometimes, when he wasn't with Blake, Austin sat in a small café near his pension and watched the Red Sox play the Tigers or the Yankees. In between batters he studied a Spanish grammar he had bought downtown.

His room at the Dorada, as Doña Luz had promised, was cool and fresh, very good for sleeping—even though the cries of the long black birds in the trees outside his window interrupted his dreams every morning. Sometimes he woke up so early he caught the last few whistles of the neighborhood *sereno*. Then, as he stood at his barred window, the street-sweeper appeared, and then the first delivery bikes, their oversized baskets piled high with bread.

A couple of times a week, using the rental phone in the Queen of the Yucatán café, he called Jules to see how their potatoes were doing. He also called his mother on Long Island and his daughter at her Wyoming hotel. Everyone pretended to think the way he and Fay and Blake were now living was altogether reasonable.

After making his U.S. calls one afternoon, Austin handed the phone back to the cashier and sat down at one of the plastic-marble tables. He ordered a Corona and a sandwich. There were only two other people in the little café, a couple of older women drinking coffee. Behind them a blue light drew moths, flies and beetles toward an electric grid, which electrocuted the bugs with a loud, unnerving *zzzzap*.

A young woman in high heels and a straight white skirt walked in off the sidewalk, glanced about and sat down at the table next to Austin's—even though there were a half-dozen other empty tables in the café. He lowered his Spanish grammar and watched her out of the corner of his eye. She crossed her long brown legs at the knee and again at the ankle. Even in this weather, she wore stockings. She ordered a coffee, a roll and then a small liqueur. When Austin glanced over at her she said, "Jou are estudying Espanish. Do jou espeak Inglish?"

He barely understood her. She had a tall European figure, but a round Indian face and coal-black hair.

"I'm trying to learn a little Spanish," he said. "So I bought this book." He held up the grammar and quoted from the dialogue he had been practicing in silence: *"Julio está en el patio. Pase adelante, Don Pablo."*

"Very good," the woman said, smiling. *"A-they-lan-te.* The *d* is very sof."

"A-de-lan-te," he said. She was not so much pretty as striking—though in White Pine ten men out of ten would have stopped on the sidewalk to watch her go by. "How do you know English?"

"Sometime I went to Miami for bisness, and as a child I estudy it in eschool."

"Study," Austin said.

"Estudy."

He smiled, and she smiled back. "I like to practice my Inglish," she said. "Before I espoke better, but now I am forgetting."

"Oh no, you do very well."

"You must be a good teacher. Estudy. I will learn to say that."

"What's your name?"

"Ana María Sandoval Chermalán, *encantada."* She gave him a warm, firm hand, and they shook. The pupils of her eyes were midnight black, her lids violet, her eyeliner dark as kohl.

"I'm Austin Wayman Pooler. But Wayman is just a middle name. My last name is Pooler."

"Pooler," she said, pushing the word out between her lips the way a small child blows out a candle. Austin shifted in his seat to face her and banged his knees against the bottom of the plastic table. The table, like everything else in Mexico, was too small for him.

She often came to sit in the Reina del Yucatán, she said, because she liked the little park across the street, and because she

worked nearby. "I make commercial translations to the Espanish," she said, "but I am not good enough. I need to practice."

"Practice," Austin said, smoothing out her rolled *r*.

"*A-they-lan-te*," she said, and they both laughed.

She had to go. But before she left they agreed to meet two days later at the same tables, to share lessons. Austin stood and shook hands with her a second time. As she walked out of the café and down the sidewalk, he watched her exemplary calves flex and relax, flex and relax.

The following morning he had a date with his wife. He had asked her for a few hours alone. They walked to the Paseo Montejo, then across town to the Parque de las Américas. She wore a pair of slacks and a blouse with a rounded collar. Her hair was in a ponytail. She'd probably been up half the night fucking Ricardo, he thought—though there was no sign of it in her gait, in her clothes or on her freshly scrubbed face.

They talked about Mérida. They talked about the afternoon rains and the Mayan ruins near town.

"If I didn't bring it up," Austin said finally, "would you let us talk about the weather the whole time and never mention Ricardo?"

"No, I wouldn't do that."

They sat down on a bench in front of the Pensión Dorada. "Are you in love with him?" he asked again.

"Love isn't what I'm after."

"Can't you answer a direct question?"

"I'm not in love with him," she said. "I don't know if I'd even remember the feeling with anyone but you. It's been too long."

"You'd remember."

"Maybe. But I wouldn't fall in love with Ricardo. Not now, anyway. Not down here."

She didn't look like a woman in love, he thought. She looked too brittle for that. With her large hands laced and her thin neck held aloft, she looked like a woman who would have preferred to be younger than she was.

Yet he wanted more than ever to take her in his arms. As simply as a bird alighting on his shoulder, desire had tapped him. He was silent for a few moments, then asked if she would like to see his room in the pension. "There," he said, pointing up to his window.

She looked around after stepping through the door. "No chair," she said.

"Relax, Fay. Sit on the bed. I'll sit in the window."

The room was clean and simple. There was almost nothing in it. The corner floor tiles were still streaked after the maid's daily washing. Fay told him he could sit beside her on the bed. "It's strange to think you live here," she said.

"How long are you going to stay in Mérida?"

"Longer than you want me to, I'm sure. But probably not as long as Ricardo would like. What about you?"

"Sometimes I wonder what the hell I'm doing here. I want to see Blake, but I feel like an idiot hanging around you and Ricardo. Could I hold you, Fay? Just for a minute?"

"For a minute."

She lay with her back to him on his hard narrow bed. They were silent. His cheek lay against her neck beneath the insouciant sprout of her ponytail. He got an erection but retracted his hips so she wouldn't know.

"After Mérida what would you do?" he asked.

"I might travel."

"With Blake?"

"If he wants to come. He might want to go back with you instead."

"What if you settled somewhere else," he said, "and Blake wanted to stay with me in White Pine?"

She lay perfectly still. "I don't want to answer that question."

This time he almost cried himself. Fay had torn everything apart, but he didn't want her to suffer.

After his next excursion with Blake he returned Ricardo's car, gave the key to Teresa at the front door and walked over to the Paseo Montejo to catch a cab back to his pension. He showered in the airy bathroom and changed into clean clothes. By six-thirty he was seated at his regular table in the Reina del Yucatán café, pretending to study Spanish. In fact, his eyes were probing the street like radar, on the lookout for Ana María Sandoval Chermalán.

She came twenty minutes late, stepping down the sidewalk in a navy-blue skirt, white high heels and a gauzy blouse he could see her bra through. Such blouses were common in Mérida, where both old women and young wore them to lunch or dinner or even work. They were meant to show, Austin guessed, that a woman *wore* a bra, and therefore was no Indian. But no matter if it was common practice, here before him were Ana María's stunning breasts, covered only with nylon and lace. He found it safest to look down.

"Great shoes," he said. Great legs was what he thought, but he had to say something. "Not everyone can wear white shoes."

"You like?" She turned in one knee, pushing her hip forward and glancing down the outside of her leg to have a look. Her toes pivoted on the café's shiny tile floor. "I have them from a friend, to borrow. I must keep them very clean. *Totalmente limpios.*"

"I like them, they look great. And the dress too. It's very pretty." Austin dug down into his new Spanish. *"Todo muy bonito.* Everything looks good on you."

"You are a *caballero,* you are very polite."

As they sat together at Austin's table, not all his thoughts were polite. Nothing was said about studying language, and after a beer Ana María asked him if he would like to go to an American movie. They took a cab downtown to see an old dubbed James Bond film.

"It will be good for your Espanish," she said—though in fact he understood almost nothing off the screen. They arrived early and sat through a long series of advertisements and previews. Before the movie started, Ana María got up, swung past his knees into the aisle and disappeared for a couple of minutes. She came back with a package of mints and, without asking, slipped one into his mouth. Her long fingernails pressed briefly against his lips.

After the movie she suggested a nearby restaurant, where they ate chicken mole and enchiladas in green sauce. Conversation was a little slow, but they did study language, in a way, for there was much to learn whenever anything was said.

Ana María practiced with his name, which was particularly difficult for her: "Owsteen Poohler." She wriggled her feet out of her shoes and set them to one side under the table, warning him not to bump or mark them. They were Brazilian, of the best quality.

Afterward, as they stood outside the restaurant, she said, "I must go home now." So when a taxi came by, Austin hailed it and opened the door for her. He hadn't counted on the evening ending so abruptly—but off she went, holding her peach-colored fingernails to her lips in what looked like a little kiss. She had given him her telephone number at work.

He waited a day before calling her. He wasn't sure what to do, because he didn't know how to court a Mexican woman. He didn't know if he *was* courting her.

But he called, and she laughed over the phone and they talked for twenty minutes. Maybe her boss thought she was practicing her English. Ana María said they should go dancing and she knew a good place.

"I hardly ever dance," Austin said.

"You will like to dance with me. Do you have eshoes?"

"Nothing but these running shoes."

"Then you must buy a pair of *white eshoes!*"

So he went out and bought a pair of leather shoes. Not white but *"color de café,"* a coffee brown. The largest pair in stock just barely fit him.

The music was loud and the dance floor enormous. Austin had enough cha-cha left over from high school to improvise a few steps. Ana María was all dressed up again, in a flared taffeta gown and red pumps. She had straight hair and high smooth cheekbones. She looked like La Malinche, the Indian girlfriend of Cortés.

Whether it was the cha-cha, the samba or the cumbia, she was a serious dancer. On the slow numbers his erection rose and bumped against her hip. She ignored it. She rested one hand on his shoulder and laid her fingers across the back of his neck.

He kissed her on the taxi ride home and touched her breasts. At her house she spoke briefly to the driver, who waited at the curb with his parking lights on as they kissed good night. Austin wasn't sure what to do. He let Ana María press against him, rubbing her chest softly back and forth against his own. Then she turned, opened the door with her key and disappeared inside. He had the taxi drop him in the center of town, and from there he walked the rest of the way home, thinking the whole way about Ana María. For a while he worried that she wanted something from him. Maybe she wanted to marry a gringo and live in the United States.

But he hadn't hidden anything from her. She must have seen the ring on his left hand, even if she never asked him about it. Or about his family, or where he was staying, or why he had come to Mérida in the first place. Their language problem was a filter that kept such topics at bay.

Still, he couldn't believe his luck at having met such a woman, especially in a country where he didn't speak the language. Just enjoy it, he told himself. He remembered how straitlaced he had been with Marilyn Tzobik, and how that had ended. And he reminded himself of how every night Fay was climbing into bed with Ricardo.

So the next time he rode to Ana María's house, Austin got out with her and paid off the driver, who promptly drove away. They had been kissing and making out for half the evening.

"I have a *compañera de cuarto*," Ana María said, "but I think she is not here." With the end of her fingernail she brushed one of Austin's nipples through his shirt. "Do you like to come inside?"

She had worn the same white shoes as on their first date. Inside the small one-story house she took them off, inspected them and set them in front of her roommate's door. Then she took Austin's hand, led him into her own room and stood beside him in the dark. He folded his arms around her and held her bottom in his hands. He kissed her mouth, her neck and the top of her breasts. But when he began to unbutton her blouse, she pushed him gently onto the bed and laughed softly. "Now you will close your eyes, like a *caballero*."

He lay without moving, but didn't close his eyes. It was light enough to see her take off and hang up her blouse, slip out of her bra, unzip her skirt and roll down her stockings. Only her panties remained.

He didn't know how to act or what to say. His knees shook with desire. He hadn't made love in almost three months. It almost seemed he had forgotten what to do.

"Do you know I'm married?" he asked. Instantly he regretted the question, but Ana María ignored him. She crouched beside him on the bed and put a finger to his lips. She kissed him. Her breath smelled of tamarindo, from dessert. With one hand she loosened his belt.

"What do you do about birth control?" he asked.

It took her a moment to understand, even after he repeated the question. Finally she laughed and said, "The *birs* control is *under* control."

"But I have to use one of these," he said. He struggled up and found the pack of condoms in his pocket. He had bought them that afternoon at a pharmacy.

"Pues no, hombre, no es necesario. I have the coil." She tried to take the package from his hand. Their eyes had grown accustomed to the dark.

"But we have to." He took her hands in his own. "Don't you worry about diseases? What about AIDS?"

"AIDS?" She was puzzled. Her breasts perched on her chest like little birds, ready to fly.

He had to explain it to her.

"Ese es la SIDA. But we don't have AIDS here. It comes from the U.S."

"But I'm from the U.S. *I* could have it."

She looked at him doubtfully and shook her head. "No. That is a disease of the *maricones,* and you are not a *maricón.* Because *mira,* look at this *plátano que tienes."* She slid her hand inside the front of his pants.

"I'm not a *maricón,* but I'm going to use a condom."

She sat back looking hurt. She got off the bed, went to her closet and came back wearing a robe. "You don't like to touch me. You must be a *maricón."*

"No, I'm not. I'm married and I like women. And now I like you."

"No, you don't. You don't like me at all. These *condones,* they are what the *maricones* use."

He tried to explain about diseases and condoms, but it was an uphill battle. She lay beside him on the bed, facing away, her robe held tightly about her waist.

Words were not their strong point. Finally he lifted her hair away from her neck and kissed the top of her shoulders. She didn't move or respond, but played the virgin seduced against her will. He undressed, took out the condom and put it on. Still she ignored him. He rubbed her neck, her waist, the back of her thighs. When he lifted the hem of her robe, she pinched her legs together.

Bit by bit he lifted her robe, and in the end succeeded in loosening the belt around her waist. He rolled her over onto her back and kissed her nipples, as erect as little pinecones. Though she never moved, he heard her small sharp intakes of breath and felt her buttocks go tense. He kissed her breasts, her hips, her thighs. She kept her legs pressed together for twenty minutes before allowing his hand to part them even a little. He caressed her, he licked her, he rubbed his penis over her entire body. When she finally let him touch her vagina with his fingers, it was as wet as a ripe papaya. Slowly he came inside her. She held him to her with her hands around his ass. She held him so tight he thought her fingernails might break the skin.

"Do you like me?" she asked, late that night.

"I like you very much."

"I am sorry of what I said. You are not a *maricón*. *Tú eres hombre, hecho y completo.* I am happy with you."

Ana María changed for Austin the entire nature of Mérida. Now he walked through the streets with a beautiful woman. He might have run into Fay—but what harm if he did? Ana María looped her arm through his and pointed out historical buildings, stores she knew, occasionally an important or scandalous person. She didn't ask about Austin's family or what he did during the day. The only thing she wanted to know was, did he like her?

He did. She asked him every day and he told her every day. He felt a little guilty about carrying on such an ungrounded affair—but he was a happier man. The few times he saw Fay he was more relaxed with her. He even joked a little, which made her look at him strangely. He wasn't ready to explain.

"*Vamos a la playa*," Ana María told him one night.

"*Vamos al disco*," he said. He thought she was helping with his Spanish.

"No, to Cozumel. We can lie on the beach and get tanned."

"You hardly need a suntan," Austin said with a laugh. Ana María had no tan line whatsoever, her skin was all one smooth dark bronze.

They decided on the next weekend. Austin told Fay he'd be out of town for three days but didn't explain why. During the week he took Blake to the movies and a soccer game, to a Mayan cenote and back to the little beach at Chelem, trying to store up some time with his son. Blake would miss him, he knew. All the same, he wanted this weekend with Ana María.

By seven o'clock Friday morning he was seated beside her in an old Mexican-made Dina bus with darkened window glass and torn seats, blasting their way out into the Yucatán countryside. They left the outskirts of Mérida behind, passed through a dozen small towns and entered the long flat forest. Barefoot kids and donkeys loaded with firewood shared the road with double-loaded mopeds and battered U.S. taxis. Mayan clay-and-stick houses lined the narrow strip of land between forest and pavement.

Inside the bus, because the barrier separating the engine from the passenger compartment was in places no more than cardboard, the noise was bestial. Every acceleration demanded an arduous passage through eight gears. Austin counted them, over and over. He sympathized with the driver, who was doing his best with an underpowered engine, but each time they settled into the relative calm of top gear something brought the bus to another stop: the speed bumps in a little village, a passenger standing by the side of the road waving a white handkerchief or a tiny country store where the driver paused to buy a liter of cooking oil, or a half-stalk of bananas, or a pair of live iguanas tied belly to belly at the necks, tails and feet.

Mile after mile the landscape was the same. After a long unbroken stretch of bush the vista would open suddenly onto a narrow clearing with a tile- or thatched-roofed house, kids playing around the yard, a few dogs, a metal washbasin, an old bicycle and always fruit trees: oranges, anonas, sapotes, papayas, mangoes and giant breadfruit. Ana María, who had seen this her whole life, laid her head against Austin's shoulder and went to sleep.

Near the coast the white road turned south and ran dead straight, not a curve for forty miles. In front of some of the most isolated and desolate clearings a woman sometimes stood holding a turtle in the air, or a bowl of eggs. But the driver had made enough commerce, and they didn't stop until Playa del Carmen.

There the ferry embarked for Cozumel. In the oven of midday Austin and Ana María stumbled off the bus onto streets chalky with heat and made their way toward the dock. Austin carried their only luggage, a nylon shopping bag with a change of clothes for them both. Ana María tied a bandanna over the top of her head, and Austin looked through the tourist shops for a hat. He found a green half-plastic baseball cap with an adjustable band and a DeKalb emblem on the front—but damned if he'd wear an advertisement on his head, and an ear of corn at that. He settled for the largest of the prickly straw hats, all too tight, and tugged it down onto his forehead.

Before the ferry came they walked along the blazing white beach. Ana María threw him her plastic sandals, rolled up her white pants and waded into the shallow water step by step, graceful as a heron.

The ferry approached over the blue bay. They boarded it with the other passengers and found a seat up top in the open air. A cooling wind blew in over the water. Ana María shook out her hair and tucked her sandals into the nylon bag. She kissed Austin's neck and held his hand against the inside of her thigh.

Austin no longer cared what Fay was doing with Ricardo Raigosa.

A sudden gust of wind caught his hat and swept it into the sea. It landed on the foamy water behind the boat and receded slowly into the distance. Ana María laughed and said, "Either the sombrero is very little, or your head is very big. I think you are very big." Then she put her mouth to his ear and whispered, *"Tu verga, por lo menos, es muy grandota."*

When he didn't understand, she raised her eyebrows, lowered her gaze to his lap and laughed out loud. *"Te voy a comer esa paloma,"* she said, *"antes de que vuele."* She liked to tease him in public. "I'm going to eat that paloma before it flies away."

She knew a hotel, a quiet place away from the center of town. They walked there, a third of a mile, over streets paved with tar and seashells. Had she been there before? Once or twice, she said.

In the still, sweltry air of late afternoon they lay on one of the two beds in their room at the Hotel Atlantic, completely naked, sweating, talking and laughing.

"Este macho es mi mula," she said. *"Tiene cojones de Tarzán."*

"I don't think that's in the dialogues I've been studying."

"We will estudy together. But later, *porque ahora voy a comer elote.* I'm going to eat this big *elote, y tú, mi amor, tú vas a comer bizcocho.* Do you understand? A biscuit with lots of butter."

She laughed, she was wild, he had never seen her so excited. She knelt on the bed and put her ass in the air. "You want? You like *el bizcocho con mantequilla? Tú quieres comerme, mi querido? Así, así, así. No hay como tu para comerme. Tú eres mi gringo, mi querido. Así, así."*

She moaned and cried, her head hanging down over the edge of the bed. He ate her until she came, and came again, and then she turned and lay beneath him, urging him on to his own noisy climax. Afterward she giggled and put a finger his lips.

"We are making an escandal. You are a bad man. You make me forget everything."

After lunch the next day they rented snorkling equipment and took a local bus out to the national underwater park. In the warm undulating water Ana María's hair floated behind her in chocolate waves. They swam out over the shelving bottom among hundreds of fish: angel eyes, parrot fish, blue tangs and queen triggerfish. Occasionally a small barracuda, never a shark.

Austin trailed behind her, staring at her brown body. Through the mask she looked longer and thinner than ever. God, how had he ever lucked onto this? He swam behind her, trying to breathe normally into his snorkel. He watched where her bathing suit pressed against her flesh and how the silken columns of her legs slid through the water, unfettered by gravity. She turned to see where he was, then swam on.

With a few strokes of his fins he caught up to her and took her in his arms. In the clear bright water every hair on her body stood out, luminous and magnified. Smiling through his mask, he reached behind her and untied the white top of her bikini.

She held out her arms so it could float away. Austin checked for other divers, but there were none in sight. The visibility was fifty yards at least. Pushing down below the surface, he untied both sides of the bottom half of her suit so that it opened up about her hips like a white cloth. Slowly, it floated off from between her legs. She watched it for a moment as it hung in the water, then dropped down and pulled off his suit as well, all the way over his fins. Then she took his hand and led him away, swimming past their suits and out into deeper water. She turned to laugh at him, over and over, testing his nerve.

They swam until they could barely see the three pieces of cloth, and then stopped to play. She dived between his legs, blowing bubbles through her snorkel, and caressed him everywhere. Her breasts passed in and out of his embrace like fish, and the whole time she smiled and laughed.

Finally she pointed toward their suits and they started back. He tried to keep up with her but his erect penis waved from side to side in the water, a hindrance to forward motion. By the time he caught up to her, she had rounded up all three pieces by herself, put her own suit on and was holding his behind her back. She only gave it to him when they caught sight of another diver passing in the distance.

Late that evening they ate dinner in a restaurant above the harbor. Ana María looked tired but happy. She lifted her hair on one side so Austin could see the black coral earrings he had given her. She had put them both in the same ear. A half mile out on the dark bay a launch set off from one of the cruise ships, carrying tourists to the dock.

Austin wasn't tired at all. Indeed, just sitting at the table across from Ana María and staring at her face, he was again erect. He wanted to go soon, back to the Hotel Atlantic, where they would take off their clothes and make love again in the warm night. His flesh was vibrating. He felt like a cult initiate to whom the cabalistic secrets of sex were now being revealed. He forgave his wife, silently, for whatever pleasures she had taken with Ricardo. He could not deny anyone, not even Fay, this inebriate discovery.

As they walked back to the hotel it was still 80 degrees out. Along the sidewalks families had gathered outside their stucco houses to escape the heat. The men stood about in sleeveless tee-shirts, while the women sat on cane chairs brought out from the kitchens. A few kids still ran up and down the sidewalks, ignoring the televisions left on inside.

Austin didn't say anything. He was wondering who this woman was who strode along beside him, her arm in his, her plastic sandals scuffing the street. One of *them* really, one of these Mexicans of Mayan stock. The only difference was, she was taller and more assured than they were, and she had picked up some English. Anyone could do that.

And what did all this mean to her anyway? All this laughter and sex and broken talk? As they passed families in the street— *buenas noches, buenas noches*—the women looked her over. Inevitably they looked at Ana María before they looked at him. No, she wasn't one of them. This was not how a Mexican woman behaved.

At the hotel she wanted to go for a swim in the little pool out back. Austin told her to go ahead, that he'd join her in a minute. Instead, after she went out, he took her small leather purse into the bathroom and locked the door.

She had a driver's license. That surprised him a little, but the name on it was Ana María Sandoval Chermalán, just as she'd said. She was twenty-five years old. There was a Mexican Cédula de Identidad, as well as a number of papers Austin could not understand. And there was a surprising amount of money. Before closing the purse and joining her outside, he poked around one last time, sliding his finger into a little side pocket. He touched something there and pulled it out. It was a worn white business card bearing the name and address of Ricardo Raigosa Menéndez.

From the door he could see her standing in her white two-piece suit at the edge of the pool, waiting for him to join her.

"Ana María, *ven.* Come here for a minute."

"Austin, let's swim."

"Come here."

When she got close he took her wrist and pulled her inside. He closed and locked the door and rolled down the windows. She stood upright in her best posture, her long hair pinned up on top of her head. She looked puzzled.

He opened his palm and showed her the white card. He said, "Ricardo Raigosa Menéndez, a real son of a bitch."

She crossed one arm over her breasts and reached for the nylon bag with her clothes in it. Austin picked it up and flung it across the room.

"*Es mi tío,*" she said. "He's my uncle. He is a friend of my family."

"Sure, and I'm Juan Dominguez. What did he do, hire you to take care of me so he could fuck my wife in peace? You goddamn cunt. You *puta.*"

"*Yo no soy puta.* Give me the bag."

"You little moaning piece of dog shit. You want your clothes? I ought to rip that suit off and kick you into the street. And what about all this money?" He grabbed the wad of folded oversized bills from her wallet and threw them into the air. "He pays you to fuck me, right?"

She stepped toward the bathroom where she had hung her dress after dinner. But Austin grabbed her, spun her around and threw her onto one of the beds.

"Austin, please. *Me duele.*"

"I was so hot for you. I spent all day looking up your ass. Quit that moaning. Cut that shit out."

He stared at the small mound of her genitals beneath the white cloth of her bathing suit. She moved her hands to protect herself from his gaze, and the gesture enraged him. Grabbing a pillow, he swung it against her belly, then climbed on top of her and beat at her flailing legs.

She screamed like a howler monkey, sat up and took a bite out of his side.

"FUCK!" Austin yelled, and leapt off the bed. He put one hand where she had bit him, then grabbed the pillow and fell over her face. She stopped screaming and didn't move. His side felt as if he'd run into a pitchfork. He unbuttoned his shirt and tried to see where she had bit him, but it was too far around under the back of his ribs. Slowly, afraid of suffocating her, he lifted the pillow. Her feral black eyes glared up at him.

He was sure someone would come to investigate after their screams, but there was no sound from any other room, nor from the distant office. All he could hear was a pair of barking dogs and the hum of the underground pump next to the pool outside.

He stood up and tiptoed in front of the mirror to look at his wound. It bled, though not freely. Ana María watched it, and him, with a hard distant look. He held a towel to his side to stop the blood and turned off the overhead light in case anyone should come and knock on the door. There was still enough light to see from the lamp outside. He stood beside the bed.

"That bastard Ricardo planned this whole thing, didn't he? That's why he sent me to that pension. He knows everything I've done. *Talk*, damn it."

"He doesn't know everything. He doesn't know we come to Cozumel—unless you told Fay."

"So you know all about Fay."

She lowered her eyes.

"And he paid you all that money. You're on his payroll. And you fuck him, don't you?"

"No, I do not. Ever since Fay, I do not go to Ricardo."

"But before that? Before that you sucked his dick and he filled your wallet with money."

"*No, no. Eso no es justo.*" She rolled away from him and began to cry.

Austin spun her around to face him. "Don't turn away from me. Look at me." He lifted the towel from his side and found a solid circle of blood. "Mother of whores. You took a piece right out of my side."

"I had fear."

"I *was afraid*. What kind of bullshit English is that, anyway?"

She was silent, her hands at her waist.

"If you were a virgin, I'd tie you to a rock and cut your heart out the way the Mayans did. I'd throw you down one of those cenotes."

She tensed and looked toward the door.

"For godsake, I don't mean it. But you deserve it. How long have you known this asshole Ricardo?"

"From when I am fourteen."

"Fourteen! That's a little girl. I guess when Ricardo wants something he just buys it."

"My family is very poor. My father is dead."

"So you became Ricardo's whore."

"*No,* I was never a whore. Please do not say that. Ricardo, he gives me money for my mother and he pays the *alquilo.* He has a lot of money. And I work for him."

"Yeah, on your knees. Keeping guys like me happy so Ricardo can fuck whoever he wants."

"Please, Austin. Please give me my clothes."

He picked her dress off the hook on the back of the bathroom door and threw it to her. Then he stood next to the bed staring at her. "Go ahead, change."

"But you are watching."

"I'm watching all right. I'm going to watch every little move your ass makes from now on."

She took off the top of her bathing suit, lowered the dress over her shoulders and reached up underneath it to remove the bottom of her suit. "My *calzoncillos*," she said.

"Forget it. Get some air on that cunt."

She sat down again on the bed, her knees drawn up and her dress tucked around her ankles. Outside, in a room across from the pool, someone turned on a radio, scanned the dial and settled on a mariachi station.

"Never I am a whore. Don Ricardo is the only man I go to—and now you."

"But he sent you to that café."

"Yes. But that is because he is in love with la señora Fe."

Austin rolled open the slats of window glass and looked outside. At the foot of the pool, beyond an adobe wall, an abandoned city lot was entirely covered by morning glory vines, their solitary white flowers spattered over the dark vegetation.

"How do you know that?"

"Because he tells me. And because he does not love me anymore. Never he comes to my house at night. Not since la señora Fe comes from America."

"And she loves him?"

"No."

"How do you know?"

"Because she does not want to marry with him. He ask her and she tells him no. And he is afraid of you. He is afraid that . . . *tiene miedo que la señora vuelva con usted a los Estados Unidos.*"

"He's afraid she'll leave him and go back to the United States."

"Yes, so he sends me to the café. I meet you and you are a gentleman. I hope for la señora Fe to go back to you, and for Don Ricardo to come to me."

Austin paced the hotel room, the towel still held to his side. A bit of breeze entered through the front windows.

"His mistress then. Maybe not his whore, but his mistress. And what about when his wife was alive?"

"La señora Beatriz was very beautiful, but she does not like the sex."

"What do you mean?"

"She likes only to be a mother."

"So he bought you."

"I was his meestress."

"Not meestress," Austin said. "Mistress."

"I am sorry to bite you. I was afraid."

"Yeah, I'm a big mean gringo."

"No, you are a *caballero*. You are . . . you are more a gentleman than Don Ricardo. And I do not come to Cozumel with you because Don Ricardo tells me. I come because I like you. Don Ricardo does not know."

Austin pulled a pair of her underpants out of the nylon bag and tossed them to her. She raised her feet enough to slide them on, then worked them up over her hips. Her dress fell back in place, but she no longer clutched it to her ankles.

Sitting on the other bed, Austin thought about the last couple of weeks. Ana María turned her head toward him but he didn't look over. She must have liked him, he thought. She couldn't have faked all that. She could not have faked what happened last night, or today in the water.

"Would Ricardo ever marry you?"

"No. Don Ricardo wants a woman like la señora Fe, who is white. *Así es en México.* I think in la USA it is the same. Men do not want to marry with a brown woman or a black woman."

"Sometimes. If they're pretty enough or smart enough."

"I am pretty in my family. I am tall." She smoothed her dress over her knees, her palms pressing against the soft cloth.

Everything Ana María did with him, Austin realized, went against her own best interests. After all, he wasn't going to marry her either, or buy her a house or look after her mother. She had a better chance with Ricardo. In the end she wanted the same as Austin, for Fay to go back to her husband.

"You tell Ricardo about me, don't you? What I'm up to."

"Yes. Except for Cozumel."

"And does he tell you about Fay?"

"Sometimes. Because he is in love he wants to tell me."

"Tell you what?"

Ana María shook her head. *"No, no es correcto."*

"What do you mean *correcto?* If you don't tell me I'll cut your goddamn heart out."

She stood up and went to the window by the door. She could have unlocked it and run outside, but she didn't.

"He says that she loves the sex. He is surprised. He can't believe it, because she is a gringa. He says that she will not marry with him but she loves the sex."

"Fuck her anyway." Austin jumped up, unlocked the door at Ana María's elbow and flung it open against the wall. "Go on. You want to walk, do it. You want some money, here." He threw his wallet on the bed and stepped outside. The image of his wife in bed with Ricardo now seared his heart. He pulled off his running shoes, ran across the patio and jumped into the swimming pool.

Ana María gave him a towel when he came back, and after

he stripped off his wet pants and shirt she wrapped him in a sheet. "Wait," she said.

She came back in five minutes with a handful of leaves. She tucked her hair behind her ears, told Austin to lie down on the bed, and put a few of the leaves in her mouth. After chewing them to a pulp she placed them against his side. It stung for a moment and then stopped hurting. She crouched beside him, holding her fingers against his ribs. Her dress had ridden up over her thighs. Soon her fingertips dropped to his waist, to his hips, to his erection.

"*Así es, Austin. El hombre no puede esconder su deseo.* You cannot hide desire."

"*Así es, Ana María.* I'm sorry I got angry and hit you."

"*Tú eres caballero. Yo sé que tú sufres por tu mujer y por tu hijo.* I know you suffer for them. *Te voy a lamer.* I'm going to kiss your eyes, *tu ombligo, el hueso, hasta los cojones.*"

"Take off your dress, quick. And talk to me in Spanish. Tell me anything. You smell like leaves."

Austin sat in the Queen of the Yucatán café with his wife and son, drinking coffees and Pepsi Cola. Along the back wall the electric grid fried an occasional bug. The television on the counter was tuned to a Mexican soap opera.

Fay looked more relaxed at the café than she ever had at Ricardo's. The three Poolers, sitting at one of the plastic tables, looked like an expatriate family at ease in Mexico. Austin wore a white Mexican shirt and dark leather shoes, and Fay a summer dress and sunglasses. Blake sat between them. He paid as much attention to the conversation as an adult—until Austin pulled some Mexican bills out of his wallet and said, "How about buying a comic book down at the corner? And then maybe you could read in the park for a while."

"Are you going to talk about me?"

Austin nodded. "We probably will."

"I guess so. Can I go by myself?"

"Sure. But look both ways when you cross the street."

They didn't start talking until after he had walked down to the little store and returned on the park side of the street.

Without ever looking across at them he lay down on a bench and began to read.

"He likes being independent," Austin said.

"Sometimes."

Austin felt constrained. Fay was bound to see that he was steering the conversation. "How did he feel about me going away for three days?"

She sipped her coffee. "He's gotten used to seeing you every day. Where did you go?"

"If it's all right," Austin said, "I'd rather explain that some other time. I will tell you—but I have something else to say. I've decided to go home."

For a moment she considered the news in silence. "So we have to decide about Blake."

"I'd like to take him with me."

Fay looked across at their eight-year-old son, still stretched out on his concrete bench in the park. "Is it because you want to be with him, or is it a way to put some leverage on me?"

Austin hesitated. He felt he owed her the truth—especially after not telling her about Ana María. "You know I want to be with him. But probably it's a little of both."

"That second reason is a mistake."

"But, Fay, you don't even know what you're going to be doing in another month. Do you?"

The bug zapper popped behind them and the television droned. "I have some ideas," she said. "But to be honest, I may have gotten in a little over my head here."

"Ricardo's in love with you, isn't he?"

She looked at him quickly. "How do you know that?"

Everything about Fay attracted him, from the upright way she sat in her chair to the low-cut dress she wore that exposed her tanned shoulders. In such a warm climate it was impossible to tell if a woman was being seductive just because she wore such light clothing.

"Just guessing," he said. "I can see how he looks at you. Of course, anyone would."

She ignored the compliment. "I suppose he is. I know he is. I warned him at the start and he tries to hold it back. But he's been making me nervous. I'm almost ready to go back to the States myself."

"And do what?"

"Travel around, to start with. And I'd like to do it with Blake."

Austin moved their empty coffee cups to one side. "We could fight over it," he said. "That's what most couples do. But I think he's old enough to choose for himself." He felt deceitful saying that, knowing what Blake had already told him at the baseball stadium.

They called Blake back to the café. He looked both ways, twice, and sprinted across the street to join them.

Fay was perfectly evenhanded as she explained the situation to him. He could either fly back to Maine with his dad, she said, and spend the summer on the farm with his friends, or else he could stay here in Mérida for a little longer and then go back to the U.S. with her. Austin watched her as she spoke, all her attention on Blake.

"How much longer?" the boy asked.

"Maybe a couple of weeks. I can't promise you exactly."

"And then what?"

"Then I'd thought about buying a camper and going out West. We could see the Grand Canyon and some other places. I think it would be fun. But so would spending time with your dad on the farm."

Except for her having left White Pine, Austin had always loved her for how fair she was.

Blake sat between them, his *fotonovelas* rolled up in both hands. Brown hairs, almost blond after so much sun, lay across his arms and legs. The top of his head looked uneven where a local barber had cut his hair too short.

"Blake . . ." Austin began.

"I'm *thinking*." He was close to tears.

Austin regretted their plan. It was unfair to ask so young a child which parent he wanted to go with. Either way he couldn't win, because he had to reject one of them. They should have talked it over and decided for him.

"I'll go with Mom."

Austin looked away. He hadn't expected this.

"But I want to be there for the harvest. All right, Dad? I want to ride on the harvester with you." Though he tried to sound enthusiastic, Blake's look was troubled. His eyes never moved from his father's.

"That'll be good," Austin said. He rested his hand on Blake's shoulder. "We'll have a great time when you come. And I'll be right there at our house any time you want to talk to me. You can call me every night if you want."

"Can we, Mom? Can we call Dad on the phone?"

"Of course."

It all made Austin sad. Somehow he had gotten in the position of having his son look after him, and nothing was more unfair than that. He wanted Blake to be free: free of care, free of terrible choices and free of growing up too soon.

SIX

Blake sat in the back of the Mercedes with Ricardo's two daughters, Sonia and Isabel. His study of Spanish was effortless, he picked up word after word without even trying. If they drove for twenty days, Fay thought, he'd speak the language.

They cruised up the east coast of Mexico, headed for a family reunion at Ricardo's father's house in Veracruz. The two-lane road was dotted with villages, towns, banana plantations and an occasional view of the sea to their right.

"Es tan azul," Blake said, for the second time. "Is it warm like at Chelem?"

"I'm sure it is," Ricardo said. "It's all part of the Caribbean."

Blake wanted to stop and go swimming, but Ricardo was intent on the drive. They only stopped once, for lunch.

Through long stretches Fay and Ricardo remained silent in the front seats. It was Fay's doing. Ricardo initiated several conversations but she let them all drop. She was thinking about Blake's choice.

At the start she thought he had simply chosen her over Austin. But it was more tactical than that. Blake's first desire was to keep his family together—and Fay, who had not yet fully persuaded herself of the fact, had apparently convinced him that she was never going back to the farm. So he had decided to remain with her and help lure his father away.

That saddened her. She saw that to keep his family together Blake would give up his home, his school, his baseball team, all his friends—everything he had grown up with. Neither Fay nor Austin had been willing to sacrifice as much.

Ricardo sped through the raw flatlands of Campeche and Tabasco. Fay was apprehensive. She should have told him she had already decided to go back to the U.S. Instead, she was now traveling deeper into Mexico and deeper into his life. Her mind was headed in one direction and her body in another.

Ricardo, cushioned in the thick front seat of the Mercedes, looked smooth and relaxed. His white shirt was as fresh as when he had put it on this morning. His face was shaven and his moustache brushed. He looked like the same man she had met on Nantucket last summer—but he was not. At least he was not the man she had imagined him to be.

They had met at the yacht club tennis courts. Though dressed in English whites and wielding a four-hundred-dollar racquet, he wasn't that good a player. He had a powerful forearm but no control, and had trouble keeping his shots in the court. "Oh dear," he said once with a disarming laugh, after hitting the ball long. "I've got all the right equipment, I just can't play the game."

She liked how polite he was. He was attracted to her, she was sure, yet he had never allowed his eyes to run down her body. Her flesh seemed to be the last thing he was interested in. Eventually his prudence drove her to small feats of exhibition-ism: instead of flipping up the tennis balls with her racquet, she bent over and retrieved them with her hand. She smacked her brown thighs with her palm and even jumped the net, her legs flashing, after taking the second set.

The next day he took her to Le Languedoc for lunch. He wore a blue blazer, a pair of white flannel pants and tasseled oxblood loafers. His English was refined and his manners European. His smooth skin was the color of his race, part Spanish and part Mayan. A team of UN observers would have denied that he was flirting with her.

Two nights later they met at a party, not entirely by accident, and wound up driving to the beach in Ricardo's borrowed Jaguar. There, in a transition as smooth as the Chopin nocturne that was playing on the tape deck, Ricardo parked and put his arm around her. Before they ever kissed for the first time, he invited her to Mérida.

"I'm married, Ricardo. You know that." They had already talked about their families.

"You could bring your son. My daughters are not much older than he is."

Fay laughed. "I can see myself explaining that to Austin."

His free hand fluttered briefly in the air. The other was around her shoulders, drawing her to his side. "Mérida is lovely all year round. If you grow tired of the cold in Maine, a vacation near the sea would help you through the winter. The blue of our waters is famous."

She let him kiss her. His lips were smooth and soft as a young boy's. After a few minutes of delicate kissing he opened her blouse and unhooked the front of her bra. Her breasts, once released, felt as if they might float off her chest into the cool Atlantic air—yet Ricardo didn't touch them. He had the air of someone who, after opening a package at Christmas, is content to view the contents in the box.

"I suppose I just get on a plane in Boston?" she said finally.

"You fly from Boston to Miami, and from there to Mérida, where I would meet you at the airport with flowers. Mérida is a city of flowers. I would be your guide to the Yucatán. I would take you to ruins larger than Egypt's, and to ancient Mayan wells so deep that people scuba dive in them. I would hang about your neck a black coral necklace more beautiful than pearls."

The soft ends of his fingers traced where the necklace would hang, just above the top of her breasts. Fully aroused, she waited for him to touch her nipples—but he didn't do so. At least not until the following night.

For the next few days he talked to her as if Austin did not exist. He told her how happy he would be if she would visit him in Mérida. There would be no commitments or expectations. Their weeklong madness ended when Austin flew down from Maine. The few times she saw Ricardo after that she kept her distance. But later that year, in the depths of the Aroostook winter, she thought seriously about his offer. Twice she called him on the phone, just to hear his voice. She told herself it was just to hear his voice—but she couldn't deny the sexual thrill of talking to him in secret. Both times he told her, quite calmly, "I hope you will come."

To Fay, when she went, Mérida was a last-minute point of escape. Ricardo met her at the airport with an armful of flowers, but he didn't rush her into sex. If he had, she might have gotten on a plane the next day and flown back to the States. He courted her instead, and let her warm to him slowly. But once they began making love he acted as if she had moved permanently into his life.

That was the assumption she read on his face now, on the way to Veracruz. He was a rich and powerful man, accustomed to getting what he wanted. Sure of himself, he was convinced that Fay would want him, and that she would forget her entire history with Austin.

At times she was drawn to such aplomb, and at times repelled by it. Now, though close to him in his car, she felt an enormous gap between them. His countenance had an impermeable look to it, almost as if waxed.

Upon their arrival in Veracruz Fay was introduced to Don Javier, Ricardo's father, and to Javier's second wife, Consuelo.

"*Mucho gusto en conocerle,*" Consuelo told her at the door. It was a formal greeting, delivered by a robust, white-skinned, black-haired woman in her early sixties. Consuelo held Fay by the elbows for thirty seconds, staring at her the whole time. Finally she placed her hand on Fay's back and led her to a small leather couch at one end of the living room. There, with a backward wave of her hand, she momentarily dismissed the others and called out to a maid to bring them cake and coffee.

In those thirty seconds, apparently, Fay had been judged and accepted. "We are so happy," Consuelo said, and: "This is your house." As it turned out she didn't speak much more English than that, and the two women were hard put to keep the conversation going. They managed to do so by speaking each in her own language.

"*¡Qué bello es tu hijo!*" Consuelo said. "*¡Y que lindo su nombre!*"

Bello. Fay understood that. "I know he's glad to be here," she said. "With all these cousins. And with *boys* his own age."

"*Ah, los primos. A veces son pícaros y malvados. Pero no, de verdad, son buenos muchachos.*"

"*Muy buenos muchachos,*" Fay said. She understood that, too: very good kids.

Eventually Consuelo introduced her to the rest of the family, calling them over one by one. Ricardo's older sister, Elisa, was the first to disengage herself from the group and come over to be presented. Then a younger sister and her husband, and then the two brothers, Guillermo and Luís. It never took Consuelo more than a lift of the finger to catch their attention. Her couch, Fay saw, was the throne of a small empire.

Luís had created a scandal this year by leaving his wife and family behind and bringing a mistress almost young enough to be his daughter. Consuelo was icily polite to this girl, and didn't introduce her to Fay for almost an hour.

Fay wondered what she had done to enter so completely into Consuelo's good graces. Perhaps it was enough to have come from the United States and to have a beautiful son. But no. That thirty-second appraisal had not been a mere formality. Consuelo liked her.

But if Consuelo knew more about her life, Fay thought—or even about what was in her heart at this moment—she would hold a different opinion altogether. Fay was married to another man, and her stay with Ricardo was adulterous. And on top of that she had already decided to leave Ricardo and go back to the States.

Tomorrow, no matter how bad the timing, she would tell Ricardo her plans. Or at least she would prepare him for the news.

After dinner, following a brief word with Don Javier, Consuelo summoned her chauffeur and left the house. She was gone for about an hour and returned without comment.

It intrigued Fay to discover a woman in Mexico who was so clearly in charge, who had her own new Chevrolet and a man to drive it, and who came and went as she pleased.

After Consuelo retired, the rest of the family seemed more relaxed. They sat around the dining-room table drinking Johnny Walker Red and Coca-Cola. There was no choice of beverage, just the one bottle of whiskey along with a tray of Cokes and a bucket of ice. The night was hot and Ricardo had stripped down to a sleeveless tee-shirt—something Fay had never seen him do in front of anyone at home, even the maid. Don Javier was telling jokes. Luís was there but his girl had gone to bed. The two Raigosa sisters sat in chairs pulled back from the table. They attended, but were slightly removed from the group.

Fay stood up and told Ricardo she was going to take a little walk to cool off. He rose as well and took her elbow. He escorted her halfway across the room, where he said, "You must wait until the morning. It's not safe at night."

"In this neighborhood? Certainly it's as safe as yours. Besides, there's the *sereno,* and I'll only go a block or two."

"No, you may not do this."

"What do you mean, I *may* not?"

"In Veracruz it's different. It's . . . it's not safe for a woman alone to go out in the streets."

"Ricardo, that's ridiculous. This is the fanciest neighborhood I've ever been in. Look, I'll just go as far as the corner. And please let go of my arm."

He dropped his voice, released her arm and turned his back to those at the table. "Fay, this is my family. You must understand about Mexico. A married woman—even if we are not exactly married—does not go out to walk the streets alone. Certainly not at night."

"What are you talking about? I just saw your stepmother go out and no one said a thing about it."

"That is completely different. Consuelo is an older woman, and no one imagines that she goes out at night to find a man."

"Of course not. And I'm certainly not going out to meet anyone either. Outside your family, I don't know a single person in Veracruz. Ricardo, be reasonable. I'll just go for five or ten minutes."

He took her arm again and led her farther from the table. "You will not go out."

Fay stared at him, disbelieving. *"Let go of me,"* she said under her breath. Slowly he did. "I'm not your wife and I'm not your mistress. And if your family doesn't understand, that's too bad. I'm sure Consuelo would. I've never allowed a man to tell me when I can go outdoors and when I can't, and I'm not starting now."

She came within seconds of telling him her plans to go back to the States. But before she did he softened.

"Please, Fay, it would be a disgrace to me if you went outside now. It would shame me in the eyes of everyone here. I beg you not to go."

That surprised her, for she would never have thought that Ricardo would beg for anything. The very words were foreign to him, and she could see in his face that he had humbled himself to say them. So in the end she didn't go.

Instead she said good night to his family and went upstairs to her bedroom. She washed her face in the sink, undressed and put on a nightgown. Then she drew back the tent of white mosquito netting and sat down on the bed.

Ricardo had a confident, almost arrogant bearing that both attracted and repelled her. He showed the easy grace of money since youth, of growing up in a family that had kept the same servants for forty years—servants who, in their ancestral villages, had servants of their own. He was often peremptory, and rarely considered anyone's desires or opinions other than his own.

Fay had yielded to him on almost everything. Only on the question of sex had she made a stand. Ricardo, who had never once used a condom before meeting her, now knew better than to initiate sex without setting one first beside the bed.

Through the open window she heard the tapping of the palm fronds and the *sereno's* distant whistle. It was intolerable to her that Ricardo should forbid her to walk on the streets alone. Yet he had commanded, and then begged, and in the end she had given in. And now, though she found the desire reprehensible, she wanted to have sex with him. It didn't make any sense, because she was still angry at what he'd said. Nevertheless, a warm breeze raised the hairs on her arms, and desire rolled up her limbs like waves on a beach.

Instead of fighting the desire she gave in to it. She turned off the light and let herself be aroused, and the longer she sat on the edge of the bed the more excited she became. The cloth of her nightgown weighed nothing, it felt as if it might float off her shoulders. Downstairs she could hear voices around the table and, finally, footsteps on the stairs.

Ricardo stepped into the room and closed the door behind him, not bothering to lock it. Standing alone in the middle of the room, with hardly a glance at her, he began to undress: tee-shirt, shoes, socks, pants. He stripped off his underwear and stood completely naked only a couple of yards away from her, his hands at his sides. His smooth brown uncircumcised penis was still rising from its sheath.

He let it rise. He presented it. He put one hand beneath his testicles and held them from below. Then, with a perfunctory and efficient technique he had long since mastered, he took a condom from the dresser and put it on.

She sat upright on the very edge of the mattress. Ricardo approached and parted her knees with his own, standing so close that his prick jutted into the air only inches from her face. His hairless chest rose and fell with the delicacy of a young girl's. He touched her mouth and throat with his fingers, then looked away toward the far wall as if to remove himself from all sensation. Save for the state of his penis, he hardly seemed aroused at all.

Her own desire had vanished like a body off a cliff. It was dead, she didn't know where it was. Slowly, carefully, she took him in her mouth. It was like licking an inanimate object. It was like practicing, as she had done as a teenager, on a small waxy cucumber or a leftover hot dog.

She thought, Neither one of us is interested in this act. She took him once as far into her mouth as she could, then withdrew and caressed him with her hand until his breathing came harder. She stroked him faster and faster, cupping his testicles with her free hand until he came. His buttocks clenched, his penis throbbed and semen flowed out into the tip of the condom.

For almost a minute he kept his eyes closed. Then, as simply as if rising from the dinner table, he retrieved his pants, put them on and went into the hallway. Fay heard his bare feet on the floor, then water running in the bathroom. She sat on the edge of the bed waiting for him to come back.

She realized, finally, that he was not at the sink but in the shower. It was ten minutes before he returned, wrapped in a towel and carrying his pants in one hand. His dark hair was slicked back from his forehead. He hung up his pants, folded the towel over the back of a chair and climbed into the opposite side of the bed from where Fay still sat. Before lying down he reached up and arranged the mosquito netting over both of them. It fell over her legs. "Time to sleep," he said, and then he did.

Ten minutes later she let herself down onto the floor beside the bed. She lay there in her nightgown, perfectly still, without a pillow or sheet. The tiles were hard but cool. Far into the night Fay remained on the floor, listening to the dogs, the *serenos,* the distant whistle of boats in the harbor and the first roosters. Even a neighborhood like this had roosters. In time her disgust and anger subsided, then her incredulity and finally even the notion that something strange had happened in this room. She had simply discovered something new about Ricardo—something, it now seemed, that she had always known.

Finally, before the first light, she got back up on the bed— but not to sleep. She just lay there until it was time to get up.

The day after their return to Mérida Fay walked into their bedroom at Ricardo's house and found him looking through the top drawer of her dresser. She kept her traveler's checks there, and her and Blake's passports.

"Are you looking for something?" she said.

"Ah, Fay. Yes, I'm looking for the girls' school records. I can't seem to find them anywhere."

They both knew that when Fay had moved in, the dresser was perfectly empty.

"Perhaps they're in one of the other drawers," she said. "Let's take a look." Elaborately helpful, she insisted on a complete search through every drawer, including the top one. "Nothing here," she said.

"Well, they're sure to turn up. And if they don't, I can get copies."

That same afternoon, after Ricardo had gone back to work, she hid the two passports and tourist cards in a pocket in Blake's suitcase. Then she took a cab downtown and bought two tickets to Miami for the following day.

The morning of the flight Ricardo went to work early. He left the car with Fay, as he sometimes did, so she could take Teresa shopping. Fay packed her suitcase and managed to get it into the trunk of the Mercedes unseen. Then she told Blake they were leaving.

"Today?"

"Sssh. Yes, now. Just throw everything you can find into your suitcase and I'll take it out through the kitchen. I don't want everyone to know we're going."

She felt bad about asking Blake to be sneaky, and about walking out on the two girls and Teresa without ever saying good-bye. But if Teresa knew they were going she would call Ricardo instantly. So Fay told her they'd be right back. *"Vamos un ratito,"* she said, shaking the car keys. Teresa nodded, and Fay and Blake walked out the front door.

They took the Mercedes only as far as the Paseo Montejo, where they parked it, left the keys under the seat and caught a cab to the airport.

She had cut the time too close, for a long line of passengers wound across the Mexicana lobby, and there was only a single agent behind the counters to check them in. But after six weeks in Mexico Fay knew what to do. Indeed, Ricardo had taught her. Choosing one of the older porters, she slipped him a folded twenty-dollar bill. That brought him to attention fast. It was five times his daily wage.

"Blake, tell him we're late."

"*Vamos de prisa,*" the boy said.

She opened her hand with a second twenty in it and pointed with her chin toward the lone Mexicana agent. The porter carried their bags to an empty check-in space, told her to wait there and reached out for the second twenty. She trusted him with it. It passed from her hand to his and from his to the agent's. The agent gave a brief, expressionless nod in Fay's direction, and for a moment she thought she had given away forty dollars for nothing. But a couple of minutes later he locked his drawer, raised his hand to the next passenger in line and stepped over to take care of Fay and Blake. No one said a word to the rich gringa in the expensive traveling suit. One woman even smiled knowingly. A couple of people came to stand in line behind her, but the agent waved them off.

She never completely relaxed until the plane had taxied, turned and sped down the runway. Once they were airborne her heart lifted with each flex of the great wings. She hugged her arms to her chest as they banked over the city, the plane rising, her life rising, her fear of Ricardo falling away. Blake pressed his forehead to the window as the plane headed up through the clouds.

Ricardo was going to be unhappy. In her top dresser drawer she had left him a courteous note explaining where he could find his car and apologizing for her sudden departure. She had wanted to be honest with him but couldn't. Not after that night in Veracruz, and not after finding him with his hands practically on her passport.

Fay and her son disembarked from the plane into the Miami airport and tramped along with the other members of their flight through a maze of glass-lined corridors. Television cameras monitored their first steps into the drug-smuggling capital of the world. Immigration stamped their passports and then they waited. The bags were slow in coming.

Blake wrestled his own suitcase over to the Customs counter. The agent asked Fay where she'd been in Mexico, where her hometown was and how long she'd been abroad. Though she had nothing to hide he made her nervous. He searched both bags minutely, glancing up at her frequently as he did so. For a moment she thought he was going to pull her into secondary and have her strip-searched. They had done that to Austin once on the way back from Peru.

"Did you get to see the ruins?" the man asked Blake. He was sandy-haired, thin, still freckled at thirty.

"Yeah, we went to Uxmal."

"Did you like it?"

"It was okay. I went with my dad. We saw some baseball games too. Where Fernando Valenzuela used to play."

"Bringing anything back in your pockets?" the man asked.

Obediently Blake turned out the pockets of his shorts: a couple of hundred-peso coins, a clay whistle shaped like a bird, a gum wrapper and some sand.

"I'm only kidding, kangaroo." The agent smiled, reached across the table and tousled Blake's hair. Blake jerked his head away and stepped back.

Fay hesitated. She didn't want to get mixed up with Customs, but she didn't like it. "You ought to let kids come to you," she said. "They don't all want to have their heads rubbed."

"Just part of the job, ma'am."

"Bullshit. You see a cute kid and put your hand out. You wouldn't have reached over and rubbed my head, would you?"

"Just calm down now," he said. "I was only trying to be friendly."

"Then tell him a joke or something. Learn how to juggle."

Blake stood to one side, his expression neutral. Fay knew he was embarrassed. No kid wanted one of those crazy mothers who flew off the handle and got angry at people in public. She kept quiet until the agent passed them on.

The source of her complaints, she knew, had nothing to do with customs, but with how she had failed to settle anything with Ricardo. She had left him secretly, the same as she had left Austin in Maine. She didn't want to think she was running from one place after another, but so far the start of her life beyond White Pine had not gone smoothly.

They spent three nights in an off-season hotel in Miami Beach. Outside, the noonday sun rang down on the flat ocean like one great metal plate against another. Where the waves slogged onto the beach, the air, the water and the sand were all the same temperature. Yet Blake crawled through the torpid wash like a crocodile, and was happy. Fay only wished that Austin were there to play games with his son. He was much better at it than she was, and the two of them could have gone on for hours.

Wielding a red pen, Fay worked her way through the recreational-vehicle classifieds. The one she liked most read," '74 Winnebago Brave, 23 ft, air, auto, 57,000 miles. Clean, dependable, and aging, like us. Worth more than we're asking: $5000. 555-4379."

She bought it. White and gold, it sat on an immaculate, grass-bordered concrete driveway in front of a stucco house with metal awnings. In deference to the tidy neighborhood the camper's tires had been covered with vinyl jackets.

"No oil stains on the drive," the man said. "It's a very nice engine."

"And the brakes?"

"Never any problem. No squeaks at all."

"How about the miles per gallon?"

"Not so good there. But better than those new ones that eat you alive at the gas station."

Frank and Lily Gershfeld from New York. Both short and slight, they looked too frail to have ever traveled around in such a vehicle. But the stickers on the Brave's rear window proved how far they had roamed since Frank's retirement: Mount Rushmore, Banff, Seattle, Big Sur, Baja and Mazatlán.

Blake stuck his head out the door. "Hey, Mom, there's a bathroom in here! You can even take a shower!"

"Frank's eyes are going," Lily said, "so I better drive you." Her voice was unalloyed Bronx. She perched her tiny form on the driver's seat and slowly, while constantly checking and rechecking her mirrors, backed out into the street. "The steering's easy," she said. "It's power assist. And you've got power brakes too. It's like driving a car, only bigger. Trust your mirrors. Sometimes I send Frank to the rear window when I'm backing up. Watch these curbs now—see how I give them plenty of room?"

"I think I can handle it," Fay said. "I've driven lots of trucks."

"Good for you. Where'd you learn to do that? I'll bet you love this little Brave. You always have your home right with you, and cleaning up is a breeze. If Frank's health were better I'd just as soon live in here and go from camp to camp."

Fay took over the wheel and drove back to the Gershfelds' house, where they settled on $4,750. "You're getting a deal," Lily assured her.

Five years ago Fay had set up her own account with the money left to her by her father. The $4,750 took a bite out of it, but not a large one. Within twenty-four hours the First Bank of White Pine had wired the money to the Gershfelds' account, and the following morning Fay registered the Winnebago to her hotel address. By midafternoon she and Blake were cruising north on the turnpike over the flat Florida scrubland. Blake explored every cranny of the camper, reporting back about the tiny cabinets, the toilet, the cold blast from the air conditioner and the big bed in the far back where he could lie down and watch the highway unfold behind them.

Though the countryside looked alien—pale green vegetation, heat rising off the white pavement, a summer drought in progress—Fay was happy in her new movable home. She was now completely in charge. After years of wanting to leave White Pine, and after what had turned into an awkward stay with Ricardo, she was finally on the move and could do as she pleased. She could pull over any time she wanted and go to sleep, or drive far into the night. Rolling down the turnpike, she loved every mile.

They stopped once to fill up with gas, and again to buy food for the tiny refrigerator. Blake liked to fix his own snacks, eat at the folding table and then wash his own dishes, all while Fay drove. That was the thrill of it.

After dark they stopped at a giant roadside mall to buy sheets, pillows and blankets. Fay, who generally hated malls, loved this one. It was no different, in fact, from any other—but she loved the idea of shopping at nine in the evening in some place she had never been before and to which she would never return. Ice-cream cones in hand, they walked back across the enormous shiny parking lot to the Winnebago. They studied it, looked at it from all angles, held hands and leaned against the door.

Fay couldn't get over it. I should have done this months ago, she thought. It was a thousand times simpler than going to Mexico.

In Orlando, only minutes from Disney World, they found a giant RV park with campers, vans and trailers from all over the country. It was like a village with its own culture. In the next bay a family had settled in for their entire monthlong summer vacation. Across the road a retired couple in a sixty-thousand-dollar Pace Arrow lived like royalty, sleeping in late in the mornings, playing bridge every night and cooking little micro-wave steaks for themselves and their two poodles.

Fay drifted through Disney World, mildly entertained. Because Blake loved it, she tried to stay enthusiastic. In fact, she was happier in the evenings when they returned to the RV camp to swim in the pool and cook dinner in their miniature kitchen: hamburgers, Rice-a-Roni, pizza, all meals of Blake's choice. Eager for the illusion, she imagined that the burdens of parenthood were now slowly droping away from her. An eight-year-old was easy, he was almost a partner in travel.

Soon after dark she lowered the bed from above the two front seats and helped Blake climb up. She was glad he had chosen to come with her instead of returning immediately to the farm. She didn't want any of this to be hard on him—though some of it already had been.

Standing on the floor, she was tall enough to lay her cheek beside her son's on the mattress. For a long time they rested neck to neck, like a pair of horses in a field. His hair smelled of chlorine from the pool. On his small tanned chest the circles of dark skin around his nipples were no larger than a pair of buttons.

"Let's just live here," Blake said. "Can we?"

She kissed him on the forehead. She had never been good at reading him stories at night the way Austin did. Instead she liked to lie or sit beside him as he settled into bed and drifted toward sleep. Sometimes he told her things about his day. Sometimes they didn't talk at all. For Fay it was enough to get close to his sturdy little body. His bottom teeth were slightly crooked, his eyelashes long, his hair as curly as his father's. He had smooth, clean skin that, whenever disfigured, healed almost overnight.

"I think we do live here. For now anyway. We live in this funny little house."

"It's a great house," Blake said.

"And if we go somewhere else we'll still be in it."

"I love you, Mom." He still said that sometimes, as directly as a four-year-old. "Tomorrow can we ride the boat across the lake?"

"Yes, we can. Tomorrow and the next day and the day after that." She wanted to make up to him for the hard times she had put him through in the last few weeks.

"And can we call my dad again?"

"Yes. We'll call him tomorrow night." They had spoken to him twice already, so Austin knew they were back in the States.

Blake closed his eyes and Fay watched him until she thought he was asleep. But then he opened his eyes once more and said, "Could Dad come and stay with us? And go to Disney World?"

She thought about it. "You can ask him," she said. "But don't be disappointed if he can't come. After all, he just went home and he's got his potatoes to look after."

"But if he wants to?"

"You ask him," she said. "And if he wants to, I'll talk to him about it."

Blake closed his eyes again and fell asleep with a long sigh and a shake, like someone dying in a movie. His breath smelled of cookies. He had forgotten to brush his teeth. She had forgotten.

Austin wanted to come. The minute Blake asked him he said yes. So Fay got on the line with him, they talked it over and a day later Austin flew into the Orlando airport.

He emerged from the plane wearing khaki pants and a flannel shirt. Fay understood that the shirt was his disclaimer about the tropics. Just because he had gotten used to Mexico didn't mean he was going to like Florida.

Blake crawled all over him. Fay gave him a soft embrace, they picked up his luggage from the carousel and walked out into the blinding light of the parking lot.

Though she had told Austin he could come, she was not entirely glad to have him. After all, she had only gotten her first taste of freedom days ago. Less than a week had passed since her escape from Mérida, and here was Austin changing his shirt in the back of her camper. She didn't want to feel like a chauffeur. She wanted to feel the heady rush of abandon as she sped down the nighttime highway, the road ahead, the road behind and every decision hers.

But she had made the offer. She had made it for Blake and would not retract it.

She hadn't thought Austin would come. For the second time that month she was surprised by the alacrity with which he had abandoned his potatoes. Of course, Jules was on the farm, but in past years Austin had always acted as if only he could properly oversee the crop. How quickly he had changed his tune, she thought, when she left to visit another man.

Was it possible that she had used Ricardo and Mérida simply to spring Austin loose? Or more to the point—having seen how her husband had reacted the first time—would she ever take up with another man simply to make Austin jump? She didn't want to think so.

Austin took Blake off to Disney World that same afternoon, leaving Fay at home in the RV park to read and think. She was glad of the time alone. She wasn't ready to patch everything up with Austin and pretend they were all in Orlando on some kind of vacation.

That night she knew Austin would want to sleep with her. He was subtle about it, but he wanted to. After reading Blake a story he came and sat on her bed and massaged her toes through the sheet. Her little room was partitioned off from the rest of the camper by a folding door. It was almost midnight. "Austin," she said. "Palm out."

No palm to the heart, no subtle variation at all. And he knew better than to argue, for the First Rule of the Palm forbade all inducement or persuasion.

"Will it always be like this?" he asked politely.

"I don't think so. But I need to get used to you for a while. And I need to know this is still my adventure. I want to make every decision and feel like I'm still in charge of things."

"Fay, you're in charge. I'll do whatever you like." He laughed. "I just wanted to lick your toes a little, like a humble servant." Through the sheet he had clasped one of her feet in his hands. Gently.

He really was a good man. Ricardo was a thug beside him.

SEVEN

Austin drove through the hot July night, the only one awake in the camper, his windshield spattered with bugs. They were headed west through the flat Florida panhandle, leaving Disney World and the whole East Coast behind.

Blake lay where he had fallen asleep on the floor, surrounded by comic books and the remains of an Arby's dinner. Fay, after covering him with a blanket, had gone to sleep herself. She lay on the bed, her motionless bare calves visible to Austin in the rearview mirror.

They had spent two more palm-out, altogether chaste days in Orlando and then started for the Southwest. Fay wanted to make the trip in one long drive. She led off at the wheel after dinner, then traded places with Austin. Now, under the influence of half a quart of truck-stop coffee, he drove on automatic, letting his mind run loose.

It never ended, he thought, this job of letting your wife be. Letting her get angry or bored or blue. Letting her be attracted to other men. Letting her wander. Letting her go to sleep on her own after you had driven and flown fifteen hundred miles to be with her and keep your family together. You never mastered the game because every week there was a new set of rules.

Any day of the year—any summer afternoon or late winter night by the fire—some worry might overwhelm her. The two of you could suddenly have nothing to say, as if you had no history together, no children and no home. Or it could be worse than that: One day she might leave a note on the kitchen table and move into town. Or it could be worse than *that:* one day she might leave and never come back at all.

Marriage itself never gave you the least guarantee about anything, for intimacy came and went on a schedule no one could predict. Sexual desire flared up or died down, now for one, now for the other, rarely in step. For more than a year after Maggie's birth, and again after Blake's, Fay had lost all interest in sex, her desire channeled into breastfeeding and child care.

Yet there had been other times, for days or weeks at a stretch, when she was insatiable. Perversely, she seemed to want Austin most when he was least available. During planting or harvest he would come back from the fields to find her in bed, a dreamy look on her face, her clothes scattered about and some erotic book open on the bedside table. Sometimes she went a month and hardly thought about sex at all, and then the mania would come over her and she'd want him morning and night. She'd pull him onto the bed, sit on his chest and read to him from a book of women's fantasies, finding a bony spot along the curve of his ribs to rub herself against while she read. "Get it up," she'd say with a laugh. "The Beast is hungry."

They called their marriage the Animal, and sex itself, the Beast. Feeding the Animal and feeding the Beast were related but not the same.

"The Beast loves blood," Austin said once, burying his face in her menses.

"The Beast loves danger," Fay said, slipping off her underpants in an empty Sheraton conference room where the National Potato Council had just met. Sitting on the polished table, she circled his legs with her own and drew her panties across his teeth like dental floss.

Before X-rated movies were shown at the White Pine drive-in, before *Penthouse* and *Hustler* were sold face-out at the local 7-Eleven and before women's magazines started priming their readers for multiple orgasms, Austin and Fay had considered themselves the sexually enlightened couple of the north country. Living in a small town where no one ever mentioned the act in public, it was easy for them to think they were the preeminent local authorities on the subject.

Eventually, even in the northern reaches of Maine, sex opened up as a public topic, allowing the Poolers to laugh occasionally at their own earnest sexual history: their first nights on the seat of Austin's truck, their stolen weekends at the Hallwick house on Nantucket, their first oral sex, their first anal sex, their first experiments with Tantric self-restraint. They had read a lot of books.

Tonight, as he drove through the Florida panhandle, the mere glimpse of Fay's naked calves and ankles were enough to arouse Austin. But he might just as well have been watching some girl at the beach. Twenty years of marriage didn't guarantee that he could caress his wife when he wanted to. It didn't even guarantee that he knew who the woman asleep behind him was. Their whole past seemed to have evaporated. Indeed, when he thought about their times in bed he could hardly remember what they'd done.

That was crazy. He could remember plenty of details surrounding their sexual life: the way Fay liked to tease him in the midst of a party, making oblique references to everything erotic; the way she massaged him and pretended, as if she were a professional masseuse, to be mortified by his erection; the way she laughed and spread her legs in bed, saying "Go ahead, look. What *is* it you see down there?" He could remember lots of peripheral details, but when he tried to call up his memories of the sexual act itself, they had all disappeared.

He could not remember, for example, what they had done about birth control the first time they made love. Perhaps nothing—but how could he have forgotten that? He could remember the gold chain he had removed that night from Fay's neck, and how he had dropped it into a little coiled heap on the rubber floor mat of his truck, next to a botany research paper on *Phytopthora infestans*. The paper had been typed on Eaton's Corrasable Bond, and was held together with a green oversized paper clip. All that was as clear as yesterday—yet he could not remember what had followed.

Tonight, twenty years after their honeymoon on an island in Penobscot Bay, he could still remember how a gull with only one good leg had alighted on a post and stared at them, its balance perfect in spite of its dangling bad foot. He could remember the thick rounded corners of the hotel's dining-room tables and the blue chenille bedspread in their upstairs room—but he could not remember sleeping with his new bride. He could remember how they stood on the balcony in their underwear, kissing each other in full view of a lobsterman in the cove below. Austin could go back that close. He could see the muscular brown curve of Fay's leg draped over the bed, and her pouting imitation of Jeanne Moreau. But the actual sex from that time had entirely vanished from his memory.

Halfway through the tunnel under Mobile Bay, Fay appeared and sat down in the passenger seat. She was wrapped in a blanket. They passed through garish Mobile on an almost-empty highway. The signs led on to Baton Rouge.

"How about if I drive for a while," she said.

"You don't want to stop? We could stay in one of those rest areas."

"No. I want to keep driving until we get there."

He pulled off onto the shoulder and they traded places. Within minutes she had the camper back up to sixty.

He sat beside her in the dark. Miles down the road, out of a long silence, she said, "I know I've hurt you, Austin. And Blake too. I don't want to but I'm doing it."

He nodded. As always, he was moved by her feelings: by the ache in her voice and the downturned corners of her mouth. If he chose to he could see all this from her point of view. But he didn't want to—or at least he didn't want to admit that he could. Almost against his will he sympathized with Fay; he loved her and couldn't help it. But if he started looking at things the way she did, what chance was there she would ever come back?

"I don't want to feel like a bad woman. Doesn't it ever seem to you that what I'm doing is right?"

Austin wrapped himself in her blanket. "I don't know. Tonight all I can see is that you want to give up our life at home for a camper and a highway and no time to lie down together. Maybe some morning I'll wake up and understand how important this all is to you."

Fay's voice softened. "You could do that right now if you wanted to."

After so many years she knew him too well. "Maybe I could," he said.

After driving the rest of the night, Fay took Austin out for breakfast in a truck stop halfway through Louisiana. They had passed New Orleans, one of the few cities he had ever wanted to visit.

Blake jumped up hungry for breakfast: he wanted grits. "True grits," he told the waitress. Austin, with the circumspection of an anthropologist, ordered a bowl for himself. After a diligent sampling he concluded that it was an emergency substitute for people with no potatoes—but his smiling son ate two servings doused in butter. By 8:00 A.M. the temperature on the rotating sign at the edge of the truck stop read 88 degrees. A few desultory mosquitoes waded through the clammy air. The sun was purple.

Austin bought a junior-size football in the gift store and passed it around with Blake in the parking lot. Blake had a surprising arm for an eight-year-old, but he couldn't catch well. He dropped the ball every second time. "It's too hard," he said. "It hurts my hands." Austin threw gentle lobs and still he dropped them. "Let's go, Dad. I'm no good at football. I don't like it."

At a toy store outside Beaumont, Texas, Austin bought a soft Nerf football, and whenever they stopped after that he and Blake played a little catch with the new ball.

Houston, San Antonio, Ozona, Fort Stockton. The drive through Texas was longer than from Boston to Cleveland. Past San Antonio and the hundredth meridian the land grew dry and stark. The temperature reached 102 but the humidity was only 10 percent. Austin drove for five hours, gave the job back to Fay and tumbled into his bunk. Within minutes he was asleep. He hadn't shaved or brushed his teeth since Orlando.

*　　*　　*

"We're almost there," Fay said, and laid a hand on her husband's shoulder. The camper was parked in a roadside rest near Carlsbad, New Mexico.

Austin stumbled out into the fresh air, the cells of his body still doing sixty miles an hour. He could feel the change in altitude. On the fawn, arid ground beyond the rest stop, each isolate bush and clump of grass grew apart from all other vegetation.

"Isn't it great!" Fay said, cupping her hand over her eyes. She had changed into a sleeveless shirt and a pair of shorts.

"It's clean," he admitted.

Fay laughed and tapped his chest with her knuckles. "Don't be so cautious. There are hardly any people here. You'll love it."

"I'm perfectly fond of people," Austin said. "I just don't like it when they all jam in together and create places like the south Bronx."

"*You* look like the south Bronx! You better shave and shower, darling, or they might not let you into the caves."

Opening up from the top of the mesa, the Carlsbad Caverns descended eight hundred feet toward the basin floor. Only one hundred feet down, the air was as cool and humid as on the Maine coast. The Poolers stayed the first day until dusk, when hundreds of thousands of bats flew out of the cave entrance, darkening the sky with their unerring chaotic flight.

On the second afternoon Fay went down into the caves by herself. Austin and Blake watched a movie at the visitor's center, played gin rummy in the Winnebago and passed the Nerf football around in the parking lot. Blake had polished his throws and could catch the softer ball with some consistency.

They were still throwing when Fay appeared at the end of the lot with a young man carrying a pack frame almost as big as he was. Skip Wilson was only 5'4", with smooth light skin and a rising shock of black hair. Fay had already invited him to dinner. "He's like us," she told Austin. "He doesn't know where he's going next. He's on the road."

While Austin cooked dinner at the RV campsite, Skip took Blake off to play catch. Fay set out the plates and silverware, then watched the nighthawks tear past in search of insects. The sun was in the cottonwoods, and the afternoon heat was finally letting up.

Over dinner Fay told Skip that she and Austin had a daughter about his age.

He looked doubtful. "I'll be twenty next month."

"She's got a summer job in Wyoming," Fay said. "She's nineteen."

Skip took a long look at the snapshot Fay showed him of Maggie, then glanced back and forth from it to Fay. "I can't believe you have a daughter as old as I am. You two could be sisters."

Fay laughed freely. "Every mother loves to hear that."

"No, really, you do. You guys aren't anything like my parents. My dad couldn't throw a football if you paid him, and my mom weighs almost two hundred pounds. They never do anything but watch TV. Have you ever been to Terre Haute?"

"Corn country," Austin said, ready to believe the worst.

"From a thousand miles away," Skip said, "I can tell you exactly what they're doing at this instant. TV every night—they even eat dinner in front of it. And I've got two younger brothers who are stuck at home. I don't know if they'll ever get away." He glanced at Blake. "This is the greatest thing you could do for a kid, traveling around like this."

He picked up Maggie's photograph and had another look. It was clear he found her attractive. Austin didn't tell him she had a boyfriend at college—and maybe another one by now in Wyoming. He didn't tell him she was 5'10" either.

After dinner Skip drank decaf with milk. He offered a sip to Blake and asked Fay, "Is that all right?" A purple light hung below the mesas and the distant Guadalupes, and the first evening breezes spun the cottonwood leaves.

"Tell me what you do every day," Fay said. "What's it like? Where do you stay?"

"I've got a tent, but it's so dry out here I hardly use it."

"You just travel around?"

"Hitchhiking, usually. I came out to the Southwest last summer too and went all through New Mexico and Arizona."

"What's the best place to go?" Fay asked. "The best desert place of all?"

"Chaco Canyon," he answered, without hesitation.

"I've never heard of it."

"You've never heard of it?" At first Skip was incredulous, but then he laughed. "I guess before last year I hadn't either. It's a beautiful wasteland where the Anasazi had an empire. Thousands of people lived in a canyon where today there's no food and hardly any water."

That night, though invited to stay in the camper, Skip took his sleeping bag and unrolled it next to the dry creek bed under the cottonwood trees. The next morning they all left for Chaco Canyon together.

As Skip had promised, the land at Chaco was barren. The approach to the canyon was forty miles of dirt road, and inside the park there were no restaurants, no gas stations, not even a soda machine. There was only one source of water in the whole canyon, a faucet outside the visitors' center.

Skip was a quiet traveler; he led them to the canyon and said nothing. He didn't read the little guidebooks Austin bought or explore anything systematically. He took Blake and climbed up a crack in the canyon wall, and for an hour the two of them sat on an outcrop looking over Pueblo Bonito, their faces lit up by the afternoon sun.

In the most isolated corner of the park's campsite, as the sun dropped toward the rim of the mesa, the four of them ate dinner on a concrete table. Ten feet beyond, the world was air and rock and creosote bush, nothing more.

Skip told them he was going to walk out to the Wijiji ruins as he had done the summer before, and camp under the stars. He invited Blake to come along—if his parents would let him.

"Can I?" Blake said.

"There's no one out there?" Fay asked.

"Not at night. There's nothing except the ruins. It looks like the start of time."

"What about snakes?"

"We'd sleep inside the walls. Snakes don't like a place with the smell of people all through it."

Fifteen minutes later Austin and Fay watched their son disappear through the scrub of a side canyon with a nineteen-year-old boy they had met only the day before.

"You're not worried, are you?" Austin asked.

"I don't think so. Are you?"

"No. He seems like a dependable kid."

Austin cleaned off the campsite table and stretched out on it with a book. Fay sat in the doorwell of the Winnebago, stripped to her bra and shorts. The temperature was still 90 degrees. The lemon, almost level rays of the sun blew against her tan shoulders.

"Imagine," she said, "how the Beast would sweat in this heat."

Austin put down his book. She had surprised him. "Sometimes that Beast comes around on such delicate little paws," he said, "you hardly know it's here."

At the start they were like friends who had known each other since childhood and only now decided to have sex. Austin unbuttoned his shirt and jogged Fay back into the camper over the carpeted floor, pushing against her with his bare chest. Their kisses, the first in months, were long and delicate, slow as a journey over sand.

The sun had set. Austin massaged her body with his forehead. He played the Beast with No Hands, pulling down her shorts and panties with his teeth. She raised her hips to help him, and with each turn they worked their way farther back into the Winnebago, away from the door and the campground. When he mouthed her nipples through her bra, she bit him back on the shoulders and neck. She held his lips between her teeth.

Her hair, even in the middle of the desert, smelled like high tide at the beach. They had begun to sweat. She rolled him over and took off the last of their clothes. Then she crouched above him, pinning his arms down with her knees and trailing her breasts across her face. She teased him. She liked to get on top and flatten his cock with her belly and pretend she didn't know it was there. Then she'd browse around it with her hips, her thighs, the crack of her ass, her cunt. All the while she licked his nipples, over and over, as if that were the last known act of sex. Austin moaned like a bear in a cage, until finally she raised her pelvis and tipped him inside. Inch by inch, she swallowed him. Even in the dark he knew her body: the narrow girlish waist, the long globes of her bottom, her faintly bowed legs and peasant ankles. Below one breast was a strawberry mark the size of a dime. Riding above him, she had turned her face to the ceiling. She rose above his penis until he almost slipped out, then sank down on it again. But she wouldn't let him come. Whenever he got close she held herself completely still.

"Not yet," she said.

"Please, Fay. Please."

"Not yet." She liked him to beg.

"Fay, I love you. I've always loved you."

"No. Not yet."

She ground herself against him, slow as bread rising. Her back was arched, her neck as long as a gull's. She grew perfectly still and silent. She was coming.

That had always been her way. She sat above him clamped as tight as a coiled spring, breathless and blind. He lifted and sank below her in a long glycerin rhythm. Deep inside her he could feel the rubbery mouth of her uterus. Her climax went on and on—until finally she fell down onto his chest, gasping and out of breath. She leaned forward so he could stroke her hard and fast and come himself, in an instant. Now she bent to his face, kissing him and moaning. He covered her mouth with his own. He wanted her breath inside him.

They lay without words. Austin's spine curved back down onto the rug, and finally he opened his eyes. The desert night had fallen around them like feathers. "Where are we?" he said.

"On the floor somewhere." She moved her arm and tapped something wooden in the dark.

"I've lost track of north."

"That would be rare," Fay said.

"I have. I don't know which way we're pointed."

Austin never lost track of his directions. Even in his dreams she knew which way was north. But now he laughed. "Maybe we could stay here for the rest of the trip. Skip could drive and Blake could bring us food and water. I'd cover your ass with a towel. No one would know what we're up to."

"Don't move," she said. Yet a moment later she adjusted her own hips, allowing a trickle of semen to run down onto Austin's belly where it pooled amid the hairs. "You're like rock inside me. How long do you think you'll stay this way?"

"Days. Maybe weeks."

"Oh dear. Pride goeth before a fall."

"All right, maybe only minutes. But think of the miracle. Even if it gets soft, it always comes back hard."

"How sweet of it," Fay said with a laugh. "But how commonplace. I had my heart set on an everlasting erection."

"A man is a lowly thing, inadequate to the needs of women. What you want is a statue."

She kissed his eyeballs, pressing her lips to them as hard as if they were marble.

"I want to talk," she said.

"Good. Me too."

"Austin, I'm not trying to leave you. You're the most adequate man I've ever known. All those women who get tired of their men—I'm not like that. That's not why I can't go back to Maine."

By now, he thought, he could have said this for her. But he had to hear it—and let her say it—over and over.

"When I went up to White Pine I was twenty-two years old. I can hardly remember what I was like back then. I was a girl. But I knew that marrying you and living on your farm was one and the same thing, and I stretched out in Maine just like we're stretched out on this floor. I had no idea where north was, so I made your north my north for all those years. Sometimes I can hardly believe they're over."

She was close to crying. She raised herself up and dropped Austin's penis, now soft, onto his belly, then lay beside him on the rug. They lay toe to toe, with her chin close to his shoulder.

"I don't want to die in Aroostook County," she said. "I know that sounds dramatic, but that's what came to me one night last winter—that I was going to die up there. Maybe not for forty years, but die all the same in a place that wasn't my home. Well, it became my home, but only because of you. Now, before it's too late, I want to choose something myself. And you can be with me when I do it, but I can't let you take over."

"Not even in sex," he said.

"Austin, I'm sorry."

"That's all right, I like it. I've always liked it. It's as if you're having sex with something beyond me, something bigger."

"I am. It's the Beast. It's the wind and the desert."

Austin held her to him, speaking past her into the dark. "Sometimes I have this fantasy," he said, "where I sneak up on you in the woods and find you lying there all alone, naked, with your eyes closed and your legs apart. You're masturbating, and I stay hidden and watch. It's as if you're having sex with the whole world."

"And you like it."

"I love it."

They lay without talking, perfectly warm on the carpeted floor. A few minutes later Austin said, "Sometimes I even think I could watch you have sex with someone else and not be jealous, because it would just be you and the world. I love to see you excited."

"You're an amazing man."

"You've never thought of anything like that?"

"I've thought of everything. I just don't admit it the way you do."

"Don't get me wrong. It's only a fantasy."

She took his genitals in her hand, as naturally as if reaching into a bowl for a piece of fruit. "No other men for me," she said. "Not for a while anyway. I think I learned a lesson with . . . that guy in Mérida."

"A highly inadequate guy, if you want my opinion."

"I was lucky to get away when I did."

Fay gave him a slow soft kiss, then laid her cheek against his arm. Her breaths grew slower, her muscles trembled and fell slack. Austin's own heartbeat dropped to its smoothest slowest pace in months—but he didn't go to sleep. Disengaging himself from her arms, he stepped out naked into the dark and took a piss on the sandy ground. There was north, with the Dipper pointing the way toward Polaris. The heat of the day had risen upward and the earth was cooling. Pegged to the top of the night sky, Arcturus and Vega trembled as if loosely mounted. Far away, the coyotes lifted their primitive ascendant cries from butte to butte.

In Tucson Fay bought a truck. They were staying at a trailer park on East Speedway and had been there for a week. One afternoon she disappeared in a taxi and came back driving a 1977 Toyota pickup with Arizona plates.

"Seven hundred dollars," she announced. "I talked this guy down from a thousand."

"You could have a career with the Gypsies," Austin said. "Buying and selling."

"Is that what they do?"

"It used to be horses. Now it's cars and trucks."

"Are there really still Gypsies?"

"Sure, they're all around. They just look like everyone else."

"I'd like to meet a Gypsy."

"I'm sure you would."

"Stop it, Austin. Not like that. Just meet one, the way I met Skip."

Skip had left them after Chaco Canyon and headed north to Mesa Verde. The Poolers had come south past Canyon de Chelly and the ruins at Kayenta.

To Austin, buying a second vehicle looked like a domestic act. Fay said she could pull the Toyota behind the camper, but she didn't look around for a tow bar. Austin kept his thoughts to himself. That was his job in Tucson. He had no other.

The truck did make it easier to get around. They drove out to the Papago Indian Reservation and to the stark San Xavier Mission. The dry, styptic heat of the desert, which every after-noon hit 105 and sometimes 110, defined the form and colors of the city. Though banks and office buildings sometimes estab-lished tiny oases of bluegrass and clover, most houses simply had desert for lawn.

Fay loved the heat. She wore shorts, a pair of flip-flops and a polo shirt. In the evenings a loose skirt. Some days she went to the university or to the air-conditioned branch of the public library. Mostly she studied botany—as Austin had in college. Here it was all plants and shrubs of the desert.

Every third or fourth evening Austin called home to Jules. The weather had turned hot and dry, Jules said. Hot was eighty. Jules had already dug the first new potatoes for the Boston market.

"Just one thing," Jules said. "I had some trouble with that purple paint. I don't know if the wood was wet or what happened, but it blistered up pretty bad. I had a couple of boys do the scraping so I could repaint it. But just one thing. Earl didn't have the right tint for that heliotrope anymore, so I had to use custard yellow. We were lucky. It covered in one coat."

Once again Austin kept his thoughts to himself. He might have been in training. "I'll be back before harvest starts," he said. "What's Charley Stoddard up to these days?"

"The way the bird sings, he's offering three-fifty a hundred for new potatoes."

"Shit, who's going to sell at that price?"

"Hard to say. You know Black Pete, don't you? He lives out behind the Starr plant?"

"Do I want to hear this?" Austin said.

"Probably not."

"Come on, come on."

"Cathy and I took in a movie last night and then stopped over to the Caribou Bar for a drink. Pretty good movie, about this family that lives out in the woods."

"Just tell me."

"Well, we got talking to Black Pete, who said they've been unloading semis over at Starr's in the middle of the night. The noise keeps him up. So one night he snuck over and took a look and wouldn't you know it, every one of those trucks had a PEI or a New Brunswick plate."

"*Goddamn* that Charley Stoddard," Austin said. "That plant sits in the middle of ninety thousand acres of Maine potatoes, and he has to buy from those sneaky little Canucks."

"Seems like it."

"Every potato grower out there has got a transportation and storage subsidy and a floor price to boot. The Canadian government sets them up so they can dump their potatoes on us, and those fiddleheads in Washington just look the other way."

"Doesn't seem right, does it?"

"If people knew what the hell was going on . . ." Austin finally caught himself. There wasn't much point in giving this tirade to Jules. "If I had enough dynamite, I'd blow up the damn plant."

"That would be the Mexican revolutionary style, would it?"

Jules had a way with hotheads, including his boss. All the same, it was twenty-four hours before Austin cooled down after hearing the news. When he got back to Maine he'd have a talk with Charley Stoddard.

Midsummer in Tucson. Within an hour of sunrise a dazzling heat and light covered the city, and by early afternoon the streets shone like metal. After sunset it cooled slowly. Austin and Fay either cooked dinner in the camper or ate tacos and enchiladas at Carlita's Cafe. Afterward they sat outside in the trailer park on a couple of webbed lawn chairs, drinking coffee. Sometimes Blake watched television at a friend's.

A dry wind filtered through the park, carrying the sounds of city traffic. The canvas awning on a nearby trailer flapped and billowed, and the palm fronds clicked in the trees overhead.

"Blake likes it here," Fay said. She looked at Austin over her cup of coffee. "Don't you think?"

"I think he's glad we're together."

"I thought the heat would bother him, but it doesn't seem to."

"And you?" he asked. "Does it bother you?"

"I can take it. I like how you can wear almost nothing here even at night. They should make Tucson a big nudist colony."

Right now she was wearing only a tee-shirt and a loose pair of shorts. Barefoot and no underwear. Ever since Chaco Canyon their love life had flourished, and one reason was certainly the heat. Late at night, after Blake was asleep in his loft, they often lay naked on Fay's bed, talking about their children and Tucson and the desert.

All this was not exactly what Austin wanted from his marriage, but it was a great step above Mérida. They talked without ever using the future tense, and steered clear of topics that might wind up in an argument. Austin figured if their conversation turned into an argument, he had already lost it.

Deep in the desert Southwest, living in an RV park in the middle of a big city, he was happy with his son and in love with his wife. It didn't make sense for him to be content living this way, but he was. Every morning he got up and found some project to do. He wrote long letters to Maggie, took Blake swimming every day in one of the city pools and talked to Fay about everything except her plans. Every night they lay down together he was grateful to be with her. Mérida had scared him.

Under the rattling palm fronds he set down his coffee cup and withdrew a tiny gift-wrapped package from his shorts pocket. He handed it to Fay.

"What's this?"

"Go ahead, open it. It's an anniversary present, just a little late." Their twentieth wedding anniversary had passed while Fay was with Ricardo in Mérida, and Austin trying to find her.

She unwrapped the box, holding it at a little distance as if suspicious of what she might find inside. But there, mounted on black velvet, were two emerald earrings.

"Austin, what is this? They're not real."

"Of course they're real."

"What are you doing?"

"Repenting for past sins. I saw them in a jewelry-store window the other day. I went by again and they were still there, so I bought them."

To Austin, jewelry had never been more than an announcement of wealth. "If you want to wear a sign," he once told Fay, "why don't you just pin some hundred-dollar bills to your dress? Make 'em thousands if you have to."

For their wedding he had given Fay a gold band but no engagement ring. All through their marriage he had bought her clothes, delicate underwear, bath soaps from Paris, perfumes and scarves. But he would never have blown good cash on trifles like rubies or diamonds.

The year after her husband died Lina Hallwick had come to White Pine for Christmas—humbling herself to travel, for only the fourth time, to that desolate terminus of the nation. Austin's father had also died that year, and the big yellow house had passed on to Austin and Fay.

On Christmas morning, among gifts of flannel bathrobes, cookware, a bicycle and a pair of cross-country skis, Lina handed Fay an expensively wrapped rectangular package. A pair of gloves was Austin's first guess. Or stockings. But the box turned out to be from Tiffany's, and inside was an emerald necklace.

The necklace looked as out of place in the Pooler living room as a silver creamer on a canoe trip. But Fay was delighted. She stood before the hall mirror, turning back and forth. She couldn't get over how beautiful it was.

Austin, however, took the gift as a personal affront. He couldn't stand the way Lina looked on from one side, full of approval, implying that something had finally been done to rectify her daughter's station in life. Austin glanced at the stones. "They're just as green as grass," he said.

Lina lifted the necklace from her daughter's neck. "You do like emeralds, don't you, Austin?" She knew how he felt about jewelry.

He only hesitated for a moment. "Not particularly. And you better not drop that thing in the meadow next spring or you'll never find it."

Fay burst out crying. Lina withdrew to her room and didn't come out until supper, when she wore a black dress buttoned to the neck, as if in mourning. Austin apologized but it was too late. He had already ruined both Christmas and Lina's visit. It was not the first time, his mother-in-law's stiff shoulders implied, that he had displayed the boorish nature of someone obsessed with tubers.

Now, five years later, Fay put on her earrings and ducked into the camper to see how they looked in the mirror. And from that moment she wore them always. She wore them to the supermarket and the library and the Desert Museum, and she wore them to bed. Only now and again she took them off and held them in her palm to look at them.

Two little green rocks, Austin thought. He still didn't believe in jewelry—but what he believed in seemed less and less important these days. The fact was, he liked the earrings on Fay and they made her happy, which made him happy. All it took was cash.

Eating one night at Carlita's, Austin and Blake met a local farmer.

"A farmer," Austin said. "From around here? You mean a rancher?"

"I grow pecans. I own some land south of town."

After dinner Austin invited him back to the park for a cup of coffee. Ramon Carbajal was about sixty with thick, silvery-gray hair that erupted behind his temples and swept back over his ears. He wore a snowy white shirt and several turquoise rings. He didn't look like he'd spent his life in the fields.

They were still talking about agriculture when Fay came back from the library with a new book on xeric landscapes. Ramon rose and offered her his seat, as polite as a Spanish hidalgo. Austin brought out another folding chair, and the three of them wound up talking long after Blake had gone to bed. That night, for the first time, Austin heard his wife explain to a third party what she was doing in Arizona, and why she had left her home in Maine. She told the whole story without once looking over at Austin. She sounded like she was practicing.

Ramon was the first person they had gotten to know who actually came from Tucson. He had been born there and knew the city from when it was only a tenth its current size. He told them he had some free time in the next few days and would be glad to take them down to Sahuarita to show them his groves.

When the time came Fay didn't go. She had signed up for a plant-identification tour and didn't want to miss it. So Austin and Blake drove south with Ramon along the Santa Cruz River in his new Chevy pickup. The vehicle was untouched by rust, scratches or mud, and the bed was covered with a fitted black tarpaulin. It was not exactly a working man's truck. As he drove through the parched landscape dotted with cacti and feathery green trees, Ramon had a spare elegant look. He spoke with a restraint that verged on sadness.

"In this country," he said, "water is everything. Your wife understands that. She has learned a great deal already about our plants."

"I think it's true what she told you. She'd like to live here."

"And you?"

"I'm a potato farmer. I live in the same house where my grandfather was born, on a farm with some of the best potato soil in the world. You'd have to see that soil to believe it." He looked out across the arid valley, allowing Ramon to guess at his distrust—even his disdain—for such impoverished land as lay before them. "Fay wants to leave Maine, but it's different for me. I've got ties there that most people can't understand. My family has lived and grown potatoes on the same ground for almost a hundred years."

"I understand," Ramon said, nodding gravely. "Over the generations a bond is formed between a family and its land. I feel that way about my groves, for example, because the property we are going to visit was given to my ancestor, Emilio Carbajal de León, in 1705."

Austin wrestled with the fact that this polite understated Hispanic with a creased desert face and a gentleman's pickup had owned his land for almost three hundred years. It made the Poolers look like rootless vagabonds.

"And your family today?" Austin asked.

"Both my sons are grown. One lives in Houston and works with oil. The other lives here in Nogales. He helps arrange for the Mexican workers during harvest."

"And your wife?"

"Ah, here's the turn for Sahuarita. My wife is a quiet woman. She's devout."

Sahuarita was warehouses, a few homes and an old gas station. "From here it's only a couple of miles," Ramon said. They drove past row after row of pecan trees on either side of the road. The plantations were strictly symmetrical, and some were flooded with water. Ramon turned through an iron gate, drove another few hundred yards and parked in front of an adobe block house set between the trees and the river. A black-haired woman and two children appeared at the door.

"They're from Michoacán," Ramon said. "Dependable, but no English, I'm afraid." He spoke to the woman briefly in Spanish, then led Austin and Blake into the trees.

The temperature dropped and the glare disappeared. Green pecans four, five and six to a cluster dotted the graceful branches. The leaves looked like white ash leaves. But what brought Austin to his knees—literally—was the loamy river-bottom soil, devoid of rocks. He dug his hand in and lifted out a tuft of grass, its thin prolific roots supporting a ball of spongy soil. He held it to his nose. Its moist rich smell was one he had never expected to find in Arizona.

"Beautiful," he said. Briefly he laid one side of his face against the ground. "Beautiful soil. You've worked this for years."

"Many years."

At the caretakers' house they sat in the shade of the nearest trees. La señora brought them lemonade and *sopaipillas*. Her husband was out inspecting the pumps.

The soil of Ramon's great-great-grandfathers had gladdened Austin's heart. "You've made something fine here," he said.

"Yet one of my sons cares nothing for the land, and my wife hasn't come here for fifteen years. Your wife, Fay, is more open-minded. Even if she no longer wants to live on your farm, she's interested in everything."

Austin glanced at Blake and fell silent. He wondered if he had already said too much in front of his son.

Ramon called softly toward the house. "*Señora, por favor, tráiganos más limonada. Y que venga Manolo con sus tiradores.*"

The woman returned with a second pitcher of lemonade, and her young son brought out two homemade slingshots. He held one out silently to Blake.

"Take it," Ramon said. "You can shoot at birds by the river. Maybe you'll see a coyote. Do you know any Spanish words?"

"*Buenos días,*" Blake said.

"*Buenos días,*" the other boy answered, thinking he was spoken to.

Once Austin and Ramon were left to themselves, Austin found himself complaining about what he had meant to leave unsaid. "Everything I live for is in Maine, and Fay wants to leave. She already has."

Ramon considered that statement. "There are many ways a woman can leave her man," he said. "Years ago my wife found God, and I've hardly known her since. She sleeps in my room—occasionally even in my bed—but it's God's embrace she dreams of. You are lucky to have a wife who still loves you."

"Is it so clear that she does?"

"Quite clear."

Behind Ramon the light from the riverbed danced through the trees. They heard the rubber twang of slingshots and the voices of the two boys, Blake speaking English and Manolo Spanish.

"You find my wife attractive," Austin said.

Ramon inclined his head, acknowledging that was so. "She's a charming and beautiful woman. But part of her attractiveness is how she feels about you. I could see that. I hope I have not offended you."

Austin finished his lemonade and set down the glass. "What if you were married to such a woman," he said. "One who loved you but who wanted to move away from Tucson. Let's say she wanted to move to the far northern corner of Maine—and she didn't just *want* to, she was going to do it no matter what. But she said that if you wished to follow her there, she'd let you."

"*Dios guarde.* I understand your winters are savage."

"Long and twenty-below, night after night. We never think anything of it."

"And in the spring you have bugs," Ramon said.

"Black flies worse than piranhas. Mosquitoes like helicopters."

"Are there no good points?"

"Of course. We're hundreds of miles from the nearest big city, and the land is the most beautiful on earth."

Ramon shook his head. "I don't see how I could survive in such a place." Then he broke into a smile. "All the same, for the sake of a beautiful woman men have done things a good deal stranger than that."

EIGHT

August in Aroostook County. Austin and his son flew up the valley in the little commuter plane from Portland, deciphering the towns from above. White farmhouses stood out from the potato fields like dice on felt. The flawless skies, rinsed clear of dust and smoke, stretched east over empty New Brunswick.

Jules Derosier met them at White Pine's diminutive airport, a narrow concrete runway bordered by potato fields and poplars. When Blake skipped down the stairs from the plane Jules slung him onto his hip as if the boy were five years old. Blake hooked his fingers behind the hired man's thin muscular neck. Neither one bothered to speak.

With adults Jules maintained a certain distance. He would sooner have danced the tango at the county fair than lay his arm around Austin's shoulders—yet with children he was affectionate. He let them hang from his arms two and three at a time, and never asked them any of those dumb questions like how did it feel to be eight years old, or what did they like about school?

Jules wore the look of bad news. "We just had five days of rain and fog."

Austin understood what that meant as plainly as if Jules had named the disease. It was late blight. "How many fields so far?"

"Two. One Katahdin and one Superior, both tablestock. I knew you'd want to see them right away."

Late blight was a misnomer. The fungus could spread during any stretch of cool wet weather and had made an appearance in Austin's fields almost every year he could remember. The same disease had caused the Irish potato famine of 1845. Austin, who battled peach aphids and Colorado potato beetles with equanimity, had always been unnerved by the invisible spores of *Phytopthora infestans*. Drifting through his fields with the wind and rain, they made him aware of chaos.

Jules had already sprayed both fields with Ridomil, twice. "We should have started earlier," he said. "We should be on a schedule."

"No sense in spraying until we have to," Austin said. It was an old argument.

The two fungicide applications had prevented the spread of lesions from the foliage to the stalks and tubers. Austin and Jules drove directly to the fields and inspected them, then tramped the neighboring fields as well, occasionally scrabbling out a few potatoes. They found no leaf roll, no spindle tubers, no wilt or scurf—and most important, no additional signs of late blight. Blake tagged along behind them for a while, then fell asleep on the front seat of Jules's truck.

Between fields Jules filled his boss in on other farm news. The oat crop had made seventy-eight bushels to the acre—no record, but a good return. Compared to harvesting potatoes, oats were no work at all: there was no grading, no washing, no bagging, no storing. Even the combining was hired out to a guy from Limestone who did custom work for a percentage of the crop. All the same, oats to Jules were simply a nuisance. "This is Caribou loam," he said. "This soil was made for potatoes."

"That's true. And I want to leave it as good as I found it."

Between them it had long been understood that if Jules ever managed to finance a hundred acres of land and some machinery he would immediately strike out on his own. That was the independent Aroostook way. But Jules had six kids, no capital and no land. He was fifty-three years old, and unless the declining Maine potato industry staged a comeback soon he was unlikely ever to farm on his own.

By the time they returned to Austin's house, the moon was already casting shadows across the lawn. In Tucson Austin had dreamed of these moist eastern nights, heavy with oxygen and charged with the drone of tree frogs and insects. Jules leaned against the side of his truck, holding his protuberant Adam's apple between thumb and forefinger—a sure sign he wanted to talk.

"So what's it like out there?" he asked. "They raise any potatoes?"

"Not that I saw. It's too hot and dry and the soil's too alkaline. Scab would kill you."

"Doesn't sound like much of a place."

"Tucson's an oven—though right now they're having monsoons."

"Monsoons." Jules's tone of voice betrayed his instant suspicion of the word.

"It rains so hard the streets flood," Austin explained. "The whole city stops until the water runs off."

"So how about Fay? What's she think of it?"

Fay was the hidden backbone of the conversation and had been there from the start. "She likes it," Austin said, admitting no more than the obvious.

"Think she'll stay awhile?"

Jules was rarely so insistent. Austin opened the cab door and lifted his sleeping child onto one shoulder. "Awhile," he said. "At least awhile."

In fact, he didn't believe Fay would ever come back. Not to walk across the mown summer lawn, not to watch the trucks unload at harvest, not to stand under the hemlocks in winter while the snow fell.

On Saturday morning Austin drove over to the Northcountry Fair to meet with Margo Umphrey, whose seven-year-old son had invited Blake to spend the night. The two boys took the string of tickets Austin bought for them and headed for the nearest ride. Margo and Austin talked for ten minutes on the sunny midway without once mentioning Fay's name.

As he set out for the produce displays Austin felt lightheaded with freedom. After three weeks of steady child care he finally had some time to himself. He whistled his way over to the old wooden hall and found it filled, on the next-to-last day of the fair, with wilted flowers, soft-nosed squashes and sagging tomatoes. After five days on display even the medal winners looked like culls.

Except for the potatoes. Dozen of varieties and hundreds of farm entries were on display—though for the first time in years Pooler Farm was not represented. Last year Austin had won ribbons for seven different varieties: Katahdin, Belrus, Russet Burbank, Green Mountain, FL 657, Red Pontiac and Yankee Chipper. This year the application deadline had come and gone while he was living in a mobile-home park in Tucson, Arizona.

In the dusty potato wing of the exhibition hall the talk was all spuds. Austin visited with Frank Nutter from Caribou and Bill Thibodeau from Mars Hill. Either they hadn't heard about Fay's aberration, or they had nothing to say about it. Austin finally relaxed. Nothing in the world was more comforting than the repeated earthy details of potato talk.

Back on the midway he bought a dollar's worth of French fries, heavy with salt and oil, and ate them as he walked. He clocked his baseball pitch at sixty-eight miles an hour and shot one out of three with a basketball. At the House of Miracles he saw a five-legged calf, a pair of Siamese twins and a woman covered with hair from crown to heel. As far as he could tell, everything was authentic.

A barker took hold of his arm outside the burlesque tent. "Hey, mister, a fellow like you oughta take a look inside." The man dropped his voice. "Just three dollars for the hottest show this side of Bangor."

"This side of Bangor?" Austin laughed. "What have they got in Bangor?"

"We got completely naked girls inside, you'll think you're in Paris, France. You'll go home so charged up your wife won't know you."

"Sometimes she doesn't know me anyway."

"You can't go wrong for three bucks."

"You mean to tell me you've got a strip show going on in there at eleven-thirty in the morning?"

"Mister, I personally guarantee, out of my own pocket, if you don't see any pussy in there I'll refund your money. In fact, I'll double your money."

The tent smelled of hot canvas. Austin felt his way in through the dark, following a baffled entranceway. Underfoot the grass had all been trampled. Hanging from the peak of the tent's main room, a single light bulb illuminated a chest-high plywood stage. A portable stereo system, perched on a wooden carton, played Jerry Lee Lewis's "Great Balls of Fire," while two fat middle-aged women danced side by side in a pure state of nature. They made the plywood shake under their bare feet. Even at this hour of the morning a dozen men stood close around the stage, staring up at the women's abundant white flesh.

When the song ended one of the dancers leapt back in a stout pirouette and exited through a curtain. The second woman waited, expressionless, for the next song, staring over the men's heads. She wasn't that old, Austin saw, just fat. Indeed, she had quite a pretty face. When the music started she smiled briefly at the small audience and gave them a passable bump and grind.

At the end of the song she asked for a volunteer. "No, none a' you," she told the first few men to raise their hands. "You all look too horny. Give me an oldah fellow." Her accent was Portland, maybe Lewiston. She teased the little crowd, warming up to this part of the show. Still entirely in the buff, she knelt down on the stage in front of an old man in overalls. She lifted the eyeglasses off his bald head, hooked them over her own ears and said, "Theya now, that's much bettah. I can see much bettah with these speck-tacles." Her knees rested only inches from the old man's nose. "But you probbly can't see anythin' atall without them, can you? No touchin' now."

Once prompted, the old man lifted a tentative hand toward her legs. She slapped it down. "Oh, I've got a bad boy heah. I shouldah known bettah than to pick this one." She folded up his glasses and slid them along the inside of her legs, spreading her

knees wide and leaning back to expose herself. She rubbed the
lenses all over her sexual organs, then buffed them up on her
pubic hair and set them back on the old man's face. The audience
broke into a cheer. The woman stood up, gave a curtsy as if fully
dressed and walked off the stage. As she left, the barker entered.

"That's it, gentlemen, the best show this side of Bangor, the
hottest show this side of Gay Paree. We promised it and you've
seen it. Come back in thirty minutes and we'll have an all-new
program. Step right out now if you would, that's our show for this
hour."

Austin trailed the little group out into the sunlight, and with
only a couple of steps joined the crowd on the midway: women
with strollers, kids eating cotton candy, teenage girls clutching
each other's belt loops. Year after year this same stream of
fairgoers had passed within twenty feet of the burlesque tent and
never guessed what went on inside. Austin himself had never
guessed.

Climbing up into the almost-empty grandstand, he sat down
to watch the contest on the track below. Stump Daigle's boy was
rolling a loaded barrel of potatoes up a narrow plank onto the
back of a truck. It was an outdated skill made obsolete by
winches, automated harvesters and bulk loaders. In his youth
Austin had competed in this same contest, but more than a
decade had passed since the last time he rolled a full barrel of
spuds onto a flatbed.

Scarcely a minute behind him, Lauren Sorrell climbed up
the concrete aisle of the grandstand. Austin stood up to say
hello—but they didn't touch. He never knew if they should or
not. He hadn't seen her since the day he painted his potato house
purple.

She was smiling widely. "Guess where I just saw you come
from!" She laughed, pleased with her find.

"The exhibition hall?"

"No, the burlesque tent! Now what were you doing in a place
like that?"

"I'd never been in there before. The guy grabbed my arm."

"Oh, Austin."

"He twisted it. He made me go in. He said my education wasn't complete without it." Austin could never resist Lauren's broad smile. It made him laugh and tell jokes.

"And what did you see in there?"

"I don't think I can talk about it so early in the day. It wouldn't be right."

Lauren tapped him with her fist and laughed. "You guys are all the same." She sat down on the bench and pulled at Austin's shirt until he sat down beside her. She wore a sleeveless green blouse and a short white skirt, beneath which her thighs flattened out on the wooden bench. The poised column of her neck shone in the heat. "Charley goes every year, the brute. Afterward he tells me about it, but I never know if he's making it up. Do they really have naked women in there?"

"They sure do. There were two mother-naked women dancing on a little stage. Enormous women."

Lauren rested her palms on her skirt. Ever since the birth of her first child she had fought the battle of flesh. "I've got this new exercise machine," she said. "It's supposed to give me legs like Jane Fonda's, but I don't use it much. Luckily Charley never seems to mind."

"Charley is a prince among men."

"With the gut he's riding he better not complain."

Austin looked down at the sparse crowd. No one sat closer to them than forty feet. "Where is Charley?"

"He's around, you'll see him. I hear you two had a little argument over at your place."

Austin nodded. "I guess we're fated to argue."

"You are. You've been doing it since junior high when we all started kissing."

Lauren pinned her hands beneath her legs. The barrel-rolling comments of the announcer below took up the slack in their conversation.

"We'll never get past that history," Austin finally said. "Will we? I mean me and Charley."

"Nope, you never will. In my house it's like weather at a picnic. It's always there. Now tell me about Fay. Is she coming back?"

There it was, the question everyone wanted to ask. Lauren, of course, was the one who dared.

He told her the truth, that he didn't think Fay would ever return.

"So what are you going to do?" Lauren asked.

"I don't know. For now the same as usual—desiccate, tune up the harvesters, hire the crew and bring in the potatoes."

"And Blake?"

"I have him, at least for now. But Fay and I haven't settled that. We haven't talked about it yet."

At that moment Lauren's husband appeared at the bottom of the grandstand and climbed straight up toward them over the benches, his cowboy boots abrading the wooden planks.

"Home again, home again, Austin. How about it, did you bring your family back with you this time?"

Lauren stood up next to Charley, her hands on her hips. "Don't get into it," she told him.

"Blake came," Austin answered simply. "Fay's still in Tucson."

"One down and one to go. That's not too bad. Just keep fishin', you'll reel her in." Charley snapped his wrist as if casting a lure. At his office the walls were covered with pike and Atlantic salmon.

Austin stood up. "I don't keep Fay on a hook," he said.

"Obviously not."

"And the news I hear is that you're still buying Canadian potatoes and unloading them at your plant in the middle of the night."

Charley tucked his thumbs behind his big Starr Foods belt buckle. "For someone who's been out of the County all summer you're sure up on the gossip. Maybe Rose told you. Of course, I hear she's leaving too. A couple more years and you'll be the only Pooler in town."

"Shut up, Charley." Lauren wheeled on her husband. "You don't have the courtesy of a goat. Fay can come back whenever she's ready. And as for the plant," she told Austin, "it's closed down for a two-week cleanup. So the two of you see if you can't relax. Come on, let's go down, I'm hungry."

They sat on folding chairs in the Maine Potato Kitchen as Lauren ate a baked potato with sour cream. The noisy rides and music of the fair engulfed them.

"I hear you've got some late blight," Charley said.

"Shit, Charley, you don't know when to stop." She took hold of her plate as if she might throw it at him. In Aroostook County commenting on a grower's potato diseases was about as polite as asking how his herpes was coming along. Lauren dropped the rest of her potato in a trash barrel and stalked out into the midway.

"Come on, you two, we're going for a ride."

Austin did not want to go on any rides with Charley Stoddard. What was Lauren up to? Charley balked and she gave him a push. "Don't be so chicken," she told her husband. "Even little kids ride these things."

"You know I can't."

"Come on, Charley. Try it this once."

He followed them reluctantly to the Screaming Mimi but would not get on.

Lauren pulled her tickets out of a little clutch purse, motioned Austin forward and climbed into the cage behind him. A teenage attendant lowered a steel bar across their laps and closed the door. To see anything, Austin had to peer out through the holes stamped in the metal walls. The motor geared down and rotated the cages another notch and then another, lifting them above Charley's head.

"He'd puke his guts out in here," Lauren said. "I know he's jealous but he didn't have to be such a prick about Fay."

Inside the cage the floor was littered with food and gum wrappers, a couple of pennies and an earring. The steel bar that locked them into the seat smelled of metal and sweat, a bittersweet odor that clung to Austin's hands.

He wanted to take this crazy ride with Lauren. But now as always Charley made it hard for him to relax. Through the metal cage Austin could see a piece of his face staring up at them. It was ridiculous, because Austin had been friends with Lauren his whole life.

On the other hand it wasn't ridiculous, and Charley was right to worry about them.

They rose to the top of the circle. Lauren's short skirt rested in disarray over the muscles of her thighs. She tucked a foot behind Austin's ankle and said, "Sometimes Charley makes me so angry I could shoot him."

"Or he could shoot me."

"Hell, he can't see us, don't worry about it. Let's rock this thing."

She began to swing the cage like a kid on a playground swing. Below them the motor kicked into a steady rhythm, and they dropped down the back side of the circle. Sweeping through the bottom only inches from the loading platform, they caught sight of Charley as they went by. The wheel accelerated. Forward and back, they rocked their cage until it stood them on their heads. Finally they made their own turn, a circle within a circle. All around them people were screaming and laughing. Austin stopped worrying about nausea and Charley and what he was doing here, and put his hand on Lauren's knee.

They slowed and came to a stop at high noon, hidden from everyone. Lauren bent over and kissed him as naturally as if they were still in high school. During the cage-by-cage descent down the back side of the circle she straightened up her skirt and pulled out two more tickets from her purse.

The attendant didn't want to take them. "Sorry, you have to go through the line again."

She held the bar down and gave the boy a five-dollar bill. He stuffed it into his shirt pocket and closed the door.

Charley strode up to the board fence not ten feet away. He looked ready to protest, but turned and stomped off into the crowd instead.

Lauren bent forward, observing her husband with the cool curiosity of a dog confronting a toad. Then she leaned back against the cracked upholstery of the seat as the cage began its ascent.

"I'm going to pay for this," she said. "But I'll lie about it. You will also lie, Austin. If you don't I'll shoot you."

"I'll lie," he said, unsure about what.

The ride began again with girlish screams, the shriek of metal, a thundering lift and fall. The cage vibrated like a Model T and Lauren started laughing.

Twenty minutes later, after walking separately down the midway and out the main gate, they drove west out of town in her big yellow Fairlane with LAUREN plates. They passed corduroy potato fields, woodlots and meadows. Farther on there were farmhouses with battered tile roofs and slanting porches, and a string of abandoned fields grown up to goldenrod and thornplum. Ever since Austin was a boy, Maine potato acreage had been shrinking.

"The last time," she reminded him, "it was you who dragged me off."

"Sort of."

There were no cars on the road. He sat close to her, kissing the side of her mouth as she drove. He put his hands on her breasts. After years in which they had barely shaken hands, the ancient vein had opened between them.

At her parents' camp on Bear Lake she spread a pair of quilts on the floor and opened the windows to the water. The miniature cottage was surrounded by birches and white cedar, and the odor of balsam hung in the blue air. Austin held her from behind, his hands lifting her breasts.

"Charley made me angry with all that talk about Fay," she said. "But that wasn't the only reason. I wanted to see you."

Austin felt his history had been broken into little shards. He didn't know what to think of this sporadic, decades-long adultery with one of his oldest friends.

She rolled away from him and knelt to undress. A few strands of gray had shown up in her hair. They made love so infrequently that between each time they aged perceptibly. Lauren pulled off her white Sears underpants and tossed them into the corner. She laughed, showing her wide front teeth. *"Now,"* she said. "I've been wet for an hour."

"No more kissing? No making out?"

"Now," she laughed.

He teased her, brushing her vagina as if by accident with the back of his hand.

"Austin, don't be cruel."

"To a heart that's true?"

"It is," she whispered. "It's true. Come. Come all the way in. Now kiss me and talk to me."

Austin's wife rarely spoke in the midst of sex. Once aroused, Fay disappeared into an aching private silence, sometimes coming and sometimes not. Lauren, in contrast, came noisily and almost at will. She liked to be entered at the start and then, after the first flush of passion, to talk with Austin inside her—with Tab A, as she had once said, fully inserted in Slot B.

"Don't come," she said.

"I won't."

"I've had something to tell you for years and years, ever since the last time we did this. I should have said it then."

He knew what it was.

"I love you, Austin. I'll always love you. Sssshh, I'm not going to come between you and Fay. You have your family and I have mine. And I'm not going to give mine up. You know that."

He worked her with the measured cadence of an oarsman, stroke and stroke. Her hips rose off the floor, then the small of her back.

"Don't come," she said again. He paused and let her down onto the quilts. Her full breasts rose and fell as she caught her breath. The afternoon was hot for Maine, and the sunlight fell across their calves. Gently, like a retriever with a bird, he took her neck in his teeth. She spread her hips wide apart, opening herself to him completely. She was as wet as an otter.

"Tell me about Fay."

"No, I don't want to."

"You do. And I want you to. What if you leave White Pine and I never see you again?"

"I can't leave my farm," he said. The subject of Fay, introduced at such a moment, had brought him to the edge of tears. "It's hopeless."

"And she won't come back?"

"I don't think so. She swears she won't. And how could I live here without her? What would Blake do?"

Lauren's hair had fallen onto her shoulders. They lay face to face in the hot afternoon, a film of moisture between their chests. From the lake came the slap of tiny waves. Miracle of August, there were no flies or mosquitoes.

"If you ever left it might be easier for me," she said. "I wouldn't think of *this* every time I saw you. But I don't want you to go. I can't imagine not running into you at the supermarket or the post office with that sweet boy of yours hanging around your neck."

"Telling me every five minutes he wants to go," Austin said.

Lauren shook beneath him, as if from a chill. "I could give this up," she said. "Year after year I always think we have. But I never want you to go away."

Imperceptibly she slid from speech to tears. Her face was wet, her chest was wet, her cunt drenched. He could no longer distinguish her flesh from his own, and he understood less than ever what sex meant to this friendship.

"I love you," he told her.

He hadn't said those words to her in almost twenty-five years, yet they fell from his lips without effort. They rolled down over her neck and shoulders like a liquid. He anointed her with them, whispering them over and over. Beneath him she had started to hum.

Lauren showered in the tiny wood-paneled stall next to the bathroom and came back chilled and white, for there was no hot water. "We're going to lie," she said again, patting herself down with a towel. Already she had a distant look. Austin knew what it was: the thought of her husband and their two teenage children still at the fair.

"You were upset about Fay and you needed to talk," she said. "The fair was too noisy so we drove out to the reservoir and took a long walk. We never even held hands. Right?"

"Right."

"He'll never ask you, but just in case."

She did sixty miles an hour on the curving two-lane road back to town, and barely spoke. Sometime in their past he had probably been the one to act this way, Austin thought. But tonight, as she hurried back to Charley to soothe the waters, his feelings for her were on the rise.

She parked on a side street in the last light of dusk. "You aren't going back into the fair, are you?"

"I guess not," he said.

"I'm sorry, Austin. I hate to be this way, but it's going to be a lot harder on me than it is on you. Believe me, I'm going to pay for this."

They parted as they had met, without a touch. Austin stood to one side of the entrance gate with his hands on the chain-link fence and watched her go. In an instant she disappeared into the crowd.

He was unhappy. Everything about the fair looked stupid now. Half of it was just a traveling carnival anyway, run by the Scolo Brothers of Worcester, Mass. The name was on every truck and trailer. Inside the fence electric cables snaked from one camper to another, laundry hung from makeshift lines and two men ate quietly at a card table, oblivious to the noise from the midway. Next Saturday they'd be working a new crowd in Houlton or Waterville.

At the far corner of the fairgrounds Austin turned north across an abandoned field. More than a decade had passed since potatoes had last been grown here, yet he could still make out the furrows beneath his shoes.

Brushing some young box elders away from the fence, he peered in at the cattle barns and livestock pens. This was an old part of the fair, one that had nothing to do with tractor pulls or out-of-state amusement companies. Nothing had changed here since Austin was a boy: not the barns, not the water spigots at the end of each set of stalls, not the bare light bulbs shining under their dented steel shades. Teenagers moved from stall to stall carrying buckets of water, replacing soiled bedding with new hay and calling out to each other through the darkness.

Austin continued along the fence until he discovered the exact grassy spot he was looking for. There, behind the last barn, on the Saturday night of fair week exactly twenty-five years ago, he and Lauren had made love on a blanket. Lauren liked the danger. As people walked among the lighted stalls not sixty feet away, she raised her skirt and lowered her underpants in a single smooth gesture. Austin dropped to his knees beside her, his jeans around his ankles and his white backside exposed.

Afterward he had buried his drooping rubber under a clump of grass and stuffed Lauren's panties into his back pocket. She did without them the rest of the night—teasing him when they ran into friends by swirling her skirt.

They were barely eighteen. Lauren had fine chestnut hair, long legs and a famous chest. She was the Ford dealer's daughter, the Potato Blossom Queen and the editor of the high-school yearbook. Everyone knew, long before that night at the fair, that she and Austin were lovers. Indeed, all spring and summer they had kissed their way through White Pine in full public view, electrifying the town. They had what everyone wanted.

And now, a quarter of a century later, Austin wanted that girl back. He clutched the chain-link fence and said her name out loud: "Lauren Sorrell." But she was far away. She had vanished into the fair's bright lights, looking for an angry husband and two children.

He had loved her. He'd been an idiot to let her go. Maybe all these years Fay was the wrong woman—the one destined to abandon White Pine for some distant city. Lauren would never have needed to do that. But now, like Austin himself, she lay buried under the inescapable fact of a twenty-year marriage.

He ran back across the field, dodged the traffic on Grant Street and sprinted the last two hundred yards to his truck. He drove west out of town, out past velvet fields and potato-storage houses as squat and dark as bricks. For the second time that day he drove past the valley's westernmost fields into the Big Woods. At the village of Malling he turned south toward the state park at Squamac.

In his lifetime Austin had probably climbed Mount Squamac a dozen times, but never at night. The park gate was open, the ranger's house dark and still. Austin left his truck by Squamac Pond, took his six-cell flashlight and set off up the narrow canopied trail. He climbed hard, flashing the beam uphill through the wholly black night.

Halfway to the top he surprised an antlered buck on the trail before him. It froze briefly in the posture of a god, then leapt away into the darkness in four ethereal arcs.

Twenty minutes later the path leveled out onto a rock escarpment and the sky grew lighter. The trees were scraggly; at the very top of the mountain they grew no higher than two or three feet. The black land below rolled away to the east, north and west, sporadically embossed by the greenish imprint of mercury-vapor lamps. Though White Pine lay hidden from sight, the powerful track lights at the fair were reflected in the clouds above. Bear Lake, where Austin had gone with Lauren, lay due north. To the west there was nothing but the Allagash and Saint John rivers, and a hundred miles of untenanted forest.

He reached the granite top of the mountain and sat down, looking out over the countryside he had known since birth. To the east the secret tubers lay thick in the soil. To the west the trees grew faster than they could be lumbered.

From far down on the flank of the hill a Canada lynx gave two long shrieks, raising the hair on the back of Austin's neck. And only a minute later, in complete contrast, the tremolo call of a loon floated up from Squamac Pond. Lynx, loon, buck, pine forest and potato fields: these were the indispensable elements of Austin's world. He might leave them behind for a while to walk through the Arizona desert or swim in the Mexican sea, but his home was Aroostook County. He had to live here.

A big Mayflower van stood in Rose's drive surrounded by packing blankets and cardboard boxes. Jack Dossett's new car rested by the curb: a cream-colored, leather-upholstered Lincoln Continental as out of place in White Pine as quiche Lorraine at a potluck. Its New York license plates were framed by the inscription DOSSETT POTATOES—LONG ISLAND'S OWN.

As Austin approached the house Dossett himself pushed open the front door and stepped out onto the lawn. He wore a flannel shirt, gray Dickie workpants and a pair of delicate little shoes designed, perhaps, for dancing. For hard floors anyway, because the soles had been cleverly tucked away under the pebbled black uppers. Dossett's gut kept his shiny belt turgid.

Rose came out as well, wearing a pastel blue dress and a pair of running shoes the same color. After embracing her son she slid her arm through Dossett's. If she had anything to say she didn't seem pressed to start.

"So that's it," Austin said. "You just put everything in a truck and go. Are you really selling the house?"

Rose nodded. She had told him as much over the phone.

"I'm building a new house for us," Jack said. "From downstairs you see the potato fields and from upstairs the ocean. How's your crop doing, Austin?"

"So far so good. If the weather holds we might have a record year."

"Of course, big yields send the price down."

"Tell me the truth," Austin said. "How much do you worry about potato prices?"

Dossett laughed. "Not much. Sometimes I think about you and your friends up here in the County."

Dossett was a satisfied wealthy man who did and said what he pleased. No one intimidated him: no surly gas-station attendant, no fancy *maître d'*, no secretary of agriculture. He had grown up poor and come into his fortune only within the last twenty years—but since his money had the grace to come from the land he regarded it as old money. Anyone who took exception to that view was likely to find himself backed into a corner and subjected to a fervent discourse on soil, sustenance and the nature of true wealth.

With her arm linked in his, and apparently without a second thought, Rose was now ready to move away from White Pine and take up Dossett's life in the fashionable Hamptons. She crossed one ankle over the other and leaned against her new man. Her unfocused look and acquiescent stance betrayed a sexuality Austin might have expected in a seventeen-year-old girl. The image suddenly came to him of Dossett's full naked belly spread out over Rose's midriff, his buttocks pumping rhythmically from above.

He shook himself and looked away. He couldn't think things like that about his mother. But since the last time he saw Rose her hair had grown longer, her eyebrows had filled out and her face looked smooth and relaxed. All that, apparently, from sleeping with Jack Dossett, the old pork belly. What else could have brought about such a change? Austin tried out the words in silence: My mother's getting laid. My mother's getting laid and she likes it.

At the same time that Austin had been left by Fay, Rose had joined Dossett's ascendant path. Nothing lifted one up or cast one down in life as quickly as winning or losing a mate.

Rose finally stirred and asked him if he'd heard anything new from Fay.

"She doesn't want to live here any more than you do," he said.

"Austin, don't pout." She stood directly in front of him. "I've lived my whole adult life in this town and now I'm moving to where Jack lives. Forty-five years ago I did the same thing for your father."

Austin had never noticed before how Dossett's whole front stuck out. It wasn't just his gut but his chest as well. He was a healthy old bugger. Rose was probably lucky to get him.

"When the ship starts sinking," Austin said, "I guess it's women and children first."

In the long pause that followed, Dossett took advantage of his chance to slip away. "I better check up on those movers," he said, and high-stepped it across the wet lawn.

Austin watched him go. "Tactful, ain't he?"

Rose pointed her finger at her son's chest. "You can sing the blues and moan all you want about Fay, but don't start in on Jack. You should be glad I found him."

"Yeah, I should. I guess I am." He took her arm and they headed for the sidewalk.

"You don't think Fay could get tired of being alone," she said, "and come back?"

"I don't think so."

Rose bounced along the sidewalk, the rise and fall in her step exaggerated by her connection to Austin's arm. He slowed down for her. They passed through sunlight and shade, through the green heart of summer. With her free hand Rose patted the bun of her long white hair. "Jack likes it this way," she said. "I'm not going to cut it."

"You never were, were you?"

"Don't be so jumpy, Austin. You make out like everything I do is treason."

"Sorry. I start thinking about Fay and I can't see anything straight."

"I know it's awkward for me to go off with another man. But it doesn't mean I've forgotten about your father."

"Of course not. I never thought you should wear black or anything. I just hate to see you leave town so fast."

"Five years is not so fast."

They walked another block in silence. Frank Whisby came by with his dog, both man and animal suffering from arthritis. Elizabeth Goss waved from her front porch, her dentures in her lap. The noonday residents.

"And out there in Tucson," Rose asked, "how were you two getting along . . . in bed?"

"Pretty good," Austin said after a moment. He was embarrassed. The last time he had talked about sex with his mother was the summer after high school when she asked him if he was being careful not to get Lauren Sorrell pregnant. "Fay and I still sleep together if that's what you mean. Not all that often, but some."

Rose sighed, a kind of soft breathing hiccup. "Maybe I shouldn't say this . . . but Jack and I have a wonderful time in bed. I don't think I ever knew what it could be like. Of course, I was never unfaithful to your father in all our days. But this is something new to me."

The idea made Austin's neck prickle. He thought the role of sex in marriage was altogether vital—but he didn't want to imagine his mother naked again, lying under the chesty Jack Dossett. He didn't want to figure out if what she was telling him was that for the first time in her life she was having orgasms. Fine, his mother could have orgasms. But he didn't want to think about them.

"What if you were in my position?" he asked. "What would you do?"

"I'm not in your position," Rose said. "I'm not a man, I'm not a Pooler and I'm not that crazy about potatoes. But if it were up to me I wouldn't let a wife just float away. I'd think about going to Arizona."

"It's desert. I could never grow potatoes there."

"Then take a break from farming. You've got enough money."

"It's not just the money."

"No," Rose agreed, "it's not. It's your work, I know. But on the other hand, think about your marriage. And about sex."

It was remarkable how easily his mother now brought up this topic. Her whole personality had been refurbished down at Dossett Estates.

"So for the sake of fucking," he said, "I have to give up everything else?"

Rose disengaged her arm from his. They rounded a block and headed home in silence. Approaching the house, she had her final say on the matter. "You're lucky to still have a choice about it. That might not last forever."

Austin pumped a couple of dollars of gas at the Short Stop—enough to get him back to the farm where he had his own tanks—and picked up one of the women's magazines displayed next to the register. The title story read, "A Lifetime in the Kitchen: Experts Say It's Worth a Million."

Goddamn, a lifetime in the kitchen. What garbage. He opened the magazine and skimmed the table of contents: "Is One Man Enough?" "It's Your Money—You Decide." "Let Him Wash the Dishes—He'll Love You for It in the End."

Austin tipped the magazine back into the stand and took off for home. What the hell did washing dishes have to do with a marriage anyway? For twenty years he and Fay had passed the job back and forth without argument or fuss. Often the one who didn't cook washed—but not always, for their kitchen styles were diametrical. When Fay prepared an elaborate meal she abandoned her dirty bowls and pans as if she were Julia Child on TV. Austin cleaned up everything as he went along—though, as Fay pointed out, his meals often amounted to little more than elaborately garnished potatoes. In any case, if the dishes sometimes lay in the sink overnight no one threw a fit about it. Every year during harvest they ate off paper plates for almost a month.

Sink politics—it was ridiculous. A marriage was sex and children and work and common courtesy. When Fay came in cold and exhausted after a three-hour teachers' meeting Austin ran her a bath. When he stayed out planting until midnight she left him a dinner in the oven wrapped in tinfoil. And if she didn't he wolfed down some bread and cheese and a head of Bibb lettuce, and crawled softly into bed so as not to wake her.

Though the dishes argument had never gotten a toehold at Pooler Farm, the word was out in ten thousand convenience stores around the country that men had anchored women to a degraded life.

Austin drove home pissed. He should have gone on to his next job—replacing a dead starter on one of the bulk trucks—but instead walked out into the nearest field. Slowly, amid forty acres of robust and healthy Kennebecs, his composure returned.

In a woodlot at the far end of the field Austin started a doe and her half-grown fawn. Side by side they bounded into the open from beneath a stand of tamaracks and fled cross-row to the top of the ridge. Among the trees Austin found where the deer had been lying, on a matted circle of grass and leaves still warm to the touch.

Though he had often stumbled across such evidence of nesting deer he had yet to see one actually curled up on the ground, for at the first scent of man or dog they fled. They rested here one night and there the next, almost as homeless as fish.

Year after year Austin had dismissed half the events of the world as the sad consequence of people who had no home. The turmoil of the Middle East was mostly homelessness. The governments of Central and South America, having cut their people off from the land, were now paying the price in chaos and revolution.

Austin wanted his son to grow up in the same yellow house he had grown up in himself, on the same farmland the Poolers had worked for almost a hundred years. But Fay was pulling their lives apart like wet newsprint. Choose between the two, she said: either your family or your land. Sitting under the tamaracks where the deer had lain, Austin tried to imagine making such a decision. He couldn't.

On the Sunday of Labor Day weekend, shortly before starting her second year at RISD, Maggie flew home to White Pine. She got off the plane wearing a man's shirt, a blue bandanna and a pair of baggy white shorts. First she hugged her father, then picked her brother up by the waist. Angling toward the grass next to the runway, she began to spin Blake around and around.

"Say uncle!" she cried.

Blake only laughed. He relaxed in her arms, letting his neck hang back.

"Say *uncle!*"

"I can't be beat!" he said. "I've never been beat!" He laughed through ten wild circles with a madman's high-pitched laugh. "I always win! It's a family tradition!"

He was right, for Maggie always got dizzy first. Even when Blake had been small enough for her to swing him by the feet he could always walk a straighter line afterward. And now, by pacing out onto the runway and slapping down his sneakers with the precision of a London bobby, he proved it was still so.

Maggie collapsed. "Oh God, why do I do it?" Nausea played over her face as she lay on the grass. A few passengers smiled as they passed by. The Poolers were renowned. No one would have thought it strange if they had played this game in front of the courthouse at midnight.

"I'm the king of the spin!" Blake said. He ran over to his sister, slid up against her like Carl Yastrzemski going into second and tumbled onto her chest.

"*Blake,* take it easy. I'm a girl."

"So what?"

"So I'm tender in places."

"She's gonna puke, Dad. She's sick from spinning!"

"I am not. Poolers don't puke. It's a family tradition. Not from spinning around anyway. Come on, get up."

Blake clung to her neck as she sat up. Even when she stood he wouldn't let go of her. He said, "Maggie, Maggie, your pants are baggy. Did you ride a lot of horses?"

"Blake, Blake, you made a mistake. I did something lazy boys like you don't know anything about. I worked. I waited tables."

"I'm not lazy. This year I'm going to work on the harvester. You waited for tables?"

"I waited *on* tables. I was a waitress in a big hotel. I had to wear cowboy skirts and a big hat."

"You mean cowboys wear skirts?"

"Give me that head, you little wildman. How long has it been since you had a nuggie rub?"

Austin watched his children tussle. Maggie looked like her mother. She could almost have been Fay twenty years ago. Her hair shone with youth, her smooth brown shins reflected the sunlight, even her knee-length shorts looked like the ones Fay had worn at Wellesley. It hardly seemed possible to him that Fay when he had first met her was only a year older than Maggie was now. A quiver swept down his back. He felt as if he were dropping through time, like a coin through the ocean.

They drove home past clapboard barns and sheds, old houses proudly kept and acre after acre of flat potato land. The mailboxes along the road were mounted on antique plows or links of welded iron chain. They bore some of the oldest potato names in the County: Umphrey, Daigle, Pelletier, Hedstrom, Bugbee. Such families never sold their land.

"You ever going to get rid of this old bucket, Dad?" Maggie sat by the passenger window, floating her right hand in the wind. "Every year the same old truck. In Wyoming they'd have retired this thing to a museum by now."

"Sure, because they don't have any history out there."

"And that old checked shirt. Don't you want to buy some new clothes?"

"Not really. This shirt's almost as old as you are. Of course, I only wear it on Sundays."

"And you've got your same old haircut."

"And the same big ears," Austin said. "And the same old farmhouse and the same old farm."

"Ay-yuh." Maggie gave her downstate imitation.

"I'd just like to hold on to the same old family."

She looked away and for the rest of the trip home gave her attention to Blake. He held hands with her, played with her hair and all but climbed out of his seat belt into her lap. At the farm he led her off to look at his treasures: a six-foot snakeskin hanging from the barn rafters, the remains of a dead owl and his latest fort under the hemlocks. When the two of them returned to the house an hour later their eyes were dark.

While Austin cooked dinner his children played and talked in the next room. Eventually he heard their muffled laughter. He envied them their secrets and covenants, their blood-relatedness. The eleven-year difference in their ages meant nothing, for everything between them was a game. Maggie, Maggie, your pants are baggy. Blake, Blake, you made a mistake.

After dinner they played Chinese checkers in the living room. Blake's contact with his sister was careless and unceasing. He hugged her neck and draped himself across her lap. Austin wanted to hug his daughter as well but didn't know if he should. In the last year their embraces had become less and less frequent.

Year after year, he thought, you raised a daughter without ever thinking of separation. She was a child, she ran in and out of your arms as simply as a screen door opening and closing. You knew everything about her: her friends, her classmates, her resentments, her ambitions. All through high school you stayed close—but when she went off to college you had to guess at the news or pry it out in little pieces.

And now Austin found it harder than ever, because of how much Maggie looked and moved and talked like her mother. If Fay had been with them he could have taken his daughter in his arms and swung her around the living room the same as always. But without Fay that seemed perilous. Maggie felt it too, he was sure. The distance between them was more than just that of a girl gone off to college.

After checkers Maggie read her brother a bedtime story. She didn't come down for almost an hour, by which time Austin already had his hands full of potato peelings and celery stalks, making the big new-potato salad he fixed every year for the Aroostook Grower's Labor Day picnic. Maggie joined him at the kitchen table.

"Did you hear from Tom out there?" Austin asked.

"We wrote a few letters."

"Is that all? I thought you two were pretty close."

"Dad, you're not going fuddy on me, are you? I *told* you what we'd agreed on for the summer."

"I think your term was 'open range.' That sounded pretty relaxed."

"Not everyone worries about me as much as you do," Maggie said.

Austin and his daughter sat face to face at the kitchen table, cutting up the new, almost skinless potatoes. "I just like to keep up," he said.

"I'm not holding back anything. Do you want to know who I went out with this summer?"

"Of course not." Though he did.

"Times have changed," Maggie said. "I'm not going to get married when I'm nineteen—not to Tom or anyone else. I might not get married until I'm thirty."

"I married your mother when she was twenty-two."

"Maybe that was too young. Look where she is now."

Austin laid down his knife.

"Oh, Dad, I'm sorry." She came around the table and stood beside him, holding his arm.

He had meant to keep away from the topic of his marriage, but now that it had risen into the conversation he let it come. "Out of the entire USA," he said, "she has to get interested in the desert."

"That's what she wrote me about this summer—all about plants and ecology."

Austin waited for her to say something else, but she didn't. She simply stood beside him with one hand on his arm and the other on his shoulder. Though not quite an embrace, it was enough for him to let go of the feeling that she too was leaving him.

Ten days before the onslaught of harvest the Aroostook Growers held their annual Labor Day picnic in the Veterans' Park in White Pine. This gathering marked both the end of summer and the start of an absolute hiatus in the town's social life—because from early September until the close of harvest no one in White Pine scheduled conferences, parties, potlucks or any other community events. At the start of harvest the public schools, which had opened in August, closed again for a month.

On Labor Day morning, under a sky as blue as cloth, Austin drove into the park in town. Growers from up and down the valley stood in small groups beside the Aroostook River, talking about fungicides and desiccants, prices and politics. This year everyone was angry at the Canadians. Mel Bennett sat behind a card table selling buttons and bumper stickers with the message NO FREE TRADE WITHOUT FAIR TRADE.

As Austin helped set up the food tables, three different friends came by to ask if he knew what Charley Stoddard was up to over at Starr Foods. Lauren was at the picnic, though Austin had yet to catch her eye. Charley was there too, walking around in his cowboy boots and jeans, joking with one group after another.

"Why don't you ask Charley himself," Austin suggested to old Henry Miles. "He might tell you straight out. Maybe there's nothing he's ashamed of. He doesn't act like there is."

"I might do that," Henry said. But in the next thirty minutes he never went near Charley Stoddard. Most likely Henry had a Starr contract he could not afford to endanger. It was the Aroostook way: don't stick your neck out.

No one stuck his neck out about Fay either. At least not to Austin. Perhaps they feared a ruinous story, but no one so much as mentioned her name.

After hamburgers, hot dogs and potato salad the men got together for a couple of softball games. Austin asked Maggie to join his team; she had played third base in high school and could hit either fast pitch or slow. But she refused to be the only woman on the field. It made Austin sad. He knew she could outrun and outfield half the men there. Some of the older guys, rounding the bases, puffed as hard as the old steam engines on the Bangor & Aroostook line.

Austin left the game himself when Rose showed up for a final good-bye. She got out of Jack's cream-colored Continental and leaned against the side of the car, her back to the picnic. "We just drove out to the farm to have a last look," she said.

"Mother, don't tell me you're going nostalgic on me at the last minute."

Jack stood beside her, still wearing his dapper city shoes with the recessed soles. "You've got some beautiful land, Austin. I can understand why you don't want to give it up."

"We didn't go into the house," Rose said. "I didn't want to do that. But I walked out around the barn. You know I always loved that field. I used to watch the sun come up over the potato plants there."

Austin took her arm. He tried to imagine if the time would ever come for him to make a last visit to Pooler Farm and then vanish. South, of course, where everyone went.

Blake and Maggie came over to the parking lot to say good-bye. And after embracing her grandmother Maggie leaned against the car and put her arm around Austin's waist and they held each other. It was simple. There was no awkwardness, or any danger. Austin inclined his cheek against her head.

Rose knelt and had a few private words with Blake. She gave something to him, which he glanced at and stuck into his pocket. Then she stood up, called Maggie to her and asked the girl to hold out her hand. She pulled off her wedding and engagement rings and laid them in her granddaughter's palm.

"I know you don't think about this now," Rose said, "but someday you might. And it's a gift with no strings. If you ever go wild and pawn the diamond I won't get angry—though the wedding ring should stay in the family. It's inscribed."

Maggie held up the ring and turned it as she read the tiny inscription: TO ROSE FROM WILLIAM, LOVE FOREVER.

"Sometimes love does last forever," Rose said. "Now I'm going to get into the car so I don't start crying." She sat inside on the spacious leather seat, holding hands through the open window with her embarrassed grandchildren.

Jack took Austin's arm and the two men half embraced. Dossett spoke in an undertone, his back to Rose and the children.

"You're looking at a hell of a choice, Austin. I'd never want to leave my land either. But if you and Fay ever need a place to stay I own a couple of houses on the beach. Bunch of cokeheads in one of them—I could boot 'em in a minute."

"I can't imagine . . ."

"Just in case." He clapped Austin on the back and slid behind the wheel. Austin walked around the car and kissed his mother good-bye. Then she and Dossett drove off, headed south on Route 1.

NINE

Under a flat meringue light Tucson sweltered through afternoon temperatures of well over 100 degrees. The feathered branches of tamarisks, acacias and little-leaf palo verdes hung motionless in the still air, casting a languid shade on the walkways of the university. But shade was little defense against the heat, so until sundown most people kept to the air-conditioned buildings and cars.

Except Fay Hallwick, who stepped out of the University Library and slapped across the campus in a pair of blue flip-flops. After only a month in the Southwest her brown hair had been streaked blond by the desert sun, and the lines around her eyes had deepened. From a distance Fay still looked twenty-five, and even up close polite men guessed she was in her mid-thirties. She was forty-two. But in recent months—ever since leaving her home in Maine—she had taken to rounding off her age to the nearest decade.

Turning the corner on a hedge of spiny ocotillos she came face to face with another traveler in sandals and dark glasses. It was Skip Wilson, bare-chested and tanned, his white tee-shirt slung over one shoulder. He surprised her once again with the two cardinal facts of his appearance: he was extraordinarily handsome and only 5′4″ tall. He had the hairless chest of an adolescent. He shook hands with her and called her Mrs. Pooler.

"Fay, please. And it's Fay Hallwick. I'm still married, but I'm taking back my own name."

"Fay Hallwick," he repeated, as if fixing the name in his memory. When they had first met—at Carlsbad Caverns and on the way to Chaco—he hadn't called her anything.

"Austin and Blake went back to Maine. I'm living in a trailer park."

"So you're going to stay in Arizona?" he asked. His dark hair shone in the sunlight. It looked hot enough to kindle a fire.

"I think so. I'm still getting used to the heat."

Skip didn't say anything. It unnerved Fay how long he stood in front of her without saying a word, his hands in the back pockets of his shorts. Finally she asked him if he'd like to join her for dinner.

Compared to Skip, Fay led a stable accountable life. She owned a Winnebago camper parked off East Speedway, a little pickup truck she drove around town in, a refrigerator stocked with food and an adequate supply of clothes, books and tapes. Skip slept on the couch of a friend's apartment and owned no more than what fit inside his knapsack. Yet Fay thought of Skip's life as perfectly reasonable and her own as capricious. The difference was their ages.

In the parched miniature kitchen of the Winnebago she prepared a cool supper of tomato slabs on a bed of lettuce, along with two bowls of cold gazpacho soup bought the day before at a deli. Skip waited outside under a palm tree, reading a book. He read the way Blake did, completely absorbed, and never looked up until she emerged from the camper with their dinner.

They balanced the plates on their laps. Fay wondered what her neighbors thought about her and Skip, eating outside in the heat. From the roof of every camper and mobile home except hers, Duo-Therm air conditioners droned like giant locusts.

"So how do you do this hitchhiking?" she asked. "You just stick out your thumb and off you go?"

"Sometimes. Sometimes nobody stops."

"What if you get stuck in the desert?"

"I always take water, my sleeping bag and a little tent. If I get stuck somewhere I make camp and wait it out."

Beyond the Italian cypresses that lined the park the sun was turning the western clouds a deep rose. Fay set her tin plate on the ground next to her chair. "In my whole life," she said, "I've never hitchhiked anywhere. In fact, I've hardly ever picked up a hitchhiker."

"You picked me up."

"But we'd already met."

"Which is one way to get rides—by meeting people. In fact, that's why I like it. It's not just getting from one town to another."

Fay stepped into the camper and brought back a couple of beers. "Twenty years ago," she said, "I married someone who always knew exactly what he wanted to do. Austin's a good man but he's not too big on adventure."

Since running into her at the university Skip had not once mentioned Austin's name or asked about Blake. He set his plate on the ground, picked up his beer and rested it on his knee. "But you came out to the Southwest. That's an adventure, isn't it?"

"It's a start."

He opened his beer with a focused careful pry of the metal tab, making Fay wonder if he had ever drunk one before. He took a sip and set the can on the ground. He asked her, "How'd you like to make a little trip the way I travel? We could hitch up North where it's cooler. With you along we'd get plenty of rides."

Two days later Fay drove her pickup over to Skip's house on Yavapai Road. She had Blake's sleeping bag, and Skip had borrowed an old knapsack for her. They took a bus to the end of the line on Oracle and started hitching.

At eight in the morning the temperature had yet to reach 90 degrees. Fay stood behind Skip on the road's wide asphalt shoulder, her thumb cocked up at the same angle as his. She felt ridiculous.

"All commuter traffic," Skip said. "We need a traveler." A steady stream of cars passed by at speed.

Though he had repeated to her that hitching would be easy with her along, no one picked them up. Fay was in an agony of embarrassment. She felt too old to be doing this. Someone, she hoped, would pick them up and carry them away from town into the desert, where she would feel more relaxed.

"Look them straight in the eyes," Skip said. She did, but no one looked back. Another hundred cars went by, and nothing.

"I can't believe it," she said. "All these people."

"It might be the wrong place or the wrong time. Let's walk up to that doughnut shop and get something to eat."

They set their knapsacks down inside the door and ordered doughnuts and coffee. Skip swung left and right on his leather-topped stool, clearly enjoying himself. "We didn't get very far before our first meal," he laughed.

Both of them were dressed in shorts and running shoes. Skip wore a baseball cap against the sun and Fay a round straw hat. She thought everyone must be looking at them, but she didn't survey the booths and the other customers the way Skip did. So afterward, back on the road, she didn't know who Skip was talking about when he said, "This guy'll pick us up."

A tan late-model Ford accelerated out of the doughnut shop's parking lot, swept across the highway and stopped ten yards in front of them. Skip opened the front door for Fay, threw the two knapsacks in the back seat and jumped in after them.

"Where you kids headed?" the driver asked. He was over-weight but no older than Fay. He wore a pair of brown-and-white cowboy boots and tan slacks the color of his car.

Fay hesitated, hoping Skip would answer from the back seat. When he didn't, she said, "To Gallup." In fact, they didn't have a destination, they were just headed north.

"You ought to go over to that San Carlos Lake. You could take a swim and cool off. I'd drive you up there myself if I wasn't turnin' off to Florence. A day like this, about all I can think of is water—but it's work, work, work and no time for fun."

He was probably a salesman, Fay thought. For a metal door and window company it turned out. He souped up the car's air-conditioning, which blasted out of the console vents across

Fay's bare legs. She froze in silence until he asked, "Got some goose bumps there? Want me to turn this down?"

He didn't seem to notice the difference in her and Skip's ages. He talked so much it was hard to tell what he noticed. "Great country out here," he said. "Though I'm from Missourah, where ever'thing is green. The only thing green out here is money, but there's plenty of that, thank God. Tucson's gettin' big. Real big, maybe too big. But you want to make a little money here you start buyin' and sellin' house lots. Real estate—that's the action in this town. Where'd you two meet up?"

"Traveling," Fay said.

"Is that right? Must be nice. Someday I'm going to take off and travel around like that myself. Get me a little boat and go up to Lake Powell."

On his left hand he wore a wedding ring a quarter of an inch wide. "Do you have any children?" Fay asked him.

"Sure, got two little girls under five, cute as cactus. Tear the house apart and pull your eyes out." He laughed and looked across at Fay. "How about you?"

"I've got a grown daughter and a boy of eight."

He talked about business for a while: thank God for the cheap labor around here; and then about the desert heat: thank God for air-conditioning. He was polite up to the very end of the ride, when he reached across the front seat and patted Fay's leg. "Don't you two get in any trouble now. I wouldn't want to read about you at the checkout stand."

Too cold to be angry, Fay jumped out of the frigid car and watched as the salesman drove away. By now they were far from town at an empty intersection in barren country. A couple of cars sped by as Fay started into the scrub, her knapsack over one shoulder. "I froze that whole ride," she said. "I'm going to change into some long pants."

Skip looked the other way as Fay stood behind a sparse pair of four-wing saltbushes. When the road looked empty she dropped her shorts and struggled into a pair of corduroys.

The cars here went by at sixty, seventy, eighty miles an hour. Most of the drivers looked straight ahead as they flashed past, though some glanced over and one even waved. After a while Fay relaxed. She stood behind Skip and stuck out her thumb, but she didn't much care if they got a ride. She liked it where they were.

Twenty minutes later a big pickup with double rear wheels and a bed hitch pulled to a stop in front of them and backed up. They threw their knapsacks in back and this time Skip jumped in next to the driver. He was straight cowboy, born and raised in Tulsa, not much of a talker. He hardly looked old enough to drive, but he was on his way to pick up a trailer and two horses on the other side of Winkelman. Skip got a few sentences out of him about the weather and a couple about hunting bighorn sheep. A rifle hung on the window rack behind them. Twice the cowboy stared past Skip at Fay and she practiced staring back. He was so young it wasn't that hard.

Also, she was no longer embarrassed. This was what she wanted: to go from car to car and person to person to see how people lived in the desert. She loved rolling down the road in someone else's truck, going somewhere she'd never been.

The ride ended at the iron-tubed gates of Three Mile Ranch. Fay and Skip stepped out into the heat and the cowboy turned west onto a flat dusty drive. Where he was headed didn't look like horse country: no shade and not much grass.

Now it was hot. The sun flattened the landscape and made the air quiver. Within minutes of leaving the cowboy's air-conditioned cab, Fay felt the sweat start down her neck. But she didn't mind. She liked being out on the road, surrounded by desert.

A couple of miles back on the trembling asphalt highway a dot appeared. A semi. It grew larger, its wind deflector gleaming in the sunlight. Finally it blasted by, hot tires shrieking, the wind from its passage strong enough to knock Fay off balance. Two more cars passed in tandem, then the road was empty.

They ate a couple of doughnuts and drank water from one of Skip's plastic bottles.

"There's nothing out here," Fay said.

"Just scrub and dust."

"I'm glad I came. This morning I didn't think I could do it, but now I'm getting used to it. They just pick you up if they want to, don't they?"

"Sure. Sometimes they're curious, or else they want to talk to somebody."

"Do women ever stop?"

"Not for me. Maybe with you here."

But none did. After thirty minutes another pickup took them as far as the Salt River Canyon, and by late afternoon they stood outside a miniature truck stop 180 miles north of Tucson. It was cooler. Partly forested hills rose up on both sides of the road. After an early dinner while it was still light, Skip led them another mile down the highway past sandy ground spotted with cedars and prickly pear cactus. They climbed over a barbed-wire fence and followed a dry wash away from the road. Behind a shallow outcrop of rock Skip unfolded his tent fly and spread it on the ground. "It won't rain," he said.

"What about snakes?"

"I wouldn't walk around at night. Actually snakes aren't the problem, it's scorpions. But they won't bother us if we don't bother them. Check your shoes in the morning."

Skip had forgotten his candles, so they had no light. By nine o'clock they lay side by side barely three feet apart, stretched out in their sleeping bags on top of the tent fly, staring up into the night.

Skip took a drink of water and passed Fay the bottle. "I hear astronomers come to Arizona from all over the world for these skies," he said.

"I can't remember the last time I slept outside like this with no tent or anything. If you tried this in Maine, the bugs would eat you alive."

They addressed the sky, not each other, and spoke almost in a whisper. Skip rustled around in his sleeping bag and unzipped it partway. "Too hot," he said. A pair of trucks whined along the road behind them. "Do you think your husband will come back to Tucson?"

"I want him to," Fay said. Far up the wash, almost too far to hear, a coyote sang.

"I think you're great to travel around like this. You act so young. You're like someone I'd meet at a party."

"I feel young. At least on this trip I do. But sometimes out here all I can think about is that I've got two children and twenty years of marriage behind me, and a husband who doesn't want to leave the farm he grew up on."

"But you don't want to live there anymore."

"No."

She let it rest at that. There was no way past this huge topic. The two of them lay on their backs, neither one speaking or moving, until they slept.

When she woke the next morning Skip was already stretched out on top of his sleeping bag reading a paperback Thoreau. She put her shorts on inside her bag, walked a hundred yards up the dry wash and peed in the sand. She looked for a pool of water so she could wash her hands and face, but everything was dry.

Back at the campsite Skip went on reading. Fay hadn't thought to bring a book, so instead she went for a walk.

She had even forgotten to bring her plant guides. She could have used them now, for after identifying the mesquites and agaves and buckhorn chollas, the burroweed and catclaw acacias, there were dozens of smaller plants she wasn't sure of. She found penstemons, desert asters and locoweeds, but had to guess at the exact species.

After following the wash for a mile she turned uphill. There were no trails, just scrub and rock and scaly banks. The vegetation thinned as she climbed higher. Thirty minutes later she stood on the barren ridgetop looking down on the tent fly far below. She could even see Skip stretched out on the dark square.

Sitting on the rock top of the hill, Fay pinned her hair up with a clip so the sun could bake her neck and shoulders. The land stretched out below her in a beige roll of ridges and dry arroyos. She closed her eyes against the brightness and for some time sat perfectly still—until she heard a tiny scratching sound. Scarcely a yard away from her leg a two-inch lizard ran out from under a rock. It darted to the left, held its pose, darted again and scurried back into hiding. It lived there. She sat still a long time, waiting for the tiny reptile to come out from under its rock again.

In her new life Fay wanted to be as empty as the desert, as attentive as an animal. She wanted to get by without having a book, without investing in house lots, without securing a titled position in some firm. Yet she feared that to lure Austin away from Maine she had to offer him a complete new life—one not simply imagined but achieved. And this week, instead of finding a job and a place to live, she was sleeping outdoors and hitchhiking around the back roads of Arizona.

She was drawn to the desert; it was why she had come to the Southwest in the first place. She wanted to sit quietly on top of a hill and let the parched air fill her nostrils, the tiny scratch of a lizard fill her ears, the wide pale earth fill her eyes. She sat quietly, but her thoughts could not be curbed. Memories of Blake, held in check by yesterday's travels and this morning's stiff climb, now engulfed her. She could almost feel him beside her: his restless shoulders, his compact chest, his sneakered feet.

Only three days ago Blake had flown home with Austin. But before they left, Fay had taken her son for a last walk up into Sabino Canyon. There giant saguaro cacti marched down the flanks of the hills to the edge of the city, and a river flowed out of the mountains. There had been a monsoon the day before.

Mother and son knelt by the water's edge and dunked their heads. "Let's jump in!" Blake said, and a moment later they were both flopping around in the current like a couple of muskrats. Thirty minutes later, after drying off completely, they jumped in a second time.

In the half-shade of a willow Blake rolled onto his stomach. He rested his hands on the ground and his chin on his hands. He breathed out slowly like a dog in the midst of a dream. "After I go," he asked, "what are you going to do?"

"I might go back to school," Fay said. "How about that? We'd both be students. I'd like to study botany, the same as your dad did in college."

"Here?"

"Yes, here. I want to live in Tucson."

Blake buried his face against her. She held him as he cried, and lifted him onto her chest. He had the same milky smell as when he was an infant.

She waited until he had almost stopped crying. "After the harvest maybe you could come back and live with me here. Not in the camper but in a regular house. We could live in town or even out in the desert."

"What about Daddy?"

Fay took a breath. "I've asked him to come too."

"But he doesn't want to." The boy broke into sobs again, louder than before, his small chest heaving. She lay back and let him cry.

In that moment she knew she could never leave her son. Before Blake, all her plans were chaff. She'd go back to White Pine and make the best of her life there for—what would it be? Nine more years. She'd get her job back, or some other job.

Blake cried on her chest until he fell asleep. His very weight upon her made her decision seem inevitable. She couldn't think beyond him. His hair and his breath fell onto her neck.

But he was no longer a little boy, and his weight slowly crushed her against the gravel below. He grew heavier and heavier until finally she had to roll him gently off her chest onto the ground. He gave a long breath and his eyelids quivered, but he slept on, his cheek pressed flat against his arm.

Fay sat up and went to kneel before the river again and dash her face with water. And there, freed of Blake's weight, she knew it would be senseless to go back to Maine. She might decide now to sacrifice herself for her son, and to enter again into the Aroostook round of potatoes and winter, potatoes and winter. But eventually she would remember. Eventually the same feeling would return: that she was going to die up there without ever knowing what she would have done with her own life. And she'd have gotten no further away from that feeling than when she had moved into town last April.

So when Blake woke up she never told him of her indecision. She didn't tell Austin either, and the next day her husband and son flew out of Tucson, headed for Boston.

Fay and Skip caught a ride through the Apache town of Whiteriver, and another headed east on 260. Past the village of Trincayo Fay sat in the front seat of an ancient Renault, talking to a retired prospector and shepherd. He was bald, short of breath and seventy-eight years old, but all fired up by the chance to tell her about the old days. He talked a mile a minute and drove at half that speed. He claimed he was headed for his girlfriend's for "some venison and Jack Daniel's, and then some rockin' and rollin', 'cause I ain't too old for that yet."

Skip kept a straight face in the backseat but later, by the side of the road, both he and Fay laughed.

Late that afternoon a ranch owner let them off in the middle of San Adolfo. A faded sign in front of the municipal building read SAN ADOLFO, THE BEST LIVABLE LITTLE CITY IN ARIZONA. There was a Sears Catalog Sales store, a Western Auto, the Apache County Museum, the shell of an old high school, a drugstore gone under and a few old stone buildings, one of them a hotel. The main street of town was as peaceful and empty of traffic as a meadow. At fifty-eight hundred feet the air was notably cooler than in Tucson.

Fay rested her knapsack on the sidewalk and considered the Hotel Apache. Its green awnings and plain stone face looked like they hadn't changed in decades. Finally a man came out of the front door—the first sure sign that the hotel was still open.

"How about a night in there?" Fay said. "I could use a bath myself."

Skip looked doubtful. "I don't know. I didn't bring much money."

"I'll treat you. Just one night and then we'll camp out again."

Though the idea clearly went against Skip's grain, in the end he agreed. He let Fay talk to the clerk, fill out the guest card and choose a room with twin beds.

The lobby, the stairs, the hallway and everything else in the hotel looked like 1940. Room 8 on the second floor was clean and somber, with two high beds, a double set of dresser drawers and a skeleton key for the door. The charge was sixteen dollars a night. After Skip showered, Fay soaked in the tub for almost an hour.

Appended next door, the hotel had its own restaurant. The wooden floors were dark with age; the ceiling was stamped metal. The walls were crowded with buffalo, deer and fox heads, an outstretched eagle and a half-dozen paintings on black velvet.

The handwritten dinner menu offered five entrées, all served with either mashed or fried potatoes, either corn or peas. A waitress stood by the table until they made up their minds. She wore a western skirt and a cotton blouse open at the throat. There were only a couple of other diners. Crystal Gayle was on the jukebox, then Ronnie Milsap.

Fay had stopped worrying about what she should do with her life and was cheerfully curious about the town of San Adolfo. Also about the Hotel Apache, the young waitress and Skip himself. The waitress returned with two bottles of beer and poured them into glasses.

"Pretty girl," Fay said, as she headed back to the kitchen.

Skip looked after her as if he hadn't noticed. "She's kind of skinny," he said. The girl was slender but not skinny. Like Fay, she was considerably taller than he was.

After dinner they walked a few blocks to the edge of town and stood next to a barbed-wire fence, looking out over the high flat plains and the starlit skies. The temperature had dropped into the seventies.

"That was quite a civilized meal for a camping trip," Fay said. "Don't you think?" Skip didn't answer. Not then or all the way back to the hotel.

By the time she stepped out of the bathroom he was already in bed. She lifted back the sheets of her own bed and climbed in. Skip never looked over. He remained perfectly focused on his paperback Thoreau, holding the book within the lighted ellipse of the nightstand's shaded lamp. Fay wished again that she had brought a book. She lay on her back and stared at the ceiling as Skip read.

Finally he slipped a piece of paper into his book, closed it and laid it on the table. "Shall I turn out the light?" he asked.

Side by side in the darkened room they lay on their backs, the same as the night before only farther apart. Headlights played briefly through the high window and a diesel engine wound down outside the city limits. It was the endemic sound of the West, Fay thought: the same throaty lament they had heard last night. Her legs stretched away from her under the worn white sheet, her toes rising like miniature obelisks at the foot of the bed.

"You were right," Skip said. "That was a pretty waitress."

Fay hesitated. It might be safer at this point to simply go to sleep. But she was curious. "Do you have any girlfriends in Tucson?"

"I had one in Terre Haute, but we kind of split up. She talks about coming out here but she'll never do it."

"Why not?"

"Her family's there and she's going to college. Anyway, I think she's glad I'm gone."

"So she can go out with someone else?"

"No, so I'll leave her alone."

"How do you mean?"

He didn't answer.

"Oh, you mean in bed."

"Yes. Except we never got that far."

"What's she like?" Fay asked.

Skip got out of bed wearing only his underwear. He found his wallet in the dark, then got back into bed, turned on the light and handed Fay a snapshot of Mary Ellen Tarvis.

"Very pretty," Fay said. It was a high-school picture taken against a swirling gray background. "How long did you go out with her?"

"Almost two years."

"And she still didn't want to do anything?"

"She read all those *Time* and *Newsweek* stories about herpes and AIDS. She thought sex and disease were practically the same thing."

"There are certain dangers," Fay said. "Getting pregnant, for one."

"She had the pill. Her own mother gave it to her but she wouldn't take it."

"So you never made love?"

Skip reached out for the photo and put it back in his wallet. "We did other things."

Again Fay paused, unsure if they should be talking this way. But he seemed to want to. At least he was looking straight at her. "What other things?"

"Kiss and . . . you know." He lay facing her, his sheet pulled up over his shoulders.

"I'm sure I know," Fay said, laughing unevenly. A sudden wave of desire had taken her by surprise. Or partly by surprise. "But tell me."

"Mary Ellen would kill me if she ever found out. I've never talked to anyone about this."

"Do you want me to turn off the light?"

He didn't answer. She reached out and clicked the switch, casting them into complete darkness.

"You're embarrassed," she said.

"I'm just waiting a minute." He sounded out of breath, as if he had just come back from a run.

"You never made love to her."

"No."

"Have you ever made love to anyone?"

"No."

How simple it would be, Fay thought. No one would get hurt—in fact, no one would have to know. She lay motionless under her sheet, letting the river of sex run through her. Pure desire took over her lips, her limbs, her chest, almost convincing her it would be right to sleep with this boy. But no, she couldn't do it. Later it would not look the same.

She was too aroused, however, to simply cut off their talk. "What did you do with her?" she asked.

He was silent for almost a minute. The entire room was silent. Finally he said, "We used to play something called the Naked Corn Game. It was in the fields at night. I've never told anyone this."

"My lips are sealed." She could see him now. Her eyes had adjusted to the dark.

He leaned on one elbow and faced her. "We'd go into a field of corn at night and take off all our clothes. Everything, even our shoes. We'd leave them on a blanket inside the first row, where we could find them again. And then we'd hide."

"From each other," Fay said.

"You could walk or crawl or do anything you wanted. You could sneak around in circles or just hide and listen. It was better to be still—that way you could hear the other move and you didn't get cut by the leaves. But Mary Ellen could always outwait me. I'd have to hunt her down. Whoever saw the other first was the winner."

"And there was a prize?"

"Yes."

Fay had to squeeze it out of him. "Like a kiss or something?"

"We'd go back to our clothes and lie down on the blanket. The winner got to kiss the loser all over for twenty minutes."

"All over?"

"Above the waist."

"What a game!" Fay said. "I think it's the greatest game I ever heard of! Though I'd rather be the loser."

"Yes, she always let me win."

"And when you kissed her would she kiss you back?"

"A little. After the twenty minutes was up."

An unmuffled truck drove slowly down the main street of town. Then the room was silent. Fay was in too deep already—but she asked, "This was Mary Ellen Tarvis you're talking about? The one who didn't like sex?"

"She liked some things. She was the one who invented the game in the first place."

"She was a clever girl," Fay said. "She knew what she wanted."

"Maybe . . ." Skip almost sobbed getting his sentence out. "Maybe . . . we could play that game here."

Of course. Fay should have known it would come to this. She had led him on and teased him worse than his girlfriend. For a moment she couldn't speak. Skip leaned back against his pillow; it was too dark to make out his expression.

"I wish I could," she told him. "If I didn't have a husband or kids or anything else. If I were free and we were traveling around together I'd play any game you wanted."

He didn't say anything.

She almost wished she'd said yes. She didn't want Skip to think she had turned him down because he was too young or too short or too inexperienced. "You're a very attractive man, Skip.

You're going to be a great success with women and I wish I could be one of them. It excites me to think about it—but I can't do it. I should never have started talking like that."

"It's all right," he said.

Another set of headlights played against the far wall, lighting up the room enough for Fay to see the disappointment on his face.

"I'm attracted to you," she told him. "But I have to say no. It's different when you're married."

"I understand," he said.

Instead of explaining about her marriage, she wanted to tell him all over again how much he had aroused her. But she held it back. "I'm glad you offered," she said. "That took courage. And one of these days some girl is going to be crazy about you."

"Hey," he said with a short laugh, "you don't know what you're missing. In that game you could have been the loser."

"Thanks, Skip. I know I led you on. Can we get up in the morning and still be friends?"

"Sure. I didn't invite you along just . . . for that, you know."

She knew, and she liked him even more for making a joke about it when he was hurt and embarrassed.

They stopped talking, and eventually Skip dropped off to sleep. Fay heard his breaths grow long and steady. For a while, in the warm, windless room, she thought she might be up all night. But her desire slowly drained and her worries receded, and then she slept as well.

The hotel restaurant had stopped serving breakfast by the time they checked out, so the room clerk directed them a couple of blocks down the street to Gwen's, where you could get breakfast all day. A cop in a black-and-white cruiser watched them as they left the hotel and walked down the street to the little restaurant. Twice he drove past as they ate, and each time Skip stopped talking until he disappeared.

After breakfast they walked out to the edge of town. The same cop pulled into a 7-Eleven across the street and started doing some paperwork in his car.

"What the hell does he want," Skip said.

"I don't know. There's no law against hitchhiking in this state, is there?"

"Not on a road like this."

But the minute they stuck out their thumbs for a ride he started his engine.

"Shit," Skip said. "We better give him some story." He looked as guilty as if he had been up all night playing naughty games with Fay.

The cop pulled up next to them, headed the wrong way on their side of the road. He didn't bother with his lights.

"Morning," he said. His smile turned up the bottoms of his long sideburns. He wore a khaki shirt and pants, a badge, a gun, a radio and some other paraphernalia. He hung a tanned arm out the door. Fay looked in at his nameplate: T. J. Paley, Deputy Sheriff.

"On your way out of town?" he asked.

Fay waited a couple of seconds to see if Skip would say anything, but his jaw looked as tight as a pipe vise. "We were just leaving," she told the cop.

"Hope you had a restful night at the Apache. The old place has seen better days."

"We thought it was nicely kept up," Fay said. She gave the cop an unwavering look—to interfere with the steady shuttle of his eyes between her and Skip.

"I'd like to see some ID if you don't mind." He looked faintly amused. "Let's see. Fay Pooler, White Pine, Maine, hair brown, eyes brown, forty . . . forty-two years old. And Edward Wilson, Terre Haute, Indiana, hair brown, eyes brown . . . and twenty years old the day after tomorrow, how about that? Well everybody's of legal age here and it doesn't seem like anybody's breaking any laws. Mind my asking where you're headed?"

By then Fay had a story ready. She told the sheriff they were headed up the Coronado Trail and from there over to the Petrified Forest National Park. Her daughter was going to drive down from Wyoming with a car to meet them.

The cop laughed softly. "I suppose that might be," he said. "But before you leave town let me give you a little advice. It isn't like the East out here. We got miles and miles where nobody lives at all. Last year a couple of hippie types hitched through town and some of the local boys out by Snowflake gave 'em a ride. They beat the piss outta him, and she never would say what they did to her. So tell you what I'll do. You stand about a hundred feet up the road and I'll get you a ride with somebody I know is safe."

And he did. A few minutes later a natural-gas foreman stopped and gave them a sixty-mile ride north. He said T. J. Paley had been deputy sheriff in San Adolfo for fifteen years and he was a damn good man. Skip looked off to the side. The foreman surveyed the two of them and raised his eyelids faintly.

Fay looked back at him. She even gave him a smile. She was sure now, in the bright cool morning, that she had done the right thing the night before. Everyone they met, of course, was going to assume the contrary. The deputy sheriff had, and now this foreman. She answered their looks and let them think what they pleased. After all, they weren't that far off. And in her new life she hoped not to worry so much about what other people thought.

TEN

The Aroostook autumn closed in fast under clear night skies and pockets of morning fog. The lakes cooled, the earth cooled and with a businesslike applause of wings the first geese flew south.

Austin and Jules worked their fields with a boom sprayer and Diquat solution, softening the potato vines in preparation for harvest. Within days the plants began to die, turning an unearthly purple-grey. When disturbed, they gave off a fine ashen dust.

A week later the harvest began on schedule. State and county officials graced the day with animated speeches about the everlasting glory of the spud, and inspectors for the anti-bruise campaign drove from farm to farm checking on conveyor belts and drop heights. As they did every year, the public schools closed down so the district children could help bring in the crop and earn some pocket money.

Austin, like most of the big Aroostook growers, could have harvested all his potatoes mechanically, but he still let hand crews take care of the farm's smaller and more isolated fields. Though it was not an economical way to get the job done, he hated to think that barrel harvests might disappear altogether, as they had in Idaho.

For over a century the 165-pound barrel had been the industry standard. Before the pickers came into the field, a tractor-mounted digger scooped up the potatoes and dropped them on top of the fluffed soil. Workers then picked the spuds into woven baskets and dumped them into barrels marked with colored tickets. A flatbed truck with a crane lifted the barrels off the field and carted them away to storage, where each picker was credited according to the ticket on the barrel. As a child working for his father, Austin had earned twenty-five cents a barrel, the same as everyone else. Eventually he made ten, sometimes twelve dollars a day.

Barrel crews still picked some of the County's crop, but most growers drove automated harvesters and loaded directly into trucks. And Austin, though sentimental, was no fool. His three Lockwood harvesters were all new, as were most of his 32,000-pound bulk trucks.

At the start of the third week of harvest a solid rain stopped work on Pooler Farm, and the crew took a short vacation. Three days later, when the fields were again dry enough to harvest, Austin rose before light, woke his son and started breakfast. Blake came down to the kitchen just in time to hear the radio announcer on the Morning Spud Special report that "Austin Pooler's crews will start an hour late this morning, but they *will* be digging potatoes. That's the word from Jules Derosier out at Pooler Farm."

"Hey, Dad," Blake said, "we're on the radio again! I bet everybody knows about our farm, don't they?"

"Maybe everybody in the County."

"I'll bet everybody in the world. Are we rich?"

That was a question Blake had been asking in the last six months or so. He wanted to know who was rich and who wasn't—though he had yet to figure out all the ramifications of wealth and poverty.

"Kind of," Austin said.

"How much money do we have?"

"It's up there. You want some fries?"

"Nah." Blake got down a bowl, filled it with Wheaties and underfed the cereal with an inch and a half of milk. "What's 'up there'? Do we have a thousand dollars?"

"We do."

"Do we have ten thousand?"

"Not in my wallet," Austin said. He wasn't used to talking about that kind of money with his eight-year-old son. "But we've got a big crop coming in and we own a lot of land and equipment."

Blake ate his cereal silently, fastidiously. "And does Mom have a lot of money? Is she as rich as . . . we are?"

Austin stirred up his home fries in the iron skillet. "Legally I own all the land," he said, "and your mom owns all the farm equipment. But we don't think of it that way. At least I never do. I figure we're all in this together."

Blake dug his spoon around in the soggy last flakes near the bottom of the bowl. When he saw his father staring at him, he said, "Hmm," just like an adult.

Though mist still hid the bottom of the valley, up on the Barton field the sky was clear blue. The brightest autumn foliage had already passed; some of the trees were almost leafless. In the spring the leaves emerged and in the fall the trees themselves. The morning sun rose full yellow over the ridge, lighting up the moist and steaming potato rows. Austin took a few paces into the field, put his hand into one of the furrows and balled up a fistful of soil. It crumbled freely, which meant the harvester would run without clogging.

"You going to climb right on this morning?" he asked Blake. "Or if you want you can hang out in the truck." Blake sometimes read or slept under the cap in back of the pickup.

"If we had Mom's camper," the boy said, "we could park it next to the field and I could do anything I wanted. I could even take a shower."

"You really liked that shower, didn't you?"

"It was tiny."

"But today . . . are you going to read or work?"

"I'm going to work," Blake said. "I'm going to work all day, just like you." He scrambled up the ladder and stood on the narrow steel platform of the picker table, ready to go. None of the crew had even arrived yet.

Austin checked the oil and hydraulic levels on the big John Deere 4250 that pulled the harvester. The first of the bulk trucks approached on the road below the field, and Annie Pelletier, who picked culls and looked after Blake when he was on board the harvester, drove in, parked and tied her bandanna on.

"There's that potato boy," she said, approaching along the edge of the field. "Looks like he's raring to go this morning."

"He says he's going to work all day," Austin reported.

"Oh no. My little meadow mouse? He has to take his nap after lunch the same as always."

"Not today," Blake said. "Today I'm going to work as hard as Dad."

"I'm sure you will. Because when you work on the table you work twice as hard as he does anyway. All he has to do is drive the tractor straight. But a picker can never relax. What do you think would happen if we snoozed on the job?"

"I don't know," Blake said.

"I'll tell you. Next winter someone down in Boston would run his fork up against a hot chunk of limestone instead of a baked potato. Which is why meadow mice have to take their naps every day—to make sure that doesn't happen."

Stan Jackman parked his car and jumped up on the table next to Blake. Annie climbed up as well, and the bulk truck moved into place below the boom. Austin let his tractor warm up for a couple of minutes, and they began.

The harvester's digger nose burrowed along through two rows at a time, scooping up a prodigious stream of earth, potatoes and dead vines. The vines were shredded and blown to one side. The potatoes, hydraulically shaken clean of soil and small rocks, rode up the side elevator's rubberized belt. Tuber-sized rocks and clods of earth, along with sliced or rotten potatoes, had to be culled by hand. That was the pickers' job. Annie, Blake and Stan hovered over the endless stream of potatoes that flowed past their table onto the bulk boom and down into the bed of the waiting truck.

Austin set the hand throttle and steered his tractor down the long furrows. The truck driver adapted his position according to the flow of potatoes, aiming for a balanced load. Austin, when everything went smoothly, could let his mind wander as he drove to the wooded end of the field. There they turned and started back.

The heat from the tractor engine welled up around his legs. At the end of the eighth row he took off his jacket and threw it to one side. He checked on Blake, but the boy never looked up from the river of potatoes. Annie laid a finger below her eye: she was watching out for him.

The tractor vibrated, the belt drives clanked on the harvester and the potatoes flowed. When they topped out one truck, another took its place. As soon as the sun dried out the ground's surface, dust swirled up behind the harvester. They covered an acre an hour.

Austin had grown up with the Barton field and knew its entire history. His great-great-grandfather had cut the field out of second-growth timber and plowed it for the first time in 1896 using an old wooden plow: a metal-tipped bullet of a plow with no moldboard to get hung up on rocks or roots. In subsequent years—first by oxen and then by tractor—the field had been steadily plowed and disked. Its rotation now was potatoes, oats and hay.

This season alone the field had been worked many times. So far it had been disked, fertilized, planted, hilled, cultivated and sprayed. And now, from the feel of it, they were harvesting a good fifteen tons to the acre. It seemed to Austin as if the potatoes that came out of Aroostook County could feed the world. All up and down the valley he could make out harvesters and trucks inching their way across the mottled tan fields.

The air was still crisp. A few puffball clouds drifted by to the south and were gone. Crows and blackbirds hopped among the dead vines on the field, looking for the worms and grubs turned up by the digger nose.

Without interrupting the tractor's steady progress, Austin stood up to stretch his legs. The wind, blowing across the disturbed soil, brought to his nostrils the greatest farm smell in the world: healthy Caribou loam and a stream of *Solanum tuberosi* rising to the open air. It was the benchmark of all odors.

* * *

Just at noon Cathy Derosier drove onto a corner of the field. Cathy catered the lunches for the entire Pooler crew—a tradition most growers had abandoned. Austin throttled down his tractor, turned off the ignition and jumped to the ground. But along with lunch Cathy had brought a message from town: Otto was at the White Pine airport.

"Otto? Not Otto Struckner?" Austin stepped back from the card table Cathy was setting up to hold lunch. "Not *that* Otto?"

"Struckner, that's right. He sounded foreign."

"Oh Christ in blue," Austin moaned. "I can't take care of Otto now. I'm in the middle of harvest."

Cathy held out her hands. "I didn't know who he was."

"You know him. He's from Germany." Austin looked at her in dismay, as if she could rescue him from this jam.

"You don't mean that old kraut who used to visit your father?"

"He used to visit my *grand*father before that. But he hasn't been here since Dad died."

"Well, he's at the airport and he wants a ride."

"Jesus, I'm in for it now. He and Dad could talk about the good old days until their lips went numb. Have Jules send someone over to drive this rig, will you? I'll probably have to take Otto home. You'd think he put in twenty years working here instead of a couple of months."

Austin grabbed some bread and apples and told Blake to jump in the pickup. He hated to pull off in the middle of the day. He *hated* it. He got into a harvest rhythm and liked to stay in the fields from sunup to sundown. The last thing he wanted to do was go to town.

As they passed through White Pine on the way to the airport, it looked like a town under siege. Clods of earth thrown off by the cleated tires of oversized farm machinery lay spattered on the pavement, and clusters of potatoes had rolled into the gutters as if washed there by the tide of harvest.

When Otto first came to White Pine, in the late summer of 1943, Austin had not yet been born. With more than a fifth of the county's workforce away in the war that year, the Air Transport

Command flew two hundred German POWs into town to help get in the potatoes, and the harvest ran all the way to November. Otto Struckner, along with the five other prisoners assigned to Pooler Farm, picked into barrels under the surveillance of an armed guard. After a couple of weeks the guard joined in the harvest as well; the prisoners, after all, could hardly run off into the Maine woods and live on berries and roots. Otto had driven a half-track for the German Wehrmacht, and before the end of harvest Austin's grandfather had promoted him to driving a flatbed between field and potato house.

Otto spoke some English and wanted to learn more, and it wasn't long before he and Austin's father struck up a friendship. At the end of November the POWs were still living in some old ATC barracks, so the Poolers invited Otto to Thanksgiving dinner. Austin's grandfather, who had twice been mayor of the town, shrugged off the criticism that he was fraternizing with the enemy. He thought Otto was an ambitious young man who had worked as hard as any Mainer to get the crop in, and who ought to have a little more exposure to American ways.

Otto went home after the war and worked for Volkswagen. In the late fifties he returned, however, as VW introduced its small, curious fifteen-hundred-dollar car to the American market. Austin, who was in high school by then, joked with his friends about how comical Otto looked in his little slate-blue bug with no hood and a folding sunroof—a car that might evaporate if it ever got pinned between two harvest trucks. The neighbors could hardly believe Otto had driven a toy like that all the way up from New Jersey.

In the last twenty years Otto had made three different trips from Germany to visit Pooler Farm at harvest. Austin never thought much about their German visitor—but he had never had to look after him. His grandfather had done that, and then his father. Now it looked like Austin's turn.

He found Otto in front of the small airport building, sitting on his luggage with an overcoat over his shoulders. It was not that cold. He claimed to have sent a letter two weeks ago about his arrival, but no letter had come. Since his last visit he had aged considerably. He was balder, fatter, and his ears had sprouted tufts of gray hair. He looked and moved like an old man. Twice in the first ten minutes he called Austin by his father's name, Anthony. And his English, though still admirable, now carried more of a German accent. He laced his fingers across his potbelly and gazed at Blake.

"So the next Pooler is growing up. That is good. Please, I have forgotten his name."

"Blake," Austin said. "He's already a good worker. He's been up on the harvester all morning."

"Yes, yes, I know. Everything is automatic now. Not like when I picked potatoes for your grandfather. Those were the days when men worked hard and Maine potatoes were the best in the world."

"They still are," Austin said.

"Yes, yes, of course. But also then, the most famous. I took a bushel with me after the war, to Germany. Perhaps even now they are growing Pooler potatoes in Memmingen."

Austin had heard that story a half-dozen times. He listened patiently and waited in vain for Otto to bring up the subject of Anthony Pooler's death. Surely Otto must have remembered that Austin's father had died. As they drove back to the farm, however, Otto spoke only of his own relatives. "Nothing is left of my family," he explained with no particular emotion. "Kristina finally divorced me and went to live in Stuttgart."

Austin knew that from Otto's last visit. "How about your daughters? How are they?"

"Who?"

"Astrid, and . . . who was the other one?"

"My daughters. Yes, Astrid, and now the other has also gone to Stuttgart. I forget her name. She has four children and two husbands. And Franz, my old friend, also decides he must live in Stuttgart. What do you think of that? The whole world is moving to Stuttgart."

Blake looked back and forth between Otto's face and his father's. Even an eight-year-old could tell that something was wrong with Otto Struckner's conversation.

Austin carried their visitor's bags into the guest bedroom and returned to the kitchen. "I have to get back to the fields," he said. "I've got a crew waiting."

"Of course, of course. Tomorrow I will help, but now I am tired. I flew at night to save money. While you are gone I will take a nap."

Austin stood by the door, ready to duck out. He didn't want to get caught up in some discussion, but he told Otto, "Fay isn't here, you know. She's on vacation. And Maggie's away in college."

"A vacation during harvest?" Otto looked squarely at Austin for the first time, but only for a moment. He slid out of both his overcoat and his suit coat, revealing the wide pair of suspenders that held up his pants. "Well, we have a house full of men." He glanced around the kitchen, even opened a couple of drawers as if looking for something. "Without Fay you need some help. Tonight I will cook dinner. I will cook the same potato pancakes we ate in 1943."

When Blake and Austin returned home that evening, however, they found Otto still asleep on the couch. Austin covered his portly form with a blanket and cooked the potato pancakes himself. Otto slept on, undisturbed by conversations, the radio, the smell of cooking.

After dinner Austin read to Blake out loud from Jules Verne. Otto slept through that too, and by the end of the chapter Blake was nodding. Austin let ten minutes pass and then carried his sleeping boy upstairs. He pulled off his shoes and blue jeans and tucked him into bed.

The next morning Otto was the first one up. He wanted to drive a truck for harvest the way he had during the war. More than forty years had passed since then, Austin reminded him, and a modern bulk truck carried three or four times the load of an old flatbed with barrels. Austin didn't add that Otto was advancing into old age and showed it.

Austin left his visitor at home that day. Otto didn't like it but did not complain outright. And this time, when Austin and Blake returned after dark, he had dinner almost ready. He didn't look as confused as he had the day before. He said he had taken a long walk through the woods and fields, and that his heart had been lifted up by the beauty of the land. Those were his exact words: "My heart was lifted up." He spoke them as simply as if reporting the weather.

"You have a wonderful home," he went on. "Maine is still so pure and unpolluted."

"Maine is great," Austin said. "But it's not as clean up here as it used to be. When I was a kid I drank out of the rivers. Not anymore."

"But compared to Germany. The Rhine is now worse than the Hudson. We have toxic wastes and expensive housing and Turks who slit your face for the pleasure of it. All is changed. At least in White Pine you live like your father. Your house is the same, your fields are the same, everything."

Since Otto's last visit, Austin thought, a great deal had changed on Pooler Farm. Anthony Pooler had died of a heart attack, Rose had moved to Long Island and Fay was living in an RV park in Arizona. Otto's tunnel vision of the past, in which his own picking days glowed luminously at a comfortable distance, had started to grate on Austin's nerves.

"Potato growers are having a rough time of it these days," he told his guest. "Every year more of us go out of business. People move down to Bangor and Portland, and our kids leave the state. In the last twenty years we've lost more than a thousand farms in Aroostook County, and now the Canadians are dumping potatoes on us at a price we can't match. Plenty has changed up here, believe me."

"But the potatoes," Otto said. "At least you have the potatoes." He went on as if Austin hadn't spoken. "I remember how hard we worked to get in the crop. From dawn to dusk, six days a week. And on Sundays the guards let me walk in the woods by myself. I always remembered that."

Austin looked Otto straight in the eye and told him that too many Aroostook fields had been ruined by farmers who planted nothing but potatoes, twenty and thirty years in a row. He said taxes were up and acid rain was killing the fish, and if people didn't look out, the whole County might go to hell in a handbasket. Finally Otto noticed Austin's agitated state and sat back from the dinner table, his eyes properly focused on Austin's own.

That was all Austin wanted: to be sure the old burgher could still pay attention.

Otto sat up straight, positioning his small, neat head over his drooping chest and oversized belly. "I would like to drive a truck," he said. "Or if not that, to pick some potatoes. I always helped your father when I came back for the harvest."

Austin was not going to let Otto drive one of the big trucks, but after some hesitation he told him he could take the pickup over to the Blasing field where seventy-year-old Andy James, a Malecite Indian who had worked the Pooler harvest since before Austin was born, was supervising a crew of school kids and semi-retired workers.

Early the next morning Otto rumbled off in the Power Wagon, and that night he surprised Austin by reporting that he had picked fourteen barrels of potatoes—and also that he remembered meeting a Dan James in 1943, who turned out to be Andy's brother. After a half-day's work Otto's speech and vision were both clearer. Austin, who had initially wondered if his visitor was showing the first signs of Alzheimer's disease, enjoyed Otto's enthusiastic report on the old-fashioned barrel harvest.

During the week that followed Otto went every day to pick spuds by hand, working up to twenty barrels a day. Austin did not point out that at the going rate, if the farm had been paying him, he'd scarcely be making enough for dinner at a good restaurant. But in the evenings after Blake went to sleep, Austin sat around with Otto talking potatoes, just as his father had done.

In spite of his big gut and soft hands, Otto looked the part of an old farmer. He parked his rubber boots inside the kitchen door when he came home, then showered and came down wearing fresh clothes. Though his memories were out of date, Austin could not resist his enthusiasm for the harvest. And when Otto showed concern over Aroostook's diminishing harvests, Austin detailed his complaints about Charley Stoddard and the other local processors who were buying Canadian potatoes.

"That is despicable," Otto said. He stood up and paced across the kitchen, his hands on his suspenders and his flannel shirt popped open over his belly. He looked as worried as if his own livelihood were in danger. "Tomorrow I will pick only in the morning. Then I will drive to the border to see who is bringing potatoes and where they take them."

Austin didn't want him to stir up any trouble—but he did want to know who was bringing in what from Canada. So for the next few days Otto parked on the U.S. side of the Woodley-Homeland border and took notes. Truckloads of potatoes were coming in, all right. Otto followed one truck to the Starr plant and another to Route 1, where it turned south. On the fourth day he left the local border and drove down to the Bridgewater and Houlton crossings. Even more Canadian potatoes were coming through there.

"Goddamn," Austin said. "Stoddard's the worst of the lot, but all the processors are buying Canadian."

"Is there nothing we can do?"

"I don't know. I've got four, maybe five more days before we finish digging. When everyone's crop is in, maybe the growers can get together and stir something up."

ELEVEN

In early October Fay drove out of Tucson on Interstate 10, east toward Deming and Las Cruces. Cotton and hay grew next to the Rio Grande as far south as El Paso, then the land reverted to scrub. The buff-colored plains hunched under the incessant wind and pale skies. Van Horn, Odessa, Midland, Big Spring: the towns scarcely made a dent in the dry expanse of mesquite and creosote bush. All the land was fenced, though none of it looked fertile enough to raise cattle. The more desolate the terrain, the more Fay liked it.

A week later she stood between Rose Pooler and Jack Dossett in the midst of an ornate cocktail party on eastern Long Island, in a house overlooking the manicured greens of the Maidstone golf course. Jack had insisted on buying Fay a dress for the party and had chosen it himself off the sale rack of a little shop in Amagansett. The price of the dress, marked down 30 percent, had come to $560. Austin would have liked it, Fay thought—but he would also have calculated, out loud, how many tons of potatoes it would have taken to buy those few ounces of cloth.

Rose held her wineglass by the stem. She wore a pair of black heels, open at the toe, and a long skirt. She looked as if she had lived her whole life next to the expensive ocean—though in fact she had left White Pine only weeks before.

"I want to leave too," Fay said. "Do you think that's wrong?"

"Austin will be unhappy," Rose answered.

Jack Dossett stepped into the conversation. "Right or wrong, the fact is that Austin's tied to his farm like a tail to a dog. He might not leave no matter how much he loves you."

A tall, fortyish ear-nose-and-throat man from Columbia Presbyterian sidled into the conversation and shook Dossett's hand. He clearly wanted to meet Fay, but when he started to introduce himself Dossett clapped a hand on his shoulder, spun the fellow around and said. "We're having a talk here, Hendricks. Besides, this is a *woman*. Nothing you could handle in a million years." With a rough shove and a laugh he pushed him toward the back of the room.

Rose shook her head. "Jack says whatever he wants, but they invite us to these parties anyway."

"What do you think?" Fay persisted. "Am I crazy? Am I going to ruin everything forever?"

Dossett frowned. "What the hell's forever? Maybe when you're young you think like that. You think the future's made out of crepe paper or something. But then you get a little older. You see your friends die and your wife die and you figure, this is it."

"So I should go to Tucson?"

"Go if you have to. No one says you can't change your mind later. If you want to come back, come back. There's no magic forever in front of you, there's just now."

"Jack Dossett, philosopher," Rose said.

Dossett patted his chest with a laugh. "Plato, Kierkegaard, Jack Dossett—all famous names in one circle or another."

Fay stopped next at her sister's. During the summer Carolyn had left Amherst and moved into her boyfriend's old farmhouse in Conway. His house was in the midst of renovations, and Fay slept in a guest bedroom where chunks of plaster as big as dinner plates had fallen from the ceiling.

After dinner the two sisters sat in the kitchen. Stefan, Carolyn's boyfriend, was out of town.

"What are you doing over here in the Berkshires?" Fay asked. "Don't tell me you're going to start fixing up Stefan's house after doing all that work on your own."

"Mine's rented out and it's good money. But this was Stefan's idea. He wanted me to come so badly I finally said yes. Did you know Archibald MacLeish used to live up the road? It really is beautiful out here."

"Am I talking to the same independent Carolyn Hallwick who always said a man could just as well fit into *her* life?"

Carolyn rested her hands on the table. "I'm not quite that same woman, because I'm older. Thirty-five may seem young to you—but you already have children. And since Stefan isn't that eager about kids, I thought we better have some give and take here. The funny thing is, it was probably Austin who convinced me to do this."

"Austin?"

"I found him in the middle of the night going through my desk, trying to find your address. He broke a dish and busted out a window with his flashlight. I was angry at the time, but for days afterward all I could think about was how attractive it was that he wanted you so much."

"Sure, he wanted me back," Fay said. "But how about wanting me enough to leave Maine and live somewhere else?"

"It is asking a lot of him," Carolyn said. She pushed her plates and glasses to one side, clearing the table between them. "It's asking more than Stefan asked of me."

Fay nodded. She had thought it over a thousand times. "Maybe it's something Austin can't do."

"Of course, when he was here, I argued from your side. I told him he should give up his farm."

"What did he say to that?"

"He didn't want to talk about it. I don't think he could imagine it."

Fay sat back from the table. "I don't want to get caught up there. That's one reason I brought the camper—so I'll have my own place to sleep."

Carolyn's eyebrows rose. "You're not going to sleep with Austin?"

"Not in the house or in my old bed. I don't want to fall back into any routines."

"Presto, you'd be living there again."

"Just like that. As easy as sleepwalking."

The two women cleared the table, washed their dishes and moved to the screened porch behind the house. Though it was only seven o'clock, dusk was already closing down over the pasture.

"Did I tell you I'm taking back my name?" Fay said. She stopped to slip a jacket over her shoulders. "I never did like Pooler."

"You did at the start."

"I didn't."

"Sure you did. I remember you walking around the day before the wedding saying, 'Mrs. Fay Pooler. Mrs. Fay Pooler of White Pine, Maine.'"

"Oh God, I didn't."

"I guarantee you." Carolyn chuckled. "But if you've put up with Austin's name all these years, maybe now he should adopt Hallwick."

"Are you kidding?" Fay laughed along with her sister. "He'd never change his name. If it were Shitlips, he wouldn't change it. He'd tell you how Ebenezer Shitlips had come over on the *Mayflower,* and how the Shitlipses settled Bath and Augusta and how the Shitlipses built the railroad up to Canada."

They laughed in unison. After a moment Carolyn announced, "Shitlips, the first family of Aroostook potatoes!"

"I swear to God, it wouldn't slow him down at all. He'd put it right on his ten-pound bags: 'Something good that's good for you. Shitlips's Maine potatoes.'"

Ten minutes went by before they could look at each other without giggling. Even then Fay couldn't let it rest. She gave her sister a sly look and said, "No one can eat just one. Shitlips's Potato Chips."

At RISD Fay found her daughter and two friends living off-campus in a rundown apartment. Crumbs lay on the counter beside an empty mousetrap, class projects littered the living-room design tables and textbooks lay open on the carpeted floor. The kitchen was painted lime green. Fay thought it looked like fun.

Maggie took her for a walk through the campus. "And Wyoming?" Fay asked.

"It was beautiful. I liked it."

"Enough to go back next summer?"

"Maybe. But they're a little behind on the arts out there. Actually I was thinking about working in a city."

"Like Portland or Augusta."

Maggie knew she was teasing. "Get serious, Mom. I mean New York or San Francisco."

Fay watched her daughter as they walked: she had the skin, the grace, the neck of youth. Fay circled her slim waist. "What did your father say about that?"

"I didn't bring it up."

"Poor Austin. Everyone wants to leave his farm and live in a city."

"Not everyone."

"No, maybe not Blake. How did he seem?"

"He's only eight. He doesn't understand."

"Sure he understands," Fay said. "He knows that I want to go and your father wants to stay."

They sat down on a bench. Maggie wore a black silk blouse and black pants. Her wardrobe already looked like New York.

"He cried a few times," she said. "I don't think he cares who lives where, he just doesn't want you to split up." Maggie's chin stuck out. She looked like an eleven-year-old trying to be brave.

Fay put her arm around her daughter's shoulders. "You feel the same way, don't you? You'd rather I didn't leave."

"I don't know what I want." She dropped her head to Fay's shoulder and began to sob.

It was as bad as having Blake cry. It was worse, because Maggie was older. Fay pressed her daughter's head to her own and wondered if this havoc would ever end. So far, all she had to show for her plans were these desolate admissions from her children that they didn't want her to leave home.

* * *

By the time Fay drove into White Pine, the boxcar graph in front of the courthouse showed the harvest at 90 percent complete. The streets of town were muddy and the parked cars covered with dust. No one gave Fay's Winnebago a second look.

After twenty years in White Pine she was once again an outsider. Here downstaters and out-of-staters were all the same: They came and went. The County, and those born in the County, endured—but Fay wasn't one of them. She knew that now and so did they.

The house wasn't locked. The front door of the Pooler farmhouse had been built without a lock and none had ever been installed. Fay stepped inside and looked around with the curious eye of a traveler. Everything looked small and strange. She went upstairs and sat down on her son's bed. A pair of pajama bottoms and a tee-shirt had been stuffed under his pillow. Suddenly nothing mattered except seeing Blake and holding him in her arms.

There were suitcases and clothes in the guest bedroom and a letter addressed to Otto Struckner on the bureau. Fay hadn't thought about Otto in years. She tried to read the letter, but it was in German. It wasn't like her to read someone else's mail, and it took her a moment to realize why she was upset that Otto was here. Though she knew it was unreasonable, it offended her that life had not stopped in this house once she had left.

She pulled a couple of trunks up from the cellar and filled them with clothes. Everything went in together: sweaters, summer dresses, coats, slips, skirts. Then she packed books, dishes, pictures, lamps, a television and a hundred smaller items into cardboard boxes. She stacked both trunks and boxes next to the kitchen door where no one could miss them.

Austin's truck pulled up outside—but it was Otto who got out and marched up the kitchen path. He looked older, heavier, full of purpose.

"Fay, how good to see you!" He took her hand and pressed it between his two rough palms. "Austin will be happy. He will be so glad to have you back. And Blake! He has waited for you every day this week."

Her heart softened toward Otto. But it was Blake she wanted to see. "Where is he?" she asked. "Is he with Austin?" She tried to sound relaxed but her voice betrayed her. She had come so far it seemed unfair not to see Blake *now*.

"There is no need to worry. He will be so happy. Austin took him to a friend's house today and soon they will be home. Blake has been working hard this year. He even helps us fix dinner."

Fay made herself calm down. She even managed a smile at the thought of Blake and Otto and Austin all cooking dinner. "I'm sure you've been eating potatoes," she said.

"Oh yes, potatoes! No dinner without potatoes! We make them every way—mashed and baked and boiled and fried, and in salads and soups. Here we never tire of potatoes!"

"And potato chips." Fay almost laughed.

"Blake likes the Ruffles kind. Sometimes I take him shopping and we eat a whole bag right in the truck."

"So Austin never finds out."

Otto held back a smile. "On occasion your husband can be a bit . . . insistent."

"He's a fanatic," she said mildly.

"Yes, he is a wonderful, fanatic man. A true Pooler."

Did Otto know she was leaving Maine? He didn't seem to. She didn't want him to take sides when the moment came.

Fay didn't know whether to stand or sit down in her own house. Finally she sat down at the kitchen table while Otto told her all the harvest details: how the Pooler yields were the best ever, how Jules had sprained his ankle but was still driving, and how Otto himself had picked over two hundred barrels of potatoes with the school kids. "Look at these hands," he said, "they are as callused as they were in '43."

On cue she looked at his hands. But she had only been giving half her attention to what he said. She was listening for Blake's arrival. All through the drive from Tucson she had tried to keep the memories of her child from overwhelming her. But now all she could think of was his brown, milky hair, his crooked front teeth and the playground odor of his body as he undressed at night, letting his clothes drop to the floor.

At the sink Otto began to peel potatoes. "I know Austin believes this to be a crime," he said. "To cut off the skins. But

Blake likes very much the way I fix them, completely white and creamy. I think mashed potatoes are his favorite."

Fay turned away so he wouldn't see her tears. All her control was breaking down.

Just after dark Austin and Blake drove up in the flatbed. Fay heard them coming. She stepped outside the kitchen door and stood on the stone path, her hands at her sides. Blake didn't bother with the truck door. He scrambled through the open window, jumped to the ground and ran full tilt up the walk.

"Mom! Mom! You're back!" He threw himself against her. His hair was tousled, his new overalls too large. "You brought the camper! Let's go for a ride! I want to sleep in my bunk bed!"

She glanced at Austin but had no chance to speak. Blake perched on her hips, his arms around her neck and his face only inches from hers. "I pick potatoes now!" he said. "I work on the table with Annie. We pick out rocks and clods. Rocks and clods, rocks and clods! Did you bring me a present?"

She had: a robot arm with a pistol grip and curving plastic fingers. She carried him inside, his heart beating against her own, and gave him the toy. He stayed in her arms and reached around with the plastic arm to pick things up: a piece of paper, a spoon, a small potato, then his father's ear. He pulled Austin toward them.

"I've got you, Dad."

"You do," Austin said. "How are you, Fay?"

She nodded and leaned against him, letting down her guard. "I'm fine," she said. "It's good to see you." She put an arm around Austin's waist and he helped hold Blake. For five minutes they ignored Otto's presence.

At dinner she and Austin hardly spoke. Instead they focused on their son, who was almost too excited to eat. All through the meal he moved back and forth between them, touching first the leg of one, then the hand of the other, creating his own bonds between them.

Otto was considerate. After dinner he washed the dishes, cleaned up the kitchen and retired to his bedroom to read.

Fay and Blake played checkers in the living room. She couldn't get enough of him. She kept hugging him and kissing his neck and pressing his hair to her face. After checkers she took him upstairs, climbed into bed with him and told him everything she could think of about her trip across the country. He lay with his head against the crook of her neck. "Keep telling me, Mom." It was an hour before he fell asleep.

Fay and Austin, both wearing heavy sweaters, sat down in front of their yellow house. The limestone steps were cold to the touch.

"You tore up my flower beds."

"I'm sorry, Fay. I went crazy last spring when I didn't know where you were."

Without a thought, without the least struggle, she forgave him. Her heart wasn't going to seize up over bulbs and flowers. She had bigger worries.

The afternoon clouds had drifted off. It was a cold soundless night, without insects or wind. "And the harvest?" she asked.

"Two more days."

Good. This was the timing she had aimed at ever since leaving Tucson. She hadn't wanted to arrive in the middle of harvest and find Austin up to his neck in potatoes. "How are the yields?"

"Great, the best in years. But prices are down. Every processor in the County is buying Canadian spuds—especially that worm Charley Stoddard."

"Poor Lauren," Fay said. "Everyone complains about her husband."

"She gets by. She never takes sides on the issue. At least not in public."

There was a miniature catch in Austin's voice, so small only Fay would have noticed. "And in private?" she asked.

This time the pause was in his breath: a hesitation slightly longer than his normal rhythm. Fay hadn't come outside to talk about Lauren, but now she studied her husband's face.

He sat upright on the stone step, his curly hair grown longer and his ears protruding. During their honeymoon Fay had called him the handsomest man in Maine. That was stretching it, even then. He had always been unkempt, and she saw now that he would have a craggy old age.

She said, "You know that smell Lauren has?"

"What smell?"

"Austin, relax. It's a sweet smell, like cardamom. Maybe it's her perfume. You know it."

He didn't say anything.

Fay reached out and held the collar of his shirt between her fingers. "One night years ago," she said, "when you came home late and went straight into the shower, I got up and smelled your shirt. There she was."

He was silent for a while. "I guess I shouldn't deny it."

"You better not."

"Why didn't you ever say anything about it?"

"I don't know," Fay said. "It was a long time ago and I wasn't sure. Did you do that all the time? I can't believe you did."

He held his arms to his chest. He didn't speak.

"Tell me you didn't, Austin."

"You know we're friends. I've known her my whole life. And mostly it's just that. Sex is just a little part of it."

"How little?"

"Tiny. Only six times in twenty-five years."

"You counted. And was one of those times this summer?"

He dropped his head and gave her a disconsolate look. She stared at him, merciless. He had kept this secret from her their whole marriage. "Goddamn you, Austin. *Was* it?"

He nodded an admission. "That's why I never told you. I was afraid you'd blow it up into something it wasn't, like an affair."

"If it wasn't an affair, what was it? What *is* it?"

"It's a friendship. It's some kind of friendship I don't know what to do about—but it's never been a threat. No more than Ricardo was."

"Don't start canceling scores," Fay said. He had gotten his chin up a little, but she wasn't ready to let him and Lauren slide. "What happened this summer?"

"I ran into her at the fair. Charley was there too, for a while.

"And then?"

His countenance fell once again. He looked like he was reporting an accident in which someone had been maimed.

"Then we drove out to her parents' camp at Bear Lake and made love. We hadn't done that in six years."

Fay wanted to know what kind of lover Lauren was, but she didn't want to ask.

"Think of how long we've been friends," Austin said. "And most of that time sex didn't have anything to do with it."

"Sex always has something to do with it."

"Maybe it does. But after this last time I think we're all through with sex."

"You might think that now," Fay said coldly, "and feel differently about it later."

"Is that true about Ricardo?"

"I haven't known Ricardo since I was three, we don't live in the same town and no, I won't feel differently about it later."

She tried to maintain her dignity, but already it was fading. Because at heart she believed what Austin said. She didn't think Lauren was a threat. The threat to her marriage was not another woman but Pooler Farm.

Fay stood up. She had forgotten how cold it could be in October. Winter lay in waiting just over the hill—an insinuating guest who would sidle in the next month with a few picturesque snowfalls, then grow blustery and refuse to leave until April. Before all that began, however, Fay would be out of the County.

"I saw your trunks and boxes," Austin said.

"So you know I'm not staying."

He stood up beside her. "I guess I do." He peered across the dark valley.

"So what are you going to do?"

"I've thought about it a lot," he said. "But could we wait to talk? You know how I get during harvest. The end is only two days off. Could we wait until then?"

"Sure," Fay said. "We can wait." She stood with her hands on her hips.

"But what?"

"I don't mind waiting a couple of days to talk. But if we do, I think we should also wait on any visits to the camper."

He looked puzzled.

"I mean at night."

Austin turned to the Winnebago. "You're going to sleep in there?"

She had surprised him. "Yes, I think I'll be more comfortable there."

"You don't have to do that, Fay. I'm not going to attack you just because we lie down in the same bed."

"I'd *rather* sleep out here." She wasn't going to tell him what she had admitted to her sister, that she was still afraid of getting caught by the farm.

"And when you leave here?" he asked.

"I'll go back to Tucson."

"And do what?"

"Live there."

"And work?"

"Eventually. I might go back to school first."

"Jesus, Fay, what kind of life is that?"

"My life. The one I'm going to invent. The one I've already started."

The topic of Blake never came up that night. Fay was glad that it didn't, for she might have fallen apart. All her plans and rehearsed speeches still fell short of that one dire topic.

The next morning she woke with the first light to the sound of Austin's flatbed pulling out of the drive. She dressed and walked over to the house and found Blake still asleep upstairs. She drank a glass of orange juice and continued packing.

Otto had left as well. She wondered what he thought of all this. What would he say when he figured out that instead of joining Austin at night, Fay was sleeping in her camper in the driveway?

At nine o'clock, an hour after the sun had crested the ridge and lit up the kitchen windows, Blake tromped downstairs barefoot, his pants dragging on the floor. He fell across Fay's lap.

"Bad dreams?" she asked.

He lay across her legs head down, without responding. He resisted when she tried to lift him up, though he allowed her to scratch his back through his tee-shirt with the ends of her nails.

When she finally got him to sit down at the table, he held his head between his hands, his chin only an inch above his plate. He didn't want cereal, he didn't want French toast, he didn't want eggs and fries. Finally he settled on pancakes.

"Are you packing?" he asked, looking over at her trunk and boxes.

She didn't want to answer that with Blake in such a dark mood. She pulled her chair up next to his and sat beside him without speaking.

"Are you?"

She had long feared this talk. But there didn't seem any way around it. Finally she said, "Yes, I've been packing my things."

Blake looked at the pile of her belongings, his eyes set and sharp. She had never seen such a cold look on his face.

"Do you want to talk about it?" she asked.

"No."

She was sure he wanted to—but there was no point to it until after she had talked with Austin. So she seized on what Blake had said: no, he didn't want to. She didn't want to voice or even think about the inconceivable choice the three of them might have to make about where Blake would live.

The silence between them filled the room. She ate half the pancakes off his plate until he said, "Don't," and ate the second half himself. Fay fell back on routine: she washed the dishes, cleaned the stovetop and swept the floor. It was cowardly not to talk, she thought. So be it, she would be cowardly for a few more days.

When Blake opened the door and stared outside, Fay heard the plaintive mewings of a cat—and realized she had been hearing them for some time. She had heard them but they hadn't registered. She stood behind Blake at the door.

"That's the one with kittens," he said.

"Does she want to be fed?" The cat was pacing in front of the barn.

Then Fay saw what had happened. She could see the blood. Austin or Otto must have run over the kittens without knowing it when they left this morning. Over the years it had happened twice before, once to Fay herself.

The mother cat paced back and forth, crying pitiably. "I think the kittens have been hurt," Fay said. "I'm going out to look. I don't think you should come."

He didn't say anything but stood at the open door in his bare feet as she went out to the barn. She was right. At least two kittens had been flattened into a mass of blood and fur. The mother cat would not come close enough to be comforted. Fay shooed her off, took a flat-point shovel from the tool room and scooped up the remains of the dead kittens.

Blake was still standing barefoot in the kitchen door. "Don't look," Fay called back to him. "How about going upstairs and putting on your shoes and socks?"

He closed the door without a word. She carried the bloody mass on the shovel to the little graveyard beside the barn where a family dog and a few lesser pets lay buried. The mother cat whined but didn't follow.

She dug the hole deeper than she needed to, then dropped the kittens in and covered them with soil. The leaves were gone from the trees overhead.

Dark shadows from the limbs mottled the ground. At one end of the graveyard Pete the Irish setter had a stone engraved with the date of his birth and death—but the kittens got only a chunk of white limestone from a pile of rocks behind the barn. Fay set the stone, then stood for a while with one foot on her shovel, looking across the harvested rows of the nearest potato field.

She found Blake in his room upstairs. He had divided all his clothes into two piles on the bed: sweaters, coats and long-sleeved shirts on one side, warm-weather clothes on the other. He had folded them. Even his underwear and socks had been folded and divided equally between the two piles.

He didn't look up when she entered the room, but continued with the division of his goods. He picked up two stuffed animals, a monkey and a horse, held them in an exaggerated pose of indecision and lay one on each pile.

Fay sat down on the floor beside the bed.

"This pile is for White Pine," he explained. "And this is for Tucson."

After the animals he started on his toys, pulling them off his shelves and out of the closet: a plastic space station, a dump truck, a punching bag, a box of Legos. Soon they covered the bed in two almost indistinguishable piles. Blake turned his back to it all, slumped onto the floor and cried.

Fay lifted him into her arms and held him to her chest. He cried and cried. She didn't try to stop him or tell him there was nothing to worry about. He was right to cry. They should all be crying, she thought. Austin should be crying out on his tractor, and Maggie down at RISD. And Fay herself, here on the floor with her eight-year-old son, should be crying too.

But she couldn't. She was afraid that if she cried at the farm even once, she would never leave.

TWELVE

The long campaign was finished, the last potatoes lifted from the soil, the dead vines chopped and scattered. The entire crew relaxed on the dusty grass at the edge of the woods, telling harvest stories. Cathy Derosier had brought beer and pumpkin pies.

"How about Bud Budiman the mummy?" Annie Pelletier said. Bud had showed up one morning with his head half-swathed in white, the aftermath of a car crash.

"At least I hit a tree," Bud said. "Imagine fallin' eighteen inches off a tractor step and bungin' up your foot."

Everyone laughed. Only a week ago Jules had sprained his ankle by jumping down to the ground from his John Deere. "It's all healed," he claimed. "I can't even remember which ankle it was." In fact, he was still limping.

Austin stood up to announce that harvest bonuses would be at least 10 percent this year and maybe as high as 15 percent. "There's not a harder-working, more efficient crew in the County," he said. "If those Canadian growers would ease up, I think we could make some money around here."

"Damn Canucks," one of the men said.

"They'd work for nothing up there just to put us out of business."

Austin opened a beer. "Sometimes I think we should do something about it."

"Damn right we should do something about it," Annie said. Annie read the papers and complained regularly about both Canadian lumber and potatoes.

Jules was skeptical. "You know Washington never listens to us up here. They don't want to rock the boat with Ottawa."

"That's usually true," Austin said. "But Otto here has got an idea that might get their attention. You all know Otto. He picked his first spuds on Pooler Farm before I was born, and he's seen some interesting things happen in Europe. Otto?"

The old German planted himself in front of the group. "I don't know if you heard about the French dairy farmers a few years ago. Prices for milk fell so low in France that no one could make money, and the government would not talk to the farmers. So some of them got together and poured their milk in a ditch. There was a great scandal, but everyone listened. And prices got better."

"So you think Austin should dump his potatoes in a ditch?" Annie said. There were some laughs. Everyone knew Austin Pooler would be the last person in Maine to throw good potatoes on the ground.

"We talked about it last night," Otto said. "It is a crime to throw away food—but what the Canadians are doing is worse. If we could dump the potatoes at the border it might stop the Canadian trucks from coming through. And then everyone would listen. If the newspapers reported that, even Washington would have to pay attention."

The crew talked about it for almost an hour, and in the end Annie Pelletier said, "Hell's bells, no one on this crew is going to lose out, because all we do with potatoes is pick 'em. So sure, let the growers go over there and close down the border. I'm for it."

For five straight hours that night Austin talked on the phone, trying to enlist support from those who mattered: the other White Pine growers, all of whom were smaller and poorer than he was. Getting their attention was easy, and everyone agreed that something had to be done. But wasn't this dumping idea against the law? And didn't they have enough troubles already? At first some of them thought he was joking. They could hardly believe Austin planned to throw away some of his potatoes—Austin Pooler, who had always been such a fanatic about wastage, bruise control and the role of potatoes in easing world hunger.

He talked to more than thirty farmers and asked the more receptive to call their neighbors. He pledged that if others would bring a few barrels, he and Jules would load up an entire flatbed with spuds and they'd dump the works in front of the Customs building.

Almost no one committed himself outright. They all wanted to know who else Austin had talked to and who had already agreed to go. The natural conservatism of the Aroostook farmer, something Austin had always respected, now confounded him. In the end, after all this talk, he didn't know if two farmers would show up or a dozen.

Early the next morning he loaded twenty barrels onto a flatbed and had Jules fill them with a bin piler. But he was worried. He felt like a teenager giving a party. He was afraid no one would come—or worse, that only two or three farmers would show up. But the first trucks turned into the drive at eleven-thirty, and within the hour twenty-three pickups were parked in front of the house and around the barn.

The sun came and went behind isolated clouds. Austin stood on the back of his truck wearing khaki pants, a pair of rubber workboots and a red wool shirt. He addressed the men—and occasional women—who stood around their trucks. "I know the County's in trouble," he said, "when this many people show up on a day's notice to throw away good potatoes."

Only a couple of men laughed. The rest looked up at him soberly, wondering if he really meant to carry this through. A single negative voice might have persuaded them all to go home and return their potatoes to storage. But only Austin spoke.

"I've never done anything as crazy as this, and I wouldn't be standing up here now if there was any other way to get the politicians to listen. I think it's a sin to dump good potatoes on the ground—but I think it's a bigger sin to let the Canadians keep driving Aroostook growers out of the potato business.

"I'm not sure, but this idea might be a little against the law. So let's not put ourselves in a bad light. Let's be real courteous—especially if we run across some Canadian drivers. We'll just go up to Woodley-Homeland and dump the potatoes in one pile where they'll do some good. I see some guns in your window racks. That might look like trouble to someone, so let's leave them here. Jules can lock them up for you in the barn and you can pick them up this afternoon."

Austin had rarely made such a long speech. But with the crowd's full attention he went on. "I want to thank Otto Struckner for keeping an eye on the border for the last couple of weeks. He's the one who tipped us off about how many trucks are coming across with Canadian spuds. Of course, if it wasn't for him, Jules and I would probably be down at the packing shed this morning with a calculator, trying to figure out if we made some money this year. Instead we're getting ready to throw away some of the potatoes we worked so hard to grow."

There were a few more laughs and some friendly groans.

"As soon as we pull out, Fay's going to alert the local papers and a couple of the radio stations." Austin tried to mention Fay's name without the least stress. He wanted to imply that of course she would be helping out. "What do you think, are we ready?"

They paused. He couldn't tell if it was Fay's name that held them up, or some hesitation about starting for the border. A few people glanced toward the Winnebago, but then they looked around and began to nod at each other in agreement. Jules locked a few rifles and shotguns in the toolroom, then joined Austin and Otto in the cab of the flatbed. They drove out onto Pooler Road and headed for the top of the ridge.

Austin drove in silence. The day was mild and the air perfectly clear. Directly overhead, puffball clouds cruised upright through the sky like candled eggs. In all the valley only a couple of potato harvesters were still at work, inching their way across an upland field west of town.

The road topped the ridge, turned sharply and descended to the east. They passed Jules's house and the crumbling, slate-roofed remains of an old barn. All this was Pooler land.

Behind them the string of trucks stirred up a plume of dust. Austin geared down and held his speed to twenty-five. Even after the iron bridge, where the road turned to asphalt, he drove no faster.

The autumn foliage was done for. The landscape had turned brown and grey. Every year after harvest Austin woke up to discover that fall had passed him by and winter was upon them. And every year he suffered a bout of gloom as soon as the last of his potatoes were under cover. Though there were plenty of jobs to do after the harvest—bedding down the machinery for the winter, picking up rocks from the fields or overseeing the packing house—an inevitable, weeklong depression came over Austin and literally sent him to bed. Jules had long since become accustomed to running the farm on his own until Austin emerged from his house and showed an interest again in the family business.

This year was different. The graceful sloping landscape, passed countless times before, now sent chills down Austin's back. He wanted to stop the convoy, assemble the drivers and take them for a walk out into one of the potato fields beside the road. He wanted to stand with them among the leveled furrows on the soft chewed earth.

They would think he was mad. After all, they had just finished a solid month in their fields. But unlike Austin, they hadn't been away for most of the summer. He wanted to remind them how beautiful their land was, even in this drab season: the quiet ferny streams, the occasional patches of rye, the upright stands of larch and fir.

Close to the border the limestone subsoil gave out, and most of the cleared land was in pasture rather than potato fields. The border cut an arbitrary line across the bushy flank of a hill. The road wound up from the valley floor and spilled into a tiny lap of flat land that held the Customs house and an asphalt parking lot.

The Canadian crossing, with its own set of white wooden buildings, stood two hundred yards up the road.

Austin drove into the parking lot, put his flatbed in reverse and inched backward. A single car with Maine plates sat in the gateway, its driver standing with one foot on the ground and the other in his car. A blue-uniformed Customs official watched the line of pickup trucks pull into the lot and park at different angles.

Austin stepped down from his truck. He didn't know the Customs man, but greeted him with a handshake. Dillworth, the plastic name tag on his jacket read.

Dillworth was confused. "Are you going across with those potatoes?"

"That would be a switch, wouldn't it? No, we'd just like to close down the border for a while and stop some of those Canadian trucks from coming through."

Dillworth tried a laugh, until he saw that Austin was perfectly serious. His clipboard jerked in his hands. "You wait here," he said. "I'll be right back."

Otto stepped up beside Austin and said quietly, "There is nothing to talk about. Don't wait for trouble. If you've got the chance, start dumping."

Austin motioned to the nearest men to climb up onto the bed of the truck, and told Jules to back it up. *"You,"* he said to the driver of the car still parked on the border. "If you want to wind up on the U.S. side of these potatoes, you better move now."

The man scooted his car forward, and Jules backed into the mouth of the one-lane bay. The truck had barely stopped moving when Will and Bass Norton grabbed the first barrel, tipped it and let 165 pounds of handsome tablestock Kennebecs rain down onto the asphalt.

The sound of it made Austin sick. Bruised and studded with grit, the potatoes fanned out in an uneven circle.

A half-dozen men jumped up on the flatbed to help. They tipped a second barrel, then a third and a fourth.

Dillworth's boss strode out of the Customs building, one hand on his service revolver. "What the hell's going on here? Austin Pooler, is that you?"

It took Austin a moment to place him: Doug Melvin, a guy he'd played ball with at the Y. "Sure is," Austin said. "How you doing this afternoon?"

"*Hey,* quit dropping those spuds off that truck. What is this crap? I've got people coming through here day and night." His hand still rode on his gun.

"Take it easy, Doug. There's no reason to get hotheaded and haul that pistol out. And I wouldn't call these potatoes crap, either. They're all USDA number ones."

As he had on the basketball floor, Austin loomed over the small, moustachioed Customs official. Austin looked up at the men on the truck and motioned with his head toward the potatoes already on the pavement. The next barrelful rained down. "We can't let those cheap Canadian spuds take over the market," Austin said. "They're already putting Aroostook farmers out of business."

"I understand that. But there's no way you're going to block an international border."

Austin surveyed the men and trucks behind him before turning back to the Customs man. "It's blocked," he said. "Don't worry about it, Doug. Let's make sure no one gets hurt, because that would really make headlines. Right, guys?"

The men on the flatbed, halfway through the barrels, waved and smiled. "No one gets hurt," said Bass Norton. Bass was a teetotaler, but he sounded drunk. By now potatoes covered the bay from curb to curb.

"Look, Pooler, I don't care who you are, you can't come in here and close my border."

"*Your* border?"

"You know what I mean."

Austin took a slow breath and looked out idly over the nearby pastures. "Seems to me you could keep busy for a while. You'll probably have to write up a report about this, won't you? So you could get a head start on it right now. Or you could take yourself a coffee break. I know you come from downstate somewhere, Doug, but now you live in the County, same as the rest of us. And up here, when the potato business suffers, everyone suffers."

"They'll throw the whole lot of you in jail. Look at this, I've got traffic already on both sides. I'm going to call in the patrol."

Austin had hoped for a Canadian semi loaded with potatoes, but so far there were only a few cars. Jules moved the empty Pooler truck out of the way, and the first of the pickups backed into the crossing.

Again, Otto hovered nearby. This was not the same aging burgher who had flown into White Pine three weeks before. His face was now ruddy, his eyes clear and his paunch firm. His thick white hair swept back from his temples. He wore a brown leather jacket, sheepskin-lined, that made him look vaguely military. He told Austin, just above a whisper, "If you dump all the potatoes before the reporters arrive, they won't get much of a story."

"You think we should slow it down?"

Otto shrugged. "I think they will want some photos."

Austin circulated among the drivers, telling them to go a little slower. He had a look, as he went, at the potatoes in every truck: Katahdins, Superiors, Chippewas, Atlantics, Pontiacs, FL 1207s, Allagash Russets. Frank Nutter had four barrels of Chieftains, clearly last year's stock.

"Dump 'em," Austin told him, "but don't be the last in line. We don't want this to look like a pile of culls."

Sandra Daigle from the White Pine radio station was the first reporter to arrive. She parked her car, looked over the crowd and walked straight toward Austin. "Are you the one in charge, Mr. Pooler?" She carried a big Nakamichi tape recorder slung from one shoulder.

"I'm the one in charge here," said Doug Melvin. He stood in front of the Customs door adjusting his sunglasses, hemmed in by the growing mound of potatoes.

"Better talk to him," Austin said. "Get the dull side of the story first."

Sandra skittered around the potatoes to talk to the Customs chief. Before she finished, Tad Thorpe of the *White Pine Argus* drove up and got out of his car. He had a reporter's notebook in one hand and two cameras around his neck. Austin liked Tad. His father owned the *Argus,* and none of the Thorpes had much use for Canadian imports into Maine: not potatoes or lumber or fish.

Tad took some pictures, then started asking questions. Sandra returned with her Nakamichi spinning and Austin gave them both the straight rap, as if they'd never heard it before. He explained that Canadian imports could not be considered fair trade—not when the Canadian government guaranteed its growers a transportation subsidy, a storage subsidy, a floor price and no-fee loans. New Brunswick didn't even have real-estate taxes. And to avoid a higher duty charge, shippers often claimed tablestock as seed potatoes, taking advantage of a loophole in the law.

Austin ran through the entire litany of Aroostook complaints and concluded by naming all the Aroostook farmers he knew personally who had gone out of business within the last year. He was still talking when a state patrol car pulled into the lot.

It was Willard Smith, whose father had been a broker up to Fort Kent.

"Nice to see you, Austin." Willard got out and shook Austin's hand, then Jules's and a couple of the other men's. "You're not getting into trouble over here, are you?"

"No, we're just trying to get our names in the papers—and to make a day's dent in all the cheap potatoes coming down from PEI and New Brunswick."

Willard was cordial with Doug Melvin. He stuck out his hand, and Doug had to shake it before launching into his complaints.

"You've got cause to arrest here, officer. Trespass, destruction of property and blocking traffic at a U.S. border."

Willard gave the scene a studied look. "Trespass," he said. "And destruction of property. Is something going on here I can't see?"

"They've thrown their damn potatoes all over the ground," Doug said. "You can see that plain enough."

"Hmm." Willard took a few steps toward the pile. "Tearing up your asphalt, are they?"

Doug pointed his finger at the state patrolman. "Are you going to arrest these men or not?"

"Well, I might jot down a few notes about all this."

"Goddamn. The governor's going to hear about this."

As the Customs chief stormed away, Willard asked under his breath, "You ever play basketball with that guy? He travels with the ball and never calls himself. You're not going to destroy anything out here, are you, Austin?"

"No, this is it. We've only got a half-dozen more trucks to unload."

"Pretty good little crowd you've got—but the traffic's not so bad I've got to direct it. I think I'll wander on back to headquarters and check in. Keep things peaceable now, and don't get me any deeper into trouble than I am already."

After the patrolman took off and the last of the barrels were dumped, Austin felt a little depressed. No trucks had shown up from Canada—and if one had, he thought, it could probably have muscled its way through the whole pile. A couple of reporters had driven up from Houlton, so Austin went through his entire spiel again. One of them, a woman from the *Pioneer Times,* asked why so few women had come.

"Most farmers are men," Austin said.

"But not all. And how about your wives? Are they going to join in this struggle?"

This struggle. Austin saw how the media could create an entire movement out of one incident. "I'm sure you'll see more and more women involved," he said.

That was what it took to deal with reporters: you learned to lie and cover up what you really felt. More and more women might get involved, Austin thought—but not his own wife. Fay was less and less interested. She was so uninterested that in another week she might not even live here anymore. He struggled not to let any of that show on his face.

The Houlton reporter scribbled in her notebook. She asked him, "Will you do this again?"

He leaned back and glanced around. The other farmers, gathered in groups around their trucks, looked excited and proud. Until a moment ago it had never crossed Austin's mind that they might do this more than once. But as smoothly as if it had been planned for weeks, he explained that they'd be back on Monday with twice as many growers. "We're not going to stop until the whole state hears about this," he said. "Not until the whole nation hears about it."

T H I R T E E N

Saturday night after Blake went to sleep, Fay got into her Winnebago and drove to White Pine. She was angry about Austin's plans to do another dump. He had been on the telephone almost from the minute he got home from the border, and had called *The Boston Globe, The New York Times, The Christian Science Monitor, The Wall Street Journal* and all the network television stations. Austin wasn't thinking about leaving the County; he was digging in even deeper.

She was already in a bad mood, and the Winnebago didn't help. It was too big and slow. It didn't fit in the gravel lot of the Caribou Bar, so she parked it on a side street and walked back to the bar. Inside the Caribou nothing had changed. The same Schaeffer beer signs flickered in the windows, the same row of vinyl-covered stools tilted in front of the bar, and the same twelve-point buck with the painted smile hung on the back wall. Dan McClintock welcomed her back.

"I heard you were in town, Fay. I didn't know if you were going to come by and see us or not." Dan had tended bar in the Caribou for thirty-five years.

"Sure, what'd you think? The town's too small for me now?"

"I've seen it happen before. But hey, you look great. What a tan. And I heard about Austin's party at the border this afternoon. It was all over the radio. They say he shut Customs down cold."

"He had a little help."

"Damn right, the whole town's behind him. I always knew Austin had a crazy streak. Remember that time he ate nothin' but potatoes for forty days?"

"Potatoes and milk," Fay said.

"No butter, no salt, nothin'. I tell you, Austin's been crazy since high school. Remember that time him and Lauren got caught . . ." Dan stopped himself.

"Sure, they got caught running around the cemetery buck-naked. Don't worry, Dan, I've heard that story before. It's twenty-five years old."

"Sorry about that. What the hell, they were just kids. You want a couple of margaritas? We got a special going, two for one." Dan salted a couple of glasses for her and filled them from a pitcher. "So how's it look? You going to stick around for a while?"

Fay's hesitation lasted only a moment. "No, I'm going back to Tucson. Austin's got another dump on Monday, and Tuesday morning it's *blastons*, I'm outta here."

Dan nodded, sweeping up a nonexistent spill. "And Austin? Is he going with you?"

"You make a good margarita, Dan. Considering how far we are from Mexico."

Someone stood by her elbow, a young man with stiff brown hair and a reddish beard. He introduced himself as Bruce somebody from the *Bangor Daily News*. He said, "I heard you mention the name Austin. Would that be Austin Pooler?"

"Sure would. Austin Wayman Pooler, fourth-generation potato grower, kingpin of the County and my husband of twenty years." She gave the reporter her hand. "I'm Fay Pooler. Fay Hallwick, actually."

"I called your husband a half-dozen times, but the line was always busy. I would have driven out if it wasn't so late."

"He's organizing for Monday," Fay said.

"For another dump?"

"Much bigger than today's. They're going to shut down every crossing."

The reporter sat down next to her on a bar stool. "Could I ask you some questions about that?"

Fay inspected the young man's round face and closely trimmed beard. She tapped the bar and asked Dan to bring another pair of margaritas.

Dan looked at her. "You still got one sittin' there, Fay."

"What is this? You want to see the shade of my money?" She threw a twenty on the bar and moved the remaining margarita to one side. "How many times you ever seen me drunk, Dan? Loosen up and give me another of those two-fers. Bruce here looks kind of thirsty, and he better get into the swing of things before I start telling him about that cocksucker Charley Stoddard."

Bruce nodded seriously and pulled out a narrow reporter's notebook.

"You quote me on that and I'll have you fired," Fay said. "I've known your boss for fifteen years." That was a lie, but Bruce held back his pen. "It's the right word for Charley," she said, "it's just not right for the *Daily News*. Family publication and all that. Here, bottoms up on this margarita and earn your story. And Dan, quit lookin' at me like you were born yesterday. You think I'm too ladylike to swear in the Caribou?"

"Fuck, no," Dan said, and half the bar broke out laughing. It was a small place.

Bruce drank his first margarita and Fay her second. She told him about Charley and Starr Foods. "He's the one you should put the heat on. He was born and raised in the County but he's got the gall to buy those Canadian spuds. You know how many farmers have gone out of business up here in the last five years? And did you know we had a nine percent decline in last year's harvest? You better get some facts down in that notebook of yours."

She was already a little drunk or she wouldn't have started talking about the potato industry. After all, potatoes were the enemy. Her husband probably cared more about potatoes than he did for her. Yet as she shared her third margarita with the reporter, sip for sip, she explained to him the decline of Maine's round white potatoes and the rise of the Idaho russet. She knew it all inside out. It was as familiar to her as the multiplication tables.

"Dan, give me two more margaritas, would you? Bruce here is going to let the world know what kind of internecine battles have been going on up here for the last ten years."

She peered over at his notebook. *Internacine*, he had written, with a line under it.

Fay tapped the word with her fingernail. "It means both sides lose. Growers lose and processors lose. Wives lose and husband lose. Everybody loses and everybody suffers. Write that down. Everybody suffers."

Dan set another pair of margaritas in front of her. "These are your last two, Fay. What are you driving?"

"Hell, I don't have to drive. I've got my bed parked down the street. Haven't you seen my camper? I'm like a turtle with its shell."

She didn't mind being cut off. It was just as well, for she was already looped. She hadn't done this in years. It was fun to be drunk, but she didn't want to lose track of her tongue. If she kept talking like this, soon she'd be telling this cub reporter—and everyone else who was listening—all about Austin's old rivalry with Charley. And that would bring Lauren into it. Amazing goddamn Lauren who was so quiet and sweet but who'd been fucking her husband for twenty years.

She figured she ought to hate Lauren—but she didn't. Maybe it was because when it came to their husbands, Fay had won. She got Austin and Lauren got Charley. Fay twirled on her bar stool and laughed out loud. If *she* were married to fat old Charley, she'd have snuck off with Austin every chance she got.

"Dan, I've got an idea. I'm going to get Charley Stoddard down here so Bruce can listen to his side of the story. Straight from the horse's mouth, you know what I mean? Let me borrow your phone, will you?"

The ends of Dan's moustache turned down, but he slid the telephone across the bar. Fay dialed, and Lauren answered with a quiet "Hello."

"Hi, Lauren, this is Fay. I know all about you, but don't worry. I'm down at the Caribou Bar and I want to talk to Charley."

After a moment's pause Lauren said, "He was just going to bed, but I'll get him."

And seconds later Charley answered in his professional bass voice, "Good evening, Fay. What can I do for you?"

"Charley, I got a boy down here at the Caribou who's reporting for *The Bangor Daily News*. I think you ought to have equal time with him, because I've been filling his ear about how many growers Starr Foods is putting out of work and about how hateful your reputation is in White Pine."

"What are you talking about? Starr Foods is one of the town's biggest employers. I've got forty-five workers on my payroll. Do you know it's ten-thirty at night?"

"Sure, but Bruce here says I've made you out to be worse than the devil, and he's got a deadline. Of course, you don't have to talk to him unless you want to." With that she hung up the phone, slid the last of the margaritas to Bruce and headed for the women's rest room.

When she came back Dan was on the phone. He hung it up without a good-bye and started scrubbing the bar with his white towel.

Barely ten minutes later Fay saw Austin's old pickup turn into the Caribou's gravel lot. So that's who Dan had called. Austin pushed through the front door, glanced at Fay and then looked around to see who else was in the bar. He was embarrassed, she could tell. His ears were bright red.

"Hi, Austin. You want a margarita?"

"No, I don't want a margarita. What are you doing here?"

"You want to meet a reporter? He's already prepped. I gave him the whole history behind these dumps of yours."

Of course Austin knew she was tipsy. And he was angry about it. But she just smiled. Getting his attention these days was easier and easier.

He waved off the reporter and guided her to a booth. He wanted to tone her down. "Are you trying to get drunk?" he asked.

"You're too late, Austin. I am drunk. I'm drunk and I'm happy. You know I'm always happy when I'm drunk."

"Until later."

"Go ahead, Aust. Give me a lecture." She took his hand in hers. "You haven't given me a lecture in years. I think I've missed them."

"Damn it, Fay."

He got no further, for at that moment a second truck pulled up beside the bar and crunched to a stop. They heard Charley yelling, then Lauren pulled open the bar door and rushed inside. *"Austin,"* she said, "your *truck!"*

There was the clash of metal. They made it outside in time to see Charley Stoddard backing up for a second assault on Austin's Power Wagon. Austin ran for his truck, but before he got there Charley hit the Dodge a second time. The direct blow lifted one side of the pickup clear off the ground.

"You piece of fuck," Austin yelled. He jumped into the protected passenger door of his Dodge and slid across the seat. He started the engine, put his elbow through the shattered door window to clear the glass and took off in reverse. Charley tried to hit him again but only caught his front bumper.

Fay heard Austin bay over the roar of the V-8s. He swerved, caught Charley on the front fender and howled at him through his shattered window. The parking lot was too small to build up any speed, but the two trucks backed and came at each other head to head. Water sprayed, Charley's hood buckled and loose gravel pelted the other vehicles in the lot.

The bar crowd was on the sidewalk, some of them cheering. Dan said, " 'Ford Tough,' my ass. Austin's going to make mush out of that truck. These guys have wanted to do this since high school."

Charley tried to turn around and attack rear end first, to protect his radiator. But Austin caught him in mid-maneuver, rammed straight into Charley's door and blasted him halfway across the front seat. *"You son of a whore,"* Charley screamed. *"You shit."* He was too pissed to be hurt. He jumped back behind the wheel, but with his hood sprung he could only see behind him. Austin turned as well and the two trucks hit rear-end-on. Charley's pickup snapped a spring assembly and sagged hard to the right.

Austin had begun to laugh. They could all hear him. They could see his breath streaming out into the night. "A bastard new Ford!" he yelled. "It's dead! It's dog meat, you'll never drive it again." They collided backward over and over, water hoses steaming and engine oil dripping onto the gravel. Five minutes later it was all over. Both engines, long since drained of coolant, had seized up from the heat.

Austin climbed out of his window, wild as a jackal. His hair stood up in shocks. He had cut his left hand on the glass. He sucked the wound clean and spat out the blood, then walked over to Charley's pickup and looked inside.

Charley sat dazed behind the wheel. With Austin's help he opened the door and climbed outside, and the two of them stood on the chewed-up gravel lot surveying the wreckage of Charley's truck. He had bought it from Lauren's father only six months before: a stepside half-ton with a custom paint job, chrome roll bar and overhead halogen lights. He shook his head, disbelieving. "What have I done?"

"It's junk," Austin said. "But so's mine."

"Sure, but you've had that truck for twenty years. What's the blue book on it? This thing cost me twelve thousand dollars, dealer's price."

The two men stood side by side, their necks drooping. Austin sucked on his hand again and spat out the blood. Charley held his left arm at an awkward angle away from his body.

At the edge of the lot under a neon beer sign, Lauren stepped up and slipped her arm through Fay's. Lauren looked tired, her eyes were pouched and dark. "It's the same old story," she said.

She must have understood what Fay had meant on the phone. "They're like a couple of roosters," Fay said.

"It's been worse since you left."

Lauren's chestnut hair had come unpinned from where she usually wore it on top of her head. Only weeks ago, Fay thought, Austin had been making love to this woman. Yet she wasn't jealous of her. Instead she held Lauren's arm against her own and thought how, in a matter of days, this would all be settled. Across the lot the men were talking about trucks and fighting, while only a few paces away the women talked of love. All the world over it was the same, year after year.

Lauren turned to Fay. "I know a lot has happened, but I hope you stay in White Pine."

"I can't do that," Fay said. "I have to go."

Fay let Austin drive her back to the farm in the Winnebago. She stretched out on her bed in back, drew a quilt up to her chin and enjoyed the luxury of the quiet ride. She felt a little tipsy still from the margaritas. Outside, above the chill windowglass, the skies were clear.

Austin parked on the drive and walked back into the camper. He knelt beside her in the darkness. "Are you asleep? Or drunk?"

"Mmm."

He lifted the quilt and lay down beside her. Her hands were between them.

"That's the end of my truck," he said. "It was supposed to outlast our marriage."

She didn't say anything. She didn't want to speak.

"Fay, can you hear me?"

"Mmm."

He moved her hands to her sides and rolled on top of her. "You can hear me, can't you? I know you can."

He took the top button of her blouse between his teeth, pulled back on it until it snapped, then spat it softly onto the floor.

Button by button, she let him destroy her blouse. He pulled it aside and blew streams of air across her breasts. He found her nipples through the cloth of her bra and sucked at them, first one and then the other, as long as a nursing child.

He undressed her, pulling her pants and underwear down as far as her ankles. When she raised her hands to help, he took one of her palms in his teeth and slowly bit into her flesh: softly at first, then harder and harder until she cried out.

He lay above her, perfectly still, his mouth on her cunt. She tried to open her legs but couldn't, because her ankles were still entangled in her pants. For a long time he didn't move at all, but simply held his mouth against her. Her chest rose and fell. She had lost all control over her breath.

They had played this game before, so she knew the rules. She was not allowed to respond in any way, or to look after his pleasure. She was not allowed to be responsible for anything.

Raising himself directly over her, he grazed her mouth with his own. He inhaled her breath. He kissed her but would not let her kiss him back. She knew the rules: she had to lie still. He slid his hands under her buttocks and approached her, finally, with the tip of his cock.

He entered her slowly, quarter inch by quarter inch. He withdrew and entered again, withdrew and entered. He lifted her hips into the air, filling her completely, moving through her with long cushioned strokes.

Borne up by pleasure, she closed her eyes and clenched him inside her. He rose and fell, holding his breath, holding back all sound.

She went on before him, alone, feeling her climax draw close. She knew it would come. She lay still as Austin filled and emptied her. She let it begin. It rose up around her like the desert, like the ocean. He was above her but she couldn't see him. She didn't know if he came or not.

Sometimes Austin moaned and sang in the midst of orgasm and broke into laughter at the end. Other times he gave her nights like this when she came for both of them, and when instead of laughing afterward, she cried.

FOURTEEN

Austin spent all Sunday on the telephone talking to other growers. Monday morning he got up early, ate two pieces of toast and an apple and plugged the phone in. It rang in thirty seconds. He unplugged it again, threw the damn thing on the couch and went out to the storage house to load up a pair of bulk trucks with new Kennebecs.

Jules didn't show up until almost nine. He stood between the two trucks with his thumbs hooked into his front pockets and a doubting look on his face. "You sure topped out those loads," he said.

"Think of it as an investment."

"Think of it as food."

"There won't be food on anyone's plate around here if the Canadians put us all out of business."

Jules nodded briefly but didn't respond. Austin couldn't tell if he had said his all or was simply staying out of an argument. He knew Jules thought the whole project was excessive—and Austin himself was not yet fully convinced that dumping sixty thousand pounds of his best tablestock into an asphalt Customs bay was an entirely defensible course of action.

The first couple of trucks showed up at ten o'clock and were soon followed by others. Fay never emerged from her Winnebago. Austin looked in once and found her reading in bed. Blake got up, made his own breakfast and then followed around behind Otto, who was making a list of who had come and how many potatoes they'd brought.

The drive filled up with trucks. Mostly they were flatbeds and pickups, but Shep Peters and Jim Lacroix, who had both done well this year, showed up with partially filled bulk trucks. Jim's wife brought an urn of coffee and a flat of doughnuts. Before long the trucks began to spill out onto Pooler Road.

Austin gave interviews to *The Wall Street Journal* and *Le Journal de Montréal*. But when a CNN crew began filming everything in sight, including Austin, Jules, the piling operation, the Pooler farmhouse and even Fay's camper, Austin ran them off as far as the road. "You guys film whatever you want at the border," he said, "but don't make it look like this is a Pooler Farm project. There are nine hundred Aroostook potato growers, and we're all involved."

Even as he spoke they filmed him. He knew what they were looking for: they wanted someone angry enough to beat his breast and make a stir. But Austin didn't want to look like one of those broken farmers he'd seen over and over on the evening news, a weathered corn-and-beans man posed before the flat furrows of his midwestern farm, holding on to his crying but united family. No crying for Austin on the national news. No talk about his family either.

When the caravan set out at noon there were 150 trucks. Austin took the lead, driving the first of the two Pooler bulk bodies. Otto drove the second, and Blake chose to ride with Jules, who towed the bin piler behind his pickup.

Three miles from the border a state patrol car picked them up and gave them an escort, lights flashing, along an otherwise empty road. Some of the stiff, upright houses they passed had been abandoned, and none looked prosperous. A few people waved approval. But Austin, alone in his heavily loaded farm truck, no longer cared about potatoes or international trade. He had talked himself dry the day before. He let the patrol car increase its lead. He drove slower and slower, as if in a trance. He didn't want to see anyone or talk to anyone. He just wanted to roll on past fields and pastures, mile after mile, with the heater blowing warm air across his feet.

A half-mile before Customs the first patrol car stopped next to three others. Willard Smith got out of one of the cars and came around to Austin's window. The long column of trucks bunched and drew to a stop.

"Afternoon, Austin. Looks like plenty of folks headed for the border today." Willard sounded as matter-of-fact as if he were on traffic duty at the fair. Austin only nodded.

"We want to keep a lane open, so the trucks should go up one by one. After they dump they can clear out down to the Fosdick meadow. I already talked to the widow. We'll park the sightseers down there too. They can walk the rest of the way if they want to have a look. I doubt if you'll have any trouble from that guy Doug at Customs, because the TV people have already worn him down. They've been up there for hours with those klieg lights, filming everything that moves. Their vans take up half the lot, but there's enough room to set up your bin piler and get the trucks in and out."

Austin nodded. He didn't have anything to say. It seemed that the whole project was out of his hands. After working so hard to get the press here, he didn't even want to talk to them.

Mary Fosdick sat on the front porch of the last house before the border, a blanket wrapped around her legs and a shawl over her white hair. As Austin drove by she raised a tiny American flag on a stick and shook it at him. He waved back. The parking lot, as Willard had promised, was crowded with vans, lights, cameramen and reporters. As smoothly as he could, as if it were his driving ability they had come to inspect, Austin turned around and backed his truck into the bay. Under the sunglass stares of Doug and two other Customs inspectors, he engaged the conveyor belt at the bottom of the truck's V-shaped box. Within minutes the black pavement was covered with a blanket of dusty potatoes.

As the truck emptied, the reporters surrounded him. They asked him about the County's problems, but they also wanted to know if he had any political aspirations. Did he side with the workers in Poland, or in Chile? Did he think the future for Aroostook farmers was bright enough for his son to become one? Austin answered their questions, but not very cheerfully. He could see they liked him that way: somber, long-faced, a true Yankee. In fact, all he wanted was to finish the unloading. He didn't know what had come over him.

Otto pulled in with the second bulk truck and Austin hung around long enough to hear the old German launch into an impassioned tirade about potatoes, fair trade and an economy under siege. Without actually saying as much, he led the reporters to believe he was a potato farmer himself in his native Germany, and that he had come all the way to Maine to help out his Aroostook friends.

As cars and trucks crowded into the Fosdick meadow, the afternoon turned festive. Women served sandwiches and potato salads, kids played tag, Mel Bennett sold tee-shirts and Cranky Leveque warmed up on his fiddle. Reporters were everywhere, talking to everyone. Austin had three of them around his neck when the Stoddards arrived in Lauren's big Ford, so he unloaded all three on Charley. "Guys like him," Austin said, pointing across the lot, "are why the rest of us have to dump our potatoes at the border." When Charley got out of the Ford, Austin saw that his left arm was in a sling.

Only minutes later Fay showed up with Cathy Derosier. Austin was surprised. The two women unloaded a five-gallon vat of soup, set it up on a folding table and began to serve it in plastic bowls. Austin caught Fay's eye, finally, and signaled to her with his hands cupped in front of him. She nodded, and a minute later broke away with two bowls, stepping toward him over the matted timothy and clover. Together they walked farther into the meadow to eat, out beyond the last cars and trucks.

The soup steamed in the cool afternoon air. Austin tipped up his bowl and drank. Fay ate with a white plastic spoon.

"Tomorrow the whole country will be talking about you," she said.

He laughed briefly. "Tomorrow I won't even remember this. I don't think I was made for this kind of publicity."

"Otto's into it."

"He sure is. That boy could be a politician, the way he talks about the old days. He looks more Maine than a Mainer."

Fay bent to her soup. "Charley seemed a bit riled with those reporters."

"How's his arm?"

"Broken."

"It must have been that time I knocked him across the seat. I guess I should have held back a little. I didn't think he'd show today."

"He must want to defend himself."

After lunch they walked out onto the road past the line of idling trucks, past Mary Fosdick on her front porch and up onto a little knoll from where they could see the border. The pile of potatoes had grown enormous; Jules had the bin piler pointed fifteen degrees into the air.

"For a skinny little guy," Austin said, "Jules can work the hindquarters off a mule. I ought to go down there and help out."

"Don't," Fay said. She circled his wrist with her fingers.

"No, I won't. I'd rather watch from here. If I go any closer, I'll just get depressed about how many potatoes we're throwing away."

For a time he and Fay lay back on the sunny grass, side by side. They had a lot to talk about, but so far they'd said almost nothing.

An hour later, as unobtrusively as possible, they crept out of the meadow in the bulk truck Austin had driven over, now empty. Blake stayed behind to play with friends; he'd get a ride home with Otto. All day he had avoided both his parents.

"I think he's afraid of tomorrow," Austin said. "When this is all over."

Fay leaned back and closed her eyes. "He doesn't want to take sides. He doesn't want there to *be* sides."

Without the damping load of potatoes, the big truck shuddered and bumped over the uneven pavement, jolting Fay against the passenger door. Finally she stretched out across the seat and rested her head against Austin's leg. They crossed the valley in silence, climbed past the Derosier house to the top of the ridge and descended toward the yellow Pooler farm buildings.

Austin parked in front of his equipment barn. "I'm whipped," he said. "I'm exhausted."

Fay didn't answer.

"Remember how you always fell asleep in the van on the way back from Nantucket?"

She was asleep now, her chest rising and falling. She wore an old blue sweater, one of Austin's that had got into the wash and shrunk.

He went on talking as if she were awake. "Somewhere north of Portland," he said, "out you'd go. It happened every year. It was like a sleeping sickness. And I always knew where it came from. After six weeks on Nantucket you didn't want to think about Maine. You never wanted to come back."

She didn't respond. Only her ribs moved. He bent down close to her face to smell her breath. He had once told her that the two sweetest smells he knew were the odor of new potatoes and her breath when they made love.

She had kidded him about that plenty. She had gotten ten years out of that one.

He sat quietly in the truck, fending off a drowsy sense of depression. He had almost drifted off when he heard a car turn into the farmyard. It was Lauren's Ford. Charley was driving and he was pissed. He braked to a stop and leapt out of the car, his broken arm held to his side in its sling. Austin stepped down to the ground and closed the truck door behind him, leaving Fay asleep on the seat.

Charley came on with his right fist clenched. "You never could keep your hands off her, could you?" He looked a little comic, able to gesture with only one hand.

Lauren followed close behind him, silent.

"*Could you?*" Charley drew himself up. The pointed toes of his cowboy boots curled up like Arabian slippers.

"We've been friends for a long time," Austin said.

"Don't give me that friends crap. You two have been fucking."

Austin's heart seized up for a moment, then clicked wildly. Lauren stepped forward.

"I told him," she said.

Charley went on as if she weren't there. "You can't hold on to your own wife, so you start bird-dogging mine. I hear Fay's fucking like crazy these days."

"Shut up about Fay. You don't know anything about it."

"Oh yeah? Then where the hell is she? She could learn something here."

Austin pointed toward the truck cab with his thumb. "She's in there, asleep. And she already knows."

Even as he spoke, Fay's head appeared at the window. She opened the door and climbed down stiffly onto the ground, her face still lopsided from sleep.

Charley snorted like a horse. "You always knew these two were screwing?" he asked Fay.

"Don't play so innocent," Fay said. "There was always something between them, long after high school. You knew it. The whole town knew it."

Charley glared. "You're supposed to cut that shit out when you get married."

"Yes, you're supposed to."

"Whose side are you on, anyway?"

Fay crossed her arms over her chest. It was colder and the afternoon light had begun to drop out of the sky. "My side. I'm leaving tomorrow."

"That's great. Just ignore the whole thing." Charley's neck grew thicker. "If there's any more of that shit around my house, Lauren's going to be on the street."

Lauren surprised them all. "Shut up, Charley." She grabbed him by his good arm and pushed him back a couple of steps. "You know damn well we're not going to split up now. You might moan and groan and destroy your brand-new truck, but you wouldn't even think of divorcing me."

"We'll see about that." He jerked his left shoulder, as if trying to work his arm free of its sling.

"If you weren't so pigheaded, you'd admit there's a lot more to this than sex."

Lauren stared out over the dark fields. Clearly she had more to say. The others stood mute, waiting for her.

"Austin and I have a history," she said, looking straight at her husband. "But we also have a history that never happened. If you can't accept that then there's nothing to talk about."

Charley had too much steam up to yield to his wife. He only paused for a moment. "Sure, history. You always want it pretty. But the truth is, he's just another horny guy with no morals. How about it, Austin, why don't you make it easy on everybody and leave when Fay does? You're not going to let her drive off alone, are you?"

They were past blows by now, and Austin's heart had already begun to slow down. "I don't know," he said.

"You don't know! She's leaving tomorrow and you don't know if you're going with her?"

"I haven't decided."

"You sad son of a bitch."

Charley stepped back, laughing and shaking his head. For a moment he seemed to ignore them. Then he turned and tramped across the lawn to the front door of the house. When no one answered his knock, he opened the door and yelled inside. "Anybody home? Any kids in here? Any busybodies from the Third Reich?"

"Blake's with Otto," Fay said. "They haven't come home yet." Charley walked back across the lawn, weaving a little as if drunk. Abruptly he took Fay's arm and led her off down the drive. They stopped next to her camper, where Austin couldn't make out what they were saying.

He stood side by side with Lauren. It seemed safer than facing each other. "Is it true he'd never divorce you?"

"Never," she said. "But he could make my life hell."

Charley was inspecting Fay's Winnebago. He made a circle of the vehicle and stepped inside, followed by Fay.

Austin touched the small of Lauren's back, once, with the tips of his fingers. "Would it be easier for you if I left town?"

She looked away toward the fading western light. "Don't ask me that."

The Winnebago started. Lauren frowned and squinted at it. It was Charley in the driver's seat. He backed up a few yards and drove forward again. It was an automatic. There was nothing to it, even with one hand.

Fay stepped out of the side door and closed it behind her. "Charley's going to take it for a test drive," she announced. "He says he likes it."

"*No!*" Lauren said, moving toward the camper. But Charley was already backing out along the drive, using the mirrors, sitting upright behind the wheel. He waved at them, a smile on his face.

"What's wrong?" Fay asked.

"Where's he going? You don't know him, he's furious."

Austin caught up with him at the farm gates and banged on the driver's window. "What the hell are you up to?"

Charley opened the window halfway and fastened his seat belt. He was still smiling. "You want to get in? You want to come with me? Or are you just going to let Fay drive away in this thing and leave you behind?"

Austin ran around toward the Winnebago's single door, but before he got there, Charley popped the transmission into drive and floored it. Acceleration on the old camper wasn't much, but by the time Charley veered onto the lawn he was doing twenty miles an hour and headed straight for the house. He cleared the porch steps with a jolt and lofted the camper through the front door. Windows exploded, boards splintered, and the Winnebago disappeared under a cloud of plaster dust and blown insulation.

Before they reached him through the kitchen, they heard him singing: "Yankee Doodle came to town, Yankee Doodle dandy . . ." The camper had dropped through the planks of the living-room floor, but the joists had held. Charley stood in the doorstep like a porter on the old Bangor & Aroostook, preparing to alight. A trickle of blood dripped down onto his collar.

They walked him to the kitchen and made him lie down on the oak table. There was a half-inch cut above his temple, small but hard-bleeding. Fay cleaned the wound and taped it shut with a butterfly closure. Though it continued to seep, Charley was smiling. His arm hurt, he told them. He was in the best of humors, and when they let him, he sat up. "Sorry about the old Winnebago, Fay, but it had to go. Am I still bleeding up there?"

The drops were getting in his eyes. Fay cleaned him again and covered the wound with a gauze square, and they led him gently to Lauren's car. It was nearly dark by now. The dust had blown away, and in the half-light the back end of the camper looked like some fat missile from Loring Air Force Base that had pierced the wrong target.

Charley laughed, inspecting it from his seat in the Ford. "No more solo trips in that old bus, Fay. We couldn't have you leave Austin behind and let him terrorize decent folk, could we? Goddamn, this arm hurts."

Lauren got in beside him and started her car. She waved good-bye, then accelerated through the gates of the farm and sped toward town, her taillights drifting across the dark.

Home from the border with Otto, Blake couldn't get over the sight of his mother's camper punched through the wall of the house. First he ran up to it from behind, then inspected it from the kitchen. The camper's front end had been folded back in accordion pleats, and Blake's bed in it demolished. He stared and stared. He said, "Charley Stoddard did that? Man, I can't believe it!" Twice he burst out laughing.

Austin, an hour after the crash, felt unexpectedly peaceful. More peaceful than he had all day. He sliced up a dozen Green Mountains and deep-fried them for dinner. The telephone, still unplugged and buried somewhere under the rubble, never rang. A blow to the television set had imploded the tube, so they never got to see the national news footage of the border closing.

Aside from the plaster dust that had filtered through the jammed door between the kitchen and living room, dinner was much like any other meal. They wore their coats and sweaters to the table and talked about the Red Sox. Otto looked at them as if they were mad.

The plumbing all seemed intact, so after dinner Fay went up the back stairs and ran a bath. Austin gave the second floor a brief inspection, then told Fay through the plank bathroom door, "It's a mess."

"Come on in, Austin."

He sat down on the toilet seat and closed the door behind him. Fay stretched out in the bathtub, her eyes closed. They had talked like this many times, with Fay naked in the tub. Under the clear water her flesh looked soft and magnified. Her breasts were awash and the dark hairs of her pubis stood up like a sponge in the sea. In twenty years he had never tired of watching her body.

"This half of the upstairs looks safe," he said, "but I'm not sure about Blake's room. I don't think he should sleep in there."

"There's your room," she said, opening her eyes.

"Yes, he could spend the night in there. You could too, if you like. I'm going to sleep out in the fields."

She nodded, pushing the water up over the brown shoreline of her chest. "You won't get cold?"

"I've got my sleeping bag."

"Want to take a bath before you go?"

A few times in the past Austin had stripped and climbed into the tub with her, though it was not a comfortable fit.

"I don't think so. I'll be back by sunup."

She sat up and leaned toward him, the ends of her hair wet, the water dripping from her breasts. He knelt on the floor beside the tub. Her lips, heated by the water, were as soft as a young girl's. He kissed her mouth, her throat, her shoulder blades.

Then he sat back on the toilet seat. He didn't want to get too close to her just now. Or he did and he didn't. "We need to talk," he said. "We keep putting it off."

She looked at him.

"All right, *I* keep putting it off. It's all this border stuff."

"I'm going to Tucson," Fay said. "I don't have that much to say—just that I want you and Blake to come."

"Give me until tomorrow."

She nodded. "Did you and Lauren get to talk?"

"I'm going to sleep in the fields, not with Lauren."

"I know that. Hey, you'd be taking your life in your hands if you tried that tonight. Charley would shoot you, broken arm or not." Fay laughed and slipped back into the water, dipped her face and came up streaming. "Go ahead, Austin. Sleep in the fields and I'll see you in the morning."

Beyond the lights of the house the ground was almost invisible, for there was a full cloud cover and no moon. Austin walked across the fields with his sleeping bag and foam pad. It was almost cold enough for snow. There was no wind, or any sound of birds: no owls, no loons, no Canada geese. He paused once to take a steaming piss, adding a miniscule amount of uric acid to the soil. He had been making deposits to the same bank for forty years.

A mile from his house, sheltered behind a thicket of young firs, he climbed into his sleeping bag. Though he pulled it close around his neck, for a long time he could not get warm. His feet rested on the bare ground beyond the pad, and the dew, after wetting the top of the bag, froze over him in an icy crinkling sheet.

He tossed and turned, feeling the rocks beneath him. No matter how many rocks he picked out of his fields, the next winter's frosts always heaved a new crop to the surface. Some Idaho farmers claimed they could plow a hundred acres without turning up a rock any bigger than a robin's egg. Great. The only problem was, to farm there you had to live on those godforsaken plains.

Austin tried to think. He tried to think about his farm, and Fay, and Blake and Maggie, but nothing would stay in his mind. He told himself he had to think because he had a decision to make. In fact, he had already made it.

FIFTEEN

Austin woke with the first light, stuffed his icy sleeping bag into its sack and marched to the top of the ridge. The skies were clear, the sun only a red corona below the distant Canadian hills. When it broke the horizon he headed home.

Blake sat at the kitchen table in his pajama bottoms and a flannel shirt. Fay wore an old pair of cotton pants and a blouse tied at the waist. It was a morning like any other. The lawn was still shiny with frost, the sun sloped onto the waxed pine floor and white bowls of cereal sat on the table. Austin's wife and son looked at him with subdued identical expressions.

"I think we should live in Arizona," he said.

Blake jumped straight up in the air. "You're coming! Daddy, you're coming!" He ran around the table and thumped his head against Austin's ribs.

Fay stared at him, then rose and circled him with her arms.

"I'm a pushover," he said. "A soft touch."

Blake stood on top of his father's boots. "Today? Are we going today?"

"As soon as we're packed. We'll put everything in barrels and take one of the flatbeds."

When Otto showed up for breakfast he couldn't believe the news. He looked insulted. He wandered around the kitchen as if a bird had crapped on his shoulder. "But you'll be back next spring, won't you? What can you do in Arizona?"

Austin didn't want to talk about it. He didn't dare talk about it. He put Otto to work mounting one of the International flatbeds with twenty-inch sideboards. When that was done he backed the truck up to the kitchen door and they started loading.

An hour later Jules pulled into the drive and parked. He sat in his cab for a couple of minutes staring at the back end of Fay's Winnebago. Finally, as if he were blind, he walked up to the camper and put his hands on it.

"Mother of infants," he told Austin, who had come out onto the lawn. "This had to be Charley Stoddard. No one else could have done this."

Austin nodded, admitting as much. But he didn't want to explain it. Maybe not to anybody, ever. "I'm leaving with Fay and Blake," he said.

Jules glanced at the flatbed parked outside the kitchen door. "Where you headed?"

"South, I guess."

"South's a big place."

"Southwest."

"You got any idea how long?"

Austin stuck his hands in his front pockets. It might take some Boston lawyer a hundred legal pages, he thought, to define the offer he was about to make Jules. He looked around at the yellow buildings.

"You want to run the farm for a while?"

Jules hesitated for twenty seconds, then nodded. "I guess I could do that."

"You can use the machinery, pay the taxes and make your own money—or lose it. I might sell off a few acres, but most of the place would be intact."

Jules, who rarely showed more than a light smile or frown, looked like he was about to cry.

"I thought if you could fix up the house here and move in with Cathy and the kids, maybe Otto could live in your house. He doesn't have much to go back to in Germany."

"That's fine with me," Jules said. He was still struggling to regain his composure. "Maybe we could set him up with some potato widow. Someone whose husband has already had a coronary trying to make ends meet."

"So it's a deal? It might be for one year or twenty, I don't know."

"It's a hell of a deal."

That was their entire contract, and they shook on it. For the first time in their lives they came close to embracing each other—but didn't.

Jules helped load the truck. They roped Fay's boxes to the bulkhead, then drove over to the barn and lifted sixteen empty potato barrels onto the bed. Austin filled half of them with clothes, books, camping gear and hand tools, everything dropped in loose. He covered the front part of the load with a canvas tarp and left the last eight barrels open.

Fay made sandwiches. Austin stood outside at the end, he didn't want to go back into the house. They would call Maggie. They would call Rose. They were leaving the icebox full of food, their mail on the desk, the harvest under cover but not all sold. Jules would have to take care of it. He'd take care of everything.

Austin filled the truck with gas from the farm pumps. "You'll have some painting to do after the repairs," he told Jules.

"Custard yellow. It's an easy match."

"I'll try to come back to visit sometime. Maybe in the spring, just to smell the earth."

"Come anytime. You can stay in the house and do some work. Come back with Blake and climb around on the potatoes."

Austin and Fay let their son say the last good-byes. He leaned out through the window across his mother's lap and held out his arms to Jules. When the hired man stepped up to the truck, Blake kissed him on the cheek. "Bye, Jules! Bye, Otto! Bye, Pooler Farm!"

Austin drove to town in blinders, seeing only the gravel road before him, the round ponds, the woodlots and dark fields. He crossed the iron bridge over the creek, his tires drumming. No one spoke until they reached the packing shed. There he had the empty barrels in back filled with five- and ten-pound bags of Atlantics.

"We're taking eight barrels of potatoes?" Fay asked.

"Think of how many we threw onto the ground. Now I want to give some away."

That night they slept in southern Maine in a cheap motel outside Portland. Austin crawled into bed and slammed directly into a dreamless sleep. The next morning after breakfast he began to pass out free potatoes: to waitresses, to gas-station attendants, to toll collectors on the turnpike.

Not everyone would take a bag. A few people inspected them at arm's length, as if the spuds inside might be laced with razor blades. Austin held them up: clean, yellow-and-white Pooler Farm bags stamped with the Maine Potato seal. A mesh window showed the Atlantics inside. These same potatoes in identical bags were selling all over New England in A&P, Safeway and Grand Union supermarkets—yet Austin had to give a sales pitch now to get rid of them.

He approached people in parking lots. He repeated his story as often as a politician at election time: low prices, unfair trade and U.S. farmers out of work. He'd practiced so much in the last few days his delivery was smooth as sheet rock.

They drove across Massachusetts and down into Connecticut, plowing along through heavy traffic. "Goddamn," Austin said, three or four times, but otherwise held his tongue. He skirted New York City, crossed the Hudson over the Tappan Zee and sped through Paterson, New Jersey.

At every stop he hawked his potatoes. They spent the night in Carlisle, Pennsylvania, then dropped off the turnpike and picked up Route 50 through West Virginia. By now Austin was enjoying himself. If they were going to drive all the way across the country, he said, they might as well take some interesting roads.

Fay didn't care what road they took. Ever since leaving the farm she had been unresponsive, almost as if the trip were all Austin's idea. Finally, halfway through Ohio, she began to wake up. They barreled down the Appalachian Highway past hillside meadows grown up to box elder and hawthorn, the canvas tarp behind them spanking in the wind.

The next night they slept in Indiana. They were still giving away potatoes. They talked—though not about Tucson or White Pine. Halfway through Illinois Fay took over the wheel. She drove slowly, hanging one arm out of the window and inhaling the odor of black soil. Stands of dry corn, still waiting for harvest, clacked in the wind. Austin sat Blake on his lap and told him a story that went on for fifty miles.

Blake was happy. Sometimes he stretched out between his parents on the front seat, lap to lap. At a truck stop Austin bought him comic books, puzzles and a fancy slingshot.

They passed into Missouri. The streams were clear, the air full of birds, the two-lane roads dotted with woolly bears. Here it was still the middle of autumn, with warm afternoons and cool nights. In Jefferson City Austin gave away the last of his potatoes to an elderly waitress.

Forty miles later they lay on the grass beside a river at an empty rest stop. The scarred picnic tables and benches had been locked to metal rings in the ground. There was a hand pump for water. Across the river the naked limbs of sycamores stood white against the deep sky.

Blake went off to hunt big game with his slingshot. Fay stretched out on the grass like a swimmer off the block, her arms and legs extended and her buttocks clenched. Slowly the afternoon sun warmed and relaxed her. She turned and lay against Austin's chest, untangling the curls behind his neck.

During the last couple of days her affection for him had grown. At dinner she sat on his side of the table with one arm curved through his and her hand on his leg. She was glad to be near him. At night she held him as they slept.

These underpinnings of sex had become more important to Austin than sex itself. They were more solid than the ground beneath his feet. They were his true north.

It was still sinking in to him, mile by mile, that this trip was no visit or vacation. His whole life was on the move. Each morning he woke up surprised. But here he was with all his things on a truck, lying beside a river in the middle of Missouri. And so far he was glad he had come.

About the Author

John Thorndike grew up in New England, graduated from Harvard and farmed for ten years in southeastern Ohio. Though fully enthusiastic about potatoes, he has never grown them commercially. He now lives with his son in Boulder, Colorado, and is writing a third novel set in Arizona and Mexico.